"QUITE POSSIBLY MY FAVORITE BOOK OF ALL TIME . . .

A story about the Lewis and Clark Expedition from the Indian point of view is a very significant addition to Lewis and Clark lore."
—SAMMYE MEADOWS, Executive Director
  Lewis and Clark Trail Heritage Foundation, Inc.

"The majesty of the scenery, the wonder of the stately tribes who greet, and menace, the expedition and the expedition's mix of soldiers, ne'er-do-wells and French traders all combine to produce a strong novel about the days when Missouri was at the edge of the map."
—*Kansas City Star*

"This rich and meaningful story offers a new look at the innocence of the Native Americans who welcomed the explorers, provided them with supplies, and never guessed the hospitality would lead to their demise. Based on historical fact, *Sign-Talker* will doubtless leave the reader wishing to read more of Thom's work."
—*St. Augustine Record*

"The narrative ripples with a luminous fascination for nature, both human and spiritual, as it rains down so much sorrow and wonder."
—*Kirkus Reviews*

*Please turn the page
for more reviews. . . .*

"A FRESH AND VIBRANT NOVEL.

"SURELY THE BEST LEWIS AND CLARK NOVEL YET . . .

This is a compelling narrative, one grounded in the best scholarship and given life by Thom's powerful imagination. *Sign-Talker* is an evocation of the American West at a crucial moment in time. Thom has given voice and spirit to that moment, and in the process written a memorable book that is both good history and a good read."

> —JAMES P. RONDA
> H. G. Barnard Professor of Western
> American History
> The University of Tulsa

"Wryly observing the bumbling efforts of arrogant whites to win the trust and loyalty of bellicose Indians, George Drouillard follows along as captains Meriwether Lewis and William Clark and thirty-odd white explorers journey up the Missouri River. . . . He is a formidable character, and . . . he emerges as genuine and credible. Thom's portraits of Lewis, Clark, the much celebrated Sacagawea and other principal characters are also nicely fleshed out."

> —*Publishers Weekly*

By James Alexander Thom

FOLLOW THE RIVER
FROM SEA TO SHINING SEA
LONG KNIFE
PANTHER IN THE SKY
THE CHILDREN OF FIRST MAN
THE RED HEART

SIGN-TALKER

The Adventure of George Drouillard on the Lewis and Clark Expedition

James Alexander Thom

BALLANTINE BOOKS • NEW YORK

A Ballantine Book
Published by The Random House Publishing Group

Copyright © 2000 by James Alexander Thom

www.ballantinebooks.com

ISBN 0-345-43519-2

Map by Mapping Specialists, Ltd.

Manufactured in the United States of America

First Hardcover Edition: July 2000

First Mass Market Edition: November 2001

10   9   8   7   6   5

In memory of
Chief George "Buck" Captain

One of the two or three most valuable members of the expedition . . . a man of much merit; he has been peculiarly useful from his knowledge of the common language of gesticulation, and his uncommon skill as a hunter and woodsman. . . . It was his fate also to have encountered on various occasions, with either Captain Clark or myself, all the most dangerous and trying scenes of the voyage, in which he uniformly acquitted himself with honor.

—MERIWETHER LEWIS, *on George Drouillard*

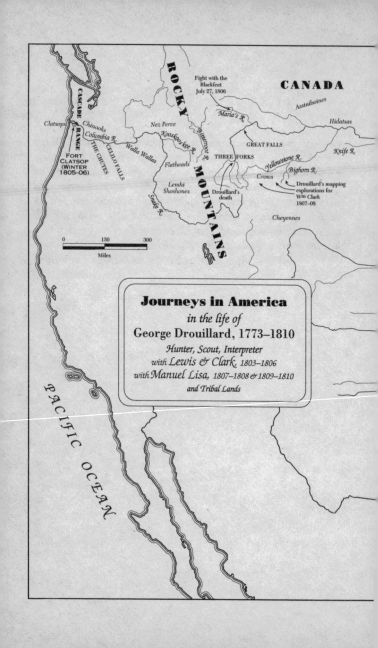

ROCKY MOUNTAINS

CANADA

Fight with the
Blackfeet
July 27, 1806

Assiniboines

Maria's R.

Hidatsas

CASCADE RANGE

Clatsops   Chinooks
            Columbia R.   Nez Perce
THE CHUTES   Kooskooskee R.
CELILO FALLS   Walla Wallas
FORT
CLATSOP
(WINTER
1805-06)   Flatheads

            Lemhi
            Shoshones

            Snake R.

Bitterroot R.

GREAT FALLS

THREE FORKS   Yellowstone R.
                        Bighorn R.
            Crows

Knife R.

Drouillard's
death

Drouillard's mapping
explorations for
Wm Clark
1807-08

Cheyennes

0   150   300
Miles

Journeys in America

in the life of
George Drouillard, 1773–1810

Hunter, Scout, Interpreter
with *Lewis & Clark*, *1803–1806*
with *Manuel Lisa*, *1807–1808 & 1809–1810*
and Tribal Lands

PACIFIC OCEAN

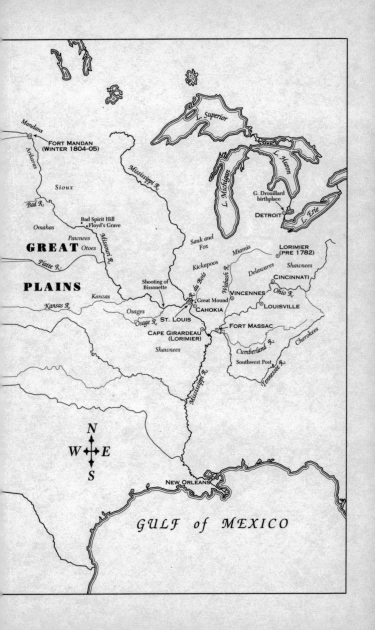

PART ONE

November, 1803–October, 1804

11th November—
Arived at Massac engaged George Drewyer in the
public service as an Indian Interpretter contracted to
pay him 25 dollars pr. month for his services.—Mr
Swan assistant Millitary agent at that place advanced
him thirty dollars on account of his pay.—

Meriwether Lewis, Journals

Chapter 1

Fort Massac, Lower Ohio Valley
November 11, 1803

An eagle soared westward above the river bluff against a gray overcast, as if leading the lean hunter toward the fort, though the fort was where he was going anyway. He would see the big mysterious boat moored below the fort, he thought. It should be there by now.

Eagles often seemed to lead the hunter, even though his personal Shawnee name was Nah S'gawateah Kindiwa, meaning Without Eagle Feathers. The name by which he was known was George Pierre Drouillard.

The tawny skin of his face was taut over jutting bone, his mouth wide, thin-lipped. His hazel eyes were paler than his skin, which gave a strange brightness to his gaze that sometimes made people uneasy, as he knew it did. It was not good for a métis—a half-breed—to make white people uneasy, so hunting and trapping alone was suitable work for him, away from the towns.

Drouillard rode a bay horse, and led an army mule that carried the boneless venison of three deer and the meat and fat of a bear, all bundled neatly in their own hides and hung on a packsaddle. He watched the silhouette of the eagle as he rode. Already he smelled wood smoke from the fort: hickory, oak. And he smelled latrine.

He sent a thought up: Without Eagle Feathers follows you, *kindiwa*. There was a reason why that was his name, and it was a sad and sorry reason, no fault of his. Still, eagles often led him.

3

Led by Eagles, that would have been a better name. If only there remained a shaman to do a new name ceremony for him, that could be his personal name. One could change to a truer name, with shaman help.

Then another name came into his memory and made him laugh. Once when he was drunk a whiteman had asked him his Indian name and he said, "Followed by Buzzards." The fool had believed him, though that would be a true name for him too, appropriate for a hunter. He was a good hunter. Not just a tracker and stalker and sharpshooter. In boyhood he had learned the voices and sounds of all the animals and birds, and could call and decoy them in their own languages. He was such a good hunter that Captain Bissell, commander of Fort Massac, employed him to bring game to the fort to feed its soldiers. He was paid for the meat by the hundredweight. He took his pay in gunpowder, lead, soap, and the printed paper that the *américains* called money. The army provided the pack mule. Followed by Buzzards. He rode along laughing. It was a laugh just slightly bitter, the taste of much Shawnee people's laughter these days.

He rode the curving path through leafless woods, and the river below was green and wide. The woods opened ahead onto a stump-studded clearing, in which the fort stood massive on its earthworks, log and stone. Originally it had been a French fort, now garrisoned by soldiers of the United States, who had rebuilt it from ruins. From its promontory on the north bank of the Ohio, one commanded a view of some thirty miles of the river, from the mouth of the Tennessee almost down to the Mississippi. It was almost like seeing as an eagle sees. There was a spirit in the place that was much older than the age of the fort. Drouillard knew this would have been a lookout place of the Ancients, those who had built the great, silent hill-mounds everywhere along these rivers, then had died or gone away before whitemen came.

But of course the eagle could look down with scorn even at this high, proud place, and see farther horizons.

Out of the woods now, he looked down to see if the big mystery boat was moored below the bluff, and it was. He had seen it yesterday while hunting opposite the mouth of the Cumberland, had stood watching it pass below with four soldiers rowing and one on the tiller and another on the bow. It was a long, black-hulled galley keelboat with a sail mast forward and a cabin in the stern. This was not quite a real ship, he thought, such as the seagoing ships he had seen down at New Orleans, but it was much more like a ship than the usual flatboats and barges that brought whitemen and their goods down the Ohio to the Missis-sippi. Days before he had seen it, he heard the rumors and the mysteries about it. People all down the Ohio were talking about the coming of this boat. Rumors moved much faster than boats, and made mysteries that had to be figured out.

A rumor said this boat had been sent by the President of the United States, and that its commander was a friend of President Jefferson. Another rumor said that President Jefferson was go-ing to take control of the Mississippi country from the Span-iards. Another rumor, or maybe a part of the same one, was that the *américains* coming on this boat intended to go all the way west to the ocean on the far side, and make a trading route all the way to the farthest place, called China.

To a solitary woodsman like Drouillard, such rumors were merely curiosities, and he could see no way they would be im-portant to him, any more than the rumors three years ago when all the whitemen had expected strange happenings just because their calendar turned to 1800 and a new century. Whitemen pre-sumed that their ways of counting time had power.

But there were two things about these rumors that made his instincts tingle, like the sound of a growl in the underbrush:

One of the soldier officers on this boat was said to be called Clark, a war name from his childhood memory: memories of shooting, houses burning, women dragging their children into the woods to hide from the Town-Burner soldiers whose leader was the dreaded *Clark*. The name was still a curse in the house of Drouillard's uncle, Louis Lorimier, for Clark had destroyed Lorimier's great trading post in Ohio and ruined him. Was this officer the same Clark, now coming again?

The other thing that gave Drouillard a frisson was that word had come that Captain Bissell at the fort wanted him to come and talk to the *américain* soldier officers when they arrived at Massac. Why would they want to talk to him?

Drouillard rode through the open gate into the fort. A sentry above the gate nodded to him, which was about as much greeting as an Indian could expect to get from a white soldier. Drouillard knew that particular soldier and sensed that if he weren't employed in bringing meat, the man would be happy to shoot him, just to be shooting an Indian. Drouillard had hunted, interpreted and guided for the fort officers for years, but many of the soldiers just hated Indians.

The quartermaster, on the other hand, was always glad to see him because the meat he brought was always fresh and well-butchered. They worked together unloading and weighing the venison and bear, and the quartermaster wrote the weights on a slip of paper for Drouillard to give to the paymaster. "Thankee, Drouillard. And by the way, Cap'n Bissell wants to see you. Got some important gents in there he wants ye to meet."

"So I hear." Drouillard finished rolling and tying the deer and bear skins, which he would flense and cure to sell at his uncle's trading post over at Cape Girardeau. He left the horse and mule hitched and took his long rifle off its saddle sling and walked across the parade ground toward Captain Bissell's quarters. Soldiers were lined up outside the paymaster's door. Soldiers were always lined up. There seemed to be something in soldier law that everybody had to do the same thing at the same time, which meant that they always had to line up and wait. Apparently, soldiers weren't allowed to have a notion to go and do something alone and get it done while nobody was in the way. Instead they had to wait until they were all told to go to the same place at the same time so that they were all in each other's way and had to wait. To Drouillard it seemed like a poor way of doing things, but it did make it possible for soldiers to stand around together complaining to each other, which seemed to be a favorite pastime of the whitemen.

Most of the fort soldiers knew Drouillard by sight as the Indian who brought in meat, and they didn't pay much attention to him. But today there were new soldiers here, the ones off the keelboat, and they watched him as he passed, and he could feel them watching him. Young men coming down the Ohio from Kentucky and Pennsylvania usually were from families that had been in the Indian troubles, and according to the rumors, the captains of this boat had been recruiting their men from those places.

The flag was stirring in the breeze at the top of its pole. One blue corner contained fifteen little pointed white designs which were said to be stars, and he understood that each star stood for a whiteman's land called a state, and that as the whitemen kept coming on into the Indian country, they kept making more states. He had heard that the old homeland of his Shawnee people north of the Ohio River was now becoming a state, and he could scarcely imagine what that meant, except that all the woods and fields and hunting grounds were being marked with lines into squares, which whitemen bought for money, putting the Indians off into tight little places and making them live there. It was a faraway and ominous thing going on back there, and he always felt it like the coming of weather.

Most of his understanding of it came from his uncle, Lorimier, who as a trader heard news from everywhere and sometimes told him about it. Lorimier would shake his head with a sad smile and say that it was something that had been going on for many generations, and that many peoples were no longer where the Master of Life had put them. Lorimier, with Chief Kishkalwa's Shawnees, had been given lands by the Spanish at Cape Girardeau near the mouth of the Ohio, many years ago, so they could stand as a buffer between the old river communities and the *américains* who kept coming down the Ohio and moving into land where they weren't welcome. But they kept coming, and were now a large part of the population, and they had army bases on the Illinois side of the Mississippi: here at Massac, and at Cahokia, across the river from St. Louis. When the *américain* officers of those posts inquired after hunters to bring meat to their garrisons, Louis Lorimier had encouraged his nephew George Drouillard to apply. By passing in and out of the *américain* forts and getting to know their officers, Drouillard might now and then hear or see things that would be useful to Lorimier and, through him, useful to the Spanish authorities. For a while Drouillard had, in a very minor way, been a spy.

But then just a few weeks ago there had come news that would affect this part of the country in ways that Drouillard, and even his uncle, could hardly comprehend yet: the United States had made a treaty by which all the lands west of the Mississippi would be under its control and governance. The treaty had been made with the ruler of France, whose name rolled like a legend up and down the rivers: Napoleon.

Drouillard, occupied with traces and tracks and streams, and the movements and seasons of game animals, with his gun and his traps, thought little of the doings of men. But there were names that came in news and rumors by the long river courses, a few names, that engaged his thought and made him wonder. Two of those names were Napoleon and Jefferson. They were in every newspaper and every rumor that came from afar. Drouillard had no image of either man, no face or figure to see in his mind when he heard their names. He could no more easily envision them than he could Nanabusho the Trickster Helper, or Kohkumthena the Grandmother Spirit. When he thought of Napoleon, what came to his mind was the French flag of red and blue separated by white; when he thought of Jefferson he thought of this more intricate flag on its pole in the center of the fort: the blue corner with fifteen white star-shapes, and its fifteen stripes, alternately red and white. Often in the last few months, while waiting to see Captain Bissell or to collect his hunter's pay, he had stood musing on the design and the meaning of the rippling, flapping flag of these *américains*. As far as he could understand it, it was the *dodam*, or totem, of their nation, as the redtail hawk was the totem of his people's nation, the Shawnee.

Now as he glanced up at their fluttering flag, he saw that the eagle that had led him along the bluff had not gone on westward, but was spiraling on the air above the fort. He stood outside the door of Captain Bissell's house for a moment and gazed beyond the flag to watch the eagle moving upward into the low, gray clouds. Sometimes Drouillard's spirit could reach that high and bring the eagle's spirit into a sameness with his own, and see as far as it could see from up there. He had done that sometimes in his life, or had dreamed that he had done it, which was the same.

Through the door he could hear the two officers who were talking with Captain Bissell. One had a hard-edged voice, one of those voices that seem to come from a place in the speaker's head right behind the nose, like the bugle horn the fort soldiers blew at certain times of day. The other was a deep-drum voice without edges, a rumble like summer thunder. Drouillard wondered which voice belonged to the officer Clark, and he was reluctant to go in and meet face-to-face an old enemy of his people, if indeed this was that same Clark. Yet he was curious to see him too. He hesitated, and watched the eagle soar higher above the flag, and heard the officers' voices.

He felt that their coming here had very much to do with Napoleon and Jefferson and the *américains'* new power over this country. When Lorimier first heard of that treaty, he had gone red in the face and clenched his teeth and fists, and cried angrily that he had grown too old to move out of the way of *américains* again, but that he probably would have to, one more time. Lorimier loved this place where all the rivers of the Middle Ground flowed together: the Missouri, the Mississippi, the Ohio, and all their tributaries; because where rivers flowed together, all their peoples came together to trade. For a trader, where could there be a better place than this? The Spaniards had given Lorimier many exclusive privileges and advantages, and he had rebuilt his fortune, and was once again a great man among the tribes. Lorimier knew about the treaty with Napoleon and the coming of the power of the United States, but surely he did not know that his old enemy Clark had arrived here in person. If it was so, he would let his uncle know it. That was the kind of spying his uncle would have hoped for.

In dreams, or in waking dreams, Drouillard had seen down from that eagle's height the coming-together place of these rivers, and all the lands around. He knew it all close down too; he

had walked, ridden, run, and paddled over all of it as a hunter and
a trapper, a trader and messenger, for Lorimier. He knew all its
creatures and plants, and the animal paths, and where lead and
salt could be found, where the medicine herbs grew. His mother,
Asoondequis, Straight Head, had taught him how to use the
plants of the earth to heal his wounds and cure his illnesses, and
she had told him: "I am only your walking mother. You only
came *through* me, from your true mother, who is Earth." She had
been called Straight Head because, in the old Shawnee way, she
had been kept as a baby in a flat-backed cradleboard which
shaped her with an erect posture and the back of her head flat.
She had raised her son likewise, so that he stood straighter, even
when relaxed, than soldiers stood in rigid attention. Some
whitemen resented the sight of an Indian half-breed standing so
proud, and so it had become his habit to stand back and attract as
little attention as possible.

Drouillard imagined the vastness of the horizons the eagle
could see as it rose higher, above the clouds. From up there now
it surely could see most of the great hill-mounds built by the Ancient People, far up the Mississippi near Cahokia, and far up the
Ohio above the Wabash. The river valleys were full of them,
square ones, cone-shaped ones, circular walls, all made of earth
and vibrant with old spirits. In his hunting he had come upon
hundreds of them, some huge, some smaller than cabins, overgrown with grass and brush and old trees, silent to the ear but
haunted with spirit music that his heart could hear. The names of
the people who had built them were long forgotten, but his
mother had told him they were built by peoples who were ancestors of the Shawnees. He had seen those men in dreams and once
in a vision: not clearly, but well enough to know that upon the
middle of their foreheads they wore something round and pol-
ished. Even in his boyhood homeland, the place called Ohio,
there had been many of those hill-mounds. In those ancient
times there must have been so many more Indian people than remained now, because those mounds would have required hundreds or thousands of people to build. Whitemen believed the
great mounds must have been built by other whitemen who had

been here long ago and then vanished, because they believed that only whitemen could do big things.

The Shawnee way was in the education his mother had given him. He had been given another education by Black Robes when he was a boy, but he had been glad to forget most of that. The Black Robes had taught him that there were many things to fear in the world, but his mother and her people had taught him that there was nothing to be feared. And in living to become thirty years old, the only fears he experienced were those that came in certain dark dreams, which returned now and then, and they were so unlike anything in his real world that he thought they were left over from the Black Robes. He had run away from them as soon as he could.

Drouillard, looking up, now saw the eagle again, so high it was a speck, and then it disappeared as if it had been only a spirit of an eagle. He had watched it as long as he could and now it was time to go in and see what Captain Bissell and the boat officers wanted of him. He was not eager, but he was curious, and maybe he would learn something that would be useful to his uncle.

As he reached up to knock on Captain Bissell's door, the latch clicked and the hinges groaned. The door swung inward and a lean soldier stepped out, paused, and turned to speak into the room. "Man out here, sir."

"Who is it?" Captain Bissell's voice asked.

"Drouillard, Cap'n," he called in.

"Ah, come in, George."

The departing soldier, not one of the fort's men, stepped out of his way, saying, "Going with us, chief?"

"I haven't been asked." So. Another one of those who call you "chief" to show they've noticed you're Indian, Drouillard thought, stepping inside. He shut the door and sidestepped to stand with his back to a wall, as he always did in a room full of whitemen.

The familiar room was hot and close, rank with tobacco smoke, overboiled coffee, and body smells, and seemed smaller because of the several big men in it. What appeared to be a black bear rose from the floor under the room's one window and came toward him. His hand tightened on his rifle in reflex, before his nose identified the animal as dog, not bear. It came with clicking toenails and sniffed his hand with a cold nose, plumed tail stirring the smoke. One of the voices, the one with a bugle edge to it, said, "Seaman, no," and the huge dog went back under the window.

The room was dim, lit from the right by gray daylight through waxed-paper window panes, from the left by burning logs in the stone fireplace, and by one candle in a glassed lantern on the plank table in the middle of the room. Much of the table was covered with sheets of paper, maps, and leather-covered books. What Drouillard noticed most keenly was not what he saw, but what he felt: the force of presences. It made his nape prickle. In the center of the force were the eyes of two big men, looking at him.

Captain Bissell sat near the fireplace. Another huge, thick-bodied man, in a pale cloth shirt, was by the back wall, hands and face as black as charcoal: a Negro. But the force was all coming from the two whitemen standing by the table in the center of the room. Both were tall, erect, broad-shouldered, and looked solid as oak trees. Their hands and faces were weathered and ruddy, their foreheads white from always wearing hats, as soldiers do.

It was in their eyes that the power was centered. These were scout eyes, hungry eyes looking for the best way through. He felt that they were seeing right through his own eyes into his spirit, though theirs was not the arrogant staring-down look that he as a half-breed got from most young whitemen.

Both of them looked to be about his own age, around thirty, so neither of them could be Clark the Town Burner, his uncle's old enemy. That was a relief.

"Gentlemen, this is George Drouillard, our hunter I spoke of," Captain Bissell said.

One of the officers, the one with short-cropped, dark auburn hair and a small, delicately shaped mouth, said, "So you're Drouillard? I wasn't expec—" His was the hard, bugle-edged voice.

Captain Bissell should have warned them to expect an Indian, Drouillard thought. "I'm Captain Meriwether Lewis," the man said. "Thank you for coming." Drouillard felt a buzzing, humming sensation such as he had felt once just before lightning killed a horse nearby. This man contained some troubling sort of medicine power.

Then the other officer, who was slightly taller and wore his thick, long, copper-colored hair pulled back in a queue, came around the table and put forth a huge, long-fingered hand, hard and rough as tree bark. Drouillard took it and felt strength come through him. This man's face was longer, more craggy, but his mouth was wider and less severe, and his eyes, deep blue, twinkled with unguarded kindness. "I'm William Clark," he said in that rumbling, soft-edged voice. "Come sit, Mr. Drouillard. Would y' take a coffee or a toddy?" Having smelled the coffee already, Drouillard chose toddy. Clark said over his shoulder, "York, would y' kindly scorch our guest some whiskey." The servant nodded, looked at Drouillard through yellow-tinged eyes and winked at him, then busied himself with mug, spoon, little cloth bags and a brown, corked jug, all at a little table by the back wall. "He'll make you what's a favorite of mine for raw days like this," Clark said. Drouillard sat on the puncheon bench in front of the table with his long rifle across his thighs, seeing no place else to put it. The officers pretended to be settling themselves and moving paper on the desk, but he knew they were studying him with so much care that it made him edgy.

Captain Clark said, "I know the name Drouillard. There was an interpreter, a Captain Drouillard, around Detroit, I recollect. . . . Saved a scout, Kenton, from the stake? . . ."

"Pierre Drouillard, sir. My father." He remembered the man Kenton from childhood, and the famous story of how his father had rescued him from burning.

"So! You're his son! And does he live in these parts now?"

"No, sir. He passed over last spring. In Ontario. He never lived out here." After having one son by a Shawnee woman, Pierre Drouillard had left to marry a respectable French Catholic woman and father a large brood of white children. Drouillard saw no reason to tell these strangers any of that sorry story.

"My condolences. I didn't know," Clark said. If this captain knew of Pierre Drouillard, perhaps he was a son, or a younger brother, of the Town Burner Clark.

Then the other captain, Lewis, who was pensively rolling a writing quill between his fingers, said, "Captain Bissell says you're from Lorimier's post, at Cape Girardeau, and related to him."

The question put Drouillard on his guard. Perhaps these officers were trying to scout out the presence of old enemies in this territory where their government's mission had brought them.

The black man had brought a pewter mug and set it on the end of the table close to the hearth, and now he bent to lay the end of an iron poker in the bright center of the coals. He straightened up, palms on the small of his back, pursing and unpursing his lips, watching the fire.

"Monsieur Lorimier is my uncle." Lorimier, like Drouillard *père*, had been one of their enemies, so he said nothing more about him.

Then Captain Clark said, "Cap'n Bissell tells us that you're an interpreter yourself. What languages?"

Cap'n Bissell sure tells them a lot about me, Drouillard thought. He glanced at Bissell, who was reaming out his pipe bowl with his penknife. Drouillard had never thought of himself as an interpreter. He was a hunter, a scout, a trapper. True, he oftentimes helped travelers and soldiers and Indians understand each other, at Lorimier's store, at the fort. He replied, "Speaking languages? Of the whites, English, French, Spanish."

"And the Indian tongues. Which of those?"

"Ah, Shawanese, Delaware. Kaskaskias and Wea of the Miamis. Ahm, Potawatomi, a little. Kickapoo, o' course; it's almost just like Shawanese . . ."

Lewis waved a hand toward the northwest. "What ones up the Mississippi? Any up the Missouri?"

This was a different matter. Drouillard tilted his head, gazed toward the wall. "I've traded with Osage, with Kansa, Kiowa, Oto,

Missouria . . ." He paused, remembering peoples who had come to the confluence of rivers with furs and hides. ". . . Ojibway, Menominee, Arikara . . . Dakota Sioux, but only a little . . ." He looked at Lewis, needing to explain something here. The black man stooped and picked up the iron poker, which now was glowing yellow and red at its tip, and thrust it into the pewter mug. The liquid hissed, sending up a cloud of steam smelling of spice, whiskey, and hot iron, which for a moment overrode all the other odors of the room. He set the mug on the bench beside Drouillard with another nod and wink, put the poker back on the hearth and returned to the back of the room. In the steam were familiar scents: nutmeg, cinnamon, clove, rare things that Lorimier sometimes got into his store by way of New Orleans.

"Cap'n, I don't know many *speaking* words of those people. But with hand talk, I can talk with about any Indian I meet. That's what I mean, sir. Don't want to make too much of it." He picked up the mug by its hot handle, inhaled the steam, blew over the top and sipped carefully at the rim. It was strong and sweet, more whiskey than anything else. The heat and fumes riled his tongue and seemed to billow through his head. Maybe he should have asked for mere coffee after all. This stuff could make one drunk even quicker than cold whiskey, and whenever he had gotten drunk, he had been sorry long afterward. "With respect, Cap'n, may I ask what you want of me? All I've ever done for your army here is bring it meat."

"And translate, and courier work," Captain Bissell reminded him.

Captain Lewis leaned forward with his hands folded on the table. "I don't know yet what we want of you, or even if we want anything of you, or whether you'll be interested in us. From what Cap'n Bissell said, you can be counted on. You might serve us well in various ways. Can you read and write?"

That was a matter of which Drouillard was ashamed. The Black Robes had taught him a little of it before he fled them. He had never used it, had turned his mind away from it, perhaps even had deliberately wiped it out with his other Black Robe memories in turning back to the ways of his mother's people. He shook his head. "No, hardly. I can sign my name so you can tell what it is, but no curlicues or feathers on it."

"Hm. All right. Would you . . . would you soldier? Join the army? I'm allowed to pay my soldiers in a land bounty, as well as wages."

That was easy to answer. Soldiers were like slaves. He had seen that at this fort. No freedom to do or say anything or go where they pleased. "No, sir. Don't look to me for a soldier."

"He's an *Indian*," Clark said to Lewis.

"War Department doesn't need to know that," Lewis replied over his shoulder. "He has a Christian name."

"What I mean is, *he* knows he's Indian."

Drouillard glanced over at Captain Clark and almost allowed himself to smile. Here was a man who seemed to understand that an Indian might well not want to soldier. Not to presume too much from a single remark, but here was something that set the one captain apart from the other.

Now Captain Lewis went on. "Then I could hire you as a civilian in the public service. Twenty-five dollars a month."

Twenty-five dollars a month! Drouillard had never needed money, or thought much about it. But it so happened that he needed money now. Since his father's death in Ontario, his step-mother Angelique had been left without means. She had been good to him, and his dear friend and oldest half sister Marie Louise kept up a correspondence. They were his family. He had been trying to earn enough to help them by hunting for the fort, and twenty-five dollars a month sounded like a fortune. With that kind of pay, he could provide enough to keep Angelique and her large brood comfortable. Suddenly he was very interested in what these officers were saying. But he was cautious. He said, "Hire me for what, Cap'n?"

"Do you know what we're about, Mr. Drouillard?" Captain Clark asked.

Drouillard crushed a tiny fragment of ground clove between his front teeth and relished the flavor of it while thinking how to answer. "Like everyone, sir, I've heard rumors."

"The rumors being . . ."

"That you mean to take that big boat up the Missouri, pass over mountains, and go down to the sea in the West, sir."

Clark laughed, a big laugh. "Sure a lot more accurate than rumors usually are! In fact, yes, Mr. Drouillard, that's largely just what we're about. And you, what d'you think of us doing that? Think we can?"

Drouillard lifted the hot mug and took a sip to hide his smile. He thought about what name to use for God. Then he swallowed and said, "Cap'n, that's a long, long way upstream. But if the Creator, and all the Indians out there, allow it, I would say the rest of it will depend on how hard you can push on."

The two officers glanced at each other with raised eyebrows, and all was still in the room. The big black dog rose, stretched, and padded with scraping toenails to the side of Captain Lewis. He fondled its ears without looking down, and finally said, "Indeed an interesting opinion. And how do you think God and the Indians will favor us?" There was a little antagonism or mockery in his tone, but he seemed earnest for a real answer, so Drouillard gave it.

"What you tell the Indians, about why you're in their country, they will have to judge whether to believe you. But the Creator will know."

Captain Clark opened his mouth and pulled at his chin with one hand as if to make his face longer. Captain Lewis's eyes sparked, his eyelids narrowed slightly, and he gave off a surge of intensity that Drouillard could feel. "Would you mean to imply that, well, that we would . . . mislead them?"

Drouillard thought that perhaps he should not have spoken that way to a white army officer who was thinking of hiring him. But if he was going to get involved with these people and go into other Indians' land with them, they needed to talk straight with each other. "Cap'n, sir, I am what you call Shawanoe. My people lived by the Ohio and along the Miami. Now your people have our country. In losing it we learned that when some whitemen talk, what they say changes between their heart and their tongue."

Captain Lewis clenched his thick jaw muscles. He glanced

down for an instant, then back up. "Interesting how you see that, Mr. Drouillard. I wonder how you know that? Captain Clark and I were at Greenville when the Indians willingly signed the treaty that turned those very lands over to the United States. We saw Little Turtle and Blue Jacket and the others sign it, and they signed it of their free will because they trusted what General Wayne told them. I don't remember seeing you there, do I? Were you a witness to some deception that we missed?"

It was true that he had not been there, but Drouillard had heard that the chiefs were held hostage and bribed and made drunk until they signed, and that they were never told they would have to leave the lands. He had heard all that bitter, sad story from Shawnees who came to Lorimier's. But to argue the point with these men who had been there was pointless.

Captain Lewis continued, "I assure you that what is in my heart is what will come from my tongue." He paused, and added, "And God will know it's true."

"Then, sir, who am I to doubt it?"

After a long moment, in which Drouillard could feel Captain Lewis's heat simmering down like a boiling pan lifted off the fire, the captain went on. "If you go with us as an interpreter, Mr. Drouillard, you should have a full understanding of our journey. You might not have heard the news yet, that the government of the United States has bought the country west of the Mississippi, up to the western mountains, from the government of France."

Drouillard felt a chill run from his jaws over his shoulders and down. So that was the truth about that treaty! *Bought it!* An angry heat flushed his face. This was talk too big for the mouths of mere human beings, who were just one of the animal families. This rigid soldier, a mere Two-Legged in a blue coat, was speaking of a portion of Mother Earth far bigger than an eagle's horizons, and he was saying it was *bought*, which was the word meaning traded for money, as when one goes to a store in St. Louis and counts out rag-money for a keg of gunpowder or a wool blanket, or perfume for a French tart.

Land belonged only to the Creator. His people did not believe that even a handful of it could be sold, though they had learned that whitemen believed they could buy it from Indians and sell it to each other and make the Indians get off it. That was the reason why his mother's Shawnee people had no homeland anymore and were scattered about in little square tracts where whitemen told them they could live. It was a reason why there was no war chief anymore who could decorate him with an eagle feather even if he earned one. It was a reason why his name was Without Eagle Feathers.

Drouillard picked up the toddy mug again and occupied himself with a long, careful sip until he felt calmed and balanced enough to think or speak. Then he mentioned something else that had sounded wrong since he first started hearing about it:

"From *France*? Sir, how does France sell a country ruled by Spain?"

Captain Clark, who was now half standing, half sitting against the edge of the table with his arms crossed on his chest, gave a booming laugh. "Napoleon," he said, as if the name explained everything. There again was the name of that soldier-king in France who was always making war over there. Drouillard looked from one captain to the other.

"Here it is about that," Captain Lewis said, fondling the ears and scalp of his big dog, which sat by him grinning and half asleep with its tongue hanging out. "Napoleon made a treaty with Spain two years ago, recovering the territory from Spain. France is strong, Spain's very weak, y' see. . . ." He paused, looking at Drouillard as if gauging how much of this a half-breed woodsman could understand or care to know. "Understand, Mr. Drouillard, before I came on this mission, I lived in the President's house. I was Mr. Jefferson's secretary, if you know what a secretary is? Aye? So I know a great deal about such things as happen in Europe . . . y' know where Europe is? And I knew how the President thought about such things . . ." Drouillard sensed that he was supposed to be awed by this information. "Mr. Jefferson," the captain went on, "didn't like France owning the territory, because Napoleon is strong and ambitious. The President is much relieved that Napoleon sold it to him. It changes everything in this country. In our particular case, it changes the way we shall make our voyage."

Sold it to him. Captain Lewis had indeed actually said that! Again Drouillard felt that shiver and flush. One man, this Jefferson, believed he could buy a country too big for even ten eagles to see over. Even though it was full of the peoples that the Master of Life put upon it to live.

And Drouillard was beginning to deduce that he himself, as interpreter, was to be the one who would have to tell that to all those peoples. He could feel his spirit beginning to lose its balance, swayed by the powerful toddy and the outrageous story this whiteman in a blue coat was telling.

"Napoleon could never have kept Americans out of this Mississippi country, and he knew that," Lewis went on. "And he needs money to support his wars in Europe. So he agreed to sell it. He knew the sale would spite England, which no doubt tickled him good. Heh heh. Now the United States will have free navigation of the whole Mississippi, and the port of New Orleans to the seas, without a by-your-leave from France, Spain, England, or anybody. Now all Americans this side of the mountains have a seaport for their goods, at last!" Captain Lewis was obviously very pleased with what his president had done, and enjoyed telling about it, even to a half-breed hunter out of the woods.

Drouillard's head was beginning to whirl with thoughts that were half new, half familiar. He had several times floated down the Mississippi to New Orleans with his uncle's cargoes of furs and hides from the Missouri country, or with lead from the mines of St. Genevieve, and had come back up in cargo boats rowed by chanting voyageurs, carrying brandies, chocolate, silks, and silver back up to the gay-hearted, luxury-loving French townfolk of St. Louis and Cahokia, Kaskaskia and St. Charles. On those journeys he had met Kentuckians and Pennsylvanians drifting in their huge, crude flatboats carrying corn and whiskey, salt pork, flax, hemp, cowhides, hardwood barrels, and sawn lumber down the river, where they would be at the mercy of greedy and hostile Spanish port officials. Of course this new control of the waterways and seaport must be important to the Americans west of the mountains.

Now Captain Clark leaned toward Drouillard, eager to say something about all this. "About ten years ago, my brother George got so damn mad he was ready to go to war to make the Spaniards open up New Orleans for Kentucky trade. He was actually raising an army, till President Washington stopped him, from fear o' diplomats. Washington all but called him a traitor over that, never mind it was George won the whole war this side o' the mountains! Well, I say, good riddance to Spaniards."

So! Then this captain is the Town Burner's *brother*! Drouillard thought. He vaguely remembered all the alarm that General Clark's invasion threat had stirred up in the Mississippi Valley: the frightened Spanish officials in St. Louis, his uncle's seething rage toward his old enemy. Drouillard recalled he had almost had his chance to become a warrior back then, as militias were formed to repel Long Knife Clark's Kentuckians. He looked anew at Captain Clark now, having momentarily almost liked him.

Captain Lewis uttered a hard chuckle, grinning, chin jutting, the first indication that he was capable of smiling. "You must admit, my friend, that things make better sense with Mr. Jefferson as our president."

"Not that you're partial, Mr. President's own boy."

They both laughed, and so did Bissell, their laughter seeping into Drouillard's fuddled perceptions of these vast, grave matters. For a moment he tensed, thinking they might be laughing at him as a gullible Indian, to get drunk on toddy and believe fantastic jokes about the buying and selling of countries; whitemen had done that to him before. But no, they were joking with each other. He realized that these might be not just two officers thrown together on the same mission, but old familiars. Indeed, they did have a way of shifting their talk from one to the other and not losing the direction of it, as members of families can do. And both had the same accent, that of Virginians.

"The fact is, Mr. Drouillard," Lewis said, "President Jefferson in his wisdom is changing this part of the world, and everyone in this part of the world will have to understand the change. As this country is a Babel—you know what Babel is?—making them all understand will be one of our hardest tasks. If you can, as Captain Bissell tells us, talk to any Indian you meet, and to Spaniards and Frenchmen as well, you will be most valuable to us. And thus, well-treated and well-compensated. But of course, you'll have to prove out. Fortunately, there's time for that."

They were staring into him again. In their minds they were making him into something they could use. Only this morning he had awakened in the woods a lone hunter with no purpose more complex than the ancient one of providing meat. Now, a few hours later, he was becoming burdened by a great piling-up of words, and he was off balance with whiskey in his head. This must have been how it was for the old chiefs when they were brought into treaty councils and persuaded to do things they never would have thought of doing.

But he was a free man, Drouillard thought. They couldn't make him into something unless he agreed, and he very well might not agree. "What is it you want me to make them understand?" he asked. If nothing came of this interview, at least he would be able to tell Lorimier what their plans were.

Captain Lewis began: "The tribes along the Missouri have to understand they have a New Father. That their earlier Father, the King of Spain, has gone. That they live on United States land now, and that they will trade with only Americans, or agents of America. That their New Father means to make a road of peace and prosperity all the way to the West. The red children can choose to participate with their New Father and enjoy his benevolence, or they can do without. Henceforth, only American goods will be traded on American soil."

It was obvious that Captain Lewis had made these statements often, because he breezed through them without pause, and apparently with no comprehension of how foolish and proud they were.

Trade with the Indians was a very complicated matter. It was interwoven with tribal enmities and alliances. Certain dominant tribes had established themselves as controllers of trade routes.

Such tribes as the Osage would trade only with Spaniards. The Sioux, far up the Missouri, preferred goods of English manufacture, and any less powerful tribes who wanted English goods had to obtain them through the Sioux. French and Spanish traders and trappers going up the Missouri were stopped by the Sioux and made to pay tribute, or were robbed, sometimes killed. Farther up was another trade bottleneck, the Knife River Mandans, eternal enemies of the Sioux and their competitors for the favors of English traders in Canada. Some tribes were bitter enemies, but for the duration of the great harvest trade fairs they would ritually adopt each other so that commerce could be done. Among the Omahas lived French traders in their third generation, their loyalty strengthened by intermarriage. In some tribes trade was entrusted to the women because they were considered smarter at such work, in others because the traders were afraid of the warriors. Captain Lewis was going to go through and tell them all to do it one way and to obey a new White Father they had never even heard of. If this was the President's idea, the President must know nothing about Indians.

Drouillard wanted to talk to his uncle. He wanted to hear him laugh over the plans of these *naifs*. Lorimier knew more about the maze of complexities in Indian trade than just about anyone, with the exception perhaps of the Spaniard Manuel Lisa. What Lorimier could teach these *américains*, they desperately needed to know. But he hated them, so why should he teach them?

Drouillard wanted to ask his uncle's opinion about accepting the officers' invitation to go as interpreter. Lorimier might be furious with him for even considering it. Or he might encourage him to go along as a spy. Or even as a saboteur, to assure that their mission would fail.

The captains were waiting for him to say something, but he was not ready to say anything. He could feel them staring at him. Finally, Lewis said, "You seem to be what we need, Mr. Drouillard. Captain Bissell says you can be counted on. Twenty-five dollars a month, and a grant of land if you stay with us the whole way. Would you consider coming with us on those terms, I mean, if we decide we want you enough?"

"How long?"

"Two years at the least. More likely, three."

"How big an army?"

"Of soldiers, maybe twenty or thirty. Some voyageurs who know the river. Perhaps forty or fifty select men, all told."

Drouillard had to put his face in the mug again to hide his mirth. Fifty men to make half a continent obey their president! He swallowed the last of the toddy, which had gone lukewarm. "I am not decided. I must . . ." He started to say *pray over it*, but most whitemen were dubious about Indian prayers, so he said, "I should council before going away so long. With my relations."

"Captain Bissell says you're not married?"

"Not married."

"Betrothed?"

"No."

"Good. We don't want married men along, or those with their hearts left behind 'em."

"Whoa!" exclaimed Captain Clark. "That'd leave *me* out!"

"Hah!" Lewis smirked and tossed his head. "Cap'n Clark's got a pretty nymphet back in Virginia he thinks will marry him if he lives long enough for her to come of age."

"Mwahaha!" Captain Bissell guffawed, and Clark blushed and grinned. Drouillard had never heard of a nymphet, but obviously it meant a girl.

Lewis said, "As for your relative Mr. Lorimier: I'd indeed like to stop and speak to him about the President's Indian trade policy. Perhaps you could subscribe for us a letter of introduction to him."

"I could do better. I could take you to him. It would be very interesting to me." He could have said amusing.

"That would be kind of you," Lewis said, "but I sh'd rather have you do us a more important service, if you'd agree to. I presume you know where South West Post is, in the Tennessee country?"

"I know the Old Trace goes to it. I've never been all the way there."

"Eight soldiers from the outpost there were volunteers for our

party. I expected them to be here to meet us, but they aren't, and
not a word's been heard of 'em. So I presume their commander
misunderstood the orders and is keeping them in wait there. Or
they've got lost or had trouble on their way here. Or, they may
have got their travel pay and deserted, God forbid. So, Mr.
Drouillard, if I gave you a letter to Captain Purdy at South West
Post, and a month's pay and some expense money, would you
undertake to go down there and find those eight fellows, and
bring them up so we can see if they're good enough for us?"

Drouillard, astonished, stole a glance at Captain Bissell, who
gave him a nod and a wink. "I told 'em I hate to let you go,
George. We'll hate eatin' beans and keg meat while you're gone.
But, hell, these're the President's own boys!"

Drouillard thought these must be *naifs* indeed. These captains, who had met him less than an hour ago, would give a half-
breed more money than he had ever had at one time, trust him
not to run away with it or drink it up, and send him some three
hundred miles through woodlands to a place where he had never
been, to find eight men whom he didn't know, who might already be lost, dead, or deserters?

There was only one explanation for such rashness, he realized: This was to test him. And talking to his uncle might be part
of the test too. Maybe they weren't such *naifs* at that. Well, he
would show them that he could be counted on. He might be
Without Eagle Feathers, but he was not without honor, and he always did what he said he could do.

Maybe the toddy had something to do with it. Despite his
mixed feelings about these powerful fools, he stood up and extended his hand.

"Write our letters, then, Cap'n," he said. "I can fetch your
Tennessee soldiers for you. As for your long trip, I can't say yet."

His answer to that would have to come from all around and
from deep inside.

Novr. 23rd 1803

landed at the Cape and called on the Commndt. [Lorimier] and delivered the letters of introduction which I had for him, from Capt. Danl Biselle, and a Mr. Drewyer a nephew of the Commandt's . . . this settlement was commenced by the present Comdt. eight years since, it has now increased to the number of 1,111 persons . . . he is a man about 5F 8I high, dark skin hair and eyes, a remarkable suit of hair which reaches now when cewed nearly as low as his knees. He is about 60 years of age and yet scarcely a gray hair; he appears yet quite active . . . His wife is a Shawnee woman, she is a very desent woman and if we may judge from her present appearance very handsome when young . . . by this woman Lorimier has a large family of very handsome Children three of which have attained the age of puberty; the daughter is remarkably handsome & much the most descent looking feemale I have seen since Kentuckey The Comdt. pressed me to stay to supper, the lady of the family presided; supper being over which was really a comfortable and desent one I bid the family an affectionate adieeu—

Meriwether Lewis, Journals

Chapter 2

Cumberland River Valley
December 1803

Drouillard sat in deep silence on the roots of a sycamore tree, suspended over the river's edge, his back against the immense trunk, waiting for deer to come down to the beach in the bend to drink. His long rifle, the finest thing he owned, lay across his thighs. His breath clouded in the dank air. The winter sun was low, screened through leafless treetops. From upriver he could hear the soldiers' voices. They were no hunters. They stepped heavy, and sniffled and spat, and talked all the time. The captains would be disappointed by this bunch from the Tennessee fort.

All seven of them and their corporal were sitting useless by a fire, up there where their rowboat was moored, brewing coffee, leaving the hunting as usual to him. They were typical of what he had seen of soldiers, never doing anything but what they were ordered to do. Their two main reasons for volunteering for the expedition were the land bounty they would be paid, and their hope of sporting with Indian women along the way. They didn't talk of that hope knowingly in his presence, they just didn't understand how well he could hear. Often they didn't even know when he was around.

Now and then Drouillard sniffed the wind. He had set himself downwind from the hoof-tracked watering place inside the river bend. Soon the sun would be down, the winter dusk deep. If no deer came because of the soldiers' noises, they would blame him, the half-breed.

27

He flexed his fingers and wrists in the cold to keep them supple for shooting.

He kept thinking about whether to go with the captains on their voyage. Every day he had decided several times to go, then not to go. He needed to talk with his uncle.

The expedition would surely cause the red peoples out there all sorts of trouble. It would be the beginning for them of what had finally happened to his people.

But the captains would be going whether he went or not, so it wouldn't do any good for him *not* to go. And he had calculated over and over the money he could earn for his father's widow and children during such a voyage: eight or nine hundred dollars, if it took three years. Unfortunately, he wouldn't get paid that money until the journey was over. They could suffer much want until the time he returned. *If* he ever returned. It might be better if he stayed and hunted for Bissell's fort and trapped and sold furs and sent them a little money at a time. Maybe go to Ontario to see them. They were all very dear to him, especially Marie Louise.

Don't think of elsewhere when you're hunting, he reminded himself.

When he put those thoughts out, his senses rushed in. He heard the scurry of small animals and the flutter of wings in the woods down to his left. A crow might warn a deer that a hunter sat here. But no crow called. Drouillard heard delicate hoofsteps and cocked his flintlock slowly, with his palm over it to muffle the click.

A doe emerged onto the beach, a stately silhouette against the shimmering river, ears an erect V, attention upwind, away from him.

His lips moved silently in the prayer that thanked the deer for her life, for the flesh that feeds the Two-Leggeds, and promised to feed her descendants when his own carcass would decay in the earth to nourish plants that deer eat. She was only about fifty paces away, so he aimed just below the top of her shoulder.

When the shot's echo had rolled away along the river and the powder smoke drifted off, she was on her knees and beginning to topple sideways, her life spirit already going out.

Megweshe, he thanked the Keeper of the Game. He heard the soldiers whoop. They knew by now he never wasted a shot, and they expected meat. They had no suspicion that the meat they ate had been sanctified by the prayer of a man they probably considered a savage heathen.

Drouillard reloaded his rifle, then went down the riverbank to butcher the doe. He slit open the abdomen and pulled out the guts. Reaching in and forward, he closed his hand around the hot heart and pulled it out. He sheathed his steel knife and took from his pouch a flint blade with no handle. It was sharp as a razor, and with it he sliced out a strip of heart muscle. He chewed it well.

Akowa, the Doe, carried in her heart the spirit of health and the wisdom to perceive the coming of evil, whatever its disguise. He ate of her heart to receive these gifts, which he would need.

In the flickering light of the dying campfire, a soldier named Potts was sitting up in his blanket, filling a clay pipe. His bedroll was closest to Drouillard's. The other soldiers, except the sentry down by the rowboat, were asleep, or seemed to be, their feet toward the fire. The Cumberland's swift water burbled and trickled, silvered by a half moon. The tethered boat rubbed and bumped woodenly against the tree roots on the riverbank, and the treetops were full of moonlight and intense star points. Drouillard was ready for sleep, his head on his knapsack, but he could feel Potts wanting to talk. Most of the soldiers said hardly anything to Drouillard, even though he was feeding and leading them. They were uneasy with an Indian in their midst, so uneasy that they never suggested he stand guard, which was fine with him.

Drouillard tried to ignore Potts, but the soldier cleared his throat softly, once, then again, so Drouillard sighed, sat up in his blanket and looked at him. Potts was round-faced, fair-haired, with a Dutchy sort of accent. He leaned toward the fire, breath clouding in the cold. He put some sticks on the fire.

Then he offered his pipe to Drouillard. That was a surprise. Drouillard took it with a nod, picked a twig out of the fire and lit the tobacco. It was harsh, dry army tobacco, but he blew a plume of smoke toward the sky to invite the Creator to hear whatever they were going to talk about. Then he turned the stem toward the four winds one by one, acknowledging all the Old Spirits. Then he touched the pipe stem to the earth and gave the pipe back to Potts with a nod. Potts had watched the ritual with interest. He took two puffs, gazed at the campfire a moment, and said, "You going west wit' us, scout?"

"Still thinking."

"Yah? Hope you come."

"Why's that?"

"Mmm. Good man. And, I like having an Indian wit' us."

"Why so?"

They were both speaking in murmurs. Potts shrugged and tilted his head, as if to think better. "Well . . . lots of Indians out t'ere, I s'pose? They might, mmm, trust us better, you along?"

"Could make 'em more sly. Most Indians only trust their own."

"Huh!" Potts was quiet, then said, "Wonder how many tribes there are out t'ere."

"Scared?"

Potts leaned closer and whispered. "Nah. Reed is, though. He frets so much about it, he's causing me nightmares."

"God damn you, Potts." The voice came from beyond the fire. "I ain't scared. Just curious about Indians. Damned if I ever talk t' you about anything again!" Reed was up on an elbow, glaring. "Just you shut up, or—"

Potts stiffened and scowled in that direction. "Don' tell me to shut up, you damnt scaredy carbuncle."

A deeper voice spoke from beyond the fire. "Reed, shut up and get up. Time you relieve Howard on watch." It was the corporal, Warfington.

Reed sighed and grunted and began to stir. Soon he had his coat and hat and shoes on, and with an ugly glare at Potts he trudged out of the fireglow toward the sentry post with his firearm in the crook of his arm and his blanket over his shoulder. Drouillard heard him stop and piss on the ground, farting defi-

ance at the corporal's authority. After a while the other sentry,
Private Howard, shambled in and got down into his bedroll
without even warming himself at the fire or saying a word.

Drouillard had been thinking of what Potts said about his
nightmares. Dreams were messages, and he had been having one
himself since the day he met Captain Lewis. It was of a flint
blade slicing flesh, and blood flowing down bare arms.

When everybody seemed settled and sleep-breathing again,
he leaned toward Potts and murmured: "What were your bad
dreams? Remember?"

Potts's eyes widened and he blew out through his lips and
passed the pipe back to Drouillard, nodding. "Of me getting shot
and cut up by Indians. Lot of 'em. Too many to fight."

Drouillard shivered. Such dreams were too much alike.
Maybe they were sharing a dream, as people sometimes do when
they camp together with wilderness all around. Suddenly a
barred owl screamed, close enough that Potts jumped and some
of the soldiers started in their sleep. Then it queried, *Hook?
Hook? Hook hook haw hooo awww!* And soon another replied
from far upriver.

Now Potts was looking at Drouillard with meaningful
intensity.

"What, Potts?"

"Uh . . . well . . . those hooters. Cherokee, down by South
West Post, act scared of 'em. You?"

Drouillard gave him back the pipe. To most tribes, Meen-
dagaw, the Owl, was a death messenger. To the Shawnees it was
a little different, an adviser. It was something to think on, that it
had come just then. He laid back, pulled up his blanket, and tried
to ease Potts with a nod. "Cherokees are superstitious savages,"
he said, doing his best to look serious.

And then he closed his eyes and went to sleep listening to the
meendagaws talking.

"Oh God Jesus Jesus Jesus!" Private Hall cried in a quaking
voice. "I can't even stand to watch this!"

Drouillard, stripped to the skin, ignored the soldier as he

stepped off the riverbank and waded in, breaking the thin skim of ice as he went. At waist depth he threw himself horizontal and swam out to the middle of the river where the faster current had kept ice from forming. His heart pounded and he gasped for every breath, but the cold was thrilling and his inner fire burned and made him feel stronger. He swam back through the ice he had broken and waded ashore. There, he stood and sluiced the water off his pale brown skin with the edges of his hands, and then he was still a moment, saying, without speaking, his going-to-the-water prayer.

Master of Life, here I am making myself clean so I will not offend and drive off the game with man-smell.

Master of Life, here I am alive because you gave me a piece of Kilswa the Sun to warm me from inside. Megweshe.

Weshemoneto. Weshecatweloo. *Master of Life, let us be strong.*

The soldiers of course thought he was crazy. He did this every morning. He had, every morning since he was a boy, except when the ice was too thick to break. Sometimes it made his bones ache.

These soldiers never bathed, or maybe they did now and then in the summer. Half of them said they couldn't swim. Maybe that was why they were afraid to bathe. Breath clouding, he stood till his skin was dry and then he put on his clothes, while the soldiers shook their heads. They didn't understand that he washed off his man-smell so he could hunt well and keep feeding them.

*Cape Girardeau
December 20, 1803*

Louis Lorimier looked at his nephew and shook his head, his lips stretched in that grin of his that looked like a yellow-toothed snarl. *"Tu, avec soldats américains?"*

"Oui, mon oncle." He explained his mission to escort the soldiers to the American captains. He had left the men camped at the river and come up to the trading post. He talked about the

captains and about their offer that he join the expedition. The old trader smoked a pipe and listened. He had pulled his long queue of black hair forward over his left shoulder, as was his habit, and was drawing the braid absently through his left hand. He was vain about his knee-length hair, which he sometimes used as a quirt when riding, or a fly-whisk in summer. Outside a window, men were standing in the cold, arguing loudly over the worth of horses they were trading.

"The *capitaine*, Lewis, visited me," Lorimier said. "He was clever, I think, in not bringing the one called Clark. It might have been difficult for us to be so hospitable, had he come. As it was, we found Monsieur Lewis quite amiable, especially after he had drained off as much of my brandy as I would have drunk in a week. He was rather too much attentive to Agatha, whom he referred to as a 'lovely nymphet'—then apologized." Lorimier shook his head again, musing. "But I am glad he came by. I now perceive President Jefferson's purchase of the territory in a more favorable light. It will be troublesome, of course. But instead of opening it up for squatters to pour in, as I feared, they seem to favor trade with the natives. Less bad."

"Or so the captain said to you."

"I believe he meant it," Lorimier said. "In truth, the *capitaine* made hints of a good prospect for me when their flag flies here. Hinting that I am well situated perhaps to become an agent for the Indians."

Drouillard sat in astonishment. He could remember from childhood the sight of this man, descendant of French marquises, setting out in war paint and feathers to raid American settlements in Kentucky, less than twenty-five years ago. And now he was speaking of becoming an agent for them! Obviously his uncle was not going to condemn him for consorting with the enemy. Lorimier had long been disappointed with his nephew for running away from the Black Robes and becoming a hunter in the woods instead of someone who could write and figure and be helpful in trade. Drouillard had been dreading his uncle's censure, but Lorimier had obviously been swayed by Lewis's talk. The old man continued:

"He offered to send Guillaume and Louis to army officer school."

Those two were Lorimier's sons. Drouillard said, "Officer school?"

"A place called West Point, in the state of New York, where they will educate officers for their army. It would be amusing, would it not, for them to make officers of the sons of their old enemy Lorimier? Ha ha! And it will give the Lorimier name much prestige in this new part of their country."

Drouillard could see that Captain Lewis had caught his uncle like a fish on a hook baited with flattery and promises. Lorimier said now, "As for you, *neveu*: they want you to go with them. Will you?"

"I am still studying on it. I would not even think of it but that I need money for Angelique and her family. But I do think of it."

"To be early in a place is a great advantage," Lorimier said. "If you go and learn that country, we will all profit by it."

"I came for your counsel about it, *mon oncle*. Thank you."

"Then you will be going with them?"

"I still need counsel from others," he said.

"*Eh bien*. Will you stay for supper with our family?"

"I have some soldiers to take care of. And before I go, I must counsel with *ni geah*."

Lorimier raised his eyebrows and said, *"Ah. Mais oui."*

He walked out of Lorimier's compound and climbed the small hillock where the Indian graves were, enclosed by a fence of cedar slats. The graves were little mounds with wooden markers, some grayed by years of weathering. Under a huge, fan-shaped elm he stopped, and gazed down at a plain cedar slab. Into it was carved the name ASOONDEQUIS. He leaned his rifle against the elm and crossed himself as the Black Robes had taught him. Though he had come to hate them and all they had taught him and done to him, his mother had cautioned him that they might be right about their god, and it was good to honor all gods, so while he was here with her he would make the gesture.

He stood with his eyes closed and remembered his mother's

face, the steady, bold eyes, the vermilion dot on each cheekbone. Then he opened his eyes, loosened the drawstring of his tobacco bag and picked out some flaked leaf. He walked around the grave, crumbling tobacco at the head, sides, and foot. Then he stood in the cold by the marker for a long while, remembering, sometimes looking east toward the Mississippi and into the sky beyond, back toward their Ohio homeland.

Because she was an Indian, her marriage to his father had not meant anything in the eyes of the Christians, and after the drunkard abandoned her to go and marry a respectable Catholic Frenchwoman in Ontario, Asoondequis had stayed with her relatives in Kishkalwa's band near Lorimier's store. They had helped her raise her son, first in Ohio, then here in the West. Here she had lived out the rest of her life on the fringe of the Indian trade, and had let Lorimier send him to the mission where he was forbidden to speak Shawnee. Then something had happened at the school, something Drouillard remembered only in dark images, in a room like a box, the murmuring voice of the man in black cloth, some caresses that had seemed comforting at first. Then being held and struggling, and pain and shame. He ran away, and his mother hid him and refused to let Lorimier send him back to the school. From then on it had been all Shawnee teaching, the prayer smoke, the Spirit Helper quest, the eagle leading him even into the sky, the strawberries in spring, the Green Corn ceremony with a drum beating and a cedar wood fire in the center. Twice she had taken him on journeys back to the Ohio country to visit relatives who had not come with Kishkalwa and Lorimier to the Mississippi. On those journeys, she had taken him still farther, to Ontario, where he had been allowed to stay awhile with his father's new French family. The children had doted on him, their Indian brother. His father as usual had smelled of liquor, but was respectable and made a good living, and was good to his Indian son. Then Asoondequis had brought him back here where Lorimier's children were his family. His mother had not married again. She had not been dead long; her grave marker was hardly turning gray yet from weather. She had not been gone long when he got the letter that his father was dead.

"Eh, ni geah," he murmured. *"Ma mère forte et triste."*

He picked up his rifle and walked down out of the graveyard. He had no idea whether he would ever be able to come back here. Her counsel to him was not apparent yet.

Riviere à Dubois
December 22, 1803

Drouillard led the column of soldiers and packhorses up the east bank of the Mississippi in a lashing sleet storm to Captain Clark's winter camp, here opposite the Missouri's mouth. The camp was a cluster of half-finished log huts. On the bank of the Riviere à Dubois, the big keelboat sat propped on wedges, two smaller boats nearby.

Captain Clark's cabin was smoky inside, with tangy smells of new-hewn oak. The rafters were roofed over with canvas. The captain's clothes were muddy and he looked very tired. He sent Corporal Warfington out with the first sergeant, Charles Floyd, to assign the arrivals to shelter and give them coffee, and said he would come and inspect them within an hour. He coughed often into a handkerchief. He invited Drouillard to have a dram, which the black servant poured for him. The servant especially seemed pleased to see him; the man hummed and smiled and draped Drouillard's damp blanket on a chair near the fire. Captain Clark looked at some mail that Drouillard had handed him from inside his tunic. The letters were limp with dampness.

Cahokia, December 17th 1803

Dear Captain,

Drewyer arrived here last evening from Tennessee with eight men. I do not know how they may uncover on experiment but I am a little disappointed in finding them not possessed of more of the requisite qualifications, there is not a hunter among them. I send you by Drewyer your cloaths portmanteau and a

*letter which I received from St. Louis for you and which did
not reach me until an hour after Floyd had set out. Drewyer
and myself have made no positive bargain, I have offered him
25.$ pr. month as long as he may chuise to continue with
us . . . I shall be obliged to go by St. Louis, but will be with you
as soon as possible.*

> *Adieu, and believe sincerely
> Your friend & obt servt.
> M. LEWIS*

Drouillard sat forward, rubbing his cold hands before the fire.
The fireplace was so new its clay was still damp. His hands stung
and prickled in the fire heat. Captain Clark brought a cup of
whiskey to his table, sat down and said, "Welcome to Camp
Wood, and thank you for a hard task done well. No troubles
along the way, I take it?"

"No, sir. Hard weather. A little trouble finding out where you
and Cap'n Lewis went from Massac."

"You had time to get acquainted with the Tennessee soldiers.
What d'ye make of them?"

He had expected that. Captain Lewis had asked him the same
question, and had gotten the same answer: "Sir, I only delivered
them. I would not judge people for you."

"Let me put it this way: Would you want to have to count on
'em?"

"Not to feed me, Cap'n. They're no hunters. Some of 'em do
talk amusing. They have many words for misery. And for
merde."

"Meaning, ah, shit?"

"Yes, sir."

The captain half smiled and shook his head slowly. "Well,
since you don't care to speak bad of folks, tell me what's good
about 'em."

The black servant emitted a short, deep laugh from the other
side of the room, where he was working grease into a pair of
boots.

"What, York?" the captain said, turning to him, fists on thighs.

"Oh, Mast' William, ain't I heard *them* words in that Clark family all my days!"

"Aye, y' have. Get better answers thataway." He turned back to Drouillard. "Any praise for those men? And let's have a smoke on it." He was filling a handsome brass pipe-tomahawk he had picked up from his table, and Drouillard guessed that the captain understood the old ritual about smoke and truth-telling. So they turned the pipe and smoked.

Drouillard said: "The corporal you can count on, but he says he has a short enlistment left. One named Potts, not a complainer. The ones named Howard and Hall don't tire easy. They might do you well if there's not too much whiskey around. It's the main thing they talk of." He didn't mention Reed's fear of Indians.

The captain nodded. "We have several already who are way too fond of whiskey. And all the bootleggers in the neighborhood have already found us."

"Corporal says one of the others is a carpenter, I don't know which one. He might help you finish this camp, anyway. That is all I can say, Cap'n Clark. I've run out of good words about them." He was not comfortable. This was like spying. But if that task had been his test, he had passed it.

The captain leaned back. "Thankee, Drouillard. Cap'n Lewis was disappointed with 'em too. But maybe some will prove out."

"Don't ask me to take back the castoffs, Cap'n. I've about had my fill of escorting."

Clark laughed. "No, we'll just give 'em to Cap'n Bissell. We took some o' his. Now, you, Drouillard: Going with us?"

"I'll tell you what I told Cap'n Lewis yesterday: I can't say yet. I need council time, without any soldiers around." He needed something he did not want to have to explain. He had his own way of seeking answers. Talking to his uncle was a part of it, but only a part of it.

"Well, if there is anything I can do that will help you decide, ask me."

Eh bien alors, Drouillard thought, there won't be a better time to ask this. "I have one need, sir. I need to get money before I can go away. Not just a little. For some needful relatives. To help them until I return."

Clark drew his fingers down his chin, and just a hint of a cautious look passed in his eyes. "What? Wages ahead? I'll have to ask Cap'n Lewis whether he has authority to do that. He's in charge of all the accounts. He has understandings with the government that I don't. Maybe a loan? Would any of those St. Louis people take a signed note? Or how about your kin, Mr. Lorimier? Could you make a note with him?"

Drouillard knew his uncle was strict against lending to relatives. He had done it too many times, and his policy now was an adamant no. He was profusely generous in other ways. He would rather give it than lend it. But not as much as he needed. "I will ask him," Drouillard said.

Clark said, "Cap'n Lewis visited your uncle. He was *very* favorably impressed. Talked on and on about him. About the whole family. Enchanted with the girls. He did carry on."

"Yes. I am blessed in my uncle and aunt, and my cousins."

"Well. Please keep thinking of us. I'll ask Lewis about the pay in advance, or loan, or whatever can be done. Might just write him about it now. Sergeant Floyd carries so many messages back and forth he sometimes meets himself. Go ask Floyd where he wants you to berth."

"No need for that, Cap'n. I'll sleep out. I'm not much for walls."

"Even in this weather? Are you serious?"

"Hunting camp. I'll bring meat." And he had other plans once away from these soldiers.

"Yes, meat. But I'm afraid this place is hunted out. Our boys bag a few turkeys and grouse, that's about it. Good luck. Oh, and aren't you due another month pay?"

"Cap'n Lewis took care of that yesterday at Cahokia."

"Good. Well, I'm going for a look at those men from Tennessee y' brought me. Rest here and warm up, if you like. York'll get you some bread and preserves, or another dram, if y' like." He slung a cloak over his shoulders, put a black *chapeau* on over his thick, copper-colored hair, and shook Drouillard's hand with a warm, strong grip, then went out into the drizzle.

Drouillard picked up his whiskey and drained the rest, head back, looking up at the peeled pole rafters and the canvas, which diffused the dim daylight into the smoky room and hissed with the drizzle.

" 'At's the boat sail," the black man said. " 'Nother whiskey, s'?"

"What? Sail? They plan to *sail* up that river?" He handed him the empty glass and York poured in a deep shot.

"Mast' Billy's a good river man."

"Soldier and sailor both, is he?" Drouillard took a long sip.

"Heh heh! He do jus' 'bout anything real good."

Drouillard wondered how a slave could admire his master so much. He said, "Such as what, does he do so good?"

The slave put his palms together and looked at the ceiling. "Well, s'. Planter. Wagoneer. Surveyor. Hunter. Talks law. Build houses, forts, anything. Boats. Maps too, real good at maps. An' can he fight!"

Drouillard was feeling mirthful and mocking as the whiskey stirred his brain, and it was odd to be talking to a Negro. It had been a long time since he had done that. He remembered a girl who had been Lorimier's servant in the war times, and a black man, a former slave, who had lived among the Shawnees.

"You've *seen* him do all those things? Or he just tells you he's good at 'em?"

York laughed deep. "I seen. Been with 'im all his life."

"All his life?"

"Yes, s'. His daddy own my daddy. Gi' me to Mast' Billy when we's both pickaninnies." York put his head back and roared with laughter, ending up bent over, slapping his knee. He wiped his eyes with the back of his wrist. "I jus' *love* t' say that to 'im!"

Drouillard blinked and wondered what was funny. It had sounded like he said Pickawillany, the name of a Shawnee town not far from Lorimier's store back in Ohio, in the war times. He said, "Cap'n *owns* you! How d' you feel about that?"

York was still chuckling. He said, "Feel? I guess I feel well 'nough. He real kindly."

Drouillard wondered if this man pretended good feelings and ignorance because that's what whitemen wanted. Drouillard himself as a half-breed among whitemen had learned to pretend in similar ways and keep his resentments and understandings to himself. Looking at York's broad black face, he felt both an affinity and a revulsion for him. He said:

"I've been thinking. Everybody going on that voyage out West is a whiteman, except you. And me, if I choose to go. Any good comes of it, all goes to them. Not to you, not to any Indians. Whatever profit, and *la gloire*, it will all be theirs. That's how it is." He shook his head and looked down into his whiskey glass.

"What's 'lugwah'?" York asked.

"Glory." He thought of eagle feathers, which had been the tokens of glory when his people had been free in their own land, warriors. "I remember a man, a slave, that got some glory. Looking at you reminds me. Let me tell you about him."

York sat down, his face eager and intent. The promise of a story made people look like that.

"When I was a boy, where my people used to live, there was a man looked just like you. Name was Caesar. Been a slave. Sometimes slaves ran off and came to hide with my people. They made that Caesar a Shawnee, adopted him into a family. He went out with warriors. He was happy shooting white folk. He got glory. Earned eagle feathers. Think how you'd look with your head all shaved except a scalplock in back with feathers in it. Big silver ear bobs. One side of your face painted red. Wouldn't you be pretty!" York had drawn back and was looking at him, eyes big with amazement, or horror. "Eh!" Drouillard went on. "Grand man, that Caesar! Had a beautiful Shawnee wife. Happy man, all his own, no one owned him. See, I wonder how a man strong enough and brave enough to be a warrior, would stay and let a whiteman *own* him." He fixed on York's eyes that hunter gaze that he knew agitated people.

York rose, went and knelt to poke the fire and add wood, taking a long time about it. His hands were shaking. Outside, men were working in the sleety rain: ax blows, talk, laughter, saws rasping through green wood. York said, as if speaking into the fire: "That all 'at story? What come of Caesar?"

Drouillard didn't know the end of the story. That had been a quarter of a century ago, in a place long lost to him. He had seen Caesar no more than two or three times. But somehow the story seemed very important, both to York and himself.

As Drouillard rode south in the cold rain, he wished he had not drunk the whiskies. Liquor got into his blood too fast and upset his balance. Not just his physical balance, but that more delicate thing in his spirit that guided what he said and what he did. By keeping his inner balance, he could rely upon himself. If he could rely upon himself, anyone else could rely upon him. If he got off balance inside, he could go too dark, or he could go too light. If he went dark he could get morose or cruel. If he went too light he might be the sort of childish fool people were looking for a half-breed to be. Or he could say things from the heart without thinking how they would sound to people who were in their own worlds. He had almost said cruel things to the slave. He had wanted to taunt him about being owned, had wanted to dare him to run away. Then, on the other hand, he had started telling his story about Caesar, with a light-headed hope that it would inspire York to free himself, to run away.

Running away was an old matter down in Drouillard's dark side. Far back in the war times he had to run away from the Town-Burning soldiers. Later he had run away from the Black Robes who tried to make him a Jesus Indian.

Most Indians believed that one's spirit had to walk in balance. For a half-breed, balance was even more crucial, but it was harder.

He rode toward the mound-hills made by the ancients, noting game trails and hoof tracks. It was almost dark when he rode up to the top of the biggest mound. From the west, across the Mississippi, a few feeble points of yellow light twinkled, sometimes entirely lost in the rain and mist, probably outdoor slash fires and wharf lanterns at St. Louis. Closer below, on this side of the river, near the oxbow-shaped lake, a few glimmers: Cahokia town, where Captain Lewis was buying provisions and trying to impress the merchants and the prominent citizens with his new authority in the territory. Nowhere else was there any light. He was alone in a world of darkness, high above the floodplain, in a place sacred to his people. The long, old songs were in the air around him but were as faint as the distant lights, and like them, they sometimes faded to nothing. Even when they were silent he could feel a hum through the soles of his feet. Long before whitemen had come to this continent there had stood here a great city of the ancient people, greater than any whiteman's city anywhere, and all its people had gone suddenly when a great death had come through. All their houses, and the temple on this hill, had fallen and rotted away, all so long ago that this old forest had since covered the mounds and town site and plazas. The story of the old city had come down through more than twenty generations, and almost everything had been forgotten, except that they were ancestors. There was nothing to show what had been here, except these hills shaped as the Creator never shaped hills, and the bones and the old clay pots, the weapons, pearls, and the copper ornaments that sometimes emerged from the dirt when rain gullied the slopes. But the descendants had kept coming here to pray, and their boys came here to seek their Spirit Helpers.

Drouillard had come for that purpose at the age of thirteen, after escaping from the Black Robe mission. The Black Robes had tried to fill his soul with fears, and had exerted powers over him that only finding his Spirit Helper had finally wiped away. On his quest, Drouillard had sat four days and nights naked and without fire, when the weather was mild. Now he hunched down in the wind and rain with a blanket over his back, and with flint and steel he struck sparks into charcloth and wadding tinder, blew into the smoking wad in his palms until flame glowed, then set it on the ground in the lee of a fallen tree and fed it dry punk from inside a log, then twigs and sticks until a good fire crackled and fluttered. Smoke swirled away into the cold, dark, misting sky. He drew a leaf of dry tobacco from a bag and rubbed it into fragments between his palms. These he sprinkled into the flames, a bit at a time, and each puff and tendril of smoke carried prayer into the heavens. He sat with the fire at his feet, his back leaning on the fallen tree, his blanket over his head and shoulders and held open to the fire, the wind from behind him.

The wind is always full of messages, he knew, but they cannot always be understood. Here the messages were under the wind, and it was not ears that heard them. They were the old songs, and they were inside him as well as outside, or they were through him as if he were but part of the wind itself.

Sometimes the songs seemed to draw the smoke of his fire into song-shapes, seemed to draw sparks up into spirals. The ancestor spirits were present and strong, but they were not fearsome. Whitemen were afraid of their ghosts; Indians invited theirs, calling on them for help and wisdom and foresight.

After midnight the drizzle stopped. Drouillard slept leaning back against the log. Two forms came to him. First was a man form with a dull-glinting ornament in the middle of his forehead. This one rose and floated over him and flew away over the Mississippi.

The other was the form of a woman. Her eyes were intense with generosity; she was holding forth something in her hands and imploring that it be taken. But there was blood pouring down her arms.

When the cry of an owl woke him, it was raining again, not a drizzle now but a blowing rain that had soaked his blanket until it was heavy. Even in the rain the little fire was still burning. On these places water did not quench fires. The sky was fading to gray in the east. Behind him the last murmur of the old songs was fading into the dark beyond the great river as if retreating from dawn.

Under his blanket he filled the bowl of his pipe with kinnikinnick and lit it with a twig from the fire. He smoked to the four winds and asked the Keeper of the Game for a good day of hunting. When he rose to get his horse, his limbs were so cold he was stumbling, but in his center he was glowing with heat.

Satturday 24th Decr.
Cloudy morning, men Continue to put up & Cover the neces-
sary huts. Drewyear returned with 3 Deer & 5 Turkeys
                                        William Clark, Journals

A private named John Colter was assigned to go out with a packhorse and help Drouillard bring in the venison. Colter was said to be a very good hunter, but he admitted that he had brought in nothing but turkeys and rabbits, and had thought the bigger game had long since been killed off in the vicinity. Drouillard told him there were more deer than one would think, and that furthermore he had seen bear sign.

Colter was compact and square-jawed, with narrow lips, a tight, mocking smile, and deceptively sleepy-looking eyes. He was one of those whom Drouillard had seen at Fort Massac on the day he met the captains. This was the one who had stepped out of Captain Bissell's door and called him "chief." As they skinned out and butchered the deer, Drouillard noted that this Colter must indeed be a hunter because he was as swift and sure with a knife as any whiteman he had ever seen. Drouillard thought the man could probably be very dangerous, but he gave off good humor and did not seem to resent helping an Indian. He wasn't jealous that Drouillard had found deer when he couldn't. Instead he went on about how good Christmas would be with all this venison. When they started cutting up the third deer, a buck with ten antler points, Colter noticed that part of the heart had been sliced away, but he didn't ask about it, so he either knew or something kept him from asking.

Instead Colter asked him, "I been a-wonderin'. How in the hell did Indians celebrate Christmas before we came?"

Drouillard looked up blank-faced from the flesh he was slicing. He couldn't believe he had just heard such a question. Colter was looking at him with that sly, mocking smile.

Then Colter started laughing. And after a while he said, "Eh, I actually made ye smile, chief!"

                    *   *   *

Drouillard could feel that snow would come before daybreak, and he was so tired that he accepted a bunk in one of the log huts. The soldiers had their Christmas Eve whiskey rations. Then more whiskey mysteriously kept coming in, and it soon became apparent to Drouillard that he could have slept better under a brush shelter out in a snowstorm. The soldiers boasted, smoked, sang, toasted the newborn Savior, gave each other tobacco, belt buckles, and scrimshaw pieces, stomp-danced to Jew's harp music, and arm-wrestled on the small puncheon table in the middle of the cabin. Some of the revelers began drifting from cabin to cabin, challenging each other to wrestling contests, their voices louder and louder. Some began bitching about being stuck in this bleak place all winter just a few hours' journey from the women and saloons of St. Louis with no freedom to go there. Drouillard had accepted a few shots of the bootleg that the men had offered in honor of his great contribution to the larder, and he was half drunk and half asleep when the inevitable fight erupted. It started when a soldier named Frazier objected to being called for guard duty by a corporal named Whitehouse, and called the corporal a pride-swollen pimple. Soon, stools and bodies were bouncing off the walls so hard that clay chinking was falling out from between the logs. Drouillard had seen hundreds of fights along the river in which rivermen, soldiers, wagoneers, and hunters broke fingers and bit off noses, and had been drawn into a few himself, but it was his policy to avoid them because too many people looked for excuses to kill an Indian or a half-breed.

So he snatched up his bedroll and rifle and slipped out of the thundering hut. A snowfall had begun. Every cabin but the captain's was alive with muffled noise. Maybe Captain Clark had drunk himself to sleep; it was hard to imagine that he couldn't hear the whooping drunks and thumping objects. Light seeped through cracks, and now and then a door would creak open and a soldier would step out to pass water, belch, hum tunes, and fart proudly into the darkness. He wanted a place to lie down and sleep. So he slipped down toward the keelboat, past a sentry who leaned dark and motionless under a corner of the tarpaulin that covered a stack of crates and kegs near the vessel. He climbed up the chocks and pry-poles onto the deck of the keelboat. In the stern cabin he found bunks built along the bulkhead, evidently to be the captains' onboard quarters. Though not furnished yet with bedding, they were strung with rope webbing. It was the quietest place in camp. He wrapped himself in his blanket, eased back onto the creaking ropes, and fell at once into a dreamless sleep.

He was jarred awake by gunfire, a crashing volley nearby, followed by whooping, hallooing, manly voices. He thrashed out of his twisted blanket, heart pounding, thinking he was a boy at Lorimier's trading town in Ohio and the Long Knife Town Burners were attacking. But then he heard what the voices were yelling:

"Good Christmas morn, Cap'n Clark!"

"Cheers, Cap'n!"

"It's the Savior's day!"

"Hip, hip, hooray!"

Stooping out through the low hatch onto the snowy deck, head aching, Drouillard stood in the early gray daylight and peered up toward the camp, which looked like a small, shabby town, smoke drifting away over it through the falling snow. About two dozen soldiers were in front of Captain Clark's cabin, bellowing and laughing and reloading their weapons. From the tones of their voices he thought some of them were still drunk. At a hoarse command, the guns were discharged skyward, with more shouts. He smelled the drifting gun smoke, smelled coffee, roasting meat, pone baking, all through the chill, dank smells of mud, river, and latrines. The flag fluttered in the falling snow. Captain Clark stood in the doorway of his cabin, in linen breeches and loose shirt, face long and pale, eyes blinking, his nose as red as his tousled hair, obviously just awakened, sleep-stupefied. Then he grinned at his men.

"Thankee kindly for your good cheer, boys. And a good Christmas day to you too." He looked up at the falling snow. "Holiday. No duties today but the guard. Big feast, thanks to our hunter. Drouillard around?"

"Here, sir." He raised a hand, annoyed at having attention directed to him. The captain stared at him, and the troops turned to look, and someone yelled:

"Ee-*yay*, Nimrod!" and more cheers and laughter went up.

"Extra whiskey ration today," the captain announced, and another cheer erupted. "Anyone may go out hunting, but sign out with Sergeant Ordway, and don't be shooting any of the neighbors' hogs. And, damn it, hunting doesn't mean hunting up the bootleggers! You do, and you know the penalty." There was more laughter.

Then Sergeant Ordway called out: "Sir, I need a word with you. And some of the men have presents for you."

"Why, thank you all. Give me five minutes, and I'll see you then. And I want to see Mr. Drouillard. Have a jolly Christmas, boys. Company's dismissed."

When the soldiers Frazier and Whitehouse slumped out of the captain's cabin, hands bandaged, faces bruised and pain evident in every move, Drouillard stepped aside to let them by and rapped on the plank door.

Captain Clark called him in, looking at him with coolness. York served him coffee without meeting his eyes, and Drouillard presumed he had upset the slave with his talk of freedom. He wondered if this grave meeting was about that.

"First, now," Clark said, "I want to know why you were on that keelboat. It's under guard because it is out of bounds except to those working on it."

"I didn't know that, sir. I was just finding a quiet place to sleep. I was in the cabin where, uhm, that happened." He inclined his head toward the departing combatants.

"Oh." The captain's expression softened. "Well, I can understand that. But now ye know. The boat and cargo are off bounds. So. Then did you witness the fight between those two?"

"I saw it start. I hope you don't mean to ask me about it as a witness, because all I saw was the whiskey in a private fighting the rank in a corporal. To me, one's about the same as the other."

"What . . . what do you mean?"

"I mean both whiskey and rank make a man forget who he really is." And, he thought, like a master over a slave too, but he didn't say that because it might make trouble for York.

"Interesting," Clark said. "Well, Frazier's sober now and Whitehouse is a private again, so I guess I've cured 'em both, eh? Now here's what I called you in for. I'd like you to do something for us while you make up your mind about joining us: Sergeant Floyd keeps so busy running courier between me here and Captain Lewis down in the towns, he's no time left for useful duties here, like helping Ordway sit on these wild men. I'd like you to take over some of Floyd's courier work, until our business in St. Louis and Cahokia is finished. You know your way around here, and we've seen you can be counted on."

Drouillard nodded, and was ready to say something, but Clark went on: "Another thing you could do for us if you take that on. We need a body of good boatmen, who know these rivers. In particular, the Missouri. We've asked Manuel Lisa to help us recruit some. You know him, I believe? You could work with him to find some who know the waters, and maybe some of the languages too, up yonder. Osage, Kansa, Missouria, Omahas . . ."

Drouillard's mind at once ranged over a number of just such men, most French-Canadian voyageurs, some métis like himself. The first one he thought of was his old friend Pierre Cruzatte, the old one-eyed fiddler, half Omaha and a veteran of upriver trade, lighthearted and honest. The thought of having along some French-speakers, someone besides pugnacious, surly soldiers, was a pleasant new notion. "I know some such as that. How many?"

"Maybe six to a dozen, depending on boats and loads. If a dozen apply, we've got time to shake out the chaff, as we're doing here amongst the soldiers. And . . ." The captain looked over the rim of the cup from which he was sipping what looked like coffee but smelled like a toddy. ". . . maybe that will be enough time for even you to make up your mind."

Drouillard felt a lift inside his bosom, a sudden mirth, a sense of relief. "I'll do those things. Carry messages. Find voyageurs. Sure . . ."

"And still hunt, when you can?"

"I will. But I won't need all that time to decide myself. You can sign me on."

"What? You *will* go? For the whole way? You're certain?"

"*Eh bien.* If I didn't go, I suppose I'd wonder from then on."

Clark was beaming, nodding. So was York. Clark said, "Got an itch to see what's out yonder? Like us, eh?"

Drouillard did want to see how it would look to the eagle in his spirit. That was true.

But his greater curiosity was about seeing these damned people try to do it. He had never seen a stranger mix of naive, single-minded, arrogant fools, extravagant spenders, hard-headed brawlers, all slaves to one thing or another—to army rules, to slave masters, to a faraway chief called President Jefferson— and all so ignorant of the minds and spirits of those wary peoples through whose lands they would be carrying their outrageous new notions. He had never seen a plan this big, this certain to fail. Everybody in the countryside was talking about this grandiose enterprise, either wanting to go or scheming for some way to profit by it. Half his heart wanted to see these strange young officers succeed in such a brave dream; half his heart believed it deserved to fail because of what land-hungry Virginia soldiers like them had done to his own people and their allies. Either way, he presumed that he was meant to go along and see it happen. His mother Asoondequis had always said that the Master of Life puts people where he has a purpose for them. He had counseled with her in her grave, with the spirits on the mound-hill, and with his uncle at the trading post. Their wisdom had not been clearly stated at those times, but they had come together now in that uplifted feeling inside him. This would require a sacrifice of all his own cherished day-by-day freedom, but he felt now that he had been put in its way, and as a talker of many languages, he might help it turn out as well as possible for the people out there who would be in its way. But all he said to Captain Clark now was:

"I would like to see that far."

Christmas 25th Decr,
I was wakened by a Christmas discharge found that Some of
the party had got Drunk (2 fought) the men frolicked and
hunted all day. Snow this morning, Ice run all day. Drewyear
Says he will go with us, at the rate offered, and will go to
Massac to Settle his matters.

William Clark, Journals

Chapter 3

When Drouillard became the captains' courier, he saw how they worked together even though twenty-five miles apart. Lewis bought supplies and merchandise in St. Louis and Cahokia, palavering with traders and officers here, and sent goods and messages up to Captain Clark at the soldier camp. Lewis was always shining in uniform, drinking, going partying. Clark stayed in the muddy camp, trained and disciplined the crude soldiers, sent them out to hunt, made them practice with their rifles, rewarded them with a little more whiskey, but punished them if they went to the bootleggers and got too much of it. He kept them busy whipsawing lumber to improve the camp and their big boat. He constantly measured the skies and the weather with his strange instruments, and wrote the measurements on paper along with lists and sketches and maps and numbers and words, words, words. All his life Drouillard had seen writing people, Lorimier's clerks and scriveners, but he had never seen anyone write and figure on paper so diligently as that Captain Clark. His fingers were always black with ink.

It was their way of remembering. Clark told Drouillard they would write each day of what was happening, all the way to the western sea. This was all for the man Jefferson, to tell him all they did, all they saw. All the sergeants and soldiers who could write would keep journals too, so that if any records got lost or damaged, there would still be accounts for the President. Clark asked Drouillard to keep a journal, but he said he could not write well enough. York made as much ink as coffee for Captain Clark. They looked alike, but the coffee was hot and the ink was not.

Drouillard, carrying letters to Captain Lewis from Captain Clark, disembarked from a rowboat near Manuel Lisa's store. Lisa was a Spanish merchant who had made considerable wealth in New Orleans. Believing in the business tenet that the closer one is to the source, the more profit one can skim off, he had then moved up the Mississippi to try to break into the old Chouteau family's fur trade monopoly in St. Louis. By virtue of being Spanish, Lisa had obtained a trading license from Spanish officials, and now had a thriving establishment on the riverfront. He had become one of the suppliers for the Americans' planned journey to the West.

Lisa's establishment fronted on a cobbled riverfront quay that ran with sewage from upslope streets; just as the great rivers of the land converged in the Mississippi Valley, the streets of St. Louis trickled mud, washwater, and chamber-pot waste down onto this broad quay, where it stewed until a rainstorm flushed everything into the river. Drouillard stepped from plank to cobblestone, stone to curb, to keep his soft-soled, delicately quilled moccasins out of the sludge as he approached the door of Lisa's store and warehouse. He breathed through his mouth to keep from smelling the stench of whitemen's civilization. A few flatboats, pirogues, and dugouts were moored at quayside, silhouetted against the vast, yellow-gray surface of the Mississippi.

The interior of Lisa's establishment was dense with the musky, rotten-flesh smell of ill-prepared hides and pelts and loud with the arguments of buyers, sellers, and clerks. As Drouillard made his way through the gloom among kegs, coils of rope, bolts of calico, hempen sacks, and shelved boxes, he heard Manuel Lisa's voice squawking rapidly in Spanish and then a deep bellow of a man in pain. From the dim depths at the back of the store two figures came hurrying up the aisle. Drouillard darted out of their way among a stack of piggin buckets.

Manuel Lisa in a black frock was in front, leading a huge, reddish-haired mulatto man in filthy deerskins toward the front exit. The giant was running on tiptoe, because Señor Lisa had a dagger point up his nostril, and by this bloody point of contact pulled him along to the front door, where he released the man, pivoted around him and with a kick sent him sprawling in the foul puddles of the quay. When the little Spaniard returned, he seemed hardly agitated. He beckoned Drouillard into his office in the rear, where they sat to face each other.

"I am surprised to see *you* here, Señor Drouillard."

"Why surprised? I come to talk further about the voyageurs."

Lisa made a sharp cutting motion with one hand. "Your haughty captain has terminated us. He will get the boatmen through Chouteau. Has he not even told you?"

"In fact, no."

"Perhaps then he was just venting his temper with me, or bluffing to make me meet his stingy terms."

"Temper perhaps. Cap'n Lewis bluffing, permit me to doubt."

"*Verdad.* And I regret he is so stingy. I would have liked to continue commerce with you."

Drouillard had watched Captain Lewis squander the government's money here in St. Louis, and thought "stingy" anything but an apt term. He had heard Lewis rant about bad faith and overcharging by several of the suppliers, including Señor Lisa. "I too regret, señor," he said, and started to rise, but Lisa shrugged, then stayed him with a hand on his wrist.

"Perhaps you could sweeten his attitude and bring him back to our establishment? I know the captain esteems you most highly." Lisa was more anxious than he pretended; all the commerce yet to come would be under the American regime.

"Señor Lisa, I do not interfere. The best I can do for you is to say nothing against you."

"Thank you for that, then." Lisa was looking at him with calculation in his glittering black eyes, which reminded Drouillard of a serpent's: large, round, and scarcely ever blinking. "Will you stay and accept a drink with me, Señor Drouillard? Don't worry, I won't tell your captain if you do."

"I will accept one, and will tell him myself."

Lisa smiled at that, and decanted rum into a fancy glass, saying, as he gave it to him, "If I can be of any service to you, or to Captain Clark . . ."

Drouillard sipped and thought. He still needed to borrow money to send to his stepmother's family, and wondered if Lisa cared enough about getting back in the Americans' good graces to lend him a few hundred dollars. But he remembered something that his uncle Lorimier once had said about Manuel Lisa: that he would never be such a fool as to get into his debt.

So he replied, "The captains are of one mind on everything. I wouldn't recommend going around one to the other."

"Of course not. I wouldn't try. As for you, Señor Drouillard, I presume you will go the whole way with them?"

"I've told them I will." He sipped the *tafia*, which was smoother and more refined than anything he had ever tasted, and set the glass down.

"You will see such sights! I envy you. I would love to be the first to see what doubtless will be wonders!"

Drouillard said, "There are Indians out there already, señor; we won't be the first to see it."

"Mhmm, yes. So. After the journey, what are your plans?"

Drouillard shrugged. He had long been a plain hunter, not used to looking far ahead, and had hardly yet got used to thinking even of the duration of the voyage. "*If* we get back, I might know what I want by then. Maybe I will have enough pay and land to start a family. Maybe I will want that by then. Who knows what one will want two or three years away?"

Manuel Lisa leaned forward, eyes intense. "It is said that far up there, the number of beaver and other fur-bearers is beyond belief. You will see if that's so. I would like you to come and see me as soon as you return. This is not an idle invitation, Señor Drouillard."

Of course it's not, Drouillard realized. For the first time he foresaw the peculiar worth he would have after this voyage. He would have a connection with the United States government, and several hundred dollars in pay, and a piece of land, but more important to a man like Lisa, he would have first knowledge of a coveted new fur country. He would be very valuable. He had often heard his uncle speak of the great advantage of arriving early in a place. That was exactly what Lisa was hinting at. Drouillard appreciated this Spaniard for making that clear. Even though Lisa was trying to catch him for his own reasons, the trader had helped his Indian mind understand what a whiteman sees when he aims forward along a straight line. Drouillard had always looked at the world and its tomorrows as an eagle looks around the horizons. But a whiteman, he thought, looks ahead just as I aim along the sights of my rifle.

"Thank you, Señor Lisa. I'll keep that in mind. Perhaps when I come back we can do business in some way. I regret your present disappointment with the American captains."

"*Buena suerte,*" Lisa said. His hand was firm but cold. "Come. I'll escort you out."

"No, please. I saw how you escorted out the man before."

For the first time ever, he saw Manuel Lisa laugh.

I bind Myself, my Heirs, & ca to pay unto Freiderick Graeter, or his Order, in the next Month of April, the just and full sum of Three Hundred One Dollars, Sixty Three Cents ⅓ in Specie, as per Amount to me delivered, for Value received. Fort Massac. 11th February, 1804

GEORGE DROUILLARD

Drouillard had not signed his name in several years, but the inked signature was not crude or sloppy. It represented him and he was pleased with the way it looked.

It was the first time he had ever signed for a debt. Mr. Graeter had been willing to write a note lending him the money for two reasons: Drouillard last year had bought his long rifle from Graeter on a word-of-mouth agreement, and had paid for it when he promised to; also, the German merchant was beholden to

Louis Lorimier in some way, and Lorimier had told Drouillard to remind him of it.

Graeter counted out the money and gave it to him, and he put it in his possibles bag, which hung from his shoulder. He had never had so much money, and it bothered him. He now had to ride all the way to St. Louis with it, nearly a hundred and fifty miles over unpeopled prairie and lawless roads. Then he would have to trust friends of the captains to transform it into some kind of a document that could be sent six hundred miles to his stepmother in Ontario. And then in two months he would have to have the same amount somehow to pay Graeter back. He was counting on the captains somehow to get him an advance on his pay, though they had been vague on that promise. Drouillard was not very worried about that. He had seen Captain Lewis sign slips of paper and get hundreds of dollars' worth of goods, with everyone understanding that the United States would pay.

The primary uneasiness Drouillard felt was that a few people here in the settlement at Massac knew he was getting all this money, and knew that he would be riding out alone with it. The witness to the signing of the note, Antoine Laselle, had a look about him that did not inspire trust. Lorimier knew him and never recommended him.

Drouillard had enough faith in his own alertness and marksmanship that he knew he would not be easy to rob, not by one or two men. Three or four might be a danger, depending on the quality of their horses and their boldness.

A good hunter knew how to be elusive prey. Drouillard looked at the winter morning sunlight slanting through a window and said, "Gentlemen, please excuse me. I should start right out if I hope to make Lorimier's before night."

They stood up and shook his hand. He would have liked to visit his uncle, and these men would fully expect him to go there.

And so he would start out on the trace to Cape Girardeau. But in the swamps he would cut northward to the old Kaskaskias Trace, and leave no trail.

St. Louis
March 10, 1804

The two captains stood stiff and proud in their blue uniforms, swords hanging at their sides, and on their heads the enormous hats that looked like upside-down canoes. The captains were looking up at the top of the flagpole in front of the Government House, where the blue and white and red French flag was starting to come down. Other American officers and soldiers stood in ranks, and nearby there were French soldiers and Spanish soldiers, all in their finery. The plaza was crowded with the townspeople of St. Louis, many of them looking as if they were about to weep, and in groups around the edges of the crowd there were Indians, colorful in feathers, fringe, quillwork, and silver jewelry, seeming to know ceremony when they saw it, but surely having no notion that their country was being sold out from under their feet.

The crowd's murmur changed to a moan as the French flag was taken off and folded by French soldiers. Yesterday in another ceremony, they had cheered when the Spanish flag came down and theirs went up. They had requested that theirs stay up until today, when the American one would go up.

Drouillard watched, and felt the emotions of the crowd change like the coming and going of breath. When the American flag went up with its familiar corner of stars, an officer gave commands and a squad of American soldiers fired their guns over the flagpole. Whoops and throaty cheers rose from Americans in the crowd, many of whom fired their own guns into the air from amidst the crowd, frightening women and babies. Some of the Indians were now talking fast among themselves and pointing up at the American flag, which was new to them and probably of a more intriguing design, in their eyes, than the French.

The dressed-up American soldiers in the ceremony were not those of Captains Lewis and Clark. These were from Massac and Kaskaskia army posts. Some belonged to Major Stoddard, an older officer who had been sent out to be a sort of soldier-governor until an American government could be formed. The soldiers who would be going on the journey were still up in the shabby little post at Riviere à Dubois: training, bored, scouring the muddy countryside for bootleg whiskey, getting into fights, challenging their sergeants, getting punished, being deleted from the roster for insurrection then restored when they repented. To Drouillard they were like a corral of young stallions within faint scent of a forbidden rutting mare, and the mare was St. Louis with its saloons and saucy women.

Drouillard had assembled about a dozen French-Canadian riverboatmen and voyageurs for the captains. These were cheerful, rowdy veterans of thousands of miles of riverways, many related to each other, almost like a tribe. They were oblivious to the notion of military discipline. They answered only to their patroon, Jean Baptiste Deschamps, who would in turn answer to the captains. Most of them at times had worked on crews under Deschamps, who happened to be related to Drouillard's stepmother in Canada. The soldiers scorned the voyageurs as motley civilians, someone at last whom even they could look down their noses at, and so in one way the French-Canadians were already serving, even though they had yet to touch an oar. Undisciplined though they seemed, the voyageurs did not loom as troublesome as the soldiers. The expedition was to start its actual journey up the Missouri in a month or so, if Captain Lewis ever decided he had acquired enough supplies, and Drouillard often wondered whether it would get a hundred miles along before a general mutiny of its soldiery.

The gun smoke from the flag salute had drifted away over the crowd, and now officers were signing papers on a little table. Speeches then began, and went on and on, in English, French, and Spanish—all three languages that Drouillard could understand, and thus could not help hearing. Had he not already heard so much from the two captains, much of this grand language about dominions, emissaries, and sovereignty would have been incomprehensible to him.

As they droned on and on, simpler and truer things flowed

through Drouillard's mind and heart: *Menoukgawmeh*. Springtime. He could feel it, and even in this stinking town he could smell it coming on the wind from the west, from that vast country to which he would be going. Leaf buds were swelling, plants were pushing up through the thawing earth, the sap was up in the sugar trees, and the great bent flights of They Who Talk While Flying were going northward.

He thought a little about the money, the debt to Mr. Graeter, which he had promised to pay back about a month from now. He still had no certainty that he could do that. Graeter might just have to wait until he came back from the journey. The good thing was that Drouillard believed in his heart that he had helped his Canada family. He was still not very good at money-thinking. Money was not a real thing in the Creator's world; even though he had signed his name and become involved with it, he had to force himself to ponder on it.

Another thing that kept coming into his spirit was the feeling of *going*. Though the boats and goods and men were all still sitting on the bank of the Riviere à Dubois, the force of going into the western country on the whitemen's purpose was already something he could feel. His tomorrows would be spent with theirs, going in a direction with them instead of living from season to season in the round world of horizons. He would be a part of the whiteman force that had kept coming westward for generations, leaving nothing as it had been before. He would be going, taking his horizons with him, and there were enough dangers ahead, the known ones and the unforeseeable ones, even the dreamed-of ones like flint cutting flesh, that he understood he might not come back. This was a whiteman thing—going in a direction and taking your life along with you—but he was becoming a part of it.

Chapter 4

The day had come that Drouillard had begun to doubt would ever come. The captains' boats had actually left the camp at Riviere à Dubois, crossed the Mississippi, and started up the Missouri, after weeks of delay. Three days on the river had brought the expedition a mere twenty-five miles up the Missouri to St. Charles, and it looked to Drouillard as if the entire enterprise had collapsed right there, under the eyes of the bewildered French inhabitants of that little town.

When he had ridden in to St. Charles carrying another of those endless messages from Captain Lewis, who was still in St. Louis, he found the boats moored at the riverside, with the enormous cargo out on the riverbank in a great heap, as it had been for so long at the Riviere à Dubois camp. Even more ominous, the soldiers were standing in a double line whipping one of their own with bundles of switches, while the townspeople moaned and wailed or just grimly watched. The soldier was John Collins, who had often been drunk and disobedient at the winter camp, as had many of the soldiers. But this was the first whipping. With each hissing slash, Collins made a teeth-clenched grimace and his eyes bulged, but he did not cry out.

The soldiers with their switches were grim-faced and seemed to be hitting him as hard as they could. Whatever he had done must have been much more serious than his misbehaviors at camp. There, he had once brought in what he said was the haunch of a bear, but which proved to be the ham of a neighbor's hog, and the captain had been required to compensate the farmer. Collins had never threatened the sergeant with a loaded gun, as Colter had one day, but Captain Clark had several times labeled him a blackguard. Collins was a slim, fine-featured, comic fellow, seemingly well-liked, and it was troubling to see how viciously his fellow men were laying it on.

Drouillard hung back until the punishment of Collins was completed, thinking dark thoughts about it. He waited for Captain Clark to treat Collins's back with an ointment and gauze, then took him the messages from Captain Lewis. It was dusk, and mosquitoes made humming, swirling clouds. Clark and Drouillard sat in the smoke of a cookfire to discourage the pests, and the captain read his mail by the firelight. His face was full of his feelings. He sighed, blew through his lips like a winded horse, and said, "Three more days? Damn, I wish he'd get up here. I'd like his judgment on a few things. Well, you need to know what this is all about. Wretched start on our voyage! We ran onto eight or ten drift logs already. Cruzatte says it's because too much load was astern." He waved his hand at the pile of cargo. "So we're reloading 'er different, to keep the bow down. I wish he'd given that advice before we started up." He pointed at the town. "Those good folk held a ball for us last night, dancing and all. That Cruzatte is lively on a fiddle, and I never saw such a little town with so many fiddlers! It was a fine time. But then that damn blackguard Collins got a bit too lusty as the wine flowed and made an ass of 'imself with some of the better ladies. When I dressed him down back in camp, he got mutinous with his mouth. Damned blackguard is what he is! So we had a court-martial for him this morning. For Warner and Hall too, for going absent from camp. Didn't whip those two, but they're confined till we move on."

Drouillard restrained himself from commenting that he had expected this kind of thing when the troops got near women and entertainment, after all those months.

Clark went on, "I'm tempted to discharge that damn Collins before we get too far up. But Cap'n Lewis recruited him and thinks he has qualities we need. We'll see, 'd reckon. Maybe he'll think things over, rowin' with his back all scabbed. Well, though," he said, brightening and flexing his shoulders, "we're on our way at last. Say, that Cruzatte you brought us is worth his pay! Even if he didn't play the fiddle so agreeable. He kept us off many more a snag than we got on. Did he tell you he joined the army? Labiche too. You look surprised, eh?"

"Yes, sir." Drouillard shook his head. He would never have expected voyageurs to give up so much of their cherished freedom, or the army of the *anglais-américain* whitemen to accept half-breeds—although, he remembered now, they had offered to recruit him as a soldier, back in the beginning; he had rejected that notion so long ago that he had forgotten. So he said only, "I will have to remember that my old friends' given names are no longer Pierre and François, but Private and Private."

Clark laughed. "You could be Private too. It's not too late."

"Thank you, sir, but no." He thought for a moment whether to make a critical observation, and decided to make it. "My people, you know, have that custom too, the gauntlet. But we run only our enemies through it. Not our own people."

Captain Clark leaned back and cocked an eye at him, an eye so dark blue in the evening light that it looked purple. "An interesting point. I'll answer it this way. When I can't count on one of my soldiers, he's not one of my people, he's my enemy, and the men's too. They understand that, and that's why they whip 'im with such relish."

"Hm. I see." And he did. It was the first time an army thing had made Indian sense to him.

Captain Clark waved mosquitoes away from his face, then stood up and walked around the fire to stand downwind in the smoke. Drouillard followed him around. The smoke stung his eyes but kept mosquitoes away. "I expect Mr. Lorimier back down from the Kickapoo town," Clark said. "Thought I'd see him come down today. Let's wait till midday tomorrow. If he shows up by then, you two can ride together down to St. Louis with the mail."

"Thankee, Cap'n. I do hope to see him before we go on up."
Drouillard knew that his uncle had gone to a Kickapoo camp
above the Missouri as an emissary for the captains, to explain
Jefferson's intentions to them. The Kickapoos had been planning to make war on the Osages, the captains had been trying
discourage them from it, and Lorimier was the right man for the
diplomacy because he knew Missouri Indian trade, and also because Kickapoo was so like Shawnee that he could talk plain
with them.

Captain Clark nodded thoughtfully. "Remarkable gent. I was
uneasy to meet 'im. Y' already know why. But he didn't mention
it at all, the war, I mean. Just said he knew my brother by repute
but never met him personal."

Drouillard had a rush of appreciative feeling toward his uncle,
and had an urge to tell Clark how Lorimier had been a better father to him than his own had been. But he kept it to himself, because he was still in a dark mood about the whipping he had
seen, and for days he had been so heartily tired of being Lewis's
messenger boy that he was sorry he ever signed on. He was glad
when Sergeant Ordway came and required the captain's attention on some matter down by the keelboat. So once again Drouillard was left in the care of York, who now had to dispense his
hospitality from a campfire under a canvas instead of his usual
cabin kitchen. But apparently he and his master were used to
camp life; he had an orderly little arrangement of iron forks,
spits, kettle hooks, and utensils, as well as a hinged box stocked
with toddy-making paraphernalia, and a coffeepot hanging over
the fire by its bail, seething away. This was the military camp for
York and the soldiers; the captain surely would be sleeping in
town as guest of some citizen or other. St. Charles, the last real
settlement west of the Mississippi, was renowned among rivermen for its hospitality. Many of its residents were the families of
voyageurs; Cruzatte and the voyageurs' patroon, Deschamps,
lived here, and two others, Malboeuf and Hebert, had lived in the
town at times in their wandering lives. So, as usual, only the soldiers had to camp out. Drouillard warned himself not to take a

toddy this time, but he was saddle-weary and peevish, and when York offered to fix him one, he shrugged and accepted, and sat on a crate to watch the servant prepare it. After two sips he found himself feeling mean again, wanting to say some of the things he had stopped himself from saying to York back at the winter bivouac.

"That captain ever whip you like that?" he asked. "The way they do that soldier Collins?"

York took a deep breath and sighed it out, looking off into the darkening sky. "Not 'xackly like 'at, no s'."

"What, then? Bullwhip instead of switches?"

"Mast' Billy don' whip me."

"I thought you just said he does."

"A man on the place do. Not hisself."

Whitemen always have people do everything for them, Drouillard thought. "You have a family?"

York nodded, momentary sadness in his eyes. "Wife."

"Like to be with her?"

"Oh, I sure do!" That came out unguarded.

"Wouldn't it be good if you could choose to stay with your wife, or go with the cap'n? You could choose, if he didn't own you. D' you know the whitemen tried to make Indians slaves when they first came? Didn't work, though. They'd run off. So the whitemen cut off their feet so they couldn't run away. So they'd just sit and make themselves die. That's why the white-men had to go get you folks. You couldn't run home, across the ocean."

York said, "You makin' 'at up?"

"No. Indian people remember way back. Eh yeh! If anybody claimed to own me, or thought he could whip me, he'd never find me."

York was sweating, brushing at mosquitoes unthinkingly. "Mist' Droor, I been hopin' you be on 'is jou'ney. Bu-But maybe you talk too much trouble."

Drouillard drained the rest of the sweet stuff from the pewter cup and put it down. He wasn't pleased with himself, tormenting a poor slave just to work out his own irritation at the masters. But he did have one more thing to say: "Think about that ol' Caesar."

The soldiers and boatmen were lifting, toting, and sweating next day, reloading the vessels to improve their trim, when Louis Lorimier rode into the camp from upriver, flanked by two young riders carrying long guns. Drouillard recognized them as his uncle's secretary and a surly Shawnee who sometimes rode as his bodyguard. Lorimier was grinning like a possum, his hat plume waving in the breeze. The horses were muddy to the chest, and walking tired, and Lorimier was flicking his mare on the withers with the end of his long braid. *"Bonjour, neveu!"* he shouted with a toss of his head. *"Bonjour, mon capitaine!"* He waded through a clutch of voyageurs who had run over to greet him.

Sitting to take a whiskey by Clark's canvas shelter, Lorimier reported that he had had an agreeable conference with the Kickapoos up north, that they had promised not to attack the Osage this season. He had played on their jealousy of the Osage by telling them that an Osage chief was going to visit the Great White Father in the East, and that if the Kickapoos honored their promise to be peaceful, they too could have a chief honored by such a journey. Lorimier was pleased with himself. He would intercept Captain Lewis in St. Louis and give a full accounting to him.

While Clark wrote a letter to Lewis, Drouillard and his uncle strolled into the town for a quick round of visits and libations with Lorimier's many friends there. Afterward there was enough afternoon left for the twenty-mile ride overland to St. Louis on refreshed horses. The trace led southeastward up over the forested bluff and then emerged onto an intensely green vista of rolling prairie broken with copses of woods. Drouillard, carrying Clark's letter about the cargo shift and the whipping, rode close alongside his uncle, knowing this could be his last sight of him for a long time.

"So, *neveu,* the *américain* fleet at last moves. And you have not changed your mind?"

"Sometimes I am ready to ask for my promise back. But I go along. They might not get much farther. The soldiers are wild, and they might desert or mutiny. They already hate that heavy boat. Their sergeant told me each man pulls about a ton. And they have perhaps a hundred times as far to go as they have come."

Lorimier nodded. "The town people did not like the whipping of the soldier. Did you see it done?"

"I did. I expect to see more. In the camp the soldiers were always in trouble, and they find this much harder than camp."

Lorimier was keenly interested in whether this voyage would succeed or fail. He said, "Do they talk of quitting?"

Drouillard shrugged. "They fall quiet when I come near. They think of me as the captains' man, since I'm their courier. Even the boatmen are wary of me. I don't like that."

Lorimier put his head back and laughed. "You like to be alone, you, the hunter! This will help you be alone! Ha ha! But I tell you, I think they will get over the trouble and succeed. You must understand the power an officer has. It is all written, in army books. When an officer may whip, or cast out, or shoot a soldier."

"Such things as your sons go to learn in the army school, eh?" Drouillard pictured the likable but spoiled boys, Guillaume and Louis, stiff-necked in blue soldier coats, with the authority to whip or shoot soldiers. He thought of soldiers now as he thought of York the slave, all probably wanting to run away, but afraid of the invisible whips, guns, and chains.

Lorimier rode along, chuckling, occasionally flicking a fly with the end of his braid. "*C'est ça, alors.* Not all bad for us. As I have said, it is good to be early in a promising place. Good also to have relations and prestige. You know that your father was a better trader and interpreter because he married your mother. And look at me. I am a shining portrait of *le pratique!*"

Drouillard thought of Manuel Lisa, saying these same things about early advantages. Lisa had seen him as being of value because of the knowledge he would gain. If his uncle foresaw that, he had not said so. To Lorimier, it seemed, he had failed for good when he ran away from school and became a hunting Indian, and apparently could never be as promising as the two soft and dissipated sons who would become officers. They had gone east earlier this month, along with some Osage headmen who needed to be overawed by the great cities and the Great White Father Jefferson.

"*Eh bien,*" Drouillard said. "Who knows what will come of all this? Sometimes it does not look so good to me." He was thinking not just of the difficulties he had seen, but those of his dreams.

"You are that dubious," Lorimier said with a slanting smile and a shake of the head, "yet you seem to be going."

"I gave my word. And, speaking of that: I gave my word too to Mr. Graeter about my debt to him. It is a month past due. But the captains keep me so busy running between them, I haven't been able to go to Massac and pay any back, or renew the note. The captains gave me no advance to pay him off with. Now we're going up the river and I have no chance to keep my word with him."

Lorimier chuckled. "*Neveu,* there are two kinds of promises. The kind you must keep as promptly as you can, and the kind you make to moneylenders." Drouillard looked at him in surprise. A promise was a promise, and he had never suspected that his uncle made distinctions. Lorimier shrugged. "I will tell M'sieu Graeter your excuse, and that he must wait. He will still be here when you return. And if he isn't, even better!"

"Uncle, you are certainly free with the honor of my name." He was not comfortable with leaving the debt untended, and knew it would linger in a part of his mind. But Lorimier knew of money things, and he knew Graeter.

Over the next rise their view deepened below and to the east. Across the Mississippi the last of the evening sun gilded the lush green woods on the slopes and top of the ancient mound-hill, and it stood forth glowing above the bottomland, which was now in shadow. The great, dusky lowland with the broad river curving through it and the sacred hill glowing in its ancient silence swelled his heart. This place among the joining rivers was the land most familiar to his feet and to his eagle's eyes. The thought of leaving it gave him an ache.

But now, below, on this side of the river, were the roofs and chimneys of the whitemen's town of St. Louis. As this valley was the place to which the river waters all flowed, this town would be the place to which all wealth flowed, if the plans of the whitemen came out as they hoped.

And he of the many languages was to help them make it so. He still wondered sometimes why the Master of Life had put him in the path of the Captains Lewis and Clark. But if the teachings of his mother were true, that was what had been done.

June 12, 1804

Drouillard had killed two bears on the prairie the day before, and he was making jerky of the leftover meat by drying thin strips on a rack above a bed of coals when a shout came from the river.

Two boats were coming down, carrying several whitemen and a boy, all dressed in skins. They came ashore.

They had been trading far up the Missouri with the Yankton band of Sioux, and had hides and furs in their vessels, en route to St. Louis. A very rugged and weathered old man was in charge of them. He introduced himself as Pierre Dorion, a patroon of the trader Loisel. He had traded twenty-five years among the Sioux. Within minutes the old man was cackling with the happy realization that Captain Clark was a brother of the great soldier George Rogers Clark, whom Dorion had aided during his Revolutionary War campaign on the Mississippi. Drouillard shook his head in disbelief. One couldn't get away from that man's reputation, even two hundred miles up the Missouri.

The captains bought three hundred pounds of buffalo grease and tallow from the traders. Then they set about persuading the old man to join them and go back up as far as the Sioux towns, where he might be very valuable as an interpreter and might use his influence to convince some Sioux chiefs to go east and meet

the President. They told Dorion about the purchase of the territory, amazing news to him, and about the President's plan to
shape all the Indian nations into a trade network. Dorion wasted
no time deciding. He transferred himself, baggage, and his dim-
witted camp boy to the red pirogue of the voyageurs, and sent the
rest of his party on down the Missouri to market their yield.

Chapter 5

Already, poor Collins was about to get whipped again. A hundred lashes this time. Just when the slashes on his back were fully healed from the punishment at St. Charles. He stood shirtless in the hot afternoon sun while the troops lined up with their fists full of whips. And Private Hugh Hall was stripped for whipping too. Fifty lashes he was to get.

Drouillard knelt a few yards away, rolling up wet deerskins to tie in bundles with wood ash, which would loosen the hair for easy removal. He wouldn't watch this whipping business. Some of the voyageurs were helping him with the skins, others were loading the keelboat and pirogues with big bundles of cooked and dried venison they had been preparing during the two-day encampment, here where the Kanzas flowed into a sharp bend of the Missouri. Drouillard had shot dozens of deer in the weeks coming upriver, and some bears. He cut the meat in thin strips and dried it in the sun on such days as this, when there was no rain.

He felt like a free man again, ranging through this vast new country, back in his natural role as a hunter and scout. Now that the two captains were together, he didn't have to carry letters and pouches back and forth between them as he had for so many weeks, and for the greater part of every day he felt as if he were roaming alone through a hunter's paradise. Being the main hunter, he was excused from guard duty at night and from the

71

labors of rowing, poling, and pulling the boats up the swift river. But he made up for it with all this butchering and work on the hides.

Over by the gauntlet line Captain Lewis was making some angry pronouncement. The soldiers were warming up their whipping arms, switches swishing and hissing in the air, but Drouillard could hear hardly any of it over the drone and whine of the flies that blackened and dotted everything, especially his butchering places. His eyes and mouth would fill with flies if he opened them wide.

He had never hunted so hard or trimmed so much meat in his whole life as a hunter, even when feeding the troops back at Fort Massac. It was because he had never hunted for anyone who was working as hard as these soldiers. He guessed every man was eating maybe ten pounds of fresh meat every day, yet they grew leaner and leaner from their exertions. They were always drenched, with river water and rain sometimes, but usually with their own sweat. They were wretched with blisters, scald foot, and boils from the constant rubbing of sodden clothes, wet shoes, sweat-slick oars and push-poles and tow ropes, all aggravated by the bites of deer flies and black flies in the daytime and the clouds of mosquitoes at night. Many had other skin problems, rashes and tumors, which the captains blamed on drinking the scummy, muddy water of the Missouri. The men used bear grease faster than he and Colter could bring it in, to soothe their irritations and discourage biting insects. They all greased up liberally but sweated it off almost as fast.

Now to add to their skin problems, these two, Collins and Hall, were about to be whipped raw with green switches. And the soldiers would whip them without mercy or restraint this time, in righteous anger:

The two had stolen from the corps liquor supply.

Drouillard knew how the men felt about the whiskey. To them it was one of the most precious parts of the cargo, equal in their minds and hearts to gunpowder and tobacco. They thought of it all day. The whiskey ration every evening was the high point of the day. It lifted their spirits and compensated for their physical miseries. And there was too little of it as it was, without selfish blackguards taking more than their share. In their meticulous preparation of the cargo manifest, the captains had determined that there was room for just a little over a hundred gallons. The soldiers mulled their liquor calculations over and over: less than three gallons per man, on a voyage that was going to last two years or more. They had figured the number of drams in a gallon and knew there was probably not enough to last the way west. They feared some of it would be used medicinally or shared with Indians and would be depleted even sooner. There would be no way to get any more when this ran out.

The whiskey was their sacred reserve, but on guard duty last night Collins had sneaked an unauthorized drink from the keg, then another, and more as it made him more careless. Then Hall had caught him at it, so Collins offered him some, and they had got quietly drunk. The captains had convened a court-martial late this morning, with Sergeant Pryor presiding and Private John Potts acting as Judge Advocate. Collins had pleaded not guilty and was swiftly pronounced guilty, one hundred lashes well laid on as punishment. Perhaps expecting to be acquitted if truthful, Hall admitted his guilt and was sentenced to fifty strokes.

Orders were shouted. Despite himself, Drouillard watched Collins go down the line. Even over the whine of flies he could hear the fierce hissing of the switches. He heard one of the soldiers shout, "Collins, you flyblown turd, y' need a flywhisk on ye! Take this!" *Shish! Shish!*

"No commentaries needed," Captain Lewis barked. "Just do your duty." The switches hissed and whistled in the air, splitting and snapping with the force; splinters and blood mist filled the air in Collins's wake, and he was grimacing and beginning to stagger. But as before, he made no outcry. When he was through, Captain Clark led him aside to anoint his tattered flesh. Then as Hall started through, Drouillard turned away, and was surprised to see the slave York squatting beside him, helping to smear the wet ash on one of the deer hides. York's headkerchief was pulled down over one eye, which had been hurt a week before when Collins, pretending to be playful, had thrown river sand in the slave's face. Captain Clark had thought York would lose the eye, but after a few days of pain and infection, it was beginning to heal.

"Eh, York, you don't have to do this bloody work. You're the cap'n's helper, not mine."

York looked at him and chuckled. "I don' mind, Mist' Droor. Ra'r be a-puttin' this treatment on a deerskin than medicine on that man's skin. Heh!" He smeared the ashy paste, which grayed his thick black hands and wrists.

Drouillard nodded. So they worked together. Hall yelped a few times as he went through the gauntlet. Drouillard shook his head. "Mean!" he said softly. "Y' know, my people never even switch a child. I can't get used to this."

York murmured deep and said, " 'N'en you never been whipped?"

"I'd kill a man who ever tried it."

York peered at him with his good eye, glanced around at the hides, bones, fly-covered guts, and bloodsoaked sand, nodded and said, "Reckon so."

Drouillard had seen the whip scars on York's broad back a few times, when the slave had stripped to swim ashore and gather cress and other greens to add to the captains' diet. He and York ate with the captains, and the four of them were the only ones free of the skin problems. Drouillard asked, "You get whipped often?"

"Not often. I been a good boy."

"Cap'n didn't do the whippin' himself, you said?"

"Had somebody c'd do it better who di'n like me. Cap'n beat the tar out o' me when we play-fighted, though."

Drouillard squinted at York. "You ever hit *him*?" The idea of the man and his slave fighting was a cheering notion.

York again chuckled deep, and shook his head. "Lucky a couple times, is all. 'Em Clark boys all, woo, watch out!"

Drouillard hadn't considered whether there might be other Clark brothers besides the Town Burner. "How many brothers?"

"Four now. Was six, till the war."

"Hm. They all play-fought you?"

He chuckled. "Oh, only Mas' Billy. Only my own boy."

My own boy, Drouillard thought. Like he owns the cap'n, rather than the way it really is.

It had taken them a month and a half to reach this river, the Kanzas. Captain Clark said they had come 366 miles in that time. The captains were always measuring and writing down. With compasses and other instruments they measured every turn in the river. Clark seemed to be able to measure miles in his mind, whether he was in the keelboat or walking on shore. Almost every day he drew little map sketches and wrote down numbers. At every river mouth, if the sky was clear, the captains measured sun and moon and stars with their strange look-through devices, and determined just where it was in the world by numbers. They seemed to see everything in lines and numbers, and they wrote something down about every living creature they saw. Lewis would kill a bird and measure its wings and legs and count its feathers and write all that down for his president. He pressed plants and flowers between papers, skinned animals, stuffed birds, and wrote everything down. It all looked like so much trouble. It seemed to Drouillard it would have been easier for Jefferson just to have come out and looked the country over himself.

Drouillard had been more hunter than interpreter so far. Five days out of St. Charles, they had met the Kickapoo hunters with whom Lorimier had counciled, and Drouillard had talked for them to the captains. The Kickapoo tongue was almost exactly like Shawnee, and the tribal name so similar to Kithkopo, the Shawnee war clan, that Drouillard suspected they must have splintered off from the Shawnees long ago. At any rate, his skill in talking with them had delighted the captains. The Kickapoos had brought three fresh-killed deer for the soldiers, explaining that Lorimier had told them to have meat ready when the whitemen's boats came up. That had of course increased the captains' appreciation of Lorimier.

All had gone so well that day that the captains gave the

Kickapoos two quarts of whiskey, and the troops had looked on, aghast, at the sight of their precious liquor passing into the hands and down the throats of mere savages. Maybe Collins and Hall had just decided to drink theirs before the captains gave it all away to the numerous Indians ahead.

But since those Kickapoos, there had been no Indians at all, and when Drouillard found their trails while hunting, they showed no recent use. For about a month now, in fact, the expedition had met no one along the river, except a fur trader named Loisel, old M'sieur Dorion's boss, returning from a winter of trading with the Sioux, some four hundred miles above. Here Drouillard had served well as interpreter, this time of the French of Dorion and Loisel. The two had given the captains much recent information about Indians, trade, and traders, which would be useful ahead, or so they hoped. Then Loisel had gone on down.

Drouillard spent his days hunting, his evenings evaluating the officers and men, or occasionally serving as intermediary between the voyageurs and the officers—a frustrating and distasteful task. Captain Lewis in particular was contemptuous of the French boatmen, whom he found disorderly and frivolous, a bad example to the soldiers he was trying to discipline. Drouillard kept encouraging Private Cruzatte to assume more responsibility for that, since he was now both a voyageur and a soldier.

Clark was easy to like and admire, but Lewis seemed a man out of balance. The energies he had expended on manipulating and flattering the leading families around St. Louis, and in buying goods for the journey, he now expended on scampering and snooping along the riverbanks after anything that might interest Jefferson. Climbing a cliff one day, he had fallen off the edge, barely saving himself by wedging his knife into a crack, giving himself and Clark a good scare. When not giddy with excitement, he was a stickler and a fretter.

Drouillard loved getting away to hunt early every morning. He would take his horse out of the valley onto the open uplands to get a feel of the lie of the new land and the course of the great river, watching the first sunlight gild the western cloud tops, then the hills, hearing the waking songbirds, watching for the smoke of Indian camps, scanning the ground for well-trodden animal paths that might lead to salt licks or watering places. Some days the game was so plentiful and tame that there was really no hunting to be done, just a leisurely, steady, long-range shot at a fully exposed deer, standing as if placed there as a gift from the Keeper of the Game. Sometimes a soldier would be sent out to hunt with him. The one named Colter was the best hunter. Others went out almost as if apprenticed to Drouillard. The good ones he could send out on tangents, to cover more ground. Far away his fellow hunter's gun would crack and the echoes would roll, and they would meet at some preselected landmark, and if both had got kills they would take them down and hang them high and safe in trees near the river where they expected the boats to get to. The soldiers loved hunt duty, a day off from slaving on oars. It was a poor day if they came in with less than four deer, a good day with six. Drouillard would usually bag a seventh near day's end, knowing that any day there was plenty of venison, the captains did not have to issue salt pork. Though there were fifty kegs of the pork, two tons of the boat's cargo, the men's appetites were such that all the pork would be gone in less than two weeks if they depended on it alone. Motivating him further to bring in fresh meat was his belief that pork, even from a fresh-butchered pig, was repugnant; salt pork from a keg was just grease—to him no better than eating from a latrine. When he brought fresh meat, the soldiers didn't have to eat such slop. For all his thoughts of slaves and soldiers, he had never seen slaves work as hard as these soldiers did on the boats, and they needed and deserved fresh meat.

When the men could row with the oars in smooth water, it was hard enough; they sat on their benches and pulled, pulled, pulled, sweating in the sunshine, nipped by deerflies, suffering blisters and strained backs. But the Missouri was not usually a smooth stream. Sometimes it was swift and shallow, chutes of tricky water racing between sandbars, with no room for oars. In such places the soldiers used long setting-poles instead of oars. Each would set the end of his pole in the mud, brace his shoulder against it, and walk toward the stern along one gunwale or the other, driving the boat forward by leg power. At the stern cabin he would have to yank the pole from the grip of the muddy bottom, carry it to the bow, turn, set it in the bottom again, trudge and push again, the boat creeping forward. In the worst shallows and the swiftest chutes, even poles would not work, and then the men would have to get out and wade in the mud or thrash through riverbank thickets while pulling the boat by ropes, as if they were canal-boat mules.

The Missouri was usually afloat or jammed with driftwood. As it undercut its meandering banks, trees, sometimes whole riverbanks of cottonwoods and willows, would slough off and cave in. Sometimes nearly the whole wide river would be choked shut with muddy piles of trees, splintered limbs, and gnarled root clumps. Although the keelboat and the two pirogues had masts and sails, seldom were conditions or winds right for such easy going. The keelboat's tall mast, in fact, was jointed near the base so it could be lowered to lie parallel above the deck, with the sail spread over it as a canopy for shelter. This inventive feature had on occasion kept the mast from being entangled or broken in overhanging trees, when the only passable channels were close to shore.

A morning rain fell steadily, dribbling and hushing in the trees. Drouillard sat under the projecting rock of a cliff, watching a deer path that led onto a mud bank churned by deer tracks. The cliff overlooked a river bend, and below the bend the river was divided by a long sandbar, whose upper end was covered by a great, tangled pile of weathered driftwood. Now and then a tree, with or without leaves, would float, bobbing swiftly and silently, through the river channels, or hang up on the driftwood pile with a crackling of limbs. Early in the morning he had come out alone, to range a few miles ahead of the boats, and had already killed a deer, which hung gutted on a tree limb a few hundred yards upstream. When the rain started, he had taken shelter here.

It was likely he would get another deer, even without moving, if he kept a view of the path.

Some blackbirds flew up in the rain. Drouillard then began to hear voices through the rain-hush downstream, then some hollow, bumping sounds. The boats were coming up into the bend. They would scare off any deer. So in a little while he would leave the shelter and go up to the carcass above, and hail the boats to take it aboard when they got there. But there was no hurry, so he waited. He liked to watch the boats.

In a few minutes the dark prow of the keelboat emerged through the veil of pale willow foliage, nosing slowly against the swift current of the wider channel. The smaller boats, first the red pirogue rowed by voyageurs, then the white-hulled one manned by Corporal Warfington's eight soldiers, appeared in the narrower channel on the other side of the sandbar.

In the bow of the keelboat stood Cruzatte and Labiche, his two métis friends who had surprised him by joining the army. Their rainsoaked clothes clung to their brawny torsos. Behind them were the twenty soldiers straining on their long oars, most shirtless and hatless. Cruzatte and Labiche each held a long, thick pike-pole with a sharp iron tip, their tools for fending off drift trees. Cruzatte ogled the river with his one good eye.

As the keelboat pulled past the sandbar, Cruzatte's high, nasal voice called a warning. Drouillard looked upstream and saw a big drift tree barreling roots first down the bend, right into the keelboat's way. The rowers, alerted by his cry, paused, looking back over their shoulders.

Cruzatte crouched, jabbed the tip of his gaff-pole into the jagged root bole, and his sinewy body arched with strain. The pole began to bend as the great weights of the boat and tree pressed together through it, and Cruzatte was nearly lifted off his footing. Labiche jammed his spike too against the roots.

Slowly the root bole swung off the keelboat's larboard quarter.

But Cruzatte was at once in action again, yelling, *"Pas encore!"* He yanked back his pole and jabbed again with it, this time at the trunk of the tree, which had begun to swing around toward the prow. And the keelboat, now veering to starboard from the force of the fending effort, was quartered by the swift current, threatening to broach with the tree coming parallel. The powerful stream had the boat and tree in its grip, carrying them sideways toward the sandbar. Drouillard's heart raced. In this moment on the muddy gray, rain-spattered water he could see the voyage coming to an early end. The weight of the tree would overset the boat or crush it like an eggshell against the tangle of driftwood. Cruzatte and Labiche were still straining to push the tree away. The oarsmen were jumping up from their places and stretching out their oars to help, all in a clamor of shouting, but apparently oblivious of the sandbar on the other side. Drouillard cupped his mouth to yell a warning, but suddenly a bellow overrode all the hubbub:

"All hands back on your oars! And *back off*! Now! Back! Back!"

It was Clark. He had seen the threat of the sandbar. The soldiers scrambled back to their places, dropped their oars into the rowlocks and pushed them instead of pulling them. Slowly, then faster, the keelboat backed out from the narrowing trap, then wheeled about stern-to in the swift channel, while the huge tree rolled onto the end of the sandbar. In a moment the rowers and helmsman had the keelboat back on course up through the river bend.

Drouillard stood shaking his head, breathing fast, as the ponderous vessel moved on up through the bend, flanked by the red and white pirogues, everybody laughing and howling to each other about yet another close escape. This would be all the talk again in camp this evening: another of those thrilling, terrible moments, and the desperate strainings and near-panics they went through almost every day to save the boats and themselves. This time they had avoided splinter-gashed hands or fearsome dunkings. Tonight they would brag, and the captains might come and brag on them all, and they wore praise like a warrior's honors. Sometimes Drouillard listened and almost envied them their frights and miseries and hard-earned celebrations.

But they weren't free, and he was. As the convoy moved on up through the bend, their laughter faded. Cruzatte's voice started up a rhythmic voyageur paddling song. Drouillard slipped out of the rock shelter into the rain to go to the place ahead where the venison hung. Those poor bastards needed meat, and they deserved it.

July 4th Wednesday 1804
The Plains of this countrey are covered with a Leek Green Grass, well calculated for the sweetest and most norushing hay—interspersed with Cops of trees, Spreding ther lofty branchs over Pools Springs or Brooks of fine water. Groops of Shrubs covered with the most delicious froot is to be seen in every direction, and nature seems to have exerted herself to butify the Senery by the variety of flours Delicately and highly flavered raised above the Grass, which Strikes & profumes the Sensation, and amuses the mind throws it into Conjectering the cause of So magnificent a Senerey in a Country thus Situated far removed from the Sivilised world to be enjoyed by nothing but the Buffalo Elk Deer & Bear in which it abounds & Savage Indians.

William Clark, Journals

Alexander Hamilton Willard was a soldier whom Drouillard had noticed at the beginning of the journey for the contrast between his daunting physique and his quiet, obedient behavior. The rawboned giant was so shy that Drouillard might never have come to know him at all if the captains had not sent him out with him often, with instructions to teach the man some hunting skills. Willard had been a blacksmith. His hands were so huge and strong that Sergeant Floyd joked, "Drouillard, you just find him a bear, and let 'im wrang its neck like a chicken. Save powder and lead."

Willard was good to hunt with in that he wasn't a talker and didn't have to be hushed all the time like some of them. Colter, and the two Field brothers, Joe and Reubin, were the best hunters among the troops. They were talkative, but not on the hunt. Willard seldom talked even in camp. But it didn't look as if he would ever become much of a hunter. He was too much a day-dreamer and didn't concentrate as one must to find sign or do tracking. He just could not concentrate, it seemed, and sometimes as they rode over the grasslands, Drouillard believed that the big man was asleep in the saddle with his eyes open.

Hunting was different here on the plains. Drouillard had spent most of his life under the gloomy green canopies of hardwood forests. Here, except in the ravines and river valleys, scarcely a tree was to be seen anywhere. Grasses waved and rippled in the wind, miles in every direction. Game on the plains had to be approached by staying in defilade, in gullies and draws, and taking very long shots. No buffalo had been seen yet. Hunting for deer, Drouillard therefore stayed much in the bottomlands, where the deer behaved pretty much as deer did anywhere.

July 11th, Wednesday 1804
Several hunters Sent out to day on both Sides of the river,
Seven Deer Killed to day. Drewyer Killd Six of them made
Some Luner observations this evening.

William Clark, Journals

"No damn fair, is it, Reubin?" Joseph Field whined to his brother, looking up from the deer hide he was flensing with his hunting knife in the firelight. He tilted his head toward Drouillard. "This feller's makin' us miss out on the fun, cleanin' all these damn deer hides!" Over by the big bonfire most of the soldiers were stomping, hooting, and capering to the fast, jiggling French tune Cruzatte played on his fiddle. Soldiers were keeping time with clapping, and a couple of voyageurs were making their tambourines sound like rattlesnakes. Captain Lewis's big dog, excited as always by the men's dancing, was bounding around in the sand as if he were one of them, and his proud and doting master was roaring with laughter at the sight. Beyond the fire were the straight edges and sloping surfaces of the long, half-faced tents of oiled linen, hung with mosquito-barring gauze, in which the soldiers off guard would sleep in rows when their party was over.

Drouillard looked up from his own work and saw that the brothers were smiling and glancing at him, joking, not really complaining. They were pretty good hunters themselves, and he had made a big impression on them. Sometimes when they didn't know he was around, he would hear them talking to the other soldiers about him, building him into a proper legend. Some of the troops had taken to calling him Nimrod. It was a name he vaguely remembered from the whiteman's religion. Captain Clark eventually had told him that in the Bible, Nimrod was the mightiest hunter of the ancient times.

"We'll be glad we got all them hides," said a man named Shields, sitting nearby. "My army clothes an' boots 'bout wore out and tore up from all this river rat work. We'll all of us be wearin' leather, come winter."

"Come winter, give me bear skin, fur side inside," said Reubin. "You notice how long we been goin' north and more north since we camped at the Kanzas?"

Shields, being a skilled gunsmith and tinkerer, spent much time near the captains, repairing things. He eavesdropped, and then talked about what he'd heard of their discussions. He said, "We got another three, four hunnerd miles more north to go. Start runnin' into Sioux 'bout two hunnerd miles, that's what ol' Dorion said."

Since he had joined the party, the old trader had talked mostly about Sioux, since that was what he knew most about. His camp boy was part Sioux. Drouillard had tried in vain to talk with the boy, who was strange and dense. Drouillard suspected that one or two of the voyageurs were playing with the boy at night. Maybe that was why Dorion kept him too, but the main thing on the old man's mind and tongue was the Sioux. His band, the Yanktons, were reasonable and probably would agree to go east. But the ones farther up, the Teton or Burnt Thigh Sioux, were belligerent, and jealous of their control over the trade in British goods from Canada. They were not likely to cooperate, even talk, with the Americans. They might even try to attack and rob them. Over and over Dorion warned them not to count on convincing *those* Sioux of anything.

"O' course," Shields went on, "ye say somethin' like that to Cap'n Lewis, he take it as a dare, an' he means to try, I reckon."

Drouillard, still working on hands and knees over the fresh deer hide that he had staked flat on the ground, listened and nodded. Unlike Shields, he kept to himself what he heard from the captains, and he heard much more, because as their interpreter he tented with them. It was true that Lewis had that cocksure idea that all the Sioux would just have to listen to him, and how could they quibble with what the Great Father Jefferson intended for them?

So here they were anticipating how they would deal with the Sioux already, while so far in all these hundreds of miles up through the plains they had not encountered Kanzas, Ponca, Oto, Missouria, Pawnee, Omaha, any of the tribes they should have met before getting into Sioux country. Since the Kickapoos in May, they had not met one solitary living Indian. It was eerie. Drouillard had seen a few old village sites, and today Captain Clark had caught a stray Indian pony. But from the very old burrs in its mane and tail, it appeared to have been astray a long time. Dorion had said there were hardly any Indians along the Missouri for a long stretch ahead, as most were up the tributaries or out on the plains hunting.

"Anyway, I want a bear fur coat," Reubin Field said. He leaned over to sit on one haunch with his elbow supporting him, and said, "Do I hear a bear growlin'?" and blew an imitation bear growl out of his rear end. Then he laughed at his own humor, slapping his knee.

"Nope, but don't I hear a hoot-owl?" Shields raised a thigh, squinted one eye, made a noise like a boot being pulled out of mud. He opened both eyes wide and puckered his mouth and said, "Oop! 'Scuse me . . ." He got up gingerly, bent forward and hurried out of the firelight down to the river. The Field brothers watched him go, then burst out laughing, hitting each other on the shoulders. Reubin, gasping between guffaws, finally managed to say, "Guess ol' Shields jes' remembered to do his laundry!"

Drouillard shook his head and grinned. *What a people!* To his surprise, he sometimes had a good time among these whitemen.

Drouillard, sleeping out, was awakened by intense, angry voices. A quick look at the low place of the moon and the burned-down campfire embers told him it was far past midnight. The voices were coming closer, from down by the river. He started to rise, and others were stirring around him. Over by the tents Captain Lewis's dog barked. Someone nearby whispered, "What is it? Indians?" Under a glory of stars, Drouillard was up on one knee on his blanket with his rifle in hand and his thumb ready to cock the flintlock. He heard footsteps coming heavily through the sand, two people walking hard, cutting straight through camp from the boat mooring toward the captains' tent. Several people were stuttering and mumbling about Indians.

Then one of the walkers, Sergeant Ordway, said loudly, "Hush, boys. No, it's not Indians. Damn good thing it ain't, by God, this son of a bitch asleep on guard!"

"I wasn't sleepin'!" the other voice said, almost whining.

"Devil ye weren't!" Ordway's voice growled as they went on toward the tents. "Think I don't know snorin'? Y're a dead man, Willard. . . ."

"Ooooh damn," someone said in the dark nearby. "Poor Willard!"

And Collins's voice, familiar by now to everyone, said, "Thank God, somebody but me catchin' hell for a change!"

Willard's trial was scheduled for eleven o'clock. Sleeping on sentinel duty was punishable by death, so the captains had to try him, instead of his enlisted peers.

Because of the trial, the fatigue of the boat crews, and the need to take some sky measurement, the captains decided to keep the camp here another day. The camp was on an island opposite the mouth of a little river that Dorion called the Nemahaw. Captain Clark took Drouillard and four other men to explore a few miles up that stream, and Drouillard soon became aware that this was another mound-hill place of the ancestors. He could hear their songs in the blowing grass, and in a sandstone cliff there were carved animals and what appeared to be a boat. Drouillard got away from the others for a brief time, lit his pipe with a magnifying glass and smoked to the Old Ones, standing atop the highest mound. He felt the spirits tingling through his feet. He was thankful that being among so many whitemen had not entirely dulled him to the subtle messages of the ancestors.

Private Willard stood trial looking like a pole-axed ox, stunned that this was happening to him. He knew he was a good soldier. He pleaded that maybe he had lain down, but he had not gone to sleep. But the captains believed Sergeant Ordway, who had caught him. They found Willard guilty, a serious offense here so deep in Indian country. They lectured him that he was to be spared the death sentence only because the party was so small and every man was needed. He was sentenced to a hundred lashes, to be meted out over the next four evenings. That meant welts upon fresh welts, enough pain, the captains hoped, to discourage any other sentry from lying down or shutting his eyes.

So that evening Drouillard again flayed deerskins to the sound of the troops flaying a fellow soldier, and he didn't watch. He smoked a final pipe that night facing up the Nemahaw River toward the mounds, thanking the Master of Life for guiding him not to enlist as a soldier. Drouillard knew he was their best sentry even though he was not required to stand guard. He knew how to sleep without turning off his senses. But damned if he would volunteer for it, because if he did, they would think they had the right to whip him for shutting his eyes. Sometimes the keenest guarding was done with eyes shut, and the ears and the nose doing the work.

Chapter 6

"

Above the Platte River

Monday the 23rd of July 1804
A fair morning. at 11 oClock Sent off George Drewyer &
Peter Crousett with some tobacco to invite the Otteaus if at
their town and Panies if they Saw them to Come and talk with
us at our Camp &c.-&c. I commence Coppying a map of the
river below to Send to the President US

William Clark, Journals

They had ridden a long way westward above the shallow, sandy
Platte, over miles of fire-blackened, ashy grasslands, and
crossed the Elk Horn Creek, to the Oto town Dorion had said
was there. They had found it, the thatched huts and racks and
tepee rings, shaded by willows, all abandoned. No smoke, no
horses, no dogs. It was obvious that the whole band had gone out
on the plains to hunt buffalo. Cruzatte, usually so cheerful, was
in a slump on the long ride back. He told of the smallpox the
traders had brought, which reduced the great Oto tribe so far that
it had had to assimilate with the Missourias and Pawnees in
order to deal with the bigger tribes to the north, such as his
mother's Omahas, and of course the Sioux. But finally Cruzatte
cheered up. "It has been good to be off that damn boat for a day!
Damn t'ing's clumsy as a house in t' water!"

July 28, 1804

Drouillard followed the spoor up the long slope through tall grass, leading his horse, which had a deer carcass tied across its rump. The tracks were easy to follow, and they told a story he already understood. The bent-down grass made a wavering line up the shoulder of a gentle rise; to him it was as plain as a road.

In the ground at the roots of the grass were the hoofprints of the elk. They were distinct because the earth had been softened by a brief rain earlier in the day: tracks broader and more splayed than a deer's, and each track with those rounded depressions at the back, like those made by a whiteman's boot heels, deeper than the rest of the track. Only the elk, of all the Split-Hooves, left those marks.

Then there was the spoor of blood drops, spattered and smeared on the grass stems. They were distinct, meaning they had been made since the rain, and the blood was a fresh new red. That freshness, and the fact that the bent grass was still straightening up, told him that the elk was not far ahead, perhaps still stumbling along, or perhaps fallen by now from weakness.

And there were the moccasin tracks of the hunters who had shot the elk and were tracking it. They ran parallel to and sometimes crossed the elk's trail, and he made it out that there were probably three. They were probably Oto or Missouria hunters. They were afoot, and there were no horse tracks.

He had found this while hunting west of the river. He was about a league from it now. He had heard the shot a while ago: that dull boom of a smoothbore, different from the crack of an army rifle. So he had set out diagonally across the prairie until he came across this trail of the wounded elk and its pursuers. He carried his rifle in his right hand, by his hip, and led the horse with his left. He walked so fast that the horse sometimes broke into a trot. The sky was a cloudy gray, the air hazy.

Captain Lewis was almost desperate by now to find some Indians along this river and give them his grand message about their new Great White Father and his expectations. This was the freshest trace Drouillard had found yet, so he hurried to catch up.

Meeting these Indians would be a delicate matter. He was a stranger, and a stranger could easily be shot at, approaching a wary party of hunters.

Instinct told him he would find them over the next hill or two, and if he did, and didn't get into a fight with them, he surely could persuade them to fetch their headmen to go and meet the captains. This, as much as the hunting, was what they had hired him for, and such a meeting was long overdue. Now the Master of Life had put his path onto this of the hunters, in this vast land, and the Master of Life arranged things when and as they were meant to be.

As he came over the rise he saw smoke above the shrubbery in a draw, and there were the Indians, three of them, their long hair hanging loose, squatting and kneeling around their dead elk.

They were butchering, piling meat cuts on the hide. He smelled cooking and saw that they had put the tongue, heart, and some innards on spits to roast over their little fire. One of them saw him and jumped to his feet with an exclamation. The other two crouched as if ready to flee into the shrubbery, glancing toward their weapons, which leaned in a bush out of immediate reach: lance, bow and quiver, and two rawhide shields. He knew they had to have at least one gun, and then he saw it, resting in the antlers of the elk's head which lay a few feet away, severed from the rest of the animal. He had caught them fully off guard, and they were in that moment of deciding whether to fight or flee.

He had to let them know at once that he had come in peace. He put his rifle over to rest in the crook of his left arm and thus freed his saluting hand. He raised it, palm forward. When he saw that they were reading his sign, he clasped his hands together, the left under the right, the sign for peace. Even at this distance he saw the tension leave them. One of the men held his right hand far out in front of himself and then drew it toward his chest, which meant for him to come closer. He led his horse, which was nervous, within a few yards of their fire, and stopped. He pointed

his right thumb at his chest, then his index finger at them, then
with the hand curved palm up made a motion from his mouth to
them. I and you talk, it said. In the meantime he asked, first in
English, then French, then Spanish, "Do you know this tongue?"
It was plain that they knew none of them, but one of the hunters
signed, *Where we live, a whiteman knows those tongues.*

How far?

Two days.

Drouillard knew he had to let the captains know sooner than
that about the Indians he'd found. So he signed: *Question: Come
with me? Meet my headmen. At the river. Half day walk up.*

The tall, slender, rather pretty-faced young man who was
doing the signing for them, tilted his head, put two fingers over
his heart and turned his wrist: *Perhaps. Question: Eat now?* He
tilted his head toward the meats sizzling over the fire.

Drouillard signed: *Eat together. Pipe first.*

"A-huh!" said the young man, with an emphatic nod and a
smile. Then he came around the fire, smiling warmly, his arms
spread for an embrace. Drouillard nodded and reached for him,
pleased but wary. If they intended any treachery, they would try
to overpower him now. He pressed his cheek against the youth's
cheek and patted him on the back, meanwhile watching the other
two over the young man's shoulder. They were smiling and
nodding.

They sat together. He filled his pipe, lit it with a smoldering
twig from their fire, presented it to all the spirit directions, then
passed it to his left, and they took turns doing the same, all
blowing smoke toward the sky. They were watching him keenly,
noting the excellence of his rifle, the colorful silk of his headkerchief, the shining pistols in the sash around his waist. These men
were in the plainest deer-hide shirts and leggings and elk-hide
moccasins, grease-stained, much patched, the quillwork designs
on the chest and shoulders faded and frayed, blood-spattered
from this butchering. The old French *fusil* with which they had
shot the elk seemed to be the only object they had of whitemen's
manufacture, other than the dingy red wool blankets of their
bedrolls. As they divided and shared the savory delicacies of elk,

Drouillard could tell they were full of questions about where he had come from and who his headman was, but their manners were too good to allow them to quiz him during the meal.

At last they finished, wiped their hands clean in the grass, smoked again, and leaned forward to hear about him and his people. He had as many questions to ask about them, but since they had fed him, he owed them answers first. So he began signing. He said he was Shawanoe, of the People of the South Wind, which they seemed to recognize, and that he was with boats going to the far end of this river. Their eyes widened. He signed: *They are Men Who Wear Hats,* which meant whitemen. They had fine goods to show, and very strong talk for the Oto headmen. Could the Oto headmen be brought to hear the talk?

The tall, pretty young man began signing. He was a Missouria, the other two Otoes. Their people were far out on the plains, hunting buffalo. These men had no horses for such hunting, so they had stayed near home to hunt food for about twenty lodges of people who had stayed behind. This young man laughed and said he was not a very good hunter. He had had the Woman Dreams, and was living and studying to become a Man Who Lives as a Woman, which was a role of good medicine and great esteem. Drouillard had heard of such a role among plains people. This youth had obvious intelligence and a promising brightness about him, and these two Otoes apparently respected him very much. He was a keen signer and sign-reader, able to perceive all the meanings of the hand signals themselves, but also feelings and nuances between the signals. Since this was Drouillard's especial talent as well, their conversation of flying hands was very satisfying, and it was more and more natural for them to trust each other.

At length the Missouria agreed to go with him to the boats, this afternoon, while the other two would take the elk hide and meat back to their people, and tell them of the whitemen's boat. As they could not carry all the elk on their backs, they gave him the rest of the meat to take as their gift to his headman. He secured it over the saddle. He gave them a carrot of tobacco for their headman, then with his newfound friend alongside, set off

walking, leading the horse toward the river. They went along in
good cheer. This had been a gift, this meeting. Drouillard had
never met a man before who was going to be a woman, but he
felt he had found a most pleasant and able first ambassador to
meet the captains.

The young Indian was awed and delighted by the big boat and
the busy soldier camp, but the captains were even more delighted with Drouillard for having finally found them an Indian.
They fed the young man and showed him watches and instruments, gave him a glimpse of the kinds of treasure the Americans could bring to his people, and plied him with sweetened
coffee served by York, whose appearance clearly mystified him.
Seaman the black dog followed him around and licked his hands,
probably because they still smelled of elk blood.

    The voyageur called La Liberté was brought into the cheerful
parley because he spoke Oto fluently. The visit went long into
the night by a campfire with a dozen or more of the soldiers and
voyageurs standing and sitting in a circle gazing on this first
"wild Indian," as they referred to him, in their midst. The youth
kept turning to Drouillard, not wanting him to leave his side, perhaps because he was the one who had first won the young man's
trust, or because he was the only other man in this whole crowd
who was obviously an Indian. Even while talking to or listening
to La Liberté, the youth would turn a fond gaze on Drouillard,
and often would reach over and hold his wrist. The captains and
some of the soldiers looked at each other with raised eyebrows
or smirks. Drouillard was annoyed at them for their presump-
tions, and thought of explaining the youth's demeanor in terms
of his Woman Dreams, but decided that would only make matters worse. This was an unsettling matter for Drouillard, who
both respected the young man's dream path and was embarrassed by it. It reminded him of Black Robe things he had long
since covered up in his memory.

    A chilly, damp wind had been blowing all evening, making
the campfire dance and flutter, giving them a welcome reprieve

from the torment of mosquitoes. The captains made plans. They decided that La Liberté and the Missouria youth should set out for the Oto town early the next day with an invitation to the Oto and Missouria chiefs and some of their headmen to come up and council, if they could be summoned in from their buffalo hunt on the plains. If the French-speaking trader among them could be brought in, he should be, the captains said. The youth asked if Drouillard could go with him to the village, but the captains insisted on sending the man La Liberté, because he spoke Oto. Drouillard was their best hunter, the captains explained, and was needed to bring in meat for all these men. The lad seemed to accept that, with a sad countenance, and leaned against Drouillard's shoulder for a moment, which caused some of the soldiers to murmur and snicker. "Better not let them two sleep in the same tent," Collins's voice came from beyond the fire, and some men laughed. Drouillard fixed his unbearable stare on Collins and lightly touched the haft of his hunting knife. Captain Lewis sighed, and sent angry looks at both Collins and Drouillard. In the awkward silence that ensued, Cruzatte volunteered in a cheery voice to play his fiddle.

"If this pretty man tell his chiefs 'bout the good-time music and dancin' we have, they will all want to come, maybe bring some women too!" he urged. The men cheered that idea. But then a cold, spitting rain began, and they could hear the hush of a heavier rain coming over the river. Cruzatte exclaimed, "Ooop! Ooop! *Oubliez ça!* Rain ruin t' feedle!"

That night the rain on the canvas was soothing. Drouillard lay looking up at the candlelit canvas while the captains sat murmuring to each other and finishing the last of their day's writings. They were talking about sending one of the small boats back with a few men to take the maps, papers, and specimens they had been preparing for the President. He presumed they would send back some of the troublesome men, such as Collins. Also Drouillard had sensed something bad with two privates, named Newman and Reed, who always hung off by themselves whenever they could. He had come upon them several times talking fast and angry, and they would nudge each other and fall silent when they realized he was near. Plainly they were up to something, and were among those who should be sent back. But Drouillard didn't consider it his duty to report suspicions. There was serious discontent among the voyageurs too, but that was Deschamps's concern, not his.

He heard Sergeant Floyd groan in the darkness a few feet away. That man, a very good man, had been very sick for several days. He was scarcely over twenty, but as wise, fair, and strong as any whiteman Drouillard had ever known. Maybe he should be sent back, where he could be doctored.

Drouillard's mind turned back to his encounter today with the Indians. How good it had been to smoke and eat with just Indians, without a white soldier or officer anywhere around. He imagined himself turning his back on these busy, driven officers and their complicated mission, and just wandering away to some Indian town, to live the way an Indian was born to live. He had often thought of that. It had been so comfortable today, sitting by a fire eating elk with just the horizons all around, without time measured by watches, without a constantly pressing purpose cutting hard and straight across the roundness of the world. It was the way his days used to be when he was a hunter alone in the woods, before he got involved with these officers and this mission of theirs which let no one rest.

La Liberté and the young Indian were talking softly. That was one way spoken language was better than hand language: you could talk in the dark. But you had to understand words of the same language to do that.

The young man's name was Wetheah. La Liberté had told Drouillard that it meant something like Good Welcome, or Hospitality. When he remembered how the young man had greeted him, it seemed appropriate. And it was more like a woman's name than a warrior's.

Drouillard smiled at the memory of something. When Wetheah had asked him what his name meant, he had replied, Followed by Buzzards.

The Council Bluffs
August 2, 1804

John Colter grinned his thin-lipped mocking grin and said, "By God, George, for every damn mile this damn outfit goes for'ard, you and me go back twenty or thirty fetchin' what-all they've lost!" They were riding along the east bank of the Missouri, leading two horses that the Field brothers had lost two days before while deer hunting on the rolling plains. Drouillard and Colter had backtracked a dozen miles or so to find the horses. In bringing them back up, they had shot a cow elk; its meat was now on the backs of the two led horses.

Drouillard snorted a laugh. "Palefaces never look back. Like poor old Willard. And now we're picking up after Rube, who picked up after Willard." They rode along laughing. It had been a comedy: The daydreamer Willard had left his tomahawk somewhere at a stopping place and was sent back afoot to fetch it. On his return, trying to cross a creek on a fallen log, he tottered and dropped his rifle in the creek. Willard was a poor swimmer, so a pirogue had been dispatched back to the creek, and from it Reubin Field had dived to retrieve the weapon. Now it was Reubin's lost horse carrying the hind quarters of the elk.

Colter said, "Be better if we just left behind all the stuff that gets dropped, and maybe drop off some more stuff when the cap'ns ain't lookin'. Like that damn stuffed beast o' Lewis's. Or your pet beaver. The more we'd drop off, the lighter that damn barge'd be. Wonder if Liberté and that pretty boy o' yours has brought the Indians up yet? I hope so, so's we can unload a few pounds o' gifts onto 'em."

Drouillard didn't mind Colter's gibes much. He had come to respect him and like him. The stuffed beast the man had spoken of was a fierce burrowing animal Joe Field had shot. Captain Lewis had skinned, stuffed, and mounted it, because he thought it was a kind of animal nobody had ever seen before, and that of course meant it had to be preserved for the Great Father Jefferson. It looked like a wide, low dog without ears and had a white stripe running back from its nose. Drouillard called it a *blaireau*. He had seen its skins in his uncle's store but had not been able to remember the English name for it until last night: *badger*. It was a bulky thing, filling still more of the boat's limited space. As for the pet beaver, it was a very young one Drouillard had caught alive in a creek one day. He released it before it suffered much, and it had become very tame for him; it acted as if it considered him its savior. When he left with Colter to find the horses, he asked some of the men to keep it supplied with green willow branches, and then it probably would stay around. He hoped it had; its coat was soft and delightful to stroke.

"I doubt the Oto are here yet," Drouillard said. "They were out hunting buffalo on the prairie. It might take days to find them. They're like another thing we have to go back and fetch, except worse because we don't know where they are."

"Yeah," Colter said. "If they'd of come up already, I guess we'd of heard a ten gun salute and bugles and drums by now. That Cap'n Lewis is so eager to show a shindig for some Indians, he's like a man clenchin' loose stools. And don't we all know how *that* feels! Well, now! Look there!" he exclaimed as they rode over the brow of the bluff and looked down on the moored boats and the camp. "Flag up on the flagpole. Reckon they're marking Cap'n Clark's birthday?" The flag rippled in the upriver wind.

"That was yesterday. So we missed the feast because we were out gathering lost horses. No, white brother, I think the flag still flies in hopes that it will draw Indians. And I don't see any down there yet."

"Dagburn, that's a pity! Reckon y'll have to stroke your pet beaver, 'stead of your perty Indian boy!"

"Ah-*huh*! Maybe the hair I stroke will be the scalp of the next paleskin who makes that joke!"

"Whoops! Mercy, red brother! Put your blade away! I was just a-tellin' m'self I'd surely never make that joke again! No, sir, why, it's not funny at all, is it?"

They rode into camp calm and cheerful as the best of friends.

*   *   *

The Indians appeared on the river bluff at sunset, as if to light their arrival most dramatically. Several fired muskets in the air, and then they rode down in dust tinged by sunlight. The troops were ordered to be on guard, ready for anything.

Two shots were fired from the swivel cannon in the bow of the keelboat to salute the thirteen Indians. The shots made an ear-pounding noise, huge billows of smoke and flashes of burnt wadding, bright in the dusk. It seemed to awe the Indians, all Oto and Missouria men well mounted, most armed with lances and bows. Some had braided hair with erect eagle feathers attached to the back of their heads, but two wore broad-brim trading-store hats, and one a plumed, three-cornered black hat. A squat, dirty whiteman, apparently their resident trader, came forward to speak. Drouillard could not see much in the deepening dusk, but he noticed that the voyageur La Liberté and the horse issued to him were not with the Indians. After a brief exchange of words, handshakes, and food, the Indians went a little way off to a fire ring and a group of brush shelters the soldiers had built for their arrival.

The troops were glum. There was not one woman among the Indians.

That night Captain Lewis worked over the speech he would make in the ceremonies tomorrow morning. Drouillard sat cleaning his rifle in the candlelight, biting the inside of his lip and waving away the mosquitoes, which were so thick that many of them got in past the mosquito gauze and whined inside the tent. Clark and Lewis talked about the distribution of the gift bundles for the headmen of varying status. Eventually they got to wondering aloud about the absence of La Liberté. The trader had told them La Liberté had ridden out ahead a day earlier and the Indians had expected he would be here. The captains guessed he had perhaps overtired his horse, or temporarily gotten lost, but they hinted at the faintest suspicion that he might have defected, since he was now in the country of a people whose ways and language he knew. Maybe, not knowing which side of the river they would be encamped on, he tried to swim his horse across the river and it had died, as had the little horse Captain

Clark captured down by the Kanzas. To Drouillard, they seemed as concerned about losing the horse as the man.

"Or maybe," Captain Clark said, "maybe La Liberté ran away to some Oto damsel he used to know. Or some new one he met."

Drouillard's guess was that he had just tired of rowing a boat all day every day for somebody else's army.

August 3, 1804

The day dawned gray with fog so thick the high bluffs nearby were invisible. The keelboat's sail had been rigged up as an awning under which the chiefs and officers would meet. In front of the awning was the flagpole with its flag of stripes and stars. The captains and soldiers were up early getting into their formal uniforms and tall hats, which had been stored in the boat lockers and not worn for many weeks. The captains opened a bale of goods already designated for the tribal leaders of this stretch of the river. Medals and flags, blankets, elegant dress coats, and bright red leggings were sorted and combined into individual bundles for the headmen. While the sergeants fussed at their squads to look their military best, Drouillard got his first look at the Peace and Friendship medals. These were stamped on one side with a picture of two hands clasped under a picture of a tomahawk and a long pipe crossed, and on the other side a profile picture of a strong-jawed man whose hair was tied in a queue behind his shoulders. "Who is the man, sir?" he asked, dangling the medal by its ribbon.

"The President," Captain Clark said.

Drouillard peered hard at it, his scalp tingling. So this was the one called Jefferson whom Captain Lewis obeyed and almost worshiped! The one who had caused all this to happen! He turned the medal to and fro in the light, and said: "Is he an elder? Is his hair white?"

"An elder? About sixty, I guess. Lewis says his hair's still red mostly. I haven't seen him for a long time. Now, George, I've a lot to do here yet. I'd like you to be with us when we talk to these people. Their trader seems to talk their tongue good enough, but I can scarcely follow his English. It's about as bad as my French, and you know how bad that is. Get Labiche there too. With English, French, Oto speakers, and your hand signs, we should be able to talk just fine."

When the Indians came in under the awning at mid-morning, they looked dignified and colorful, but a little meek. The sun had burned off the fog and shone bright on the sailcloth, making everything under it glow with intense color. An upriver breeze made the awning rustle and billow, and the Indians' feathers and fringes shivered and flounced. The interpreter, whose name was Faufon, was in moccasins, leggings, and breechcloth like the Indians, but he wore a frilled white long shirt with a sash around the waist, and a three-cornered hat. He was stocky, fat-cheeked, and cheerful. As Drouillard watched him, he felt an arm slide across his shoulders and heard a familiar voice at his ear. He turned to face an elegantly dressed young Indian wearing a deerhair crested headdress and fur hair-ties in his tight braids, and it was a moment before he recognized him as Wetheah, the young hunter he had brought in a week ago. The Woman Dreamer. He was so transformed by his finery, Drouillard could hardly believe it was he. When he smiled in recognition, the young man laughed and embraced him like a long-lost brother, patting his back and pressing his cheek against his. Drouillard saw that Captain Lewis, now stiff and trim in blue dress coat with gold braid frogging and epaulets, was glowering at him, so he patted the youth on the back and drew away, nodding, and indicated that he should go and rejoin the other warriors. Drouillard took up a stance near the gift bundles, not meeting Lewis's eyes.

The thirteen Indians were seated in a semicircle facing out on the meadow where the flag fluttered. This was the time when a pipe should have been passed, but Drouillard saw it was not to be done. Instead, Captain Lewis shouted for the troops to pass in review. The sergeants shouted at their squads to shoulder arms and march, a drum rattled, and the straight lines of soldiers, all in red-trimmed blues with their tall hats adding a foot to their height, tramped by in perfect step, as if they were two dozen bodies with one mind. The Indians leaned to each other and murmured in amazement at the sight. Drouillard, who thought drill the most unnatural thing he had ever seen human beings do, doubted that it was putting the Indians in a receptive mood. The young Missouria turned to look at him with his eyes wide, eyebrows up, and mouth down and open in a comic expression, and Drouillard could only shake his head and shrug. Then he raised his fist to make circles before his forehead, which meant "crazy." Oh damn, he thought, I shouldn't have done that. He was relieved to see that neither captain had seen him.

After the parade there was still no pipe. Captain Lewis at once stepped before the Indians and started his speech about the new White Father, the Road of Peace, and the Red Children, pausing to let the Frenchman translate into Oto. Drouillard was impressed by the patience and politeness of the listeners. Even when the captain made his veiled threat that red children who listened to bad birds would be denied trade for the wonderful American goods, the Indians stayed calm and nodded as if in full accord. It was obvious that the captain was pleased with their reception of his glowing plan.

The speech went on for a long time, and eventually Captain Lewis challenged all the Oto and Missouria to gather up a group of their principal leaders to travel to the Great Council Fire in the East and see their new White Father and the powerful nation he governed. If they went there and promised to submit to him, they would be honored with ceremonies and loaded down with such beautiful and valuable gifts as they had never imagined before now, and when they returned their people would prosper.

The unreliable traders from other countries will be no more, he told them, and the only Father to whom they could turn for protection was their new American Father, Jefferson. Drouillard translated that into French, and the trader then into Oto. Drouillard wondered if he was saying to them what had been said by Captain Lewis. *Eh bien,* he thought. They would probably make Faufon an agent of the American trade, just as they had done Lorimier. At any rate, when the speech was done, the Indians seemed to have been sufficiently impressed, and they murmured and nodded. By then it was time to take the midday meal, with the expectation that the Indians would get to make their replies afterward.

The weather held pleasant, with a refreshing breeze. The great Missouri flowed by below, and the tall yellow grasses on the bluffs waved and rippled in the sunlight. The meal was not only succulent fat meat but also a profusion of grapes, currants, plums, and berries the soldiers had been gathering during their wait in this beautiful place. York, carrying food around, was so awe-inspiring that many of the Indians almost forgot to eat when he was in sight, although these tribes had been exposed to traders long enough to know there were people with black skin. Captain Lewis's dog sat trembling near his master in anticipation of meat scraps, his patience and good manners amazing to a people whose own dogs prowled and cringed around feasts.

The Indians wanted Drouillard to sit with them, so he sat between the young Missouria and a leathery, cheerful Oto whose main interest seemed to be in the magic by which Drouillard could ignite tobacco through the magnifying lens in his compass cover. Drouillard conversed with the two by hand signs and learned a few things that made him realize the afternoon would be amusing. He and Hospitality talked about tribes and soldiers. The young man was a quick and graceful sign-talker, and didn't bother with the grim reserve that warriors affected. One thing amusing Hospitality was that the officers seemed to think these Indians they were entertaining so diligently were chiefs. Actually, they were just family clan headmen, as good a hasty collection as could be got together while the main body of people was out hunting on the plains.

The young man himself, being treated to all this ceremony, was not even a family headman. He was just a boy whose dreams and bright nature had marked him as one likely to become a spiritual leader. He wondered whether the captains had even recognized him as the person who had been here before. Drouillard put his right thumb to his chest, then put his fist over his heart with forefinger extended and thrust it away, turning it down. Then he flipped his open hand over and back.

I think no.

So Hospitality just tried to look dignified and enjoyed the joke.

In the afternoon the Indians, through their interpreter Faufon, explained that these were not principal chiefs here, and proclaimed themselves ill-qualified to speak for their people.

But they said they had been pleased to hear that these new people coming in would not be stingy, like the French and Spanish traders. "They will not give us any gift for nothing," said one of the older headmen. "We will be glad to be out from under them."

Hospitality stood up to speak. His deer-hair crest rippled like blown grass in the breeze under the awning. He was shy and his voice soft. "You please us with good advice and tell us how you want us to behave. We will try to bring our headmen to talk to you before you go too far up the river and away. Your great boat is full of beautiful presents. We will take some to our headmen, and they will want to talk to you. Perhaps they will go to see the new Great Father in your country. We are a poor people. When our hunters return they will be out of powder. Please give us some gunpowder and a drop of your milk." The Frenchman translated, saying that by "milk" he meant whiskey.

One more headman spoke. He said one of the big troubles of his people was the hostility of the more powerful Omahas up the Missouri, as well as the Pawnees who lived up the Platte. He said that if the Americans could heal those troubles and truly make the road of peace they promised, the Otoes and Missourias would owe them much gratitude and respect.

Their Frenchman concluded with a report that the Spaniards in Santa Fe had recently invited the Platte River tribes to go and trade with them there, and that a few people had set out this summer for that city, which was a journey of about twenty-five days.

Immediately, then, Captain Lewis moved to resume control of the council. He told the Indians again that they now lived on the

land of their great new American Father, who would be angry if
they traded with the Spaniards of Santa Fe, or the British from
the north. He swept his hand around to indicate the bluffs above
and this good, level bottomland, and told them that this would be
a good place for an American trading center, and that it would
be full of more and greater goods than anything they had ever
seen, because big boats could carry so much more up the Missouri than could be carried overland from the Spaniards. He said
the White Father would surely want to put a store here because it
was a place close to so many tribes that would soon be at peace
with each other.

In fact, he said, if you will send up your chiefs and have them
catch up with us there at the towns of the Omahas, we will halt
there and help you make peace with them.

Drouillard translated these grand promises, but thought: the
Creator gave me two ears, one to hear like a whiteman and the
other to hear like an Indian. Captain Lewis certainly talked like a
man who believed he could do anything, and he seemed to believe his own words. He had wealth to buy anything he needed.
But the Indian ear heard a stranger who showed up one day and
claimed he owned the Great Spirit's land and could not only
make all Indians obey his wishes, but all British and French and
Spaniards too.

And now Captain Lewis began proclaiming certain of the Indians to be chiefs.

The first was the Oto, Little Thief. Though he was not present,
and was already a chief in the eyes of his own people, he was
now made First Chief by the Americans. They set aside a bundle
of clothing, a flag, and one of the largest medals, to be delivered
to him. They made Big Horse a second chief of the Otoes and
made a bundle for him with a smaller medal. Then they gave
Hospitality a medal of that same size and called him another
second chief. Hospitality, delighted and bewildered to find himself suddenly a chief, shook the captains' hands vigorously,
seemed poised to hug them, but backed off, then stepped over
and threw his arms around Drouillard with a laugh that was almost a squeal. Then he wandered out, blinking and shaking his

head in wonderment, while the captains named four other chiefs. In response to their earlier special request, the captains had a canister of gunpowder and a bottle of whiskey brought from the boat. The whiskey was served in little glasses to the Indians, and seemed to make them happier in their befuddlement.

It was still early afternoon. Captain Lewis had Sergeant Ordway bring the air rifle from the boat. Drouillard had heard of this device but had never seen it. He had heard the captain talk about demonstrating it to impress Indians, if they ever found any Indians to impress, and now they had found some. It looked like an ordinary long rifle, but without the protruding flintlock and frizzen, and with a thicker stock. The captain, in the shade of the awning and shielded by Captain Clark, pumped a lever. Then Captain Lewis went out before the Indians and let them see him load a ball in a greased patch down the barrel and tamp it with a ramrod, while Ordway walked out about seventy paces and set up a target, a kerchief attached to two sticks stuck in the ground. The Indians' attention was called to the demonstration. Captain Lewis took standing aim; the Indians squinted in anticipation of the noise and smoke. Several smiled and turned to each other for some quick chattering, which Drouillard presumed to be wagering. With the smoothbore muskets they were accustomed to, such a shot would have been very unlikely.

Lewis announced, "Now!" and squeezed the trigger. With no smoke and less noise than a light sneeze, the shot flipped the target out of the ground and dropped it into the grass.

The whole party of Indians blinked and looked at each other, looked at Captain Lewis, looked at Ordway, who had stepped over to replace the target, and started talking rapidly. Monsieur Faufon told Drouillard that some of the Indians believed the sergeant had done a trick out there, perhaps with a snare string. All the while, Captain Lewis was putting another ball down the barrel. He waved Ordway to the side, aimed, asked Faufon to quiet the Indians' discussion and have them watch, and then squeezed the trigger again. Again the white kerchief flopped away.

If the Indians had not had their dram of whiskey, they might have realized by then that this was actually a special kind of a gun instead of some sort of a trick; as it was, it required four more successful shots to convince them that this white man was actually shooting the little target with something as quiet as bow and arrow but more accurate than a musket. By the time the demonstration was over, the soldiers had taken down the awning and struck camp. It was a good time to leave, while the Indians were still a little bedazzled and slightly tipsy. Hospitality, the new boy chief of the Missourias, caught Drouillard and pressed a cheek to his. Then he signed, *Question: See you when?*

Drouillard signed: *Far, two winters.* He held up the shivering fists that meant winter.

Hospitality nodded gravely, and gestured: *I leave heart on the ground.* Then he stood with his fellow chiefs and warriors and watched the corps in its boats and its hunters on their horses move away up the river. For a change there was a southwest wind, and the boats moved under sail, a pretty sight that these Indians might never have seen before.

Drouillard had ridden about a league when he saw the red pirogue row up close to the keelboat. A soldier climbed down into the pirogue and was rowed to shore. As the man came striding back down the west bank, Drouillard saw that it was Moses Reed, one of the shifty malcontents of the crew. Drouillard rode down the slope and met him. "Where you headed, Mr. Reed?"

Reed squinted up at him, the afternoon sky-glare in his eye. "I left my knife back there where we put up them shelters. Cap'n told me to go back an' get it and then catch up."

"Long walk. Three miles back, and then by the time you get back here they'll likely be three more miles farther up. Kind of discourages a man from leavin' things lying around, eh?" Reed apparently took it as a personal criticism, scowled, and started to move on. Drouillard thought of the distances and the descending sun. This fool probably wouldn't come back till after dark and he'd get lost and then he or Colter or somebody'd have to waste a morning going back to hunt for him. So Drouillard said, "Why don't you just get on my packhorse and we'll trot back there real quick and find your knife? If the Indians didn't carry it off, that is." He knew the captains wouldn't like that, as the long walk was part of the lesson about carelessness, but he was willing to risk a little censure for that if it could save trouble the next day.

Reed was thinking hard, then he said: "Well, you don't need to go back with me. But I'd be obleeged for the loan o' that spare horse, and I could go back quicker."

Drouillard looked at him and saw some cunning in his face. "I said I'd ride back with you. But I can't give you my packhorse."

"Why not, man?"

"First place, it's in my charge. Second, I usually get a deer or elk this time of evening, and that's why I've got this horse, is to carry meat."

"Aw, hell, Drouillard. Get a deer, you can load it up when I come back up with the horse. Be a good Injin an' gimme the borry of that horse."

"Guess you better get down there while there's light to hunt for your knife, Reed. Have a nice walk." And with a light shift of his weight in the saddle he rode away.

Reed called after him: "Goddamn difficult half-breed! Hell, it's an army horse, an' you ain't even in the army!"

Drouillard suddenly felt a tingle of danger in his back. He turned quickly and saw that Reed had raised his rifle as high as his waist, one hand at the flintlock. Drouillard reined the horse left and halted so that his own rifle across the saddle just happened to be pointed at Reed, and said quietly, "Yeah, better hold that gun with both hands so y' don't lose it too." He glanced up-river. The keelboat was far up but still in sight. He looked back and saw that Reed was considering the boat too. He sat there and waited until Reed turned and trotted on down the riverbank. Only then did Drouillard turn back north.

He rode onto the higher ground to get out of the clouds of mosquitoes, the late sun glaring from above the western horizon, grass rising and flattening like flowing currents of gold. A dark shape raced along above the northern horizon, then rose and swerved and changed shape: a great flock of tiny birds moving as if all one. He scanned the slopes and draws for game. He saw elk moving along a height, but they were on the other side of the river, so distant they looked like a line of ants on the smooth contours of the land. He tried to keep his mind clear in the hunting attitude, but he was not serene. The soldier Reed had annoyed him with his "half-breed" talk and his menace, but that was a small part of it. What was really bothering him, rising up like a bad digestion, was his part in that damned council. He remembered the eager, friendly faces of the Otoes and Missourias when the council started, and then the confusion and doubt that had begun to show as they listened to the vague promises and the veiled threats of Captain Lewis's speech. He remembered their disappointment with the medals and pieces of paper, all of no apparent use, and the dearth of other gifts. They knew the big boat was full of useful and pretty things, and they knew it was going on upriver into the lands of their enemies, the Omaha and the Sioux, who would probably get much more.

But what gnawed sharpest in Drouillard was the memory of Captain Lewis telling those Indians who would be their chiefs.

In many ways, Drouillard had come to admire these captains—even Lewis, swollen as he was with his own importance.

But what Lewis did not know, or care, about Indian people and their tribal ways, was going to defeat his own cause. Worse, in Drouillard's mind, was the trouble Lewis's ignorance was likely to cause among the Indians themselves. He imagined Hospitality going back to his people and proclaiming that a passing whiteman had made him their chief. Maybe the youth wasn't that foolish, but one never knew what would grow in a man's head. The one called Jefferson had certainly planted such a seed in Lewis.

Drouillard remembered that one of his own justifications for coming with these captains had been that he might be able to help protect them from their own ignorance.

I guess I need to tell them some things they don't understand, he thought.

And I'd better tell them before they get up among the Omaha and the Sioux, where a little stupidity will go a long way.

* * *

When Drouillard brought his horses down to the riverbank, the corral guard told him that the captains wanted to see him.

A voyageur of middle age, François Rivet, rowed him to the sandbar where the camp was being set up. Rivet was so powerful in the arms and shoulders that though it was a boat for seven rowers, he handled it easily by himself. An exuberant man, he sometimes entertained by dancing on his hands to Cruzatte's fiddling, but now he looked at Drouillard in a sullen and suspicious way, and had not a word for him. It was ominous, and Drouillard wondered if it had something to do with his being summoned by the captains.

Cookfires of driftwood smoked up the campsite, the soldiers and voyageurs squinting against the smoke but standing in its most acrid clouds to avoid the swarming mosquitoes. Drouillard kept his hands, face, and neck anointed with bear oil and elderberry in such times, and was less bothered by them.

He saw Sergeant Floyd sitting on a crate by his squad's campfire with his face drawn and white, arms crossed over his middle, so full of pain that he was ignoring mosquitoes. Drouillard sensed death near the man, and was sorry, for this was one of their best. York was coming, bringing a cup of something for the sergeant. It was said that York gave Floyd such care because he was some kind of a relative, a cousin, of Captain Clark. York gave Drouillard a strange look and said, "Cap'ns want t' see you."

"So I hear. Thanks." He walked over to where they stood by their own fire in the blue dusk, waving away mosquitoes. They were still in their uniforms from the council, and they stiffened when they saw him coming. By now he was uneasy. Everyone seemed to know something he didn't.

Captain Lewis glared at him. "George, we need to talk to you."

"So I hear," he said again.

"Let's walk down. The troops don't necessarily have to hear what we've got to say."

"Good, sir. They might not want to hear what I have to say either."

"Oh? You have something on your chest, do you?"

"With respect, sir. I'll listen first."

They walked away from the camp, down to a thicket of willow where the mosquitoes were even worse.

"Now, George," Lewis began, "I hardly know how to speak of this. I never in my life expected to have to talk to any man of mine about ... about such an *aberration*." Drouillard didn't know what an aberration was, but thought it must have something to do with the way everybody had looked at him this evening. Lewis went on, continually brushing mosquitoes away from his face. "George, you've been valuable to us. You've kept us in fresh meat, and never failed in a duty. But, damn it, now, it—this—" He took a deep breath, got mosquitoes in his mouth and began sputtering and spitting. Then he glared and said forcefully, "I'm talking about *pederasty*!"

Drouillard squinted at him through the dancing mosquitoes for a moment. "Cap'n, I don't know what that is, so I doubt I did it."

"Damn it! Buggery!" Clark blurted. "Don't play dumb!"

Drouillard stepped back. He had to control himself, to keep from going for his knife. He couldn't speak, he was so full of sudden fire.

"Yes, buggery!" Lewis snarled. "The vice of English fops and ... and papist *priests*!"

Papist? Drouillard's flaring mind tried to remember that word. Didn't it mean Black Robe? This captain was accusing him of something like that thing he had wiped out of his old memory?

Before he could find words, Lewis went on, in a hissing, angry tone: "The men are talking about you, Drouillard! You and that pretty Indian boy you brought in all moon-eyed and snuggly! And about that simpleton of Dorion's ... By God, Drouillard, I won't have—"

"*Tscha!* Damn you, Cap'n, you better *stop*!"

"What? What did you say to me?" Clark swelled up and boomed: "You don't talk to your commander that way! By God, I'll have your guts for garters if—"

"I said you better stop." He was cold enough inside to kill now and didn't care how he spoke. The officers stood as if stunned. "Listen," he said, hissing like a snake. "I'm not one of your soldiers. I'm not your slave. And I'm not one of those Catholics you hate!"

He knew of the contempt these Virginians had for Catholics; he had heard them snipe and scoff behind the backs of the wealthy Spanish and French merchants and officials Lewis was always soliciting in St. Louis.

"Listen! You say those lies again and you will look around and wonder where Drouillard went!"

They stood, barely visible in the deepening dusk, and he could feel their indignation, could feel them preparing words.

"Listen!" he went on. "I'm an Indian and you're in Indian country now. I am your eyes and your tongue. You're stumbling into a country you don't know. Without me, and Cruzatte and Dorion, you are blind and dumb. You say that buggery lie again and I am gone so quick you'll think I was just a spirit!

"Listen! I told you I have words for you. Hear this: your Father Jefferson has filled your head with such goddamn smoke and foolishness you won't get past the Omahas, and sure not the Sioux, if you try to do them as you did those few poor Otoes today!"

"Did what . . ." It was Lewis, in a low, furious, outraged tone. But they were listening, not pulling their pistols on him or calling for the sergeant of the guard to arrest him. They were not even bothering to brush at mosquitoes now. Maybe he had got away with talking back.

He said: "If I could have talked to your Jefferson before he sent you, I would have told him: Big Horse and Little Thief are as great in their nations as you are in yours. You are no one to name them to be chiefs or not, you are just a stranger going through. They choose their own leaders, by ways of knowing that you don't understand. I would tell your Father Jefferson, Indians don't go to Washington and tell a man they meet, 'You will be President.' Eh? So you can't say that in their country!"

He was amazed that they were still standing quiet in front of him, listening. They could not like this. They were important whitemen and he was just a half-blood Indian. They thought they were important even here in this country, because their President had given Napoleon some money. He hoped that now as they stood staring so hard at him, they might be considering their own ignorance, that they might know how much they needed his eyes and his language.

It would be up to them now. If he had told the truth too plainly for their comfort, or if they still couldn't see it, then they would get rid of him.

One thing was certain in his heart: they were not going to lay whippings on him. He could outshoot, outswim, and outrun any of their soldiers. If he needed a horse, he could take one out from under the very nose of any of their sentries. If this was to be the end of his part in their journey, he would vanish so quickly they would wonder if he had been just a spirit. In truth he felt that, compared with these ponderous men and their great load of Jefferson duties, he was a spirit.

He waited. He thought he felt Lewis's anger still expanding. But it was Clark who spoke. "I'm for getting back to camp. There's too much to do, t' be idling out here feeding m'skeeters."

They stirred. "Mind you, Drouillard. No boys or you're out," Lewis said.

"Mind you, Cap'n, there never were boys. And Hospitality isn't a bugger. That good young man is something among his people you don't understand."

"Well, whatever it is, it's unnatural."

Unnatural, Drouillard thought. If you want to see unnatural, see one of your white soldiers copulate with a dead doe because she's still warm. Drouillard had seen one do that while out on the hunt. But he didn't say it. He was not a bearer of tales.

"I wonder if Reed found his knife and got back," Captain Clark said as they walked toward the camp. He seemed relieved it was over. But Drouillard was still mad.

August 3rd Friday
prepare a Small preasent for those Indians and hold a Concul Delivered a Speech & made 6 chiefs at 4 oClock Set out under

a gentle Breeze from the S.E. Camped below a great number of Snags quite across the river, The Musquitors more numerous than I ever Saw them, all in Spirrits-, we had Some rough Convasation G. Dr.—about boys.

William Clark, Journals

Chapter 7

Toward Sioux Country
August 7, 1804

For several days Clark acted as if there had never been strong words, but Lewis talked to Drouillard only when necessary and seemed to be studying him coldly. Everyone had too much to do to sit dwelling on things, as the convoy moved up the winding river fifteen to twenty miles a day and the officers measured and wrote, measured and wrote. Captain Clark had become very interested in the shifting and reshaping of the river course, caused by cave-ins, silting up, and flood-throughs. He noted bow-shaped ponds that had formerly been parts of the river channel and were now cut off. He found a stretch where the river made a twelve-mile loop and came back within a quarter mile of itself, and saw that in flood times the water had flowed over that narrow neck. He predicted that in a year or two the main current would wash through and isolate the long loop. In his shore hikes he tasted and studied the varieties of grapes and fruits that grew so profusely in the bottoms, while Lewis examined and described herons, snakes, and waterfowl killed along the way, and took his navigational sightings, so solemn and intent on his instruments that he appeared to be worshiping them. Drouillard ranged the plains hunting, staying away from the captains, the troops, and the voyageurs, except in camp. He watched the boatmen's eyes and expressions for hints about which men, if any, had spread the rumors about him, perhaps to divert attention from their own use of Dorion's boy. Drouillard in the beginning had tried to

113

reach through the lad's veil and find a spark of his Sioux spirit inside, but now stayed far from him.

Reed had been gone four days, and as the expedition moved north, the officers' anxiety about him had grown. Then Sergeant Ordway came up with evidence that he had deliberately deserted. Ordway had examined his knapsack, and it was empty. Reed apparently had left not only his knife back at the council camp, but all his clothes and ammunition. It was presumed that he would head for the Oto villages, perhaps to try to obtain a horse there for his escape back to civilization.

So now Drouillard was riding out with a written order to find Reed and bring him back, preferably alive, but dead if he resisted, riding south along the west bank of the river with Labiche, Reubin Field, and a private named William Bratton, a member of Reed's squad. Bratton, a Kentuckian, was a fair hunter with some gunsmithy skills, which might be needed on this long trek.

Drouillard was glad to get away from the officers a while. He was pleased, on the other hand, that they still had enough trust to put him in charge of a mission having life-and-death importance. They had given him some of the best available men, and had entrusted him with most of the hunting horses. Drouillard was not happy that he might have to kill a man for quitting this party; he had been close himself, many times, to turning his back on it and walking away. Four nights ago he had been within an eyeblink of doing so.

Capturing Reed was just a part of this mission. The captains had also told him to summon Big Horse and Little Thief, and other Oto and Missouria headmen, and bring them north to meet the expedition at the Omaha towns where the captains hoped to negotiate a peace between their tribes and the Omahas, as they had promised. They had also told him to find La Liberté, who had last been seen more than a week ago when he left with Hospitality to invite the Oto chiefs up for the first council.

Drouillard had in his pouch a twist of tobacco and a string of wampum beads as token gifts for the chiefs.

*   *   *

He led his three men south over the familiar plains at a distance
from the river, to avoid the many extra miles of looping riverbanks. He had hunted alongside Reubin Field often enough to
know that the man would be dependable and calm in whatever
situation this mission put him. Labiche was volatile, but that was
outweighed by his realistic understanding of tribal life and his
ability with languages, so Drouillard was pleased to have him
along. Now and then it was pleasant to talk in French too.

Private Bratton was a steady and rugged young fellow, pleasant, talkative. He was one of the few soldiers with real strength
and confidence as a swimmer. One day Drouillard had seen him
swim the whole width of the Missouri to get an article he had
forgotten to put on the boat. Bratton seemed nervous about this
present task, though, and asked Drouillard, "D'you, uh, d'you
reckon we'll have to shoot Reed?"

"Maybe. He might choose that over being taken back and
whipped."

"Whew! Yeh, for desertin', it'd be way over a hundred lashes.
They might shoot 'im, even if we don't. After court-martial, an'
all." After a while he went on, "D'you reckon La Liberté deserted too, or just got lost?"

"He knows this country. I doubt he got lost. If a man gets lost
beside a river half a mile wide, I'd guess he wanted to."

"Wonder if we're s'posed to shoot him?"

"He's a hired civilian, like me. I think the army book'd say
don't shoot civilians 'less you need target practice." Behind,
Field and Labiche laughed.

"Reckon they might shoot 'im for a horse thief, though," Bratton chattered on. "That was a gov'ment horse he rode out on.
Say! When're they goin' to send a boat home with all them
written papers and whatnot, like they was sayin'?"

"Haven't heard anything about it for days."

"If I was Reed, I'd just've waited for that ride," Reubin Field
said. "Bet they would've put that dunghead on board home, just
t' get shed of 'im!"

Drouillard had never heard either of the Field brothers talk bad about anyone but Collins. Since Reed's disappearance, several soldiers had expressed their dislike and distrust of him.

After a few breaths, Bratton started chatting again, this time about Captain Lewis, who was apparently an amazement to all his soldiers in one way or another. "Say, did you ever see a feller fuss over wee particklers like he does? Like that dang flathead snake we kilt t'other day? Why, he counted every black spot on its back and measured every line on its belly, and wrote all that down! Or them birds he's always killin' and measuring their wings and even each feather, and their toenails . . . Ever see anything like it, boys? Why, if they send home to Mr. President all that stuff they've written and drawed and trapped and stuffed and flattened out 'twixt blotters, lordy, it'd be *easy* then t' haul that barge up this dang endless river—"

"Bratton!"

"'Ey, chief?"

"Even Cap'n Lewis doesn't write as much as you talk. Let's save our breath and ride. We've got maybe seventy miles to go just to get down there and start looking." Drouillard urged his horse into a trot and they moved south over the vast grassland, to seek two men who were trying to lose themselves in it. This was a time, he thought, to see like an eagle.

August 8th 1804

we had seen but a few aquatic fouls of any kind on the river since we commenced our journey up the Missouri . . . this day after we had passed the river Souix I saw a great number of feathers floating down the river those feathers had a very extraordinary appearance as they appeared in such quantities as to cover pretty generally sixty or seventy yards of the breadth of the river. for three miles after I saw those feathers continuing to run in that manner, at length we were surprised by the appearance of a flock of Pillican at rest on a large sand bar . . . the number of which would if estimated appear almost incredible: they appeared to cover several acres of ground . . . we now approached them within about three hundred yards before they flew; I then fired at random among the flock with

*my rifle and brought one down; the discription of this bird is
as follows . . .*

Meriwether Lewis, Journals

August 9, 1804

In the twilight Drouillard paced all over the old camp and
council site, stopping here and there and tilting his head or
squatting to pinch up soil and rub it between his fingers, sniffing
the air, picking up a wood chip. Field, Labiche, and Bratton had
already built a cookfire, and Labiche was cooking a turkey while
the other two halfheartedly strolled around trying to read something from the week-old tracks all over the beaten ground. Finally Drouillard told them to go and sit down because they were
leaving new tracks all over. They shrugged and sat down in the
campfire smoke, lit pipes, and commenced killing mosquitoes.

Drouillard had found one set of soldier-shoe footprints
fresher than the rest, and followed them from place to place until
their story was plain to him. He went to the campfire and sat on
the ground to eat with the others. The turkey was undercooked
and tough but flavorful enough to merit the hard chewing. The
last light faded behind the bluff and the pole shelter-frames of
the old camp dimmed to invisibility in the deepening darkness.
Wolves chorused on the distant plains. Mosquitoes whined in-
cessantly, and the men had to blow mosquitoes away from their
mouths before every bite of turkey.

"Here it is about Reed," Drouillard said when they had finished eating and sipped their whiskey ration. "He camped here
at least two nights, maybe three. He dug up his stuff, over there
by that leaning-over cottonwood. Could be he wanted to go to
the Oto town but didn't know which way to head off. He went up
on the bluff once, maybe to look for their smoke. Confused man.
Cooked a big catfish. Two days ago or maybe yesterday he set off
the only way he knew to go: down the river. Now he may just try
to walk all the way back to St. Louis, or he might turn up the

Platte and try to find the Oto town, try to get a horse. *If* he knows that's where they are. I doubt he knows. My guess is he's afraid of Sioux Indians and that's why he deserted. He probably thinks the Oto are friendly enough and hopes to trade something for a horse. Or maybe he's pining for a woman."

"Poor bastard! Imagine that!" Field exclaimed.

"Mon ami," Drouillard said to Labiche, "come daylight I want you and Reubin to go overland to the Oto town, find Faufon, and La Liberté, if he's with 'em. Get their chiefs ready to go up to meet the captains at the Omaha town. Their *real* chiefs, not those made-up Jefferson chiefs."

"How will we know 'em?" Fields asked.

"Eh bien, why not ask the Indians? I'd reckon they know who their chiefs are!" This was getting to be a sore point with him.

"Uh. Yeah."

"Bratton and I will track Reed down the river. When we get him, we'll bring him back up here, and we'll wait here for you and the chiefs. And bring Faufon. And La Liberté."

"Um, Drouillard," Reubin Field said, "don't y' think we should all go after Reed? He's got a good rifle, y' know, and he's a fair good shot."

"It won't take four of us for him. I want you to get those chiefs ready to travel while we're getting Reed. If we do one thing at a time, it'll take us a month to catch up with the boats."

Labiche raised a finger. "Could be them chiefs already headed up? Wasn't their trader s'posed to take 'em up?"

"Supposed to, but I doubt he has yet," Drouillard said. "Probably still be out after buffalo. But if they have already left, come back and meet us here and we'll all go up. Now, see, one reason I'm splitting us off is, I don't think we'd make a real good impression on the Otoes by hauling a tied-up or a dead soldier into town with us. I mean, since the cap'ns are preaching 'peaceful road' and all that. I can explain a deserter to a few headmen. A town's a different matter. Indian women don't like to see a man tied up, and might want to turn him loose."

Field stretched, yawned, spat out mosquitoes. "I look forward to goin' to a town where the women like the men runnin' loose!"

In the distance the evening songs of several wolves braided themselves through the darkness, a beautiful sound that filled Drouillard's heart with longings for something he couldn't have named. In the tones he detected the songs of the ancestors.

He was startled by a sudden outburst of yipping and squealing, much nearer. It continued madly for half a minute, then quit as abruptly as it had begun.

"What in tarnation!" Field exclaimed.

"Sound like somebody flang a litter o' pups in a fireplace!" Bratton said. "What was it, Drouillard?"

"I never heard it before."

Labiche, who had lived here, knew. "It's Little Wolf. Spaniards call him *coyotl*. That was a pack of 'em."

"Lordamercy, 'tween them and the skeeters, how we goin' to sleep?" Bratton exclaimed.

"They're done," said Labiche. "They just say good night once."

"I like the big wolves better," Drouillard said, marveling at the creatures that Our Grandmother, the creator of lives, had put to live in different places of the world. "Now, *they* sing beautiful. Just be still and listen."

August 11th Satturday 1804
about day this morning a hard wind from the N.W. followed by rain. we landed at the foot of the hill on which Black Bird The late King of the mahar who Died 4 years ago & 400 of his nation with the Small pox was buried and went up and fixed a white flag bound with Blue white & read on the Grave . . . from the top of this hill may be Seen the bends or meanderings of the river for 60 or 70 miles round . . .

                                        William Clark, Journals

"There he is," Drouillard said to Bratton. "Get down." They dismounted in shoulder-high brush a hundred paces from the north bank of the Platte. Drouillard pointed to a wisp of smoke near the riverbank, half a mile downstream. Near the smoke, looking no bigger than a gnat against the broad expanse of the roiling river and its labyrinth of sandbars, was a man. Still farther down to the east was the even greater shimmer of the wide Missouri. Drouillard kept pointing until Bratton finally made out the figure. "Cooking breakfast, I guess, maybe trying to figure out how to cross."

"God be praised!" Bratton said softly. "Don't a man look small in this country!"

"Sure he feels small by now. Well, I better go down and get him." He studied the bottomland, then turned to Bratton and said, "Tie the horses here. Then come with me, and don't talk."

They slipped through the grass parallel to the Platte, staying screened by shrubs and berry bushes until they were about a hundred yards from Reed, who was sitting on a barkless drift log facing away toward his fire and the river. To his left grew a long stand of willow slips, lightly waving in the early morning breeze. His rifle leaned upright against the log.

"Get a bead on him at full cock," Drouillard whispered. "I'm going down to say hello. If he reaches for his gun, I'll get him. If he gets me, you get him. Clear enough?"

Bratton was shaking his head. "Isn't there some better way?"

"Don't argue, eh?" he whispered. "The wind's my way and I'll go by way o' the willows. He won't know I'm there till I am. Check your primer."

They flicked up the frizzens of their flintlocks and recharged with new powder. Drouillard readied both his pistols, slipped them back into his sash, waited till Bratton had aim on Reed, then nodded, stooped, and ran down the slope toward the willows. The only thing he had to worry about between here and the willows was scaring up ground birds that Reed might hear. It didn't happen. In a few seconds he was walking noiselessly along the screen of willows, approaching Reed by his left shoulder. The smell off the man was as bad as anything short of death, Drouillard thought.

Reed looked scrawny and wretched. His jaws were dark stubble and his clothes were torn and filthy. Impaled on a greenwood spit leaning by the fire was a little bird. Some guts and wood duck feathers lay in the sand, alive with flies. Reed was gazing at the broiling bird in such a deep stupor that he might as well have been asleep, so Drouillard just walked up behind the log, snatched the muzzle of Reed's rifle and lifted it away. Only then did Reed jerk his head up and look around into the muzzle of his own piece, which Drouillard cocked with a loud click.

" 'Morning, Reed. Lost?" he said into the haunted, stricken face.

Reed rose slowly, lips trembling. Then suddenly he was sobbing. "Oh, hell," he whimpered. "Man, am I glad to see somebody!"

August 18, 1804

It happened to be Captain Lewis's thirtieth birthday when Drouillard caught up, more than a hundred miles up from the Platte, and he brought with him so much of what Lewis wanted that the captain seemed to forget all the hard words of their confrontation two weeks ago.

Drouillard had the deserter, and he also had the Oto chiefs Big Horse and Little Thief, along with half a dozen of their chieftains and some of their most esteemed warriors. The trader Faufon was with them to help interpret again. Labiche and Field had found La Liberté at the Oto town too, and he had promised to return to the expedition with them, but then had slipped away the night before they started up. They did bring up the horse he had taken. Both captains were lavish with their praise and gratitude for Drouillard.

The chiefs were greeted with a blast of the swivel gun, a display of the fluttering flag and squads in full uniform, and were offered food and a chance to rest from the hard ride. But then the captains explained that a council would have to wait until they tried and punished their warrior who had done bad.

Little Thief, the Otoes' true chief, was not little. He was burly, with long, sinewy legs and short arms, and a square, sun-fried countenance whose deep creases suggested a lifetime of smiling. His headpiece appeared to be the cylindrical crown of a Spanish army shako with the bill removed and a fan of grouse tailfeathers fixed on top like a crest, and over his shoulders he wore a yoke made of the whole skin of a coyote, head and forepaws hanging down in front, tail and hind feet down his back.

The next chief was Big Horse, who was small, lean, middle-aged. Drouillard suspected this diminutive man was called Big Horse because any horse he sat on would have looked big. He had a face that looked as if it could split firewood, divided by a line of red paint from nose bridge to chin, and a bonnet of eagle feathers so big that when the wind blew at his back it looked as if it would fill and sail the slight fellow out of his saddle. But while amused by the sight of him, Drouillard kept in mind that eagle feathers are earned by bravery.

The rest of the Oto and Missouria warriors were splendid and impressive in bearclaw necklaces, quilled tunics, shell gorgets, painted shields, feathers and hairlocks, carrying feathered coup sticks and lances. In the long ride up from the council bluff with them, Drouillard had imagined what a glorious horde they must have been before the smallpox had reduced them. He had felt drab himself, and saddened that his own people had been de-feated and driven from their homelands before he was old enough to be a Shawnee warrior. All he had to decorate himself in was his demeanor and abilities. There was no one to award him eagle feathers, no wars for which to paint his face as his mother's ancestors had done. These warriors' wildness stirred but saddened him.

The soldiers likewise were being shown at their most impres-sive in long-tailed blue coats with red lapels, cuffs and standing collars, white waistcoats and tight-legged coveralls, the wide straps of their shot pouches and bayonet scabbards crossed over their chests, every man made to look a foot taller than he was by his cockaded top hat. Most of the uniforms were patched and dingy by now, but at a distance the squads looked trim and grand, not to be outshone by the colorful warriors. Being all young men, those on both sides eyed each other both audaciously and with admiration.

Private Reed was immediately whisked out of sight to be

shaved and put in uniform for his trial, and Drouillard went straight to the boat, stripped out of his dirty trail clothes, bathed in the river with soap, even his hair, rubbed face and limbs with elderberry bear oil, and braided a neat queue down the back. By the time the troops were convened for the court-martial, he was in a clean linen hunting shirt with necklaces and ear bobs, a bright silk turban on his head, quilled knife-sheath hanging on his chest, and two pistols in the sash at his waist. The chiefs appraised him and nodded as he returned. They already knew him by reputation as a hunter; in fact, Hospitality had told them he was the chief hunter of the whole whiteman army. At least now they could see that he was no mere scruffy army scout.

Private Moses Reed too was transformed, and looked like a soldier, not a scared fugitive. He stood straight and ready to face his judgment. It was hard to believe this was the man who had broken down crying when he was caught. Reed had tried to bribe Drouillard and Bratton to lie and say they had found him lost.

Reed stood erect and pleaded guilty to deserting with a public rifle and ammunition, which meant, to Drouillard's relief, that he would not have to testify against him. Reed looked directly at the captains and said, "Please, sirs, I own up to what I did and I am sorry. I ask the captains to be as merciful to me as your oaths and reg'lations allow."

Drouillard watched the two officers murmur close to each other. Clark's left eye was twitching. The afternoon sun was low and the flag was fluttering hard in the evening breeze, a breeze that promised an evening without mosquitoes. The bottomland was broad and grassy; the sun blazed off the river. The chiefs and warriors sat watching everything while Faufon tried to tell them what was happening.

Captain Clark stood and said, "The prisoner will step forward. Private Moses B. Reed, by the articles of war the crime of desertion is punishable by death. Since you have straightly confessed to the charge against you, and since we need a man on every oar, you are to be spared that severest penalty. The court sentences you to pass through the gauntlet four times, each man holding nine switches. Thereafter you will no longer be considered a member of this body of men and you will not be permitted to bear arms."

Drouillard was looking at Reed and saw him become No Man, an outcast, just as a Shawnee in disgrace used to be put out. Reed shrank before his eyes and went pale. Sergeant Ordway removed Reed's coat and shirt to prepare him for the whipping.

Better if I'd given him a chance to run, Drouillard thought. He'd probably rather be dead than this.

The Otoes and Missourias were becoming agitated as they began to understand what was about to happen. Faufon came over to the captains. "Messieurs, my Indians beg you to pardon that man. They cannot understand men whipping their brother!"

"Well, then let's go and explain it to them so they can," Lewis replied.

Drouillard decided it was time to make himself invisible.

He slipped behind the canvas of the captains' shelter. York was there tending the cookfires, where army pork boiled in kettles, and cleaning fish. There were mounds of grapes and berries on a ground cloth. York was singing under his breath, absorbed in his work and thoughts, and didn't see Drouillard. He was shirtless in the cooking heat, the late sunlight gleaming on his sweaty torso. Three strenuous months on the river had melted the fat off him and his musculature was impressive. When he turned and reached, Drouillard saw the old whipping scars all over his back. Suddenly the slave saw Drouillard and was startled. Then he smiled.

"Hey, Mas' Droor! Heard you was back! Now we can eat somp'n 'sides fish an' pork!" He explained that Captain Clark and the troops had made a brush net and seined up nearly a thousand fish in a beaver creek and he was sick of cleaning fish. Aside from one elk Collins had shot about ten days ago, the corps had been living on fish, turkey, and beaver in Drouillard's absence.

Out in the camp now the sounds of the punishment began: the slash and crackle of the switches splintering on Reed's back, grunts and curses, gasps of agony, and the shrilling laments of the horrified Indians, who apparently were not much convinced by Captain Lewis's explanation of army discipline. York's face twitched as he heard the sounds.

"They just made another slave there," Drouillard said. "Maybe you could ask out of the job now."

York dropped his gaze and knelt back down with his fish knife, of which he was a master; he gutted, split, and scaled two bass and a pike before he said anything. Finally he glanced up, and there was just a trace of a smile on him. "I been pesterin'."

"Good! What's he say?"

" 'At he too busy t' talk about it."

"Reckon he can always say that."

"Maybe 'e won' be too busy t' whip me if I don't shut up." York laughed. "We see."

Only their first glimpse of York got the Otoes' minds off the distress of Reed's whipping. York was still bareheaded and shirtless. For a moment they were dumbstruck, but soon were exclaiming a word over and over, which Faufon explained was their word for Buffalo Standing on Back Feet. With his tight-curled poll, glittering black eyes, beard, and huge chest and shoulders, that perception made sense. Hospitality had told them the soldiers had a black man, so he was not a total surprise. At the serving of supper he had dressed and put on a headkerchief, and the Indians jovially called him Buffalo in Clothes Standing.

Drouillard sat near the captains to assist by hand language or French while Faufon did most of the translating. First the officers had to apologize for a big disappointment; the Omaha towns had been found empty, the people apparently still out hunting. So their promise of negotiating peace between the Otoes and Omahas, the main reason that the Otoes had come up all this way, was empty, unless the Omahas came back to investigate smoke from grass fires the soldiers had set north of the camp. The main council would be held tomorrow, with that hope in mind.

Then Lewis asked about the causes of the troubles, assessing the intertribal political balance throughout the new country as Jefferson had requested.

The response was a bewildering recital of petty spites and getting even, ranging from horse thievery to theft of corn, and involving the Pawnees as well as the Omahas. It went on and on, until the officers' eyes were glazed and they were squirming with the uncomfortable realization that these complaints were like old family squabbles and grudges that they couldn't follow, let alone mediate, and couldn't have done even if the Omahas had been here to give their side. Drouillard could see that Lewis was sorry he had asked, and it was hard to keep from laughing.

Captain Lewis's birthday was a good excuse for a double whiskey ration, and the cool breeze had swept away the mosquitoes, so the supper was followed by a celebration around the fires. By the time the stars were shining in the vast, clear dome of the sky, Cruzatte's fiddle was whining and squeaking, tambourines were jingling in time, a Jew's harp was twanging, soldiers with linked arms were capering and stomping around the bonfire, Rivet was dancing on his hands with his heels behind his head, and young Oto warriors were prancing glassy-eyed and yipping like coyotes. Drouillard had winds and voices whirling in his head, and the images of warriors dancing around the war post in the towns near Lorimier's old store, in the war days, when his own people were still warriors. Captain Lewis, pointing to the fiddler, was telling everyone that President Jefferson was an accomplished player of the violin, which was like a fiddle but, of course, finer, and that people sat and listened respectfully instead of dancing.

Of course. But in Drouillard's spirit was not violin or fiddle, but the old voices, the faint, ancient songs.

Sunday, August 19, 1804

Little Thief came to breakfast wearing nothing but feathers, moccasins, and a loincloth. "What the devil?" Captain Lewis exclaimed. "I would expect a little more decorum for an important council."

Drouillard already suspected what the Oto chief meant by his nakedness, and it came out in council under the awning at mid-morning, after Lewis had made his speech on peace and trade under the new Great Father. Little Thief stood and began his reply.

"I heard your message and returned from hunting the buffalo, to speak with you of peace. Peace would be good. My people have always been at peace with white traders, English, French, Spanish. You are traders and you carry many goods in your big boat. I come naked. I am poor. I must return naked. But if you can give me something very fine to take my young men, they will be satisfied to stay home and not go to war. I would like to have for myself a sun glass to make fire, as was shown to me by your great hunter, Followed by Buzzards." Drouillard hid a smile behind his hand. That damned Hospitality had told them that was his name!

Faufon said then that the Missouria chief Big Horse wanted to speak next.

The little man stood up, looking severe. He complained that the whitemen did not understand about the leaders of the Oto and Missouria people, who lived together. They had sent him a smaller medal than the one they had sent to Little Thief, even though he was of equal importance in his tribe. Then he gave the same speech Little Thief had given about peace with the traders, but added that in order to keep the young men quiet, he needed to take home "a spoonful of your milk." He hoped for enough whiskey to satisfy the young men. He also hoped to take home some of the best articles from the boat to show his people what the traders under this new flag had to offer.

The captains looked at each other, frowning and baffled. Drouillard leaned close and explained: "All the whitemen they ever knew were traders. To them you are traders because you are whitemen. They don't care what your flag is, they are only inter-ested in what you offer to trade, and your prices. They know they have to be at peace with you to get your trade. That's all."

"No, damn it," said Lewis. "They have to be at peace with *each other* to trade with us! That's what we're trying to tell them!"

"They're pretending that makes sense to them. To keep you happy. So you'll give them samples."

"No. They've got to understand the rules. Peace with each other, and no trading with anyone but the United States."

"They heard you tell 'em that, sir." Drouillard shrugged and sat back. He was enjoying this.

Captain Lewis impatiently repeated the requirements. Then he had Captain Clark pass out written certificates and explained that when American traders came along later, they would see those papers and know the Indians had agreed to the rules, and would trade fairly with them. Most of the Indians acted happy to receive a piece of paper, but one proud Oto warrior, Eyes Big as the Sky, thrust his certificate back with a frown. When he saw the indignation in the captains' faces, he probably realized that they might give him nothing for his insolence; he apologized and asked for his piece of paper. But the act had given Lewis a high place to scold from, and he barked at them so vehemently about valuing goods over peace that Faufon the interpreter could hardly keep up. It was getting hot under the awning and the mood was bad.

Little Thief rose then and said that Eyes Big as the Sky had misunderstood something and wished to be forgiven, and really did want his piece of paper.

Drouillard said, "Just give it to 'im and they'll forget this."

Instead Lewis told Clark, "Give the certificate to the chief and tell him to award it to somebody worthy of it." Drouillard could see that all the warriors were insulted by that. Little Thief, scowling, took the certificate from Clark and handed it straight back to Eyes Big as the Sky, thus insulting Lewis in equal measure. Lewis might have exploded then, but Sergeant Ordway slipped in under the edge of the awning, stooped and told the captains, "Sergeant Floyd's really taken bad. *Real* bad."

The captains tried to end the council in a little better mood, by giving the Indians a few more gifts, some whiskey, and a show of the air gun. It didn't help much.

York and Captain Clark hovered over Sergeant Floyd back in the camp. The Indians wandered around the camp, gazing at York, and at the great black dog, asking for whiskey and more presents in sign language, which the soldiers didn't understand, and everyone grew exasperated. The soldiers were afraid the warriors would carry off things, and grew grim and touchy. Captain Lewis spent a while trying to talk Little Thief and Big Horse into making a trip to see their new Great Father in the East, and invited the Indians to camp close by another night.

Little Thief made one final request. He asked to take Private Labiche back to his town to help the Otoes talk peace with the Pawnees. Had not the captain wanted all the Indians to make peace?

Lewis did not see this as the reasonable request Little Thief thought it was, and replied that he could not let any of his soldiers go. Drouillard saw a shadow of distrust and disappointment slide like a cloud over Little Thief's eyes. That night the Indians didn't hang around for fiddling and dancing.

20th August Monday 1804
we Set out under a gentle breeze from the S.E—Serjeant Floyd as bad as he can be no pulse & nothing will stay a moment on his Stomach—Passed two Islands and at first Bluff on the S. S. Sergt. Floyd died with a great deal of Composure. Before his death he Said to me. "I am going away I want you to write me a letter"—We buried him on the top of the bluff ½ Miles below a small river to which we Gave his name, we Camped in the mouth of floyds river . . .

William Clark, Journals

Chapter 8

Drouillard sat by the captains' tent, cleaning and oiling the flint-lock of his rifle, and now and then he glanced over at the new sergeant, who was being briefed on his responsibilities by Captain Clark. Captain Lewis was lying down in the tent, coughing and hacking, too sick to talk.

The new sergeant, elected by the soldiers to take Charles Floyd's place, was a sturdy, box-jawed Irishman named Patrick Gass. Drouillard didn't know him well because Gass seldom was sent out to hunt. Gass was a prodigiously strong oarsman, and the best carpenter in the unit. He spent much of his time repairing the boats and making oars and masts and tillers, fixing cracked gun stocks, or converting emptied crates and barrels into any other wooden item the corps needed. His skill with sharp tools was a pleasure to behold, but his language was a disgrace. He drove his tools with the force of profanity. He called his tools and his materials sons of bitches and sluts, buggers and turds. He had been a soldier for about five years, and his vocabulary included vile words Drouillard had never heard even rivermen use. And yet, he was educated well enough to be one of the journal-keepers. He was funny and popular, so he had received nineteen of the soldiers' votes, winning the sergeancy over two other good men, Bratton and Gibson.

Captain Lewis erupted into another coughing fit, which grew deeper into gut sounds, nearly like vomiting. Clark turned an anxious eye toward the tent, waited for a lull in the retching and hacking, and called, "Can I do something for ye?"

"No, I'll get rid of this."

This morning Captain Lewis had found a cliff composed of sandstone and some glassy-looking mineral. In pounding it, heating it, and tasting it to determine what it was, he had poisoned himself either by ingesting the stuff or breathing its fumes. Drouillard shook his head and went back to work on his rifle, thinking whitemen would kill themselves before they'd leave anything be. Lewis had taken a dose of salts, in which he had great faith for ridding him of the poison.

Patrick Gass had brought his journal notebook, and he and Captain Clark began comparing their notes for the last few days. "My writin's so goddamn messy," Gass growled. "Three or four days in the pot my ink clots up like cunt's blood and gets too thick for the pen."

Captain Clark had been depressed since Charles Floyd's death, and evidently didn't deem the uncouth Gass a worthy replacement for him. He looked at Gass as if he were a dumb animal. "Well, man, add water and stir when it gets that way. It's like this Missouri River. If it doesn't get rain, it's all sandbars and mud. Or just make less ink at a time, so it doesn't sit so long. An ink pot's really pretty simple. Not worth cussin' over."

After Gass left, Captain Lewis came out of the tent, pale, breathing through his open mouth. "Call of nature," he said, and ambled off toward the latrine with his peculiar bow-legged walk. He stopped and turned. "We should reach that haunted hill Dorion told us about in two or three days. I'm sure eager to go up there and see what all that superstition is about."

Clark raised his eyebrows. "He said it's ten miles or so from the river. You sure you'll be up to that?"

"Well, I sure aim to be better right away." He turned and went on.

"You can't keep a good man down," Clark said, shaking his head.

"Not when nature calls, anyway," Drouillard replied. Clark

laughed. To himself, Drouillard damned Dorion for having mentioned that hill. The old Frenchman had proved himself an invaluable guide along the Missouri, knowing much about distances, tribes, and the traders' names of rivers, and would surely be a most useful interpreter when the corps reached the Sioux. But it was a shame he had mentioned the Bad Spirit hill with its little devils. It was said to be guarded by knee-high demons with big heads who tormented and sacrificed anyone who came near. Dorion said the people of all tribes avoided the terrible place, that birds hovered over the hill like dark smoke, and that the birds were the spirits of those who had been killed by the demons' sharp arrows. Whatever the truth of it was, such a place was a sacred place. There were good sacred places and there were bad ones, some good to some tribes and bad to others, but in any case, it was better for whitemen not to know about them. In particular, people like these captains, Drouillard thought, who cut apart snakes and birds and tested the rocks of the earth and then wrote everything down, were much too intrusive and irreverent and should not go to spirit places. And they would, of course, want him, their own Indian, to go with them.

He did not want to go near some other nation's Bad Spirit place, not even alone and with the protection of reverence. He really did not want to go there in the company of white soldiers who were explaining everything to their Great Father back east. He said to Captain Clark, "I doubt if the cap'n can make it that far on foot. And the horses are out." Hunters were out on the plains with the horses and there was no sign of them.

"Well," Clark replied, "he'll make that choice. If he feels up to it, we'll go. Probably have horses up by then anyway. I sure hope so."

Drouillard tried another ploy. "I've sure seen elk sign aplenty. When we get the horses, I'd like to go get enough elk to feed us awhile. I'd like to scout us up some Sioux while I'm out. From what Mr. Dorion says, we should meet them any time now."

"All that in its due time," Clark said, spreading paper and uncorking his ink pot. "Meantime, we do want to see that haunted hill."

August 23, 1804

"Yeaw-hooo! Yeeeaw-*hooo*!" It was Joe Field running down the high north bank toward the boats, thrusting his rifle overhead and capering with every few steps. The soldiers, who were tediously poling the big boat into a powerful headwind, through low water channels among sandbars, had to squint into fine, stinging sand even to see where the voice was coming from, and then they made out what he was shouting: "Got me a buffalo! Yeaw-hooo! I got our first buffalo, by God!" He cavorted on the bank, holding his hat high with one hand and pointing with his rifle upstream. "Big son of a bitch! Way past that high land! Goin' to need a pack o' help to haul 'im down!"

Drouillard was standing with Captain Lewis near the hatch of the after cabin. The clouds of blown sand now and then fully blanked Field from their view. The sand was so fine and so full of dried riverbottom dirt that it stuck to their faces, their clothes, even to the sides and bulkhead of the vessel. Lewis grinned, blinking, and glanced at Drouillard. "Hard luck, George. I always reckoned it'd be you, or me, getting the honor of bagging our first buffalo!"

"Eh, Field's welcome to the honor, sir. I got my first one when I was about twelve."

"Oh?" Lewis squinted straight into his eyes, as if to gauge whether he was telling the truth. "Really!" Then he cupped his hands around his mouth, as much to keep sand out as to project his voice into the wind, and shouted to Field, "Good man! Go on up! We'll come ashore for it when we get there!" Field responded with a wave and his hat blew off. Drouillard hoped he'd be able to find it in this sandstorm. The captain shouted in the wind to the men straining on their set-poles, "Hear that? Reubin Field's shot us our first buffalo!" The men gave a cheer.

Drouillard said, "That's Joe, sir. Reubin's out with the horses."

"Right—Joseph," Lewis mumbled. Drouillard was troubled, as he often was by the captain's little slips. Lewis was a conscientious commander, careful for the safety and welfare of his men, but sometimes he seemed hardly to know them. He could glance at a soldier and remember what he was good at or poor at, but often didn't seem to know his name, after all these months on the same boat. Drouillard felt that as intense a presence as Lewis was, he wasn't all here. He was like something in heedless passage from far behind to far ahead.

It was disturbing to think of an arrow-spirit like Lewis's aiming at a round, seething spirit-swarm like the haunted hill. And it seemed to Drouillard that this storm of blinding, howling, clinging dust and sand was a warning against going there.

August 25, 1804

On the vast plain under an oppressive yellow haze, the Bad Spirit hill was visible from miles away, the only high place within all the horizons, and dark as if charred. It was a hill standing where no hill should be standing, and although it appeared bald, it reminded Drouillard of the great mound beside the Mississippi, which had been covered with trees. He was walking ahead and off the left flank of the file of seven men who followed the captains. There had been eight, but one had been sent to take Captain Lewis's black dog back to the river after it collapsed panting in the heat. The slave York looked as if he too would collapse, but he kept trudging along behind his master, clothes sodden with sweat, gun over his shoulder, chest heaving. Ahead on the other flank was Colter, striding alert even in the great heat. Captain Clark with his long legs and deep chest was a great walker too, and though drenched with sweat, he was striding along through the parched grass with ease.

It was Captain Lewis whom Drouillard watched from the edge of his eye. With every step he seemed to be losing strength. Perhaps that was because of the poison he had taken from the earth, or the medicine he had taken for the poison, but perhaps it was something beyond that. Drouillard kept hoping to see him stop and give up and turn back. But Lewis staggered on, obviously determined to investigate the Bad Spirit hill.

It was hard to guess distance on this featureless plain, but at what seemed about a league from the hill, Drouillard began to feel its force. It was like a prickling, hot pressure building in front of him. It was not the wind; it had nothing to do with the wind, which was blowing on him from his left. It was like a thickening and heating of the air between him and the hill, telling him not to come closer.

They moved on, the pressure growing. Blackbirds and larks rose from the grass or flew to and fro across their path in ever-increasing numbers. Drouillard thought he heard, under the sounds of the birds' cries and wing beats, faint, shrill voices, as if hundreds of angry women were scolding from the hill. They grew louder and louder. He looked over to the column. Lewis was still stumbling onward, the others were gasping and coming along, and no one seemed to be noticing the voices.

At about a mile from the mound he could see a cloud of what appeared to be black smoke leaning off the top, and heard Colter call out about it. Soon Drouillard saw that the cloud was not smoke, but hovering, swirling birds, the birds Monsieur Dorion had spoken of.

A few yards from where the base of the mound rose abruptly from the sloping plain, rocks lay amid the grasses. The prickling sensations on his breast and face were now intensely sharp and stinging. Suddenly the hot pressure grew cold. The shrilling voices were nearly drowning out the twitter of the birds. The stings now were not just on the front of him, but penetrating him. He stopped. He would go no farther. The captains were talking, the men were talking, milling about, starting to make their way up the slope. Their voices were loud and clear but he could not understand any of their words.

He prayed a wordless prayer of apology, turning in a circle and crumbling tobacco all around his feet. He saw York sink to the ground at the base of the hill and sit mopping his brow on his sleeves. He saw the captains climbing the slope, he saw Captain Clark glancing back down and calling something, his name probably, Drouillard thought, but the voice was an incomprehensible, quavering bellow that instantly faded away and was replaced by bird twitterings and the scolding of tiny, savage voices. The captains and the soldiers climbed on up and up. Drouillard saw Colter stop and look down at him strangely, then turn and go on up through the swarm of angry spirits. The spirits were like hornets swirling around Drouillard, held off only by his circle of tobacco, and he understood perfectly well that he was not to go onto this hill, but these whitemen seemed impervious, even oblivious, to them.

Drouillard stepped backward and felt the pressure lighten. Another step and it was less. Understanding, he turned and walked quickly away from the mound. At a hundred paces the painful swarming had eased so much that he could stop and stand comfortably. The spirits now knew that he understood them and would stay off the hill. He pinched some more dry tobacco from his pouch and cast it into the wind. He heard York's voice calling his name and asking, "What you doin', man?" He just waved away the question and walked another forty or fifty paces away from the hill, growing still more comfortable. Looking up, he watched the whitemen casually wandering atop the hill, examining things and talking or gazing into the distances. He saw Captain Clark walk along the ridge of the mound toward the east end where the birds were still swarming. Something told Drouillard he should make an offering circle around the base of the hill, so he set off at a swift trot. The mound was long and narrow. At each end and side he sprinkled a little tobacco. Half a mile of running brought him around, back to where York still sat bewildered on the ground. Drouillard was hot and the run had made him very thirsty. "Mist' Droor, you sure strange!" York exclaimed. "Run in this heat? Ooooh!"

"Eh so? Those whitemen are stranger. Climbing a hundred-foot hill in the heat."

"Oh, they jus' crazy. You *strange*."

Drouillard waited at the edge of the shrilling and swarming until the whitemen came down. They seemed to be all right, just desperately thirsty. It seemed that if they didn't believe in something, they were impervious to it. But Drouillard did wonder if they would be changed after this.

25th August, Satturday 1804
. . . The surrounding Plains is open void of Timber: hence the
wind from whatever quarter drives with unusial force against
this hill; the insects of various kinds are thus driven to the
mound by the force of the wind, or fly to its Leward Side for
Shelter: the Small Birds whoes food they are, Consequently
resort in great numbers to this place in Surch of them . . .

One evidence which the Inds Give for believeing this place
to be the residence of Some unusial Spirits is a large assem-
blage of Birds about this Mound—is in my opinion a Suffient
proof to produce in the Savage mind a Confident belief . . .
from the top of this mound we beheld a most butifull land-
scape; Numerous herds of buffalow were Seen feeding . . . we
set the Praries on fire as a Signal for the Soues to Come to the
river.

William Clark, Journals

August 27, 1804

Drouillard had walked forty miles alone over the moonlit plains
looking for young Private Shannon and two horses. He hadn't
seen a trace of the man. It had been a night bright enough to track
by. Now before dawn the morning star came up, uncommonly
brilliant. The shallow Missouri glimmered below, braiding
among sandbars. It had been a long night of beautiful solitude
and no sound but wind, water, the rustle of small scurrying animals, his own moccasins whispering in the prairie grass.

He didn't think Shannon had deserted. He was a well-liked,
agreeable lad, about nineteen, not very experienced. He had just
got lost hunting.

When Drouillard came in without him, the captains sent Joe
Field and John Shields out to continue the search, and Drouillard
slept the morning away in the cabin of the moving keelboat,
which the soldiers were pulling through the shallows much of
the time with a long rope of braided elk hide. He would half
waken to the groans and bumps and voices, then fall back into

deep sleep. He dreamed of a black eagle high in a tree that stood above a mist like clouds.

He woke to a shout in the afternoon: "Hey! Indian swimmin' over! Lookee! Two more!" "Sioux at last!" Clark cried. "That last prairie burn got their attention! Hey! Red boat, bring Dorion up!"

August 30, 1804

His heart pounded with the drum, and when the Sioux warriors trilled, his own voice broke out of him in his people's war cry, which he had never uttered in battle. The soldiers turned and looked at him, eyes big in the firelight with astonishment. He was as startled as they at his outcry.

The dancers' chattering rattles sent wave after wave of shivers through him. He had never in his adult life been so stirred.

There were about seventy warriors and boys here, so the captains had warned the men to be on guard for any trouble, even though these were Dorion's people—Yankton Sioux, who called themselves *Dahkotah*, or Allies—and were friendly. They were erect, sinewy, sharp-eyed and proud. Their chiefs were Shaking Hand, White Crane, and Half Man. Only a few had guns, cheap, rusty trade muskets; most were armed with bows, lances, clubs, hatchets, and knives. The soldiers' fine rifles would not be much advantage if any trouble broke out in the crowd; it would all be face-to-face, hand-to-hand cutting and bludgeoning, and the soldiers were far outnumbered. The only sense of security lay in old Pierre Dorion's assurances, and in his influence with them. He had Sioux wives, and sons by them; one of those sons, Pierre *le jeune*, had come to the soldier camp with all these Indians.

The captains, aside from their nervousness, were delighted. The President's grand plan for peaceful commerce hinged on co-operation with the powerful Sioux tribes, of which there were about twenty; now represented here was one of their factions, acting friendly enough so far, and thanks to Dorion and son there was no language barrier.

Today there had been plenty of talking and gift-giving and

showing off, including an impressive display of archery skills by young boys. Now tonight there was this big party around the bonfires. Tomorrow the formal *parloir*, or powwow, would continue. The Yankton chiefs had already expressed an eagerness for a reliable source of goods, as the Teton Sioux farther upriver jealously controlled the flow of British goods from Canada. The quantity and quality of utensils and ornaments they had already seen today made their eyes gleam.

The Dorions had instructed the Americans in the protocol of rewarding the dancers and musicians: tossing them tobacco, hawks' bells, beads, whistles, and cheap knives. And in the shadows outside the fire circles, some of the randy voyageurs were already trying the art of seduction by barter on the few women who had followed the warriors down. There was whiskey breath in the air.

Four tall, elegant, composed warriors held themselves apart from the rest, while staying close enough to the fires to be admired. They deigned to talk only to one another, cheerfully and with the familiarity of brothers. Dorion had pointed them out as members of a society known as Warriors Who Never Step Back. Whatever the odds or jeopardy, they never took cover or fled, but stood their ground until they won or died. Dorion said that the society had recently had twenty-two warriors but eighteen had been killed in a battle with the Crow people far to the west, and only these four survived. The captains had shown a fervid interest in this society. Captain Lewis told the chiefs that American soldiers were just such a society, and fled from no threat. Drouillard thought that was a pretty tall boast; as well as he had been able to discern, only two or three of the expedition's soldiers had ever been in combat, except for their brawls among themselves back in winter camp at Riviere à Dubois.

Now a sweaty warrior stepped out from the rest dancing around the flames, and danced a tale of his exploits in war, all told by mime: stalking, springing, crouching, striking, holding up a scalp. The soldiers encouraged and applauded him with shouts, whistles, clapping, and tossing tobacco and trinkets at his feet.

Bratton leaned close to Drouillard, breathing whiskey smell, and said, "They think they're so brave, tell 'em how we'uns went right up t' their Devil Mount 'n' walked all 'round on it! They're 'fraid to do that!"

"No."

"Huh what?"

"I'm not going to tell them that."

"Puh! Just 'cause you were afeard to go up!"

"No. Because we didn't belong up there. Believe me, they won't admire that the way you want 'em to."

And then Drouillard had to worry that Captain Lewis, with his liquor and bravado and his ignorance of Indians, might get carried away himself and brag about climbing the Bad Spirit hill. Surely old Dorion would have the sense not to translate it to them if he did. But then, it was Dorion who had told Lewis about it in the first place.

It was late at night before the Indian dancers yielded the dance ground and the corps could begin to put on its own show.

The opening spectacle was little Pierre Cruzatte, springing into the firelight like a grasshopper with his fiddle held overhead in his left hand, the bow in the right. To the Indians, the instruments must have appeared to be weapons. As he hopped all the way around the fire on bent legs, leering, his one eye rolling and bulging like a madman's, he twirled the fiddle bow and waved the fiddle by its neck like a war club. Then, stopping right in front of the three dignified chiefs, he tucked the fiddle under his chin, stomped three times with his right foot, dragged the bow over the two low strings in a mournful announcing note, which probably sounded to them like the moan of a wounded animal. That was followed so quickly with a squealing, swiftly bowed tune on the high strings that the chiefs almost fell over backward in astonishment. For the next hour the soldiers stamped, whirled, swung, bowed and cavorted, whooping and yipping, to fiddle, tin horns, Jew's harps, and finger cymbals. York was coaxed out to dance, and the sight of the huge black man dancing with the alacrity of a sprite finally overtopped anything the Indians had seen, and not long after midnight the festivities were closed. The

Sioux were ferried across in the white pirogue to their campsite across the river, with the understanding that the talks would resume tomorrow after the chiefs had held council. When they were ready, they would be brought back across and feasted again, and would have their opportunity to reply to all they had heard from the captains today. Laughter and cheerful voices echoed across the water, wisps of pleasantry through the hush of a strong and mild southerly wind.

Drouillard listened to wind and water, watching a sentry pace the riverbank silhouetted against starlit water, remembering the great, surging feeling of wildness that had made him yip and trill with the warriors. Wind and stars and wild freedom: these were expanding his spirit until he felt a swelling under his throat, like another scream wanting to come out. The captains and soldiers had done well and had been respectful; he wasn't ashamed to be seen with them by Indians. But he knew they didn't belong here.

He lay there trying to sleep. Two soldiers, Werner and Whitehouse, were still awake nearby, in soft voices revising a familiar old song to suit the impressions of the evening. They sang in murmurs:

> *"Let's go a-courtin' the big chief's daughter,*
> *Let's go a-courtin' the big chief's daughter,*
> *She ain't been loved and I think she oughterrr!*
> *Let's go down and court 'er!"*

August the 31st 1804
after the Indians got their Brackfast the Chiefs met and arranged themselves in a row with elligent pipes of peace all pointing to our Seets, we Came forward and took our Seets, the Great Cheif The Shake Han rose and Spoke to Some length approving what we had Said and promising to pursue the advice.

I took a Vocabulary of the Sciouex Language—and the Answer to a fiew Quaries Such as refured to ther Situation, Trade, number, War, &c.&c.—This Nation is Divided into 20 Tribes, possessing Seperate interests—Collectively they

*are noumerous Say from 2 to 3000 men, their interests are so
unconnected that Some bands are at war with Nations which
other bands are on the most friendly terms. This Great Nation
who the French has given the nickname of Sciouex, Call them
selves Dar co tar . . . They are only at peace with 8 Nations, &
to their Calculation at war with twenty odd.—*

*the half man Cheif said My Fathers . . . we open our ears,
and I think our old Frend Mr. Durion can open the ears of the
other bands of Soux. but I fear those nations above will not
open their ears, and you cannot I fear open them . . . You have
given 5 Medles I wish you to give 5 Kegs with them . . .*

*all Concluded by telling the distresses of ther nation by not
haveing traders, & wished us to take pity on them, they
wanted Powder Ball & a little milk.*

William Clark, Journals

The captains were so elated by the success and harmony of
their first council with the Sioux that even a night-long rainstorm at the next camp didn't dampen their spirits.

Drouillard was in a turmoil of rich and troubling feelings. He
was relieved that Captain Lewis had learned at least not to tell
the Sioux who their chiefs were. But Drouillard hoped the officers weren't fooling themselves. It had gone so well because of
the Yanktons' trust in Dorion and his son, and their fluency in the
language. Dorion had been a gift from the Master of Life, but
was gone now. Lewis had sent him back with the Yanktons to
persuade some chiefs to go next spring to meet the President.

Chief Half Man's last warning lingered in Drouillard's
memory: "I fear those nations above will not open their ears."

With no one now in the party able to speak with the stronger
bands of Sioux except by hand signs—though Cruzatte knew a
very few Sioux words—the next encounter could not be as easy
as this one had been.

But what a people! Drouillard thought. Nothing had ever
heartened him so much as seeing an Indian people free in
their own land. Again the notion whispered deep in him that it

might be just as well if this expedition failed to go farther into
that land.

September 7, 1804

Every morning, Drouillard ascended the riverbank at first light
and ranged out on the plains to take up the trail of the lost man,
Shannon, and every day he found also the trail of John Colter,
still following. Shannon had been missing nearly two weeks
now, and for a week of that time Colter had been on his track,
never catching up.

But yesterday Colter had returned to the boat. He had given
up on catching Shannon and the horses, and on the way back he
had killed a buffalo, an elk, three deer, five turkeys, a goose, and
a beaver, which he had up on scaffolds not far ahead. He had
come back to report that Shannon was apparently still alive and
moving rapidly, and to find out whether to keep on in pursuit. "I
don't know what he's livin' on," Colter had said, "unless it be
grapes. No sign he'd kilt anything but one rabbit. Bones by a
little fire. He's sure the poorest hunter in this army. But I reckon
if he gets hungry enough he can kill a horse. Maybe if he tied it
to a tree and took real careful aim he could hit his horse?"

So this morning the captains had landed at a dome-shaped hill
on the south bank and climbed it, taking a spyglass, hoping they
might see Shannon ahead from that eminence. They didn't see
him. They were descending to the riverbank when they discovered a kind of animal they had never seen before.

The creatures had made burrow holes over several acres of
the slope above the river. They were whistling to each other, apparently in warning as the officers approached. The captains
heard the whistling sound and looked over to see several of the
animals scurrying into the holes. Some then stood in the burrows with their heads and shoulders out, watching like sentinels
as the captains stooped here and there trying to see into the
holes.

The rest of the afternoon evolved into a single-minded campaign to capture one of these rodents for the President. Drouillard gazed in amazement and amusement as almost the entire manpower of the corps passed buckets and kettles of water up from the Missouri River to pour into one of the burrows, hoping to flood a few of the rodents out. The equivalent of five barrels of water were poured in, the soldiers now and then probing the ground with long poles. Eventually Drouillard found himself involved in the mud-spattered eviction effort, and he was down on hands and knees when a soaked, furry, squirrel-like face bobbed up through the muddy water in the hole. Before anyone else had the presence of mind to move, he grabbed its nape and extended the animal to Lewis. "Here, Cap'n. My gift to Chief Jefferson."

The voyageurs referred to the rodents as Little Dogs of the Prairie, finding their yips suggestive of barking. A cage was built for the specimen, in hopes that it could be kept alive until it could be sent to the President.

In this exhausting period of struggling up through the sand-bars and twisting channels, worrying about Shannon and watching for signs of the next of the Sioux tribes, one natural novelty after another distracted the officers. Captain Clark became obsessed with a fleet prairie creature that was either a goat or an antelope, with short, forked horns and of a light sorrel color. He hiked onshore whenever he could, hoping for a shot at one, but it was impossible to get near them. To steady his rifle for the long, long shots that would be needed to get one, he began carrying an espontoon, which was a short infantry officer's spear with a hilt-like cross piece behind its head. With the butt of the spear on the ground and the rifle barrel resting on the cross piece, a long, standing shot could be much steadier. But even with this, Clark failed to bring down any of the pronged-horn creatures. Sometimes he took York on the hunts with him, and one day the servant killed two buffalo. The uplift to his pride was a marvel to see. He swaggered and smiled, wordlessly declaring that no mere slave carried a rifle and killed buffalo.

One day Drouillard followed buffalo on a beaten trail and found a strong salt spring. The captains meanwhile discovered a molasses spring and the fossil backbone of what looked to be some sort of fish or whale, nearly as long as the keelboat. The "molasses" was some kind of bitumen oozing from under a blue shale bluff; it looked, even tasted, like molasses. The vertebrae and teeth of the great fish protruded from the earth of a ridge, providing the troops endless speculation on how a fish could have climbed to high ground. It also gave them much to complain about, as it was carried piece by piece down to the river and added to the burgeoning load of specimens and souvenirs that had to be rowed up the river.

Drouillard, who could marvel at an amazing object and then leave it where the Creator had placed it, just shook his head at their groans. Whitemen were slaves to what they obtained.

Tuesday 11th Sept. 1804
George Shannon who had been absent 16 days joined the boat about one oclock. the reason of his keeping on so long was he see tracks which must have been Indians. he took it to be us and kept on, his bullets he shot all away & he was without any thing to eat for about 12 days except a fiew Grapes, he had left one of the horses behind as he gave out, he had gave up the idea of finding our boat & he was near killing the horse to Satisfy hunger. &c. &c—he Shot a rabit with Sticks which he cut & put in his gun after his Balls were gone.
                                        Sergeant John Ordway, Journals

Shannon, once a handsome, tall lad with dark hair and blue eyes and wispy soft whiskers, was a dirty, gaunt-faced, walking cadaver in rags, tending to weep with relief and gratitude from time to time as York fed him marrowbone broth and fawn veal to start rebuilding him. He told of the despair he had felt when fat buffalo had wandered within yards of where he sat dizzy with hunger, with gunpowder in his powder horn but not one lead ball to fire at them.

Somehow he had neglected to think of making snares or deadfall traps, or of catching or spearing the fish that abounded in every stream; he had been too intent on catching up. Drouillard wavered between scorn and pity, then offered to take him out when he got recovered and teach him how easy it was to get food, even if it was roots, grasshoppers, snakes, and grass seeds. "And," he said, "it's really hard to mistake Indian tracks from whitemen tracks, if you know how to look at 'em. That alone would have kept you from straying off."

"Good idea," Clark said. "Shannon, if you'd just learn a few of the tricks Drouillard knows, y' might survive long enough to reach age twenty."

He sat on deck, rain drumming on the awning just above his head, fleshing the pelts of three beavers he had trapped the night before, clothes bloody and greasy, the air dank and thick with smells of beaver gland and unwashed soldiery. Near the after cabin, Lewis was dissecting some entirely new kind of hare that Shields had shot, with long, wide ears, long hind feet, and powerful legs. "It don't scurry like a rabbit," Shields was saying. "It sprangs. When it shot through the brush I thought I'd flushed a quail, till it landed and I got a look at it!"

Drouillard said, "Here comes Cap'n Clark."

The captain was muddy to the knees, drenched. He had two rifles hanging from his shoulders by their slings, and in his right hand was his espontoon, which he was using like a walking staff. Behind him came Willard, with some beast across his big shoulders, its forelegs gripped by one huge hand, hindlegs by the other.

"Damned if he didn't get one of those pronghorn goats!" Lewis exclaimed. "At last!"

A whole new animal for Jefferson, Drouillard thought. What he said aloud was, "He's some hunter, that cap'n is." It was a tribute, and he meant it. Drouillard himself hadn't been able to get within range of one of those beasts.

When Drouillard hunted, he watched as much for Indian traces as for game. The boats were a thousand miles up the Missouri now. The next populations would be Teton Sioux, who called themselves the Burnt Thighs. They were the ones known throughout the trading routes as "the pirates of the Missouri." As far as he knew, any communication with them would have to be done through the language of his hands, unless somebody like Dorion should fall into their laps before then.

Chapter 9

The three Teton Sioux chiefs came in under the awning at noon and sat to smoke the ceremonial pipe and begin the council. The moment Drouillard saw Thotohonga's eyes, his nape tingled. Thotohonga, whose name meant War Maker, or Partisan, was almost sparking with mean spirits. His eyes were like a snake's, cold and darting. He was sinewy and handsome, with jutting cheekbones and narrow chin, but his upper lip curved in a sneer over his prominent front teeth.

The principal chief, T'tanka Sapa, Black Buffalo, appeared a solid and civil man. His cheeks were pitted by pox and much weathered. He was tense and wary, holding something in, and Drouillard sensed that Black Buffalo did not want Partisan to catch him smiling at these whitemen. There was something bad between them, whether an old animosity or something particular to this meeting, and it extended to their bodyguards, who hovered outside the council circle. The third chief, T'tanka Wakan, Buffalo Medicine, seemed to be aware of the silent conflict, but revealed no sign of being on one side or the other. He would be one to watch for clues to the others.

Captain Lewis was absorbed in his own task of delivering President Jefferson's message, and wasn't aware how inadequate to the translation Cruzatte's mishmash of Omaha and Sioux was. Black Buffalo, though confused, seemed to do his best to listen and understand, but Partisan began acting like a bored smart

148

aleck in a schoolroom, glancing around, smirking, yawning, even sighing and farting to show his boredom, or to make his followers laugh. The captains' sun-browned faces grew redder than the Indians'. At one point, when it appeared that Captain Lewis's hair-trigger temper was about to go off, Captain Clark put a hand on Lewis's wrist and told Drouillard to take over from Cruzatte, using hand language. That helped.

Black Buffalo answered the peace spiel by telling of a raid in which his warriors had captured many Omahas. Lewis puffed up to scold him, but Drouillard interceded with a suggestion that some of those captives should know Sioux well enough to translate into Omaha for Cruzatte and thus establish a chain of spoken language. Partisan snarled at the idea of bringing lowly Omaha "tied-up dogs" into a high council about Sioux rights and powers.

"A reasonable idea," Captain Clark said, "but reason doesn't suit that man right now. He's a-showin' off for the constituents."

"Aye, showing off," growled Captain Lewis. "That's what we might as well do. Words aren't getting us anywhere."

So the council was terminated. A parade and drill was held, but it was by only a squad. For the sake of safety, most of the soldiers were standing to arms on the boat, which was anchored a hundred yards offshore. The council awning and parade ground were on a sandbar in the mouth of the Bad River, while most of the Sioux warriors and villagers, seemingly a hundred or more, watched from the riverbanks, their excited voices a steady drone.

Because of the eminence of the Sioux on this stretch of the Missouri, the captains had put together what they considered a generous array of gifts for the chiefs and their selected warriors. Each of the three chiefs was presented a large Jefferson peace medal depended by glossy ribbon, and an American flag. Black Buffalo was decked out in an elegant scarlet military coat and a cocked hat with a plume, and while he preened in it, Drouillard saw Partisan writhe with envy.

When Captain Lewis set up his air gun demonstration and hit the target, Drouillard saw Partisan's eyes widen with wonder like those of the rest. Even the spectators on the distant river-banks erupted in a chorus of amazement. But as the captain aimed his second shot, Partisan said something to the nearby warriors, pointed his finger at the target and pursed his lips. When Lewis squeezed the trigger, Partisan spat and jerked his pointing finger and the target twitched in the distance. Partisan grinned and the warriors laughed. Captain Lewis of course presumed they were laughing at him, and had no idea why; they might have laughed if he had missed. That ended his air gun demonstration.

"Very well," Lewis said. "Let's invite the chiefs onto the keelboat. I'll wager they'll be impressed enough by some of our inventions and manufactures. And maybe a dram will loosen 'em a bit. They're tight as bowstrings with their pride."

The chiefs, and one bodyguard who had come onboard the keelboat with them, were intrigued by the swivel cannon, the compass, magnifying glasses, telescopes, and the iron corn grinder, and by the size and solidity of the vessel itself, but they did not let themselves appear overawed. Partisan was right there ready to snort if Black Buffalo or Buffalo Medicine expressed any real enthusiasm. They had seen plenty of such things before, he seemed to suggest, and better ones, from the British traders of the North West Company, to which the Sioux had long been attached. Drouillard stayed close wherever the chiefs went in the vessel, explaining with hand signs, but trying to stay inconspicuous and study the interplay between Black Buffalo and Partisan. All three chiefs had, of course, noticed that he was one Indian among all these whitemen, and they looked at him curiously now and then. The keelboat was crowded, with so many uniformed soldiers standing at rest along the gunwales.

When Captain Lewis uncorked a half-full whiskey bottle and set out glasses, all pretense of indifference vanished. Like any Indians who had been exposed to white traders, they knew liquor very well and it had their full attention. Captain Lewis poured each chief a quarter of a glass, and a shot for himself and Captain Clark. Before the captains could raise their glasses in a salute, the chiefs had gulped theirs down and stood blinking, breathing through gaping mouths, and extending their glasses for refills. Lewis held up the bottle to show it was empty. Partisan grabbed the bottle, upended it and sucked at its neck, set it down hard on the deck and with three motions of his right hand said, *Give me another.* Captain Clark brushed his right palm down past the fingers of his left, in an imprecise sign somewhere between *Ended* and *Wiped out,* and although it was sloppy signing, Drouillard thought either message was clear enough. It was clear enough to Partisan, whose eyes narrowed as he put his fist to his forehead and twisted it away to say he was angry.

"Tell him I'm angry too," Lewis snapped. "Tell him we've a long way to go and must move on." Cruzatte, still in his mix of Sioux and Omaha, tried to tell them that, while making signs that meant *Go boat.* Clark murmured to Lewis that it might do to try a little more diplomacy, but Lewis said, "I'm mad. These are bandits. Firmness is all they'll understand."

When the chiefs began to understand that their visit was so abruptly over and that the captains meant to go on up the river, Partisan suddenly began lurching and staggering down the narrow deck, acting as if he'd had as much whiskey as he wanted, instead of the little bit he'd had. With considerable balking and manhandling, by which the Indians got an inkling of how strong the blue-coat soldiers were, the chiefs soon found themselves in a pirogue being rowed toward the riverbank by five soldiers and three voyageurs. Captain Clark sat in the stern, with Drouillard and Cruzatte squatting between him and the four surly Indians. The scores of Sioux men, women, and children lining the riverbanks were clamoring with confusion or consternation, depending probably on how they had perceived the brief tussle on the keelboat. Drouillard saw a number of warriors running along the riverbank toward the place on shore where the boat was headed.

Captain Clark said in a low voice: "Listen, Drouillard, Cruzatte. We've got these gents a little more riled up than I like 'em to be. Cap'n Lewis is having one of those days when his fuse is short. Now, before we get to shore, I hope to calm these people a

little, but let 'em know that it's not their say-so whether we
go on up the river. That we're warriors, not merchants. That
merchants will come along later, but not if they try to interfere
with us now. Can you get that across to 'em?" All the time he
was talking, the chiefs were muttering and whispering among
themselves.

Drouillard said, "There's no talking to 'em with that one
here. The others might listen but he doesn't want 'em to." Then
he got their attention and talked to them with his hands, while
Cruzatte occasionally interjected a few words.

Drouillard couldn't tell whether they were heeding his message. When the pirogue slid to a halt in the muddy shallows,
though, three warriors splashed out from shore and grabbed the
boat's mooring rope, and the chief's bodyguard, who had been
riding in the bow, jumped to his feet and wrapped both arms
around the mast. The stern swung downstream, closer to the
bank. Black Buffalo and Buffalo Medicine, faces set in anger,
clambered over the gunwale and waded ashore, talking rapidly
to the warriors who were swarming around the landing place.
Captain Clark and Chief Partisan stood in the pirogue, face-
to-face.

The captain, erect, solid as an oak and elegant in his gold
braid, blue coat, and rakish black cocked hat, made the simple,
graceful hand sign that said, *You may go.* Partisan, equally elegant and formidable in a beautifully tanned tunic with long
fringe and fine quillwork, drew himself up, every fiber quivering, craggy head held up haughty and defiant, nostrils dis-
tended, and stared the captain in the eye almost nose-to-nose.
The eagle plume standing at the back of his head quivered in the
hot breeze. Drouillard crouched, ready to spring into whatever
action would be needed, but hoping Partisan would back down
and get off the boat. Drouillard was aware of the overwhelming
number of warriors onshore drawing metal-tipped arrows out of
their quivers, and some with ready muskets, all gathering near
the boat. Black Buffalo was pacing on the shore in his new
scarlet coat and cocked hat, talking fast and pointing at Clark
and Partisan. Across the water Drouillard could hear Captain

Lewis barking out commands for the soldiers to stand to arms, to load the swivel with sixteen balls and stand ready to fire. *Merde!* Drouillard thought. I am to die because men can't talk?

Again Captain Clark made the gesture for Partisan to get off the boat, at the same time telling the five soldiers to ship oars and stand to arms. When the soldiers lifted their shiny rifles and stood up, the crowd of warriors on shore shifted about and moved back a little, some nocking arrows.

Partisan began hissing words at Captain Clark. Then the chief bumped his shoulder hard against the captain's chest, once, before stepping over the gunwale into the shallow water and side-stepping toward shore, meanwhile haranguing him and making insulting gestures. Cruzatte said, "*Mon capitaine,* I think he say you are Tight Hand, not give him enough presents. That you must leave this boat here." On hearing that, Captain Clark stepped off the boat and waded after Partisan, jaw set, face florid, eyes ablaze. Partisan hurried ashore until he was among his warriors and turned snarling at Clark.

"Sir," said Private Frazier, one of the pirogue's crew, "want us to get this Indian off the mast?"

"Never mind him yet. Drouillard, Cruzatte, come here." They stepped into the water. It was warm and the bottom was slick. "Tell this man that we are going on up the river. That we are warriors and he won't stop us."

Drouillard signed that quickly. Partisan responded by lunging close again, pointing at Clark's face and erupting in fast, jabbering, insulting tones, with belligerent gestures. Not a word of it was understandable, but the message was all too plain, and the captain, standing with shin-deep river water licking at his shined boots, reached across his waist and drew his sword from the scabbard at his left hip. Its metallic slide and ring were frightfully loud. The cacophony of excited voices fell to a murmur as the captain leveled the long blade toward Partisan's face. Partisan was looking at the blade and was for the moment speechless. Warriors were moving to vantage points with arrows ready, and Captain Lewis was shouting more orders on the distant keelboat. Drouillard reached into the boat for his rifle and Cruzatte's and brought them up. He and Cruzatte stood flanking Captain Clark.

Sometimes he had wondered how he would die; a hunter does often consider death. He had never dreamed of standing with whitemen against Indians. But this was no time to think of that. It was a time to decide where to aim. The air seemed compressed and the light was brilliant and he was cold inside. He was a Shawnee, and these Sioux were not enemies and the whitemen were not his allies, but this was how the Master of Life had put the moment together, and he could not shame his ancestors by being afraid or slow, even though there was no one anymore to give him an eagle feather.

A red figure was moving into the side of his vision. He glanced over. Black Buffalo, stately in his gift coat, lips drawn thin, strode down the riverbank to the prow of the pirogue. He grabbed the mooring rope from the three warriors who held it and shouldered them back. He shouted at the warrior who was hugging the mast, and the warrior let loose and jumped ashore. Black Buffalo threw the rope aboard. Then he stood staring at Partisan and Captain Clark, who were still poised as if to kill each other. Some warriors had waded in to the left, and Drouillard saw that he and Cruzatte and the captain were now cut off from the pirogue. Corporal Warfington, head of the pirogue's crew, said, "Cap'n Clark, sir, what should I do? Want us to shoot?"

Clark barely glanced over his shoulder, and said, "Go to the ship and ask the captain for a full squad."

"Don't wish t' leave ye here, sir."

"Go on. I mean to face down this son of a bitch. Don't act hurried, but don't dawdle."

"Yes sir. You Frenchies, row. Rest, stand to arms." The pirogue moved off across the sun-glittering water. Captain Clark stood with sword drawn, Drouillard and Cruzatte with cocked rifles, in water to their shins, with maybe eighty warriors all around them with their weapons at ready, and a hundred or more other Sioux people crowding both riverbanks, and Captain Clark meaning to stare down one proud son of a bitch. The keelboat seemed far off.

And just to make things even nicer, Drouillard thought, I need to piss.

Captain Clark kept his sword pointed at Chief Partisan but told Drouillard and Cruzatte to try to talk civil to Black Buffalo and Buffalo Medicine. "Tell them we are sorry we can't stay, but we're going on. It's not their say-so. We're warriors, not women."

The interpreters said that with hands and words, and Black Buffalo answered with flitting hands and flashing eyes.

"He says they are warriors too. That if we go on, they will follow us and kill us bit by bit. That they have another town farther up with more warriors. That those could destroy us. He says if we leave the white boat here full of gifts, they'll let us go on. Might just be tough talk for Partisan's sake, or he might mean it."

"Tell them we have enough medicine on our big boat to kill twenty towns. That if they misuse us, the Great Father in the East will send enough soldiers to destroy them in an instant."

All this threatening talk was being done under metal arrows pointing, sword pointing, guns ready. But it was talk. It used time. It was a good thing now that the translation was so bad because while it went on, the white boat reached the keelboat and then came back with a full squad of resolute blue soldiers, all with shiny guns. The warriors and chiefs who had been pressing so close around waded out of the river and withdrew a distance up the bank, where they talked among themselves. The voices of the three chiefs, all too familiar by now, were scolding and arguing.

Captain Clark blew out a long breath between his lips and slipped his sword back into its scabbard, and Drouillard eased his flintlock from full cock. So did Cruzatte. After a time the chiefs stopped quarreling and stood looking at the boatful of soldiers as it nudged ashore beside Captain Clark. One voyageur hopped off the bow with the mooring rope in hand to hold the boat there.

But then Captain Clark waded out of the river, muddy water streaming off his boots, and walked toward the chiefs with his right hand proffered. They looked at him expressionless, and no one reached out for his hand. So without a pause he turned his back on them and came back down to the shore. He looked at Drouillard with a half smile and a shake of the head and said, "Seems we're done here. Get aboard." He stepped into the stern with all the dignity that stretching, lurching maneuver allowed, and stood there, and Drouillard and Cruzatte boarded. The voyageur shoved the prow off shore and leaped aboard with the rope in his hand. The rowers dug in and the boat swung around to go out. Drouillard noticed that the captain's hands were shaking. He himself was taking some deep breaths and watching the river water seep out of his moccasins and leggings and run into the bilge, when the captain said softly, "Hullo, what's this now?"

Black Buffalo and Buffalo Medicine, each with a bodyguard, were wading hurriedly into the water after the pirogue, hands extended. Black Buffalo was calling out some words.

"These two ask to go to the big boat again, I think," Cruzatte said.

"Well! Surprise, eh? Squeeze in, boys. Make room."

The chiefs sat on bundles of the pirogue's cargo. The vessel was near to swamping with twenty-two men and about six tons of cargo. Drouillard needed to urinate so badly that he considered not waiting. He was sitting in Captain Clark's shadow.

If I moved to piss over the side, he thought, we'd turn over. If I pissed in the boat, it would sink.

"What are you laughing at?" the captain asked.

"Just things in general, sir. Wish you'd sit down."

"Would, but I'm afraid to move."

Drouillard smiled up at him. "Glad you're afraid of *something*."

25th Septr
we proceeded on about 1 mile & anchored Out Off a willow Island placed a guard on Shore to protect the Cooks & a guard in the boat, fastened the Perogues to the boat. I call this Island bad humered Island as we were in a bad humer.

William Clark, Journals

The music sounded like a heartbeat and a rattlesnake together. Warriors around the bonfire held flat drums, made of rawhide stretched over willow hoops, beating them at heartbeat pace with padded sticks. Each drum was decorated with clusters of deer and goat hooves that chattered like rattlesnakes with every beat. There was great power in the music. Drouillard could feel it all through him, passing from sky to ground.

Black Buffalo and Buffalo Medicine had invited the captains and some of their soldiers to come to the town for this feast and dance ceremony. Intimidation at the riverside had failed to cow these bold whitemen. Now, after a wakeful night on the big boat, drinking sugared coffee until their hands were trembling, these two chiefs had fallen back on the more customary way of impressing visitors, which was hospitality.

The captains had been wary of accepting the invitation to the Sioux town, fearing treachery, wanting to get past this difficult tribe and move on up the river. But President Jefferson wanted something worked out with the Sioux, and anything that might effect that had to be tried. And Cruzatte had advised the captains to accept, saying, "If you are their guest, you are safe. They honor guests." The captains had turned to Drouillard for his opinion on that, and he had confirmed it. His people, the Shawnees, would feed even their enemies if they came as guests, he told them.

So they had come to this council lodge to be fed and entertained. They had smoked the pipes and had been served roasted dog. Dog, Cruzatte had explained, was a dish served only as a special honor. The dog, a useful animal and a friend, too beloved to be eaten as mere belly-filling food, was sacrificed only to feed honored guests. The captains had wondered how they had become honored guests after all the surliness and threats they had endured yesterday by the Bad River.

"Because they know you are important whether they like it or not," Cruzatte had explained. "And also because they found you brave."

Captain Lewis, at first reluctant to eat dog, called it perhaps

the best meat he had ever tasted. Clark, who had eaten his portion only for protocol, was disgusted with it. He had leaned over
to Lewis and said, "Aren't you ashamed! Wait till I tell Seaman
what you had for supper!"

The drummers now began to sing. Their voices started high
and nasal and descended to moans and growls, the drums would
be struck doubly hard, and the voices would start shrill again and
go sadly wailing down, like wolf spirits. And they sang to the
open sky, as wolves do. This grand council lodge was circular,
about thirty feet across, made of long, straight poles leaning inward to an apex, with a ceremonial firepit in the center, and this
evening its covering was only shoulder-high, leaving the sky and
stars open to view while protecting the occupants from the wind.
Old Dorion had called these lodges tepees. The base was the Sacred Circle; the poles pointed toward the sky where Wakan
Tanka, the Creator, dwelled. "Their home is also a prayer," Dorion had explained.

About fifty chiefs, warriors, and soldiers were sitting in this
lodge by firelight, all smoking tobacco and kinnikinnick mixed
in their pipes, facing the fire in the center, and it did not feel
crowded, because of the open sky. Out beyond the music Drouillard could hear the murmur of the town people, about eight hundred living in seventy or eighty of the tepee lodges. Tonight this
whiteman visit was the center of all attention. All the way up
from the river, curious people had been staring at the boats and
hurrying along the path, watching the soldiers come up to the
town. The captains had been conveyed to town sitting on elegant
buffalo robes carried by several warriors so their feet did not
have to touch the ground.

In their parade into town they had seen the beauty of the
lodges, the orderly and cheerful demeanor of the people, their
wealth of proud men and good horses. A particular order of
Sioux men was always on duty as policemen and town criers.
Drouillard had seen one such gendarme grab two squabbling
women and propel them out of sight. He had also seen a picketed
area where the forty or fifty Omaha prisoners from the recent

raid were being kept: women, children, and elders, scruffy and fearful, and they were guarded by the tribal police.

He could feel the presence of many people outside the lodge. Often a lower edge of the cover would be raised and eyes would peer in. Now and then a child's face would appear at the top edge of the cover, where some little one had crawled up a pole to look in.

Now into the firelit circle erupted a throbbing, trilling sound, and the tempo of the drums changed, faster. In through the lodge door came a procession of richly dressed women of all ages, taking delicate half steps in time with the drums, some shaking rattles, all carrying long sticks decorated with feathers and ribbons, and each stick topped with one or more human scalps. The scalps were the war trophies of their fathers and husbands, sons and nephews, and there were many fresh ones. In a battle less than two weeks ago the Sioux from these towns had killed seventy-five Omaha men and boys, and had captured the women and children penned outside. The women began singing and filed off into two lines, one on either side of the fire, and there they kept up the same bobbing, rhythmic step, standing in place. The older women danced with a stolid dignity, only their feet moving, singing with their eyes half closed as if remembering the stories they were singing. Younger women tossed their heads from side to side in a great intensity of emotion, their long hair whipping left and right, their white teeth bared in grimaces, and they thumped the ground with their heels so that the fringes and bangles on their dresses flounced and shivered and their breasts and buttocks trembled. This dance was a celebration of their men's bravery, a serious dance of life and death and triumph, not a trivial or suggestive dance. But the soldiers in the lodge were being affected. They were young and fit and were starved for contact with women. Through a space between the dancers Drouillard watched Sergeant Ordway. He could see that the sergeant was not admiring scalps; his eyes were trying to penetrate clothing. Collins watched from nearby, mouth hanging open.

The dancing and singing lasted until midnight, when the captains announced that they must get back to their boats. The chiefs expressed disappointment. They had thought the officers and soldiers would spend the night in the town.

Certain women, Black Buffalo told them in hand language, *say they would like to have the company of you and your soldiers. They say you have strong medicine, and they like you. We have many women and few men here. Some women are lonely. You do not have to go back to your boat.*

Drouillard translated that in a low voice; the soldiers were excited enough without hearing it. He saw the longing in the captains' eyes and knew they were struggling with their own desires. Drouillard was himself full of yearning. But he felt that he had a duty to add: "Traders have been here for many years coming and going. The French pox is to be considered."

Captain Lewis said, "Indeed. That had entered my thoughts already. Thank them, but decline."

"As for me," Captain Clark said, "I'm not going to sleep where I'm outnumbered a hundredfold by people who treated me the way these chiefs did yesterday."

The chiefs were looking on anxiously, waiting for what they surely thought would be an acceptance. Drouillard had not seen Partisan tonight, and he brought that to the captains' attention. The traditions of hospitality notwithstanding, Partisan at large was an alarming thought. Lewis said, "I had rather invite them to stay with us on the keelboat again tonight. Coffee and whiskey. Tell them we wish to repay this evening's hospitality."

The two chiefs jumped at the offer. Drouillard heard them speak of Partisan in a derisive tone. The chiefs knew that the invitation to visit aboard was prestigious, and that their prestige would rise as Partisan's declined.

With the chiefs aboard, it was another almost sleepless night. The guards fretted all night over the palpable presence of great numbers of Indians on the dark riverbanks. The chiefs were up almost all night wanting to talk and drink liquor or coffee. They kept begging the captains to stay another day and night so that another part of their nation could arrive to see them, and they promised another night of feasting and dancing if they would stay. Captain Lewis kept returning to the topic of the forty-eight Omaha prisoners—women, girls, and boys—that they had taken in their recent attack. He insisted that if the Sioux would agree to deliver those prisoners to Pierre Dorion, who could then return them to their own country, it would be a good first step toward the peace that their new Great Father desired all along the Missouri. The chiefs indicated that they might do so if the captains would promise to stay another day. Drouillard felt that they were playing the agreement along only to get another delay; their eyes revealed to him that they thought freeing the captives was too silly an idea to take seriously.

Exhausted after perhaps an hour of troubled sleep, the captains at dawn saw that the riverbanks were crowded with more Indians than ever. The chiefs wanted more coffee and were reluctant to leave the keelboat, and once ashore, reluctant to get out of the pirogue. As if sleepwalking, the exhausted captains went through the necessary diplomacy, visiting the town again, writing out peace certificates, giving out more medals. Captain Clark made visits to the homes of the chiefs and elders, even startling Partisan by stopping in to see him. The man was speechless with confusion, or suspicion, but was civil because Clark was in his home.

Captain Lewis sent Cruzatte to the prisoner compound, ostensibly to give the women a few awls, but actually to find out whether they had overheard any treacherous designs the Sioux chiefs might have on the Americans.

In the course of the day, Black Buffalo again offered Captain Clark the company of a young woman, asking him to take her and not despise the people, as she would represent all her people in a spiritual connection with him. This time Drouillard found the chief so earnest and sincere that he hoped Clark would accept, thinking it might be the single key to open the door of friendship they had so wanted with this nation. The chief said the girl was a maiden. Drouillard took one look at her and said, "Cap'n, accept her and *I'll* perform your duty!" Clark laughed and turned his back on her; Black Buffalo's eyes hardened.

In the evening, after sitting through the same entertainment again, full of food, the drums monotonous, the stupefied captains excused themselves early. Partisan went down to the boat with them. He boarded the pirogue with Clark and Drouillard and several of the soldiers. As the voyageurs rowed across the gurgling, hushing river, the keelboat's little tin lantern cast a tiny glittering pathway of yellow light across the turbid water under the starry vastness. Captain Lewis, with Cruzatte and four other soldiers, stayed on the bank to wait for the pirogue's next trip. Cruzatte had talked to the Omaha prisoners during the evening. They had told him they heard that the Sioux intended to stop the boats from going on up to other tribes farther north. The captains had been careful to show no sign of suspecting those intentions, but because of Cruzatte's report, Captain Clark specifically invited Chief Partisan to spend the night on the boat, with the idea of keeping the most troublesome one where he could be watched—a willing hostage for this last, wearisome night.

Drouillard knew that was how the captains saw it. But as the oars dipped and rose and the pirogue's prow swashed across the current toward that little tin lantern, he was thinking that not only was Clark a fool for turning down an uncommonly lovely maiden, but that he had insulted Black Buffalo and his whole great people in an unforgivable way. It was beautiful and peaceful here under the silent stars on the great, tugging current of the mighty river, but the spirits were bad, and there would be more trouble.

It came at once.

In bringing the pirogue to the keelboat, the steersman went too far forward of the big boat's bow, swung the tiller and caused the pirogue to turn sideways in the current. The pirogue, heavy with passengers and tons of cargo, came down broadside on the keelboat's anchor cable, which was tight as a fiddle string.

Drouillard heard a grating and a cracking of wood, felt a tilting, and then a dull thump. In the next moment, querying voices were rising on both boats, and the huge, dark bulk of the keelboat was turning sideways and away.

Captain Clark bellowed into the darkness: "All hands up! On

the oars! You're adrift! Hey! Everybody up! Anchor cable's broke! You're adrift!"

Drouillard felt water over his feet. "We've sprung a leak, Cap'n!"

In a moment there was a commotion of voices yelling, footsteps pounding, oars clattering. Partisan, not knowing what was happening, began yelling in his language. And back on shore Captain Lewis's piercing voice was shouting from the darkness, demanding to know what was going on.

Captain Clark kept yelling to the keelboat oarsmen. "Hurry! Get 'er nose upstream and *pull*! There's sandbars just below! Don't get sidewise on those sandbars! All hands *pull*!" It was the nightmare they had avoided in half a year of struggling up this swift and tricky river: their precious ship adrift at night. And adrift not just anywhere, but in the midst of hundreds of Indians of a notorious nation. Chief Partisan all the while was bellowing something incomprehensible.

It was past midnight by the time the keelboat was secured to a tree on shore, and by that time Black Buffalo and two hundred warriors had arrived from the town, excited, shooting in the air. All the soldiers who had been routed from sleep to save the boat had dropped their oars and picked up their rifles, ready to make a last stand against overwhelming numbers of Indians. And the security of a mid-river anchorage was gone now; warriors could pour showers of arrows and musketballs down the bank into the keelboat. The locker lids Captain Clark had designed as breastworks were raised and propped, and the soldiers crouched behind them listening to the commotion of running and shouting all along the banks. Captain Lewis was still on the far shore with five men, and the white pirogue could not be used to go rescue them until the leak caused by her collision could be found and caulked. Two men were down on their knees with a lantern trying to do that. Partisan was still emitting an occasional shout but was apparently too terrified of his precarious position in the leaking boat to try anything.

Gradually the voices onshore grew calm, and finally Captain

Lewis's voice came across the hush of wind and water: "Is the boat secure yet? Lots of Indians here but no trouble!"

In the small hours of the morning Drouillard sat in the boat's cabin with the chiefs Black Buffalo and Partisan and their body-guards, Cruzatte, and the exhausted captains, with everybody trying to explain everything about the incident, hampered as usual by the lack of a Sioux interpreter. He had to collect the facts and convey them by hand language.

When the anchor cable had broken and Captain Clark yelled his orders and the soldiers began shouting and moving about on the boat, Partisan apparently had thought an Omaha war party was attacking, in retaliation for the recent Sioux raid. He had thus been screaming at the top of his lungs about an Omaha attack, and that word had been relayed to the town, thus bringing down Black Buffalo and his two hundred warriors. It had re-quired all Cruzatte's limited skill to convince Black Buffalo that there had been no such attack.

The captains, meanwhile, already irritated and exhausted, and alarmed by what the prisoners had told Cruzatte, did not believe Black Buffalo's explanation for his quick arrival in full force; they thought he must have had the warriors already gathered to carry out the interference that Cruzatte had been warned about. By now the captains were beyond believing anything favorable of these chiefs. But again they did not want the chiefs to know what they suspected. Captain Lewis said, "I mean for us to move out of here at first light. I'm going to keep these treacherous sav-ages right here under guard till we're ready to sail. Might as well invite them to drink coffee with us till then. They'll be asking for it anyway. They're too excited to give them whiskey."

"Another night with no sleep," Captain Clark grumbled, wip-ing his hand over his white forehead. "All right. But before we move on, I want to retrieve that anchor. I'll take both pirogues and start dragging for it soon as there's enough light."

28th of Septr 1804 Friday
I made maney attempts in defferent ways to find our anchor

without Sukcess, the Sand had Covered her up. after Brack-
fast we with great Dificuelty got the Chiefs out of the boat . . .
proceeded on under a Breeze from the S.E. we took in the 3rd
Cheif Buffalo Medicine who was Sitting on a Sand bar 2 miles
above—he told us Partisan was a Double Spoken man—we
Sent a talk to the nation, if they were for war or deturmined to
attempt to Stop us, we were ready to defend our Selves—we
Substituted large Stones in place of an Anchor. we came to at
a Small Sand bar in the middle of the river and Stayed all
night—I am verry unwell I think for the want of Sleep

William Clark, Journals

October 8, 1804

The last week had been, for Drouillard, a wandering in paradise.
With cold nights had come relief from mosquitoes at last. Also
left behind were the Sioux. It had not been considered safe to
send out hunters while the Sioux were hounding the convoy, and
the diet of army pork, grease, and corn meal had been dis-
gusting. But the Sioux were a hundred and fifty miles behind
now, and again he was ranging the high plains hunting fresh
meat, not letting himself regret the captains' failure with the
Sioux. He had translated and advised the best he could. The
failure had been caused by the rivalry among the chiefs, as much
as by Sioux determination to control the river trade. Drouillard
was glad it was over and that it had not ended in shooting. If it
had, these whitemen would have been wiped out, and himself
with them.

He was hunting afoot now. The last horse had been stolen by
the Sioux while the big encounter was going on, so he could not
go after buffalo. Fresh meat these days was mostly elk and deer
killed in the bottomland timbers. Several pronghorns had been
killed when, by good chance, they were caught swimming the
river on their seasonal migration. The rutting season for Split-
Hooves had begun, and buck deer and elk were reckless about

concealment, and could be called by clashing antlers together. The captains, carrying espontoons as rifle rests, had killed some game with long shots, and their good humor was being restored.

Drouillard walked the high plains with a gait that could cover ground nearly as well as a horseman. He mused on distances. According to Captain Clark the Great Measurer, they had come 1,430 miles up the Missouri since leaving the Mississippi in May. Clark always sighted through his compass at every bend and turn, and wrote down the degrees of the course, then would calculate miles to the next change, and write that down. Drouillard imagined that constant counting and measuring of the world must be an incredible drudgery. But counting and measuring were powers the whitemen were best at, and since they always ended up owning everything they counted and measured, they obviously were well served by those powers.

Somewhere along the way the captains had abandoned their idea of sending one of the pirogues back to St. Louis with their papers and specimens. Perhaps the Sioux had convinced them that they had no riflemen to spare. Some men who had expected to go back were grumbling their disappointment, in particular Reed the deserter, who was a mere oar slave, latrine-digger, and pot-walloper. Were it not for the continued friendship of his fellow malcontent Newman, Reed probably would have jumped in the river and drowned himself by now. Some of the troops speculated whether Reed and Newman were, as they put it, a "couple."

As he loped along the flank of a grassy hill, Drouillard now smelled town ruins. It was the distinctive smell of a burned-out Indian village. Recently the convoy had met a solitary French trader, Jean Vallé, who had been trading far westward in a region he called Black Hills. Drouillard had met Vallé long ago at his uncle's trading post, and some of the voyageurs knew him too. Vallé had given the captains very encouraging assessments of the good nature of the Arikaras, who lived not far ahead. The Arikaras farmed the bottoms and the islands industriously, growing corn and beans and squash which they traded to the Sioux for horses and for merchandise the Sioux got from British trading companies. The Arikaras were poor and weak now, down to a fourth or fifth of their population because of smallpox, the latest epidemic last year. Poverty and weakness made tribes more receptive and hospitable of course to newcomers, so the American captains would not be meeting the kind of arrogance they had recently found in the Sioux. It was likely that the Arikaras would agree to and accept anything the Americans said—especially if it promised to reduce their dependency on the Sioux for trade goods. That had been the practical wisdom of Vallé, another of those godsent informants the captains were lucky enough to find in the wilderness. But, Vallé had warned before bidding them adieu and going on his lonely way, always expect to find some Sioux among the Arikaras.

Drouillard veered toward the river and looked down on yet another burned-out ruin of an Arikara town. There were many like that since the smallpox; the survivors had migrated upriver to join with other survivors. One of the towns had been abandoned so recently that its fields were full of squash, pumpkins, corn, and beans ripe for harvest. The Americans had stopped there and collected enough to vary the diet. York had been able to make a pumpkin pie, gleefully remembering just how his wife used to do it.

Drouillard felt good now as he thought of York. The man seemed less and less like a slave as they came along. Though he still kept up his duties as Captain Clark's manservant, he also did his share on the oars, setting poles, and tow ropes, where his great physical strength was appreciated, and the more it was appreciated, the more he was willing to show it off. He had grown from gunbearer to hunter on his long shore walks with his master, his marksmanship becoming better under Clark's instruction. As the soldiers' respect for him grew, so did his openness and high humor. He had rigged himself out with flair, perhaps remembering Drouillard's description of Caesar the Negro Shawnee. He had been gathering muskrat skulls, hooves, mussel shells, arrowheads, Indian hairpipes, feathers, bear claws, and pretty pebbles, and had drilled and strung them to make for himself a big hank of barbaric, rattling necklaces, inventing for each a legend of magic. He wore a blue, old-style Continental Army coat, breechcloth, and handmade leather leggings and moccasins. He wore a red headkerchief, sometimes with a three-cornered black hat on top, with a buzzard feather sewed to the crown. A few times he had been permitted to range the hills hunting with Drouillard, away from his master, and those had been wonderful times for York, who still liked to think of himself and Drouillard as the expedition's only "colored folk."

"I still been pesterin' Mas' Billy. 'Bout lettin' me free."

"What's he say?"

"Like with 'em Sioux. Li'l promise, 'n' then a li'l threat."

Drouillard had elbowed him and joked, "Next time you're out alone with him carrying his hunting gun, just poke it in his back and make him put it in writing."

"Ooooh! Man! Can't do 'at!" The thought was too much for York, who didn't realize it was a joke.

Drouillard shrugged and said: "Guess it wouldn't do any good, would it? Even their writ-out promises they don't keep. Just ask my people."

Still, York was getting to be a lot more than he had been, and Drouillard was growing ever more friendly toward him. He liked to imagine him free, another Caesar.

A trace of flattened grass caught Drouillard's eye now, and a faint scent. He stopped and looked along it. Big print with claw marks. Bear.

It had been a long time, far down the river, since he had shot bear. *Makwa,* whom his people called the Brother of Man. The only bears he had known were black bears, amiable, self-contained grubbers and scavengers who minded their own business and took good care of their children, like a good Indian. They were easygoing because they feared nothing. But this track was much bigger than a black bear's track. It would be what the tribes along this river called a white or yellow bear. Yesterday Captain Clark had seen the tracks of one of these and spoke in excitement of the size of the track. An Indian who wore a necklace of the claws of a white bear he had killed had as much prestige as a man with many scalps on his pole. The captains anticipated meeting those plains bears, confident they would be less formidable before the army's superior rifles.

Angry bears, Drouillard thought. I wonder what they're afraid of, to make them angry?

Now he saw the boats. They were in a channel running alongside a big, wooded island, an island two or three miles long. He looked down on the unexpected sight of hundreds of cheerful Indians walking along the near shore of the island, watching the boats. There was a big village on the island, a cluster of the eight-sided, earth-covered lodges like those in the abandoned towns. These farming Indians lived in large, snug, permanent houses, surrounded by palisades, so different from the cone-shaped, skin-covered tents of the buffalo-hunting Sioux. This was apparently one of the three remaining Arikara towns Vallé had spoken of; it sat amidst a sprawling garden of corn and vegetables. Several small, round, tublike boats were following the keelboat and pirogues, and although he was still a long way off, it appeared to him that the boats were occupied by women.

The keelboat and pirogues were edging toward the riverbank at the upper end of the island. He saw Cruzatte heave off the bow the chained boulder that had replaced the lost anchor. It was time to trot down there. No hunting the angry bear today; the captains would be needing their hand-sign interpreter.

Chapter 10

A Town of the Arikaras

10th of October 1804
the Inds. much astonished at my black Servent, who made him
Self more turrible in thier view than I wished him to Doe . . .
telling them that before I cought him he was wild & lived upon
people, young children was verry good eating. Showed them
his Strength &c. &c.—Those Indians are not fond of Licquer
of any Kind.

William Clark, Journals

The cannon and air gun, the big boat and all its instruments and gadgets, had been acknowledged as great medicine by the Arikaras, but York was the biggest medicine of all. None of them had ever seen a black man. He pretended to stalk and be stalked by crowds of squealing children. He strutted and chuckled and growled. He lifted two grown men high off the ground at the same time, one hanging on each wrist.

He acted as if, for this day at least, he was not a slave but a king. Several Arikara men offered him their wives, believing that the spiritual power he put into them would then be transferred to themselves by a similar connection. Unable to resist, York went into a lodge with a moon-faced young beauty, whose proud husband guarded the door until York was done. That whetted his appetite for more. He wanted Drouillard to speak to them for him in sign. "Tell 'at perty gal her baby looks good, an'

170

I'm *hungry*! She looks 'licious too! Tell 'er I take 'at titty the baby not usin'!"

York was too strange or formidable for some women, who instead found the fair-haired, blue-eyed, tall and strapping soldiers better medicine. The air was full of lustful excitement. "Drouillard, tell this lady," said Shannon in a half-strangled voice, "that she's givin' me a cockstand just a-lookin' at me the way she is. D'ye know sign language for that?"

Drouillard shook his head, half smiling. "Think, Shannon: A cockstand *is* sign language."

To the captains, the goodwill of this visit with the Arikaras was a delightful contrast to the ugliness of their Sioux encounter, but they worried that fraternization might jeopardize discipline and security, so they let only small groups of soldiers at a time go into the towns, with a sergeant in charge. Guards had to stay with the boats.

Moses Reed, no longer a member of the corps, was given no liberty in the towns, and since he could not carry a firearm or stand guard, he was confined to the cooks' area, a gray, lone figure, shuffling, dispirited, cutting firewood, tending fires and carrying water. His friend Private Newman had Sergeant Ordway ask Captain Lewis if Reed might have just a few hours off to mingle with the Arikaras. The answer was such a firm negative that Newman clenched his jaw, left the village, had himself rowed over to the camp and sat smoking with Reed. That act of compassion and defiance did not go unnoticed, and Lewis declared both men confined to the cooking area.

Two unlikely looking and unexpected collaborators had appeared out of the countryside just when they were needed: both raffish French traders who had been living in the Arikara towns for years, fluent in French, English, Arikara, and Sioux, able to interpret easily in the councils. Pierre-Antoine Tabeau had the thick shoulders and powerful arms of a former voyageur, but also an impressive education. He was, he claimed, writing a narrative history of the Upper Missouri tribes. He also professed, with dubious explanation, to having sworn fidelity to the United States long ago, and said he was joyful that this would be a trade route of the U.S., not of the Spanish or English. The other trader was Joseph Gravelines, an associate of Regis Loisel. Gravelines was without pretension, and Drouillard trusted him at once. Both warned the captains that many old factions were now living close to each other in the remaining Arikara towns, making for jealousy, and cautioned against naming as supreme chief any one of the three town headmen.

But in council, Captains Lewis and Clark went ahead and did so. They gave Kakawissassa, Lightning Raven, a bigger medal than the ones they gave the others, Pocasse and Piaheto. In the uneasy silence that followed, they gave fancy coats, cocked hats, and American flags to all three. They distributed beads, combs, scissors, cloth, wire, needles, knives, and hatchets for the chiefs to give to their men and women. They entertained the three with the twangy vibrations of the Jew's harp and then gave each one two of them.

Drouillard recognized in the council two Sioux warriors who had been involved in the confrontation down at the Bad River, and found out that they had been sent up to persuade the Arikaras to stop the whitemen. They were watching the gift-giving with keen interest. They would of course go back and re-port to Black Buffalo, Partisan, and Buffalo Medicine that the boat soldiers had given the Arikaras much more than they had given the Sioux. Drouillard sat amazed that the captains imag-ined themselves ambassadors of peace. Tabeau had spent hours telling the captains just how to make the best impressions and longest-lasting arrangements with these Arikaras. Then Captain Lewis had done it the Jefferson way, and concluded the council with the usual air gun demonstration, fully satisfied with the im-pressions he had made.

On the day after the council, the three chiefs returned and told the captains everything they wanted to hear. The chiefs weren't lying; they really did want peace and trade. But as good Indian hosts, they did not want to shadow the whitemen's shining vision with the realities of intertribal life. Only Piaheto, the one they had named third chief of the Arikara nation, was candid enough to suggest that the nations along the river might misunderstand, or forget, or be unable to comply with, these promises being so politely made along the way. He doubted that the Mandans up the river would heed the whitemen's demand for peace with the Arikaras. Drouillard thought it was appropriate that Piaheto spoke thus because his name meant Eagle's Feather. In the tradition of Drouillard's own people, one could speak only truthfully in the presence of an eagle's feather. The eagle flew high enough to see everything and knew what was true.

The captains were glowing with pleasure. They had heard what they wanted to hear. The Arikaras had said they would send chiefs to meet their new Great Father in the East, even though the dangers of such long travel made them fear for their lives. Tabeau had given more information about the Arikaras, their language, customs, agriculture, and commerce with other tribes, than the captains could have hoped to learn if they had stayed here a month. They had written long into the nights to get it all on paper for the President.

Then Chief Piaheto, Eagle's Feather, positively surprised the captains by offering to go upriver with them to the Mandan country and try to talk peace with them, and also promised he would go down next year to talk to the Great Father.

And Joseph Gravelines accepted an offer to hire on as Piaheto's interpreter into the Mandan country.

What pleased the troops most, besides the lusty attention of the tribe's pretty women, was that the Arikaras would accept none of their precious whiskey. They would not take anything that would make them act like fools.

There was a celebration, with music and dancing, just before the boats were to set out northward. Through the whole three-day sojourn in the friendly towns, Drouillard had been ignored by the flirtatious women. The white soldiers and the great black man were obviously remarkable beings, but he was obviously just an Indian. Though he was the only one who understood the connection for what it meant, the women and girls looked right past him at the blue-eyed men who, not being merchants like most whitemen, must be on some long spirit quest to the far edge of the earth. The Arikaras had yearned to receive some of their magic by intimate connection.

Drouillard wondered if he would be ignored like this all across the country, and sighed.

Ten miles upstream from the Arikara towns, the evening camp was suddenly disturbed by a commotion of excited voices. Drouillard, sitting outside the hatch of the keelboat cabin, rose and leaned out over the gunwale to see what was happening.

"What is it, Drouillard?" Captain Lewis asked from inside, where the captains were interviewing Eagle's Feather, with Gravelines interpreting.

"Two women," he replied. "Followed us up." Even in dusk he recognized them. An Arikara man at Piaheto's town had been sending them among the soldiers. The man was not in sight, but the two slender beauties, apparently on their own, had walked a long way to resume their enticements. Over their shoulders they wore buffalo robes to serve them as cloaks or beds. At the edge of the camp the soldiers were strutting and jostling each other to be first in the courting play.

The captains were annoyed, but decided not to insult the chief by chasing the women out of camp as if they weren't good enough for the soldiers. Better to let them stay, with rules on the troops, than have the soldiers deserting camp all night like tom-cats, as Clark put it. The rules were no fighting over the women, or ganging up.

Drouillard felt both a yearning and a sadness. The soldiers would give the girls trinkets. In return they would get a swoop of delight, bragging rights, and probably a souvenir dose of dribble-and-burn. Gravelines and Tabeau themselves likely had passed the diseases hundreds of miles along these riverbanks. As dusk deepened, firelights brightened, the fiddle squeaked up by the cooking area, and the male and female voices laughed and giggled the wordless language of desire in the margins of the camp. Drouillard's heart cramped with a strange, miserable anger.

Fifteen hundred miles they had come; the horizons of many eagles. And yet he was still not in a place or time untainted by hairy-faced whitemen and their vainglorious ignorance. He remembered an image from a recent dream: an eagle nest in a tree above mist. From that high nest, he understood now, the eagle watched whitemen coming, and it knew something, something he yearned to know.

Now, catching the tune of Cruzatte's old fiddle, the voices of Werner and Whitehouse started up.

> *"Let's go a-courtin' the big chief's daughter,*
> *Let's go a-courtin' the big chief's daughter,*
> *She ain't been loved and I think she oughter!*
>   *Let's go down and court 'er!*
>
> *Wait! Have ye seen the big chief's daughter?*
> *Wait! Have ye seen the big chief's daughter?*
> *She looks much older than a daughter oughter!*
>   *I'll not go to court 'er!*
>
> *Might it be she's the big chief's mother?*
> *Might it be she's the big chief's mother?*
> *G'zooks! Or even his old gran'mother?*
>   *She's yours! I'll find another!"*

Over the silhouetted low bluffs on the far shore, the last lilac light was draining out of the sky, and in the deeper dark above, the first bold stars were shining. Reflecting the last light, the Missouri looked like rippling silk and sounded like a scarf fluttering in a wind. Soldier voices above were laughing at the song, and soldier voices below were fussing and joking over the women. Suddenly there came a loud, fierce, rapid argument, first in two voices, then three or four, incoherent over the singing and the fiddle.

By the time the music trailed off, the dominant voice was that of First Sergeant Ordway, bellowing over the hubbub of derisive voices: "God damn you, Newman! You—You—You are under arrest for that! By the authority of—"

"By the 'thority o' your rancid ass, y' goddamn puppet! God damn high horse Lewis got no right to make a slave out of a white man! I'll go tell that son of a bitch myself! Turn me loose, you reekin' turd!"

"Mutiny, Cap'n!" Ordway shouted. "Hold him down, Shields. . . . Get back, Reed. Get back, get back . . . You're under arrest too. Cap'n! Mutiny up here at the mess!"

When Newman and Reed were brought on board, Newman had a lump above his left eye and his clothes were rumpled, soiled with ash on one shoulder and river mud on the knees. He was scowling but subdued. Reed was forlorn as usual. They stood in lantern light, at attention, near the mast, and Lewis stood glaring at them with his hands clasped behind his back. "First Sergeant alleges that you've been impugning your superior officer, Private Newman, and repeatedly. How do you answer?"

"Sir, I don't know how I could *im-pune* when I don't even know what it means. All's I ever said was, Moses ain't no nigger, to be made a slave of. When you whipped and discarded him you said he'd be sent back on a boat. You didn't say he—"

"That plan was changed. No boat is going back till next spring. Reed's not at issue here, it's you fomenting mutiny."

"I didn't mutiny, sir. I just raised hell at what ain't right."

Lewis sighed and stood back. "Reed, he says this is because of you. How much of it comes from you we'll find out in court-martial."

"You can't court-martial him, Cap'n," said Newman. "He ain't in your damned army anymore."

Lewis's fists and jaw clenched. "Mr. Newman, by tomorrow you might not be either."

The Arikara chief Eagle's Feather stood with Drouillard and Gravelines at the hatch, watching this confrontation with anxious tension, blinking rapidly. Drouillard glanced at his profile: bony-jawed, skin creased like old boot leather, yellowed by candlelight from inside, comb of feathers in his headdress turning in the breeze. He turned his face to Drouillard, a sad eye glinting.

No use trying to explain anything, Drouillard thought, and just shook his head.

13th of October Satturday 1804
a fiew miles from the river on the S.S. 2 stones resembling humane persons & one resembling a Dog is Situated in the open Prarie . . . the Rickores make offerings whenever they pass. those people have a Curious Tradition of those Stones, one was a man in Love, one a Girl whose parents would not let marry, the Dog went to mourn with them all turned to Stone gradually fed on grapes untill they turned, & the woman has a bunch of grapes yet in her hand (Infomtn. of the Chief & Intepeter) near the place we obsd. a greater quantity of fine grapes than I ever Saw at one place . . .

We Tried the Prisoner Newmon by 9 of his Peers they did "Centence him 75 Lashes & Disbanded him from the party."
William Clark, Journals

October 16, 1804

Drouillard stood on the riverbank with Captain Lewis and Eagle's Feather in a cold northwest wind under gray skies and sighted his rifle on a pronghorn that was so far away it looked as small as a mouse. It was on the edge of a herd. If he were hunting in his own way, he would stalk in closer for a more certain killing shot, but Lewis wanted him to shoot it from here, to impress the Arikara chief with the American rifles. At this range the captain would have rested his muzzle on his espontoon. Drouillard didn't like to shoot from a rest because it interfered with the instinct. He had grown from a boyhood of killing rabbits with a throw-stick, birds with bolas, and game with arrows, before he ever had a gun, and so to him prayer and instinct had as much to do with the fate of the prey as the accuracy of the weapon. There had to be an acceptance between the animal and the shooter to allow a kill, and that was a thing of the spirit known as the Keeper of the Game. This excellent rifle only made greater distance possible.

The pronghorn raised its head and looked in Drouillard's direction. It did not run. The spirit connection was now fixed, and he squeezed the trigger. The extra-heavy powder load discharged, and the distance was so great that he had time to lower the muzzle and watch through the smoke for the result. The animal leaped almost straight up. Its herd was already in flight toward the river by the time the body fell to the ground.

"Whewee! Good!" Lewis exclaimed softly, and glanced at Eagle's Feather, who was gawking. "I think he's impressed. *I* am!"

The captains for about four days now had been working their strong impressions upon Eagle's Feather, who was the first wild Indian they had had so long as captive audience. The chief watched them respectfully as they seemed to pray to their navigational instruments and their journals. He studied, like a swivel-head owl, the strange cooperative force by which the many parts of this complicated unit moved on and on against the stream: the soldiers rowing; the Frenchmen in the red pirogue rowing nearby, but always singing or laughing or arguing; the hunters going out and then reappearing farther up the river with hides and meat; the three cooking messes setting up every evening, the tattered tents rising in the twilight; the few soldiers lining up before the captains at every stop for treatment of their boils and blisters and gashes and sprains; the constant packing and unpacking of bundles; the jolly, almost frantic lineup for the evening whiskey ration; the never-ending strain and struggle to keep the ponderous boat under control and moving on. Drouillard, only half Indian, after nearly a year with this ongoing community without women or children, still sometimes had moments of soul-clarity in which it seemed as if there could not really be something like this; he would glance at Eagle's Feather and wonder how it must seem to this man of another world, into which these strangers had so suddenly come with their alien ideas and overwhelming demands. The chief had protested and wept aloud at Private Newman's whipping. All the rest of this must seem as incomprehensible to him as had that terrible custom.

He had shot two more pronghorns, the last near a little river the chief called Elk Shed Their Horns, almost in Mandan land. As Drouillard went down the bluff to hail the boats, to get men to help him fetch in his three kills, he began hearing over the wind a commotion of excited cries. He broke into a lope along the bluff, and after a few paces he saw beyond the cottonwoods the keelboat and pirogues coming up, far below. Captain Lewis and Eagle's Feather had lingered near the antelope carcasses, to guard them against wolves, but also because Lewis had found a new kind of small prairie bird in a tuft of grass, a bird either injured or so weak it didn't fly away.

The shrill yelling was coming from the riverbank a little way above the oncoming boats, and as Drouillard loped along looking down over the last rise, he saw a swarm of quick-moving figures and he had to stop where he was to take it in and understand what was happening.

A herd of several hundred pronghorns was in the river. On both riverbanks Indians were running. When the animals tried to come ashore, the hunters headed them off, forced them back into the water, shot them with arrows. Some hunters were in the river with the herd, clubbing the animals with sticks and dragging them ashore. When he got down close, he saw that these hunters were almost all boys, not yet even of warrior age. They were having a thrilling time and were harvesting enough of the delicious animals to feed their people far into the coming winter. By the time Captain Clark came up from the boats to observe the slaughter, carcasses lay on both riverbanks for half a mile, and the boys were still swimming to shore, towing dead pronghorns with arrows protruding from them. With his usual exactness, Captain Clark recorded that the boys had killed fifty-eight. Drouillard noted ruefully, "I only got three."

At dusk the youthful Arikara hunters came from their camp to see the big boat, visit their chief, and bring loads of meat as a gift to the whitemen. Still exuberant from their great hunt, they sang and danced until late at night. Eagle's Feather obviously was very proud of them, and so was Drouillard.

October 16th
This day took a small bird alive of the order of the goat suckers. it appeared to be passing into the dormant state, the bird could scarcely move.—I run my penknife into it's body under the wing and completely distroyed it's lungs and heart—yet it lived upwards of two hours—this fanominon I could not account for unless it proceeded from the want of circulation of the blod.—the recarees call this bird to'-na it's note is at-tah-to'-nah'; at-tah' to'nah'; to-nah, a nocturnal bird, sings only in the night as does the whipperwill.—it's weight- 1 oz 17 Grains Troy.

Meriwether Lewis, Journals

Eagle's Feather observed that since there was so much meat, they had not needed to eat the tonah bird. He was sorry they killed it.

October 21, 1804

The spirit of North Grandfather grew stronger. Drouillard was wind-whipped, walking in snow, when he saw the great bear tracks.

Every year, winter had come down from the north to wherever Drouillard lived. This was not the same. The boats were moving to meet winter, up the cold, gray, endless river through a land ever more vast and bleak. The leaves blew off the trees in the bottoms and ravines, the nights were bitterly cold. The soldier tents, weakened by months of sun, moisture, mold, and wind, were now coming apart in these north winds that never stopped. The country was full of old signs of long ago life, things that the Arikara chief tried to explain, but which made the heart shrink: rocks with ancient markings that told of old catastrophes and predicted those to come; old forts where Mandan towns had been, only ruins now; a sacred tree all alone on the open plains, survivor of countless prairie fires; an oak upon which the Mandans in ceremony hung from ropes pinned into the flesh of their chests and necks. Gravelines had never seen such a ceremony but knew the Mandans and the Cheyennes still performed them. The captains listened aghast as the interpreter tried to explain it. Young men volunteered for the torture to make themselves men, but more importantly, to bear such pain on behalf of their People, so the People would not have to suffer so much. Drouillard had heard tales of these ceremonies, from traders: *okeepa,* the Mandans called it; the Sun Dance, other peoples called it. He listened and remembered the Jesus of the Black Robes who hung by his pierced flesh to take the pain of the people upon himself.

In the boat at night with the wind howling around, Eagle's Feather talking as if in a trance would tell the captains of the ancient, giant snakes and turtles in the beginnings of the world, awakening in Drouillard memories of the creation stories his mother's people told, different but much the same.

We are on the edge of the places where whitemen have come, he would think, and the magic is still so strong it could force you to your knees.

No, this was not like North Grandfather coming down as he always did; this was going closer and closer, day by day, to the home of North Grandfather. At daybreak today the freezing rain had turned to snow and looked as if it would fall all day.

And yet, bleak and frightening as the land was as it gave way from Arikara to Mandan country, the game grew more and more plentiful. Two days ago Clark, counting as always, had written that he saw fifty-two herds of buffalo and three of elk while standing in one place. Yesterday eight deer had given themselves up to Drouillard's rifle. Captain Clark had killed three, and the other hunters two. Herds of the pronghorns were crossing the river to go to their winter home in a sacred range the chief called Black Hills. These grasslands were a paradise for the hoofed animals.

Each day, Drouillard had to draw deeper and deeper for the fire inside him, the life-heat of Shawandasse, the South Wind, to keep from shrinking in the north wind. Though he had not yet seen a Mandan, he already admired a people who could live in such a treeless, merciless, wind-scoured land. Eagle's Feather said the Mandans had kept moving north to stay distant from the Sioux. Once they had been numerous enough and strong enough in their fort towns to live where they chose to live. But years ago the traders had brought the burning-up disease, the smallpox, and it had reduced them as badly as it had reduced the Omahas. Now they survived the raids of their numerous enemies because their towns were like forts, and also because they were exceedingly brave and tough. But also, it was believed, because of the sacred thing in the center of their main town—a protection they had always carried with them since the beginning of the world.

"It is something like a big barrel, made of cedar wood," Gravelines said. "It is in the center of their ceremonies. Inside it they keep their Mystery, which is only seen by its Keeper Shaman. No one else knows what it is."

To the captains, one of the great mysteries of the Mandans was something Jefferson wanted to know: Were they a people long ago come from Europe? Some of the Mandans had blue eyes and pale skin and light hair. Their fort towns were built like the ancient towns of Britain. They used round, leather-covered tub-boats like those used in an old country of Britain called Wales. The President knew a legend that hundreds of years ago a prince had crossed the ocean from Wales and made settlements on this continent. He had told Captain Lewis to learn if the pale ones known to be among the Mandans were their descendants. Above all, the President wanted a very strong friendship to be made with the Mandans, because their towns, in the great bend of the Missouri, were the major center of all tribal trade on the great plains. Gravelines said that every autumn, all the tribes of the high plains, as far away as the Crows in the west and the Assiniboines in the north, gathered at the Mandan towns, with French traders from St. Louis and British traders from the North West Company and the Hudson's Bay Company, for a trading fair involving thousands of people and every kind of food, hides, horses, and handworked goods, as well as guns, tools, and woolen blankets. One of Captain Lewis's purposes while there would be to wean the Indians away from the British companies and to make the British traders understand that this would henceforth be an American trade center.

Gravelines said the population of the two big Mandan towns was further swollen by the nearness of three major Hidatsa towns within fifteen miles. Though the Hidatsas were high plains buffalo hunters who ranged as far west as the Shining Mountains, their winter homes were in the Knife River fortress-towns, built like those of the Mandans. The two tribes lived in peace, traded and intermarried with each other, and had many of the same allies and enemies. Captain Clark was eager to learn from the Hidatsas everything they knew about the rivers and routes leading into the Shining Mountains, because that was where the corps would be going next year, and it was a land never seen by whitemen. The captains always asked Indians about the lands ahead. Even Drouillard, after every day of hunting and butchering, had to sit down in the evening and tell Captain Clark every detail he had seen of the country he had ranged over during the hunt, and the captain would make pencil notes of words, and sketches of hills and woods and streams. And the next day as the expedition moved on, Clark would be checking the sketch-maps, with his compass and telescope and calipers, to measure what he saw against what Drouillard had reported to him. The captain did the same with all the hunters who went out, even Captain Lewis. Some of the hunters were very accurate in their observations, some were terrible. Clark had found Colter and Frazier to be almost as reliable as Drouillard, and George Gibson next after them. But it was Drouillard he counted on most, because he always checked out, and also because he hunted almost every day, and ranged farther ahead and on the flank than anyone else.

Now Drouillard looked at the bear tracks growing faint as snow drifted over them. All the Indians spoke fearfully of the strong and fierce bears of the plains. An unfortunate encounter had happened yesterday, before the snow. Cruzatte, walking on shore, had seen one of these bears. In the greatest excitement and fear, he had shot at it immediately. Cruzatte's one good eye was not keen, so one might only guess whether his shot had hit the animal. It did no more than enrage the bear, which rose up and roared, and so badly frightened Cruzatte that he dropped both his rifle and tomahawk and fled toward the river. When Cruzatte realized he was not being pursued by a wounded bear, his greatest fear became that of having to tell Captain Lewis he had thrown away his army rifle. So he had turned back and gingerly gone looking for it, and found that the bear had fled in the opposite direction. When Cruzatte recounted the incident last night, it had so amused the voyageurs and troops that it became the evening's entertainment, complete with roars, growls, and pantomime, and Cruzatte had so enjoyed the attention that he had ended the evening playing music, even though it was so cold and dank that it could not be good for the fiddle. For the men it was not just amusement, it was their first eyewitness account of an encounter with the beast that was growing in their dreams and nightmares. They wondered why it was not in its winter sleep, the weather having turned so cold, and they even began ragging Cruzatte about whether he had actually seen a bear or just made it up. Drouillard himself had begun wondering that, until now, finding these tracks. If these yellow bears did hibernate, they obviously were not fully into it yet.

The reason the event saddened him was that he had meant to be the first man in this corps to encounter a yellow bear. He had wanted to meet one of these bears before any of the soldiers shot at one. It was not that he wanted to be the first to shoot one; he wanted to meet one in peace. He did not think one kind of bear could be so different from other bears, or that yellow bears by nature attacked without some kind of provocation. He had wanted to find a yellow bear and get near without bothering it. He would have been surprised if one had attacked him just because it could see him. That was not bearlike. He had come upon many bears in his life, fallen in with their amblings, gazed back and forth with them, stayed near them until they lost their curiosity and went back to their foraging.

But when he had gone hunting to get bear, which he had often done for their hides and meat and fat, the bears he met knew he had come to kill them. Bears understood men. Without words a bear could understand a man's intent, because he was man's brother. Once Drouillard had wounded a bear near the Tennessee River, and he was sure that it went everywhere within twenty miles and told all the other bears about him, because for a while all the bears would flee or hide from him, or menace him and then run.

Captains Lewis and Clark and their men shot every animal they saw. They had come two thousand miles up the Missouri River with guns banging. Drouillard himself had done much of the killing; that was his job. But when he had enough meat, he stopped shooting animals even if they were right under his gun. Captain Lewis killed animals no one would want to eat, just so he could examine them for President Jefferson. The soldiers shot wolves because they were wolves.

Almost everyone either feared the legendary bears so much he hoped never to meet one, or wanted to be the first to kill one. The bears would know that, and the soldiers' reputation would go ahead of them up the river from bear to bear, and the bears of course would be afraid or hostile. Drouillard had hoped to meet one before hostilities were established.

Now it was too late. Cruzatte had seen a bear and at once had shot at it. It hadn't been coming at him when he shot at it. At first he had said it was, but Drouillard stared at him until Cruzatte admitted the truth: it hadn't even been looking at him.

So, now the alarm would be going up the river from bear to bear about this American army. It was like what Drouillard remembered of the warriors who would talk at Lorimier's in Ohio when he was a boy. The Shawnees had learned the hard way by then: American soldiers are coming. If you don't kill them first, they will kill you.

He would have liked just to meet a yellow bear and let it see that he wasn't an American soldier.

He followed the tracks a little way, looking for droppings. After a mile he found scat. He separated it with his knife point, to compare its diet with that of black bears. Scales, bone, and hair suggested that it ate more fish and meat, maybe carrion, than blacks, which ate mostly grubs, insects, berries, vegetation. By examining scat and droppings, he could sometimes tell where an animal lived and fed in a varied landscape. Such knowledge was a small part of hunting.

He was not in a mood now to kill a bear in this forbidding place. So he veered away from its trail and headed toward the river.

PART TWO

November, 1804–March, 1806

we were now about to penetrate a country at least two thousand miles in width, on which the foot of civillized man had never trodden; the good or evil it had in store for us was for experiment yet to determine.

Meriwether Lewis, Journals

Chapter 11

"God damn, I never saw such stuff call itself wood!" Sergeant Gass complained. "Slicker'n lard, squirts when y' chop it, and gums up your saw teeth like a man chawin' raw possum!"

He was notching wall logs for the barracks huts of the fort, and though he had been a carpenter much of his life, he was having a frustrating time with the cottonwood, which was the only tree in this countryside long enough and thick enough for laying up fort walls. Drouillard watched him from a safe distance, because even Gass's great skill with an ax did not keep him from losing control of it now and then, when the bit would glance off the slick, white wood and go wild. Two men had already cut themselves with axes today. The cottonwood was so heavy with water that it required half a dozen men with carrying sticks to bring a single log from the woods to the building site, and so pulpy that its fibers pinched and clogged the teeth of a crosscut saw. Gass had already given up any hope of ripsawing planks from such a material; any flat surface would have to be hewed with a broadax or adze, which was dangerous with this slick, stringy wood. There was a bit of elm and ash growing in the woods, but it was small and would be saved for tool handles, pry-poles, and rafters. So they had to work with the cottonwood. There were two virtues in its favor: it was soft, and its inner bark was prized as horse fodder by the Mandans. And the ax-wielding

189

soldiers of Gass's fort-building crew were producing huge quantities of bark and chips. Axes chunked unceasingly and the wind was full of the smell of greenwood.

Drouillard, like everyone else, took a turn as a laborer and carpenter's helper these days. Frosts and cold, raw winds motivated everybody to get the buildings finished quickly. Every time he looked up, flights of geese, brant, and ducks were clamoring faintly, crossing the grim gray sky southward in their formations. Two miles across the Missouri, straight to the west, the Mandan fortress city of Mittuta-Hanka stood on a sheer bluff, spectacular from here: several dozen domed, earth-covered houses, protected from the plain by a high palisade, with cornfields and gardens outside. Its chief, Sheheke, had been nicknamed Big White by the captains; he was the fattest, palest Indian Drouillard had ever seen. And he was good-humored and hospitable, seemingly delighted to have the Americans build their winter home so close by. His Mandans came by constantly, going to and coming from hunting, or just to watch, often to bring gifts of corn and meat. Sometimes they brought their horses to graze nearby, and to gather cottonwood bark for their winter fodder.

And there were whitemen with the Mandans: clerks of the British trading companies, and some French-Canadians who lived and traded here. One was a middle-aged man named Rene Jessaume, who claimed that he had been a spy for Captain Clark's famous brother General Clark during the Revolutionary War near St. Louis, a statement Captain Clark believed to be an invention to gain favor. Despite that doubt, the captains had hired him as an interpreter because of his deep involvement among the Mandans. Another French-Canadian of about the same age, named Charbonneau, had come down from his home in the Hidatsa towns a few miles up, and they hired him to interpret with that tribe. That would help the captains as they tried to learn the way into the Shining Mountains from the Hidatsas who had been there.

And something else Charbonneau had said piqued the captains' intense interest: he had two girl wives, whom he had purchased from Hidatsa warriors who captured them a few years ago in the Shining Mountains. They were of the Snake, or Shoshone, tribe, which lived near the headwaters of the Missouri, deep in those mountains into which the expedition would be going next year. One of them was with child now, but would be delivered of that burden before the expedition moved on. Both could speak Hidatsa almost as well as Charbonneau could himself. As an added inducement for his hire, he had hinted, they would get not just one interpreter for his pay, but three.

Yes, Drouillard thought. What fortune these captains always had. Wherever they went, they found interpreters. Labiche. Cruzatte. The Dorions. Gravelines and Tabeau. And now Jessaume and Charbonneau and his wives. Drouillard himself, hired as their original interpreter because of his hand-signing, had not been needed so much for it, and had been free to hunt, which was his preference.

"Take it away," Sergeant Gass said. Soldiers picked up the cottonwood log he had so neatly notched, and he stepped over to the next, spiked in the end of a measuring string and walked down the log; with two flicks of the ax he marked the length, put away the string, eyed the end of the log, and began chopping out the next set of notches.

The fort was coming together in a remarkably orderly fashion out of this chaos of thunking axes and flying wood chips. Already some of the walls were chest-high. Two rows of barracking huts converged toward the rear of the fort, where there would be a smokehouse and pantry building with a sentry post on top. A high log palisade with a gate would enclose the end facing the river. A sentry on the palisade would always be looking right down over the moored boats. Drouillard remembered York bragging last winter of the many abilities of his master, one of which had been fort building, and he thought, Yes, that black man was right. Captain Clark was building the fort, while Captain Lewis was usually over at the Mandan towns doing his diplomacy. It was like St. Louis and the Riviere à Dubois camp all over again. How long ago that seemed. That had been just a camp of huts. This, being next to several thousand Indians, was a defensible fort. And it was being made very skillfully. The captain had designed and laid everything out with leveling instruments and measurers of angles. Sergeant Gass was the main carpenter, and a good half of the soldiers were as adept with a sharp ax as with a whittling knife.

Just about everything York had boasted his master could do, Drouillard had seen him do in this past year. And it was just a year. Captain Clark had greeted him this morning by saying, "Today's November eleventh. One year to the day since we landed at Fort Massac and hired you, Mr. Drewyer. And I'll say I'm damn glad we did it. Captain Bissell said we wouldn't go hungry with you along, and he sure was right!"

He remembered that day, remembered watching the eagle soar above the Ohio River. He thought of that as he helped the soldiers carry the log and hoist it onto the wall, where its notches fit precisely on the notches of the logs under it. As he walked back toward the log Sergeant Gass was notching on the ground, he saw a man and two girls coming along the shore, making their way past the Mandans who were wandering between the fort and the boat watching the activities. The man, though attired all in Indian dress, had a thick, dark beard graying at the chin and a whiteman's duckfooted walk. It was Charbonneau, the newly hired interpreter from the Hidatsa town. Drouillard guessed that the two Indian girl-children behind him were his wives, the Shoshones from the Shining Mountains. He was curious to see them, and went down, raising his hand in a greeting.

"*Bonjour,*" Charbonneau said, in a voice that seemed too small and breathy for a man of his size. "*Où sont les capitaines?*"

"*Là-bas, dans le grand bateau. Capitaine Clark, seulement. Allons-y.*" Drouillard led them down and went up the gangplank and hopped on the deck of the keelboat. When he turned, he saw that Charbonneau was still standing on the bank, looking down fearfully at the water between the boat and shore, then at the narrow plank. The devil! Drouillard thought. If he's afraid of falling in the water, he's hired on with the wrong army! He coaxed him up by offering a hand. The two girls followed without hesitation, even smiling and chattering to each other, apparently at the novelty of balancing on the narrow plank. Drouillard offered his hand to them, but they shook their heads, holding their blankets about them. He noticed that they were good wool British blankets, not old, apparently one of the benefits of being married to a trader. Captain Clark, having felt them boarding, came out of the after cabin, where he had been writing or working on maps. He was not wearing a hat, and the girls stood stock-still, struck with the glory of his red hair and high, white forehead. Below the brow his face was as brown as theirs. They began whispering to each other, and from the expression in their eyes, they found him beautiful. The captain was shaking hands with Charbonneau when York emerged from the cabin and loomed behind him, resplendent in his secondhand military coat. The girls gasped, stepped backward as if to flee, then huddled together, each with her hand over her mouth, staring aghast. York frowned, then, maybe afraid he would frighten them unduly, smiled. Charbonneau himself had recoiled at the sight of York but, whether he had ever seen Negroes or not, he must have known of them, and recovered his composure while his young wives were still speechless.

Charbonneau announced that he had come to speak of the terms of his hire, to have the captains meet his Shoshone wives, who might go with him and serve as interpreters when they reached their homeland in the mountains, and a few other matters that had occurred to him after their first agreement. So the captain took them into the cabin, which was warmed by a little barrel-like iron stove exhausted to the outside by a tin chimney tube. The stove was a bad experiment, having cracked from overheating in last winter's camp, but for the present it was the only way to warm the boat cabin while the captains wrote and drew. It stank and seeped smoke, but would keep the ink from freezing in their pens until quarters in the fort with their fireplaces could be finished.

Charbonneau understood virtually no English, so Drouillard stayed to aid his conversation with the captain. Charbonneau wanted permission to bring both his young wives on the journey, saying one would be jealous if the other went. Captain Clark replied that he was reluctant to have even one woman along, and wanted one only as a Shoshone interpreter. Charbonneau therefore began haggling; he offered to provide his own tepee lodge to shelter his family, if that would make it easier, and gave a hint that one of his wives might be available for laundering and other services, which the captain gave him no opportunity to specify. As this went on, Drouillard was making his assessments of Charbonneau and the young women. The Frenchman, he decided, was just a man who obtained as much as he could in any transaction, as traders do, and perhaps had a swollen sense of self-importance, as might a man with more than one woman at his service. One of the girls had a placid, pretty, round face and a sly way of watching Captain Clark and York intently without seeming to stare; she cast her gaze coyly around the little enclosure, as she would be expected to in a place she had never been in before, but she was really seeing nothing but Clark and York, her gaze always coming back to them. This one had opened her blanket in the warm room, and her full, ripe figure indicated that she must be the pregnant one.

The other was barely half the woman: slight, wiry, and small-bosomed, the veins and tendons in her forearms defined under the taut skin, likewise her long, muscular neck. Jaw muscles, chin, cheekbones, and brow ridge were in high relief, and her mouth was prominent: generous lips over strong, forward teeth. She was not pretty, but this angular head on its long neck had a certain elegant tension and poise. She looked like a creature of quick strength—belied by painfully bashful eyes that appeared as if they were afraid to look up at a face. And yet it was this one, rather than the roving-eyed one, whose spirit seemed to vibrate like a coiled snake.

Captain Clark had finally made it clear to Charbonneau that he could bring only one wife, and that if he chose to bring neither, he might as well stay at home with them both. Clark was, however, very interested in the notion of bringing the tepee lodge. "We won't have the keelboat to live in," he mused aloud, "and the tenting's going a-frazzle on us. O' course, we can't tote poles for the thing, but any time we mightn't find any suitable ones in the woods, why, we could rig a frame of oars and masts off the pirogues. . . . Tell him, George, we'll consider buying his lodge cover, additional to his wage, and we want him to bring whichever wife he thinks the better interpreter. Between us, I hope it's not the flirty, pregnant one. She'd be trouble amongst so many men." Drouillard translated to Charbonneau, watching his face go through all the expressions of dismay, wistfulness, anger, and helpless resignation. Then he turned to the captain.

"The little stringy one's smarter and tougher, he says, and would be the better interpreter. I think he hates to say that, sir, because he seems to prefer the other one for, well, cuddling."

"Well, how much of that would there be anyway, with thirty men about and a babe on her breast? She'll be better off staying home with the tribal women, and the skinny one going with us. Works out fine. Tell him it's a deal: the lodge cover and this skinny girl. And him, o' course. It's her we want anyway, not him, but don't tell him I said that."

He turned back to the Frenchman and announced the agreement. They went on for a while in French, and finally Charbonneau nodded and stuck out his hand to Clark. Drouillard smiled ruefully and said: "He corrects us on one misunderstanding, Cap'n. It's our little skinny one who's with child, not the one who looks like she is."

Clark looked at her and blinked. "Good God, where's she hiding it? Well, tell him to take 'em home and work out their feelings there." He picked up a pencil. "Find out her name."

Drouillard and Charbonneau talked while York and the moon-faced girl flirted with their eyes. Drouillard glanced at the thin girl and found her shy eyes on the captain. "As I make it out," Drouillard said, "she is bird, maybe crow, woman; S' Kaka Weah." It sounded similar to the part of his own name that meant Feathers: *S'gawateah.*

Clark moved his lips and wrote: *Sah ca gah we ah or bird woman.*

"Makes sense," he murmured. "Wasn't that one Missouria

fellow Ka Ga Paha, Crow's Head? And Kakawissassa was Lightning Raven."

They watched the Frenchman totter fearfully down the gangplank, his wives covering their laughter with their palms. Captain Clark shook his head and said, "I don't envy that man. Having to go home and tell one wife he's going away with the other! In fact, I don't envy any man having two wives. And Jessaume says he has others besides."

"I don't know," Drouillard remarked, fanning the air. "Man smells strong, eh, worse than beaver gland. They might all be glad to have him out of the house awhile."

Now York was laughing behind them. They turned to look at him. "That li'l gal goin' with us, eh? Good, Mist' Droor. Makes three of us color people, you, her, and me. 'Bout ten white to one color, now. Was twenty to one, just 'smornin'. And a year ago it was just me, one! Heh heh!"

Captain Clark snorted. "Why'd I ever teach you 'rithmetic, you uppity black rascal? Go make us some coffee!"

"Just don't tell that bird woman you eat babies," Drouillard said. "We'll lose us an interpreter before we've got her!"

Drouillard saw a Mandan boy walk across the snow and stop right in front of Captain Clark and give him something. Then Clark sent York into the fort. The slave returned with a small, round trade mirror, which Clark put in the boy's hand. The boy was saying something to Clark in his language. Clark made some sign. The boy made signs that said *four* and then *bear*. Clark glanced around, watching for some chiefs and elders who were coming up to the fort, and the boy ran off to where another boy was waiting for him, and showed him the mirror. They started down the bank.

Just then Drouillard heard an eagle's cry, very close, looked up, saw none, and then realized that the sound was coming from where Clark stood. The captain had a whistle in his mouth, made of the wing bone of an eagle. That was what the boy had given him. When the boy heard it, he turned, smiling, and Clark waved at him.

"Fine whistle, eh, Drouillard!" the captain called to him. "I'll keep this. I think that boy made it himself for me!"

Drouillard nodded. He thought it was a fine thing for a man to take such pleasure in a gift from an Indian boy.

December 1804

It was an amusing sight, but he felt too much sympathy to laugh:

York stood in front of Captain Lewis in the half-finished officers' quarters of Fort Mandan with his long shirt pulled up and his breeches down while the captain examined his penis.

"I'm afraid so," Lewis said. "Frostbit. Now, York, can you explain this? Frostbite in this weather I understand. Half our hunters have it in their feet and faces, and no wonder, cold as it is. But how did you happen to have this thing out long enough to get it frozen?"

Sergeant Ordway, waiting nearby for a medical consultation of his own, chuckled and said, "He was prob'ly doin' sign language to some squaw."

York clenched his jaw. Drouillard, who was here with a broken left hand, saw how much self-control the slave had to use when soldiers made fun of him. Drouillard's hand had been crushed and lacerated badly more than two weeks ago when a log was dropped on it during construction of the fort's storage room. It still ached intensely, especially in the cold, but he could move all his fingers now.

"Was just pissin', Cap'n." York said. "Took too long."

"Why?"

"Hard t' start, Cap'n. Hurt an' burns."

"You mean it hurt even before the frostbite?"

"Yes, s'."

Captain Clark, writing by the fireplace, looked up at his slave with a frown. "Damn it, York. You come down all venereal rot, you won't be worth much to me, now will you?"

"Sorry, mast'."

Drouillard looked at the slave, thinking: Aye, York, take care of that thing, it's *his* property. York was in great demand by tribal women, both Mandan and Hidatsa, who believed he must be a source of great spiritual power. Whiteness too was considered powerful medicine, and several of the soldiers, especially the blond and red-haired ones, had been welcomed most ardently by the village women. Lewis got some dry bark from the medicine chest and gave it to York. "For the frostbite, make a tea out of this bark, and when it's lukewarm, soak that blacksnake in it. You have frozen toes too, don't you? Soak them in it too, and keep massaging them lightly while they soak."

The sergeant laughed again. "He supposed to massage that other thing too? Guess he won't mind that. . . ."

"Sergeant, I presume you're here on a venereal complaint too? How many others of you?" Lewis asked the figures hulking inside the door for sick call.

Two hands went up, but a soldier named Weiser said, "Not me, Cap'n, sir. I just got me a hitch in m' hobble, rheumatism I reckon."

Most of the boils and felons and skin problems that had plagued the soldiers all summer were gone now, succeeded by colds, pleurisy, rheumatism, cuts and sprains from construction accidents, the venereal complaints, and frostbite and snow-blindness. The captains had expected severe winter in this northern latitude, but nothing had prepared them for cold this deep. This was like another world. One night there had been a display of spirit lights high in the northern sky, looking like long fringes of starglow rippling against the black sky. The captains of course had had a name for it and had written a description of it, but Drouillard believed it was a message from North Grand-father Spirit, and he had smoked a prayer pipe to it outdoors under the frigid sky.

The barrack rooms of the fort had just been roofed when winter struck, with sleet and then fine, stinging, windblown snow, and frost shimmering in the air at dawn, snow falling and drifting, and the river freezing so rapidly that the captains real-ized that the keelboat and pirogues were frozen fast in the river's edge. They had been too busy getting the fort roofed over to stop and drag the vessels ashore, and now they were fast in ice, and the captains had to worry that their hulls might be damaged or even crushed. Cold was so keen and intense at night that the water-laden cottonwood trees split open with reports like rifle shots, and outdoor sentries had to be relieved after half an hour. The thermometers, by which these methodical men measured each day's temperatures, morning after morning, made them exclaim with disbelief. Howling wind blew to drift the snow into smooth or rippled shapes like great waves. One morning Drouillard had heard Lewis exclaim that it was seventy-seven degrees below the freezing of water. The wind hissed so relentlessly through the fine cracks between logs and chinking that it was necessary at last to plaster the entire inside walls of the living quarters with clay. Once the clay had dried by the heat from the fireplaces, the rooms were so airtight and snug that Drouillard thought he would suffocate in his sleep.

The erection of the palisade across the front of the fort was in process now, and it had become an ordeal. With the ground frozen hard as rock, ditching for the palisade poles required burning fires in the ditch to thaw the earth enough to dig out an inch or two at a time.

In the hard freeze, the problem of securing food for the troops had become critical. Jessaume the interpreter had exaggerated the ability of his Mandans to provide meat. Though they had many horses and were good hunters, they were cautious about ranging far for the buffalo because of their fear of large Sioux and Arikara war parties. They brought some meat, but most of their food contribution was in corn, which they brought across the river to trade for manufactured goods. They wanted spear and arrow points and war axes that the corps blacksmiths, Shields and Willard, fashioned for them out of any metal scrap they could spare. The ringing of hammers on anvils went on every day. Visiting Mandans, fascinated with the bellows and the metalworking, were usually crowded about so tightly that the smiths could hardly work, and they had to watch for pilfering.

Drouillard had been of no use as a hunter because of his

broken hand. He had, in fact, missed opportunities to hunt buffalo on a grand scale, the way the Mandans did it: racing on horseback alongside great, fleeing herds, shooting point-blank at them with powerful short bows reinforced with sinew, bows so strong that an arrow might pass clear through a buffalo's heart. Both captains had gone out on such hunts, with parties of soldiers and Indians. Their accounts of the skill and recklessness of the Mandan horsemen were thrilling, and Drouillard was impatient. He longed to go out and ride with these free, brave, cheerful people over these spacious slopes and plains in pursuit of the swift and mighty *t'tanka*, as they called the buffalo—the *kith tippe*, in his Shawnee memory. Sometimes he stood in front of the fort and watched these people ride out, a people as yet uncorrupted by whitemen, a people still free on their own land, and his heart ached for his own people's past.

And yet, how free were they, really? They had their picketed, fortified town, and they were happy and secure within it. But their women prayed and wailed when the hunters went away, because the Sioux and the Arikaras were out there. The men were happy to go out when a dozen soldiers went out with them, soldiers with their long-shooting rifles. But their enemies were always in their minds, and it took all their courage to go on long hunts, out of sight of the towns. Their enemies were like an invisible prison wall.

Sometimes Drouillard wondered: How free is anyone? Even soldiers sleep in a fort. Even the strong, far-ranging buffalo were ringed about with enemies they feared: the packs of wolves who stalked their weak and young.

These wolves of the plains were so numerous and aggressive around the hunting camps that the captains said they usually got more than half the meat of a hunt. When the herds were far from the fort and villages, the hunting parties sometimes had to build wooden pens to protect the meat from the wolves until it could be packed home on the hunters' backs, on horseback, or on sleds. When the hunters came in from those distant hunts, they were usually frostbitten and fatigued almost to death from camping a few nights in the bitter cold.

Every ordeal of that kind increased the captains' admiration for the Mandans. He heard them tell in awe of Mandan hunters caught out in the plains with no way to make fire, surviving all night with no shelter but a buffalo skin despite cold so intense that ax heads were too brittle to use.

"I'll wager," Captain Lewis said now as he prepared a mercury dose in a penis syringe for York's venereal complaint, "I'll just bet you that you'll never find one of these Indians with a frosted cock!" He shook his head.

York chuckled. "Well, Cap'n, I do try t' keep it in warm places much as I can."

"Oh, don't you, though!" Captain Clark exclaimed.

The captains regretted the spread of the venereal complaints among the troops, but did not try to forbid or even discourage carnal relations with the village women. The officers had finally come to understand that this was a part of the diplomatic accord they wanted to achieve. It was helping to dissolve the line of suspicion between strangers and strangers. Some of the soldiers, originally after mere sexual relief, now had genuine sweethearts in Mandan families, and those families were pleased and honored, because they esteemed the Americans as brave, strong men with spiritual power.

The interpreters with their wives moved into the cabin built for them in the fort. Jessaume's Mandan wife was sluttish and overbearing, and the captains expected that the couple would not contribute to much harmony in the fort.

Charbonneau's diminutive wife was now obviously pregnant, with a hard-looking protuberance standing forth on her tough little torso. She was still so shy that it was impossible to forget that she had been a captive and a slave before the Frenchman bought and married her. With the interpreters' quarters adjacent to the captains' room, York found it easy and natural to keep an eye out for her comfort and welfare. York continued to refer to himself and Drouillard and this little Bird Woman as "us colored folks of the house," and Drouillard would look at him as if annoyed, but in his heart he was pleased. There was something he liked about not being considered a whiteman.

S' Kaka Weah, the Bird Woman, found that she liked coffee, with a great deal of sugar in it. And so York made much coffee. Charbonneau was miffed and mystified that the captain's servant ignored him to wait so solicitously upon his little wife. York did not know that in the captains' estimation this girl who spoke Shoshone, a language they would need in the Shining Mountains, was much more valuable than her husband. Charbonneau believed they were allowing Bird Woman to go along because they needed him.

Drouillard often heard the officers discussing that notion of President Jefferson's that the pale, light-haired people among the Mandans might be descended from Welshmen who had come to America some six hundred years ago.

He now and then saw some of those remarkable-looking men and women. In every detail of dress and manner they were Mandans, speaking that Mandan tongue that sounded a little like the Sioux but seemed to come from far back in the throat. But some, even young warriors and girls, had hair that was yellowish-gray or light brown, and gray or greenish-blue eyes. Families in which these traits prevailed were integrated in the age-group and apprentice societies of the tribe, not separated out by their appearance, and seemed in fact to be held in high esteem. Chief Sheheke himself, Big White, appeared to have that influence in his face and blood, though his hair and eyes were not light. The captains made their usual vocabulary list, as they had tried to do among all the other tribes, and noted that there were many Mandan words that sounded like nothing they had heard before. But nobody in the Corps of Discovery knew the Welsh tongue, so they reached no conclusions. The Mandans' stories of their old origins were hard to come by because Jessaume's English was barely comprehensible, and even his own French tongue was so out of use that Drouillard had trouble understanding him. The story was, it seemed, that their ancestors had lived in a parallel world under the ground, until a hole was seen above with light and sky. So First Man had climbed up on roots and vines and emerged onto this world. Others had followed the scout up, until a very fat woman broke all the roots and vines in trying to climb up, and all the other ancient ancestors remained stranded in that world underneath, even to the present. Some relics of the ancient times were still kept in the sacred vessel in the middle of the town of Mittuta-Hanka, where they would remain under guard until next year's ceremonies. By that time, these white soldiers would already be gone, and would miss the ceremonies.

There was one curious coincidence that the captains spoke of: the Mandan origin story said that the hole they had come out of was down at the very end of the river, where it flowed into the southern sea. According to the story Jefferson hoped to prove or disprove, that was where the Welshmen had landed.

The river was frozen solid, and it became a road between the fort and the towns. The chiefs of the various towns came down to talk to the captains, and the captains went to the towns to talk to the chiefs. Big White had gained much prestige by having the American fort closest to his town, but the grand chief of the Mandans lived in a town called Rooptahe, about two leagues north and on the same side of the river as the fort. That chief's name was Black Cat. He was eager to please the Americans, and agreed that peace among the tribes would help everybody. He smoked with the Arikara chief, Eagle's Feather, and offered to send some of his best men back down with him to the Arikara towns to speak of peace. And Black Cat told the captains that he himself might go next year to speak to the new Great Father in the East. The captains, of course, were very pleased. But one day Jessaume, with a shrug, told Drouillard something that seemed closer to the truth:

"Black Cat does not understand why the captains are going through here. He wonders why they tease the people with little gifts. He is afraid they are saving their goods for the Hidatsa. And some Mandans tell the Hidatsa that these captains are going to help the Sioux attack the Hidatsa, which is why they build so strong a fort down here. Jealousy." Jessaume shrugged. "I would not want to be those captains. They are too hard to believe. Some people think they are here just to keep the British from bringing down goods."

"Why don't you tell those things to the captains?" Drouillard said.

"I thought you might tell them," Jessaume said. "They know you a long time. They believe you. I think they do not believe me."

"I am their hunter, not a carrier of rumors. That is why they believe me."

Later that day, when York had been teasing Drouillard about being one of the "colored folks," he led the slave to the gate in the fort's palisade and waved his hand to point out the wide, bright, frozen river valley, the boats frozen fast, the distant domes of lodges at Mittuta-Hanka, and the lines of ant-size human figures crossing the river ice in all directions, carrying loads of firewood on their backs, or pulling loaded sleds, leading packhorses and dog sleds. Even in this intense, bright, hazy cold, there were more people out and moving than one would see on the mildest day in the cities of St. Louis or New Orleans.

"See what?" York asked, shivering, cupping his hands for warmth over his frostbitten crotch.

Drouillard laughed voicelessly, his breath turning to frost. "This is why I'm glad I'm not a whiteman. Look how we colored folks got them outnumbered. Wouldn't you hate to be telling so many people things that they can't believe?"

"Mist' Droor," York said after a moment, "ever' time you talk to me, I think troubles. Wish you stop that."

Drouillard said, "You're a big, important man out here. When you're being treated like a king in one of these Indian lodges, do you ever think of just setting yourself free and hiding with the Indians? You could be like old Caesar I told you about."

York was gazing out with that worried look on his face. Then he looked sidewise at him. He shuddered violently. "No, s'," he said. "I wou'n stay in a place this cold if I was its king!" And he turned and hurried back into the fort.

Drouillard remained, and kept gazing out over the immense

landscape of snow and slanting sunlight, blue sky, blue shadows, tiny figures moving. Above the domed earth lodges of Mittuta-Hanka the smoke of family fires rose. Over the town's medicine lodge he could see the three tall poles with effigies hanging from them. They were a part of the ancient mystery of the Mandan people, something to do with their original person who came up from underground. First Man, they called him, or Lone Man. He was represented by the effigy between the other two. It made Drouillard remember something from the old Black Robe teachings: Jesus between the thieves. He didn't know whether any of the soldiers had thought of that when they saw the effigies, but he had seen Sergeant Gass looking up at them with some kind of thinking going on behind his eyes.

Drouillard liked it here despite the cold; he liked these people. He had thought very often about how good it could be to step away from the whitemen here and live among a people like this, who did not have those whiteman ideas that always made them go on and on in a direction, changing everything as they went.

But no, he thought. The whitemen are already here and it will have to change now. If I do hide with the Indians, it must be farther on.

Tuesday 25th Decr. 1804
cloudy. we fired the Swivels at day break & each man fired one round. our officers Gave the Party a drink of Taffee. we had the Best to eat that could be had, & continued firing dancing & frolicking dureing the whole day. the Savages did not Trouble us as we had requested them not to come as it was a Great medicien day with us. we enjoyed a merry cristmas dureing the day & evening untill nine oClock—all in peace & quietness.

Sergeant John Ordway, Journals

January 4, 1805

Thank you, Colter, Drouillard was thinking, and he meant it.

He was sitting with a circle of very old Mandan men around a fire in the big Medicine Lodge of Mittuta-Hanka Town. By the warm, dim light of that fragrant fire, as his heartbeat kept pace with hand drums and rattles, he watched a pretty young woman come dancing toward him straddling a line of sticks laid end-to-end on the floor and ending at his feet. The young woman was stark naked, holding open a buffalo robe across her shoulders. She squatted over each stick, stood up, straddled the next stick and squatted over it, so that it was taking her a long time to come to him.

Kneeling by his shoulder was the young woman's husband, who was chanting something into his ear in a pleading, almost whining tone. Though he did not understand the words, he had already learned what the young man's entreaty was: Great Hunter! Favor me by copulating with my wife, so that she may pass your hunting powers on to me when I copulate with her!

This was what Jessaume had described as the Calling of the Buffalo ceremony. Every year young husbands gathered the greatest of the old men here and asked them to pass on their veteran skill and knowledge in this way, for three nights. When the ceremony was done, buffalo would usually appear nearby, and the young hunters, their spiritual powers enhanced, would go out and kill them. Often these old men were so feeble they could hardly walk, and could not perform the connection, but sometimes one would come back with the young woman, both looking satisfied.

Drouillard was astonished to find himself here, but Colter had changed his fortunes with the village women. On New Year's Day and the next day, most of the soldiers of the fort had been invited to Mittuta-Hanka and Rooptahe towns to make music with their fiddles, tamborines, Jew's harps, and sounding horns, and to demonstrate their ways of dancing. They had put on splendid shows, to the delight of the townspeople. Then this morning Captain Clark had called Drouillard to him. "You're to go up to

Mittuta-Hanka Town this afternoon, invitation of one of their medicine men. They want you to be in a ceremony that's supposed to draw the buffalo."

"Me? Why do they want me?"

"Well, as best I understand it, they wanted our best hunter, so they asked Jessaume who it was, and he asked Colter, and Colter told 'im it's you. Nobody will argue that, so it appears you're our man to go. From what I hear of this ceremony, Colter might be wishin' he said he was the best himself. Wish he'd said I was. It's sure something I'd like to see."

And so now the young woman was close in front of him, almost enveloping him in her outspread robe, and he, sitting, was face-to-face with something he had not seen for many months. She bent her knees in time with the drum and thrust her pelvis forward so that his face was almost kissed by it, and she smelled clean with a musky odor which he recognized as eager sincerity. Above him in the shadowy robe her breasts hovered, her shadowed face looking down at him between them, her expression trancelike, smoky light flickering warm and ruddy on the rafter poles above her. And her husband, with one hand under Drouillard's elbow, was urging him to stand up and go with her, his voice almost a cooing prayer. Drouillard was so aroused already that he was afraid he might ejaculate before she could lead him to wherever she was taking him. They went out and walked through smoky wind over packed snow and entered a smaller lodge, snug and warm with a bright fire burning in its fire ring, and there she plucked at the fastenings of his clothes and then threw her robe over a pile of bedding near the wall and lay down naked upon it, golden brown in the fireglow, and waited for him to undress.

He had never done this with a woman who knew none of the languages he spoke, and so he could not say anything about her beauty or his gratitude. And perhaps no language would be needed for that. But even in his eagerness, kneeling over her, he thought of York and the soldiers coming to the captains for venereal treatments, and before touching her he held his hand up in a question sign. She made a querulous frown, and he signed, *You sick below?* She answered so quickly her hands were a flutter. *No. Hurry. I want.* Then she reached for him and took him in.

He was quick as a sneeze, but she yelped and then sank back and sighed. He wanted a longer pleasure, but she hopped out of the bed, seeming marvelously happy, and signaled for him to get dressed. She led him back to the medicine lodge with its three effigies above it and took him in. The drum and rattle were still going and another young couple were importuning a scrawny, craggy-faced old man with snow-white hair hanging to his waist. They got him up and he went out with the young woman. People were smiling at Drouillard, and his young woman was beaming and nodding as she led him back to where he had been sitting. Her husband smiled and nodded and cooed to him, and pressed his cheek, then the couple went away behind the circle of elders as he was motioned to sit back down. He had hardly had time to reflect on that quick moment of pleasure before another fine-looking young husband brought him a pipe to smoke, then laid the trail of sticks across the floor again to him. Everybody was looking at him with great kindness and cheer, and very soon he realized that another handsome young naked wife was advancing upon him.

Snow was whirling in the dawn sky above the smokehole of the love lodge by the time he withdrew from the sweet, moist depths of the last wife. He rolled onto his back tingling and exhausted, ready to sleep for a day. But the woman's husband and other family members arrived with the daylight, all full of laughter and caresses for him, and began fixing him a breakfast of beans, corn, persimmons, and chokecherries to fortify him for his walk back to the fort. In sign language they thanked him for calling the buffalo for them. They fed him and smoked with him, and touched him so often and so softly that he had to hold back a sob because he had not been surrounded by love like this since he had lived with his mother and cousins at Cape Girardeau.

Captain Clark was putting together a map from several small maps when Drouillard came out of the snow into the fort. The captain put the sheets aside and laid out some scribble paper. "You look a bit puny," he said. "York can make some coffee, or a toddy. I'd like to make some notes about that buffalo-calling ceremony for our summary to the President. I presume you had one of their women and have the venereal now like everybody else."

"Four women, sir. I know how careful you like to be about number-counting."

"Four . . . *four*? They offered you four?" His jaw hung open.

"They offered me six, Cap'n. I didn't take on the two sick ones."

The captain had a pencil in his hand but seemed to have forgotten it. Finally he asked, "And how d'ye know that?"

"You hired me to talk to Indians, Cap'n. So that's what I did. I asked them."

13th of January Sunday 1805
a Cold Clear Day (great number of Indians move Down the River to hunt) those people Kill a number of Buffalow near their Villages and Save a great perpotion of the meat, their Custom of sharing meat in common leaves them more than half of their time without meat Their Corn & Beans &c they Keep as a reserve in Case of an attack from the Soues, which they are always in dread, and Sildom go far to hunt except in large parties Chaboneu informs that the Clerk of the Hudsons Bay Co. with the Me ne tar res (Hidatsas) has been Speaking Some fiew expressns. unfavourable towards us, and that it is Said the NW Co. intends building a fort at the Mene tar re's
                                        William Clark, Journals

Chapter 12

Hooves clopped on the river ice, and the waxed runners of the sleighs hissed and squealed. Willard had shod the three horses with cleated iron shoes that gave them protection against rough ice and good footing on smooth ice, and so the frozen river had become like a wide, level road. In places where broken ice had frozen up jagged, Drouillard rode the mare up onto shore to detour over land, where the snow lay as shallow as an inch and deep as two feet, depending on wind-drifting. The three soldiers rode on the two sleighs behind him, their talk and laughter muffled by the high collars and scarves bound over their lower faces to protect them from frostbite. They all wore fur hats and mittens, and blanket coats or rough-tailored skin coats with the hair side in. Their faces were muffled to invisibility, but he could hear them joking about how this was the way the Corps of Discovery should have come up: just wait till midwinter and come up on horse sleighs and maybe ice skates, so much easier than rowing and towing a barge. Drouillard himself wore a fur hat made from the skin of what had been his pet beaver until the voyageurs ate it, and he wore it pulled down to his eyelids, and his face-scarf pulled up almost to meet it. So he was seeing the whole vast, glaring white world through a mere slit, the only way to avoid going snow-blind on days like this. They had swiftly come down the river more than twenty miles since morning, but still had almost twice that far to go down to the meat caches, near the Heart

River. Down there, Clark's hunters had left several hundred pounds of boned elk, deer, and buffalo meat closed up tight in wooden pens, and now Drouillard and three soldiers were going down to get it before the wolves could.

Actually, only two of them were officially soldiers, Goodrich and Frazier. The other man was John Newman, the man who had been whipped and expelled for talking mutiny. He had been brought along as a laborer to help load the frozen meat on the sleighs, and push or pull when necessary. Forbidden by his sentence to carry a gun, he had been issued a broken musket and a bayonet, so as not to appear defenseless.

Drouillard knew where the two meat pens were because he had been in that hunting party, the chief hunter, as usual. That had been a nine-day ordeal: hunting and sleeping out in the most bitter cold, feet cold and beaten by rough ice, plunging after wounded game in knee-deep snow, butchering and boning meat before it could freeze solid. Captain Clark on the second day had broken through ice and gotten soaked to the hips. The hunting party of sixteen soldiers had killed forty deer, sixteen elk, and three buffalo bulls in that period, but many of the animals were so lean and meager from the winter that they were hardly fit for use. The party had hunted more than fifty miles down the river. It had nearly done in the sixteen men before they staggered back into the fort yesterday.

Drouillard had gone to sleep last night to an astonishing sound: a baby crying in the interpreters' room next door. Charbonneau's little Shoshone wife, after a long and excruciating labor, had given birth to a boy baby, her first child. Charbonneau had returned from the hunt to find himself the father of a two-day-old son. The delivery had been brought on after long labor by one of Jessaume's remedies: rattlesnake rattle crumbled to make a tea. Among the specimens Lewis had collected for the President was a rattle. Ten minutes after taking the tea, Bird Woman had given birth, with Jessaume's woman as midwife.

So Drouillard had gone to sleep to the sound of a crying baby, and had awakened to the sound of axes chopping ice. For nearly two weeks the soldiers had been trying to free the keelboat and pirogues from the grip of the frozen river. They had even tried heating water in the bilges to melt them free, but nothing was working.

This morning the pride-swollen Charbonneau had given Drouillard a look at the tiny baby while the soldiers were harnessing the horses, and he had remarked, "Eh! Little half-breed, just like me!"

And now he was thinking of that little half-breed baby as he led Frazier, Goodrich, and Newman down the frozen Missouri. Three inches of new snow had fallen last night and was blowing in fine streamer shapes across the old snow and the river ice, and the wind was cutting through his clothes, but even that bitter discomfort didn't keep him from daydreaming about that little half-breed, which sometimes he thought of as himself, long ago. If Charbonneau and his wife were actually going to come along with the captains as interpreters, as planned, then that meant this Corps of Western Discovery, as Captain Lewis now liked to call it, would have an infant member. It was getting crazier all the time. This spring they would be setting out into unknown country, two thousand miles across, surely much more dangerous than anything yet, with a suckling baby in the ranks. He shook his head, squinting into the snowglare, thinking, At least York will be happy we've got another "colored folk" with us! He was chuckling at that thought when he saw many figures come running out of a draw ahead, spreading out left and right, at least a hundred of them, high-stepping through the snow from every direction, beginning to yell and whoop.

They were Sioux warriors. Drouillard and his three men were being swiftly surrounded.

He yanked down his scarf to yell a warning to the men, but they were already yelling their warnings to him.

With the reckless courage of overwhelming numbers, the Sioux were rushing straight through the snow without regard for cover. Most of them had bows with arrows nocked, most wore shields on their left arms, some had lances, and a few carried muskets.

Drouillard, angry with himself for letting his fatigue carry him into daydreams, reined in the mare he was riding and pulled his rifle from its sling on the saddle horn. The soldiers were clambering off the two sleighs and reaching for their rifles, which lay nestled among ropes and tools on the sleighs. Newman already had his useless musket in one hand and was making it useful by attaching its bayonet.

The warriors were not shooting arrows or bullets, so Drouillard guessed that killing was not their foremost objective, although he knew very well they would start killing at any provocation. He scanned them as they swarmed down, trying to see who might be their leader. Keeping his rifle pointed skyward, he warned the three men, "Be ready, but don't shoot!"

Some warriors charged at the sleigh-horses and, with knives flashing, they cut away harness and collars, while the rest kept their weapons aimed at the soldiers. Swiftly they mounted the horses and galloped off up the riverbank through the snow. So it seemed their first purpose was robbery. A man whose bold carriage suggested that he might be their chieftain was striding toward Drouillard with a fierce expression, motioning for him to dismount. Drouillard reined the horse in a backstep. The chieftain lunged forward and grabbed the reins right under the horse's chin and tried to jerk them out of Drouillard's hand, but he kept a tight hold, and when the chieftain looked up, he found the muzzle of Drouillard's rifle pointed right between his eyes. He froze in the pose and appeared to be doing some deep thinking. Drouillard kept the rifle steady on that spot and slowly shook his head. Most of the warriors had stopped darting about. By the sleighs there was some grunting and commotion. He saw that a warrior had laid hands on Frazier's rifle to take it away from him but was no match for the soldier's work-hardened strength; he might as well have tried to pull an oak tree down by grasping one of its limbs. At that moment Newman swung his bayonet around and put the point at that Indian's throat. And Goodrich had his rifle cocked now and was slowly sweeping it back and forth at the several nearest warriors who looked ready to charge Frazier. For a moment the whole tableau was stock-still except for a few warriors who were edging around toward Goodrich's sleigh with the apparent intent of grabbing two skinning knives and a tomahawk that lay among the ropes, glinting temptingly in the sunlight.

Drouillard stared straight into the eyes of the chieftain who was still standing at the point of his rifle. He sensed as many as twenty or thirty arrows or muskets aimed at him right now. He remembered the day last fall when Captain Clark stood in the river's edge with his sword drawn and faced down the threat of three Sioux chiefs and a horde of warriors. This appeared to be just that kind of a moment. One shot by anyone on either side would precipitate a quick burst of killing, and the result would be a few Sioux dead and all the whitemen dead. The two sleigh horses were far away now; there would be no getting them back. One the captains had bought from the Mandans; the other had been borrowed from a clerk of the North West Company. The gray mare Drouillard sat on now was borrowed from the Mandans and had an unweaned colt back at the fort. He didn't intend to let these Sioux take her out from under him while he was alive.

The chieftain still had not thought out what to do, apparently; he stood holding the rein. Drouillard intensified his stare, that look no one could endure. Holding his rifle by the trigger hand only, he used his left hand to point at the chieftain's grip on the other end of the rein; then he turned his pointing hand palm up, hoping the man would understand it was a one-handed version of the sign for *Separate* or *Turn loose*. This was the moment. If he couldn't back this man down, he would have to shoot him and it all would be over. He presumed that Frazier and the other warrior were still deadlocked on Frazier's rifle but wouldn't flick his stare away from the chieftain's eyes to see.

"Mr. Drouillard," Newman's voice came quietly, "what do we do? They just took the skinning knives and tomahawk."

"If you still got that man on your spike, keep him there. Never mind the knives."

"Still got 'im."

"Good. I mean to make these sons o' bitches back off."

"God help us, man."

"I'm counting on that," Drouillard said, and he was; he had been praying fervently even while glaring and aiming at the chieftain. But that one still had not released the rein. His breath froze in puffs of frost at every exhalation, and Drouillard could see in his eyes that he wanted desperately to look around at the situation but was afraid to look away. Drouillard just barely widened his eyelids, intensifying his stare to give the impression he was about to act, and leaned an inch forward as if bracing his gun shoulder for a recoil. That brought his rifle muzzle an inch closer to the chieftain's eyes, and the little puffs of breath stopped coming out. Obviously the man believed now that he was on the edge of death and didn't want to be there.

The chieftain released the rein and stood still, sneering. Drouillard backed the mare off one step and kept the rifle on the man's eyes. None of the hundred warriors, at least none in the edges of his vision, was moving, though he heard several murmuring to each other. He listened for the squeak of any footsteps in the dry snow anywhere behind him, and heard none.

The chieftain, without looking away, said something in a quick, loud voice. It was a good, rich voice, and Drouillard had a strange notion that he could have liked this tall, narrow-faced Sioux chieftain if they had met under different circumstances; the man was certainly more careful than cowardly. When he spoke, some of the warriors began moving back a little way. Drouillard glanced over just in time to see Frazier jerk his rifle free from the grasp of that warrior, who still remained as if pinned in the air by Newman's bayonet.

Drouillard said, "Good, Mr. Newman. Draw off, now," and Newman did so. "Now, boys, we'll just ease out of here and head back for the fort. You get out of arrow range and I'll catch up directly."

"This one whoreson savage got my good tomahawk and I want it back," Goodrich said.

"Damn you," Drouillard warned, "don't bust this all up over a tomahawk—" But Goodrich had already grabbed for it, and the warrior kept his grip, and voices were rising all around. It was about to start all over. Drouillard looked down his sights at the

chieftain, narrowed his lips and motioned toward Goodrich and
the warrior with a quick tilt of his head. The chieftain said something in three sharp syllables and the warrior released the tomahawk. Drouillard nodded to the chieftain. Newman, Goodrich,
and Frazier began edging toward the river, their guns still at
ready, and none of the warriors got in their way. He would let
them get out of bow shot, maybe even musket range, then he
would follow them, but in the meantime he was going to keep his
rifle on the chieftain standing before him. He wanted to talk to
this leader in sign and ask him to have the horses brought back,
but knew the man would not demean himself that much in the
eyes of his warriors. The horses were a lost cause. Drouillard
knew if he got out of here alive with his three men, that would be
answer enough to his prayers.

As the soldiers made their way across the glaring snowscape,
he could feel his ears, face, hands, and feet freezing into numb-
ness, and he had all he could do to keep from shuddering violently in the saddle. He presumed that all these Sioux men were
equally miserable, surely as eager as he was to quit standing im-
mobile in the bitter cold. He looked at the chieftain and thought
of the few Sioux words he had learned from Cruzatte. He
nodded to the chieftain and said, *"O wash tay."* This is good. It
was easy to remember because it was like *weh sah* in his own
people's language. The chieftain perhaps didn't think it was that
good; he didn't respond. Or maybe, Drouillard thought, in his
cold-benumbed mind he had remembered the wrong words.

His three men were now about forty paces away. He saw that a
few of the warriors had lowered their weapons and now hugged
them to their chests to put their freezing hands under their
armpits. He began backing the mare toward the river, following
the other three, squinting at the snowglare. If any of the warriors
wanted to make their glory by shooting him, this would be their
last chance.

But they all stood still. A hundred or more Sioux warriors
stood watching the whitemen get away. He hoped with all his
heart that he would not have to shoot, because he couldn't feel
the trigger, and in the glare his eyes were going bad.

When he caught up with his men, he dismounted and walked with them to get his circulation going. They kept looking back but no one was following. The Sioux might yet, of course. They might follow in the dark. Drouillard estimated that it would be midnight when they got back to the fort, even later if they stopped to hunt and build a fire for a supper, which they would need to do. He hoped this snow-blindness would not make them totally blind by night. The crisis seemed to be over, but the ordeal had several hours to go. They might not even make it back. They just crunched on through the dry snow on the river ice, wrapped in thought, no one talking, until Goodrich said, "Cold out here. But not as cold as I expected t' be by now!"

"Tell ye what," Frazier said after a while. "I mean to tell the cap'ns that this here Newman is a soldier and by God he should be put back on!"

"Amen!" said Goodrich.

"Thankee, boys," Newman said in a voice almost strangled by emotion. Then he said, "Damn me, but those redskins really had us outnumbered, didn't they, though!"

Drouillard couldn't resist. Grinning, he said, "What d'you mean 'us,' white boy?"

February 16, 1805

He was almost too sore to sit up, but Captain Clark had him bent over a small tub, Newman on the other side, with their heads covered with a draped cloth. Now and then York put a heated stone in the tub and threw snow on it to make steam. Drouillard and Newman blinked and blinked their burning eyes in the steam. Captain Clark told them it would cure their snow-blindness. They talked with the captain through their drape. Drouillard told him how bravely Newman had stood up in the crisis with just a bayonet and recommended that he be returned to duty. Clark said he would bring it up with Captain Lewis when he returned. Captain Clark was supposed to be working on maps and lists, but he kept getting up and pacing, pacing until his own feet, punished by the long hunt, hurt too much to walk on. He was plainly very worried.

In a fit of temper, Captain Lewis had set out with twenty-four soldiers and a few half-hearted Mandans to go chasing those hundred Sioux warriors, with the thermometer at sixteen degrees below zero. This could be a disaster, the end of the whole enterprise and the deaths of many good men if it went wrong. Now and then Drouillard could hear Bird Woman's baby squall briefly in the next room, and the woman talking and chortling to him. Drouillard prayed that Lewis wouldn't catch up with the Sioux.

By evening his vision was almost normal and the pain gone, and he was resting with his feet in a tub of lukewarm water, when two of the Mandan warriors from Captain Lewis's war party came into the fort, supporting Private Tom Howard, whose feet were so frostbitten he had been unable to go on. As Clark began to work on him, Howard told him that Captain Lewis had decided the Sioux party was so far ahead it couldn't be overtaken. Therefore, the twenty-four soldiers were going to go on down and get the meat Captain Clark's hunters had left, and then spend a day or two hunting. Clark was very relieved, for two reasons: there would be no battle, and the meat supply in the fort was entirely exhausted.

A few days later it was clear that Private Howard's feet were recovering and no toes would have to be taken off. Drouillard's eyes and feet were back to normal. Charles McKenzie, the North West Company clerk whose gelding the Sioux had stolen, visited the fort for a couple of days, and was decent and forgiving when he heard about the incident. The subchief of Mittuta-Hanka Town, whose name was Little Raven, visited the fort. He told Captain Clark that one of the old men the captains had met there had died, at the age of 120 winters, after requesting that his body be set on a stone facing south down the river toward the hole in the ground from which all the Mandans had come.

While Captain Clark was writing this story down, Drouillard saw anguish in the face of Little Raven. He remembered the deep sadness that used to pervade the Shawnee settlements when any of the ancient elders passed away, taking with them the powerful wisdom of great age. He thought of the young women in the buffalo-calling ceremony, who had hoped to pass on some of that great power of age, and he understood the ceremony better, and felt a deep wave of humility at having been honored. In the next room he heard the nine-day-old baby trying out its voice. Captain Clark put down his pencil, and said, "Born about 1684 then. To think I met a man who lived in the seventeenth century!" This captain really loved number counting.

21st February Thursday 1805
Capt Lewis returned with 2 Slays loaded with meat, after finding that he could not overtake the Souis war party. (who had on their way distroyed all the meat at one Deposit which I had made) deturmined to proceed on to the lower Deposit which he found had not been observed by Soux he hunted two days Killed 36 Deer & 14 Elk, Several of them So meager that they were unfit for use. the meet which he killed and that in the lower Deposit amounting to about 3000 wt was brought up on two Slays, one Drawn by 16 men had about 2400 wt on it.
                                        William Clark, Journals

Drouillard stood in melting snow on high ground near Mittuta-Hanka Town, inside a circle of nearly a hundred human skulls, whose eyeholes all faced inward and seemed to be looking at him. He could hear the ancient spirit songs, not through his ears but faint inside his head, as he had heard them that cold, drizzly night more than a year ago, up on the great mound beside the Mississippi. What he was hearing through his ears was the far-away garbled talk of the geese, who were at last returning to the north. North Grandfather Spirit was retreating toward his home, drawing after him the high-flying fowl and the cold that froze everything. The captains and their soldiers were joyous at the end of a winter they had feared would kill them before it ended, a winter that had frozen their feet and faces and made them retreat into their smoky little rooms in the fort, or into the warm beds of the Mandan and Hidatsa women. Several of the soldiers were in love with the same girls, and almost every man was now taking the mercuric calomel for the sickness in their private parts. Drouillard had not contracted the disease, and to his knowledge the captains had not either, although he believed that Captain Clark had been in bed with someone during his visits up at the Hidatsa town of Black Moccasin.

These skull circles were the cemetery of the Mandan town. Off to the east stood several tall scaffolds made of poles, holding up the bodies of those more recently dead. The scaffolds kept the bodies out of the reach of wolves, and the bodies were encased in tightly sewn buffalo and elk hides to discourage vultures and ravens. There they remained until nothing was left but bones and dry skin, when their families would take them down and bury the bones, and leave the skull on the ground in this circle, where it could be visited, talked to, cried to, prayed over, and smoked to with sage and tobacco. Some of these skulls were very old and sun-bleached white, some were still nose-deep in snow. Around some the snow had melted down and the teeth and chins were visible. Jessaume had told him of these things. And on one mild day not long ago, Drouillard had passed close enough to this cemetery to see a few people sitting before skulls, and to hear them talking and singing and crying to them, a sound much like the spirit voices he heard now.

On this day, most of Mittuta-Hanka's people were across the river near the fort, watching the soldiers' great efforts to pull the two boats and the ship up out of the ice. They had started almost a month ago to free the vessels but the weather had defeated them over and over. Every day the captains more urgently feared that the spring breakup of the winter ice might crush or wrench the hulls. Finally now, with their iron-blade pikes, the soldiers had freed them, and made a windlass to pull the ice-caked vessels ashore. From here in the Mandan cemetery Drouillard could see the keelboat, almost as long as Fort Mandan itself, imperceptibly moving up the far riverbank with the soldiers laboring around it through a crowd of Mandan onlookers, the figures tiny at a mile distant. Farther up the river, out of sight beyond Black

Cat's village, Sergeant Gass had been scouting for cottonwood trees big enough and straight enough to make as many as six dugout canoes for the river voyage on west to the Shining Mountains. The keelboat, too broad and deep-draughted to go much farther up, would instead be loaded with the tons of plant and animal and mineral specimens, the notes and records the captains had been writing, and with skins of beaver trapped on the way up. It would sail home under the command of Corporal Warfington, with a small crew of soldiers whose enlistments had run out, and with most of the voyageurs. Also with them would be the two disgraced men, Reed the deserter and Newman the mutineer. The pleas of Drouillard and several soldiers on behalf of Newman had failed. Captain Lewis refused to pardon and reenlist him. The destination of Warfington's cargo—including the prairie dog still alive in its cage—was President Jefferson's office. Warfington's little crew expected to have to fight its way past the Sioux on the way back through their country. They had vowed not to be stopped.

Only the weather would dictate when the rest of the corps would leave its Mandan and Hidatsa neighbors and head west, but the stirring to move was evident everywhere. Charcoal mounds seethed, making forge fuel. Hammers were steadily ringing a mile away, *clink, clink, clink,* as blacksmiths made arrow points and war axes and repaired guns for the Indians, in exchange for bags and pots of corn. Captain Clark spent hours with interpreters and Indians, getting descriptions of the lands and the rivers ahead. Sometimes they would talk and he would draw. Sometimes they would draw river courses in the dirt and make sand heaps to show where mountains were, and he would sketch his maps from those. The Hidatsas were his best source for those western distances, because they hunted buffalo as far as the Shining Mountains, and sometimes even entered the mountains to steal horses and captives from the Shoshones. They told of a great river that would enter the Missouri from the southwest, which was known by French traders as the Roche Jaune, or Yellow Stone, which came from lands yet unhunted and full of fur-bearing animals. They told of other landmark rivers coming in from both sides, describing the distances between in terms of the numbers of sleeps, and said that at a distance which he interpreted to be perhaps four hundred miles there was a great Falling Water place, just this side of the mountains, where they would have to carry their canoes around. A hundred and fifty miles above the falls the Missouri would divide into three branches; that was the place where the Hidatsas had captured the Bird Woman four years ago. The branch coming in from the west would lead them up to the ridge of mountains that divided the east-flowing waters from those that flowed west. And from there it would be all downstream, the captains said, to the Sunset Ocean, which they called the Pacific. Drouillard had heard them talking about the route ahead so often that he could have repeated it all himself. He hoped it would be that simple. These captains, he knew by now, heard best what they wanted to hear.

One thing Drouillard heard that meant much to him was that there were many nations of Indians between the mountains and the sea who had never seen whitemen. Except for the Bird Woman's memory of her Shoshone tongue from childhood, there would be no knowledge of any of those many languages out there, and talking with those nations would have to be by hand-signing. Sometimes he would look at Bird Woman, that girl with her half-breed baby, and he would think: You and I, the Indians among all these whitemen, are going to be important.

26th of February Thursday 1805
Mr. Gravelines two frenchmen & two Inds arrive from the Ricara Nation informing us of the peaceable dispositions of that nation towards the Mandans & Me ne ta res & their avowed intentions of pursueing our Councils & advice. Mr. Gravilin informs that the Tetons, with the Yanktons of the North intend to come to war in a Short time against the nations in this quarter, & will Kill everry white man they See—

*   Mr. Gravilin further informs that the Party which Robed us of the 2 horses lately were all Sieoux 100 in number, they Called at the Ricaras on their return, the Ricares being dis-*

*pleased at their Conduct would not give them any thing to
eate, that being the greatest insult they could peaceably offer
them, and upbraded them.*

William Clark, Journals

Now in charge of the canoe-making, Sergeant Gass was on
another rampage against cottonwood. He raged to Captain
Clark: "It'll have to be caulked all over where it's wind-riven,
like here, see, and here. And that crack there'll want t' open up
when she's in the water and has weight amidships. I'll need tin
and tacks to cover cracks like that there son of a bitch. And see
how that grain runs from here 'round here? Any heavy-footed
bastard stomps down a leetle hard there, the whole goddamn
bilge'll bust!" He pointed in disgust at a half-finished dugout
canoe.

The captain burst out laughing. "Lordy, Sarge! I thought all
the smoke up here was from your wood fires, but maybe most of
it's from your language!"

Sergeant Gass's axmen had felled four of the thickest cottonwoods and were hollowing them out with fire, ax, and adze. The
muddy ground was covered with trampled, fibrous cottonwood
bark, dirty wood chips, charred wood, and tobacco spit. The cottonwood was soft, Gass's tools were sharp, the hewing was easy;
the burning was only to temper and dry the sappy wood.

Despite Gass's dissatisfaction, the canoes were, to Drouillard's eyes, beautiful things. Throughout his youth and adult-
hood he had used dugout canoes, had watched Indian men make
them, had admired that evolution of the Great Spirit's creation, a
tree, into man's creation, a graceful vessel for crossing water.

For all his irreverence, Gass was producing four beautiful canoes in the time Indians could have produced one. It was the
sharp steel tools that made canoe-making so efficient.

While Clark inspected the canoes, Drouillard hefted his long
rifle in his left hand and examined its familiar form with eyes
and fingers. This fine weapon was a whiteman creation, made
with materials and skills his own people had never had before
whitemen came. The Indians had always had flint and wood to

make fire and bows and arrows, but the whitemen had brought the steel and the mysterious knowledge of gunpowder, a kind of fuel, so that now he, an Indian, could be a more efficient hunter than Indians without rifles. His whiteman rifle was like Gass's steel tools. These were the new things of steel coming into an old land of flint, and everything would change.

"I've found two more big trees up on that island," the captain was saying to the sergeant. "Even after what goes home by the keelboat, we'll need six canoes and the pirogues to carry what we need. That means two more dugouts. Now I've got to go back to the fort and meet with Chief One Eye. He's finally consented to go down and grace us with his presence. Drouillard will take you up and point out the two trees."

"Yes, sir," the sergeant said. "We'll need more provisions to work here longer."

"Yes, you will. Drouillard'll get you fresh meat right away. Anything else? Candles? Flour?"

"If Shields could spare a sharpening file, ours is about worn-out."

"All right. I'll have one sent up. Bring the canoes down to the fort as soon as they're ready. God and weather willing, we'll be heading west before much longer!"

Every Indian man or woman Drouillard looked at was crying, and he had to clench his teeth to keep from sobbing himself. The fort stood abandoned, with its gate open and no flag on its flagpole, the first day in five months that there had been no flag on the pole, the first day in all that time there was no chimney smoke. Everything that could be moved had been taken out of the fort to be loaded on the keelboat or in the pirogues and canoes.

The snow had melted off the ground, and tiny flowers and shoots of green grass showed on the trampled slope, but the deserted fort looked more desolate in springtime than it ever had when roofed and banked in blowing snow. There was no ice on the river for the people to walk over to the fort. So the Mandan people who were here, watching the men load up the boats, had come over in their little round leather tub boats, and there were only a few dozen of them. Most of the population of Mittuta-Hanka were still on the other shore of the Missouri, and their voices were a piteous drone of weeping and farewells. The whole soldier town they had loved and cohabited with through the winter was leaving them. It was as if the Mandans had expected them to stay.

A young man and woman were coming toward Drouillard, making their way among soldiers who carried bundles and knapsacks down to the canoes. He recognized them after a moment of confusion. This was the last of the young wives who had taken him to bed the night of the buffalo-calling ceremony, and her husband who had given her to him. Their faces were terribly earnest, their eyes shining.

He stopped where he was and set his bedroll on the ground, and stood ready for he knew not what.

The man signed a greeting, *I see you.* Drouillard replied likewise.

The couple stood close in front of him, and the expressions on their faces were of the greatest tenderness. With his fist and then open palms the husband signed that his heart was too heavy to hold up. *You go. Heart is heavy.* The woman stood, not signing, but nodding in affirmation. Drouillard signed that he too was sad to go.

The man made the spiral before his brow that meant medicine, then pointed from Drouillard to the woman and to himself. He swooped his hands in the sign for *Many*, then with his forefingers crooked by his temples he said *buffalo*.

Drouillard smiled and nodded. It was true that just a few days after the buffalo-calling, a herd had come near the town and the hunters had killed many. With his right fist the man said, *I kill,* then held up his little finger, then the one next to it, then the middle one. *Three.* Then with both open hands he made the sign *Thank you.*

The young wife, whose beauty and ardor he had remembered in reveries many nights since, had nothing to say here. The hunting power had been a gift from him to this young man, and she had been only the passage for it. Still, her husband had brought her here for the thanking and the farewell.

Drouillard signed *My heart* and then *Sunrise: I am glad*. The man made two soft syllables, then stepped up and put his arms around him, pressed their cheeks together, and stepped back. The wife still stood back. It would not do for her to embrace him here.

But she did have something to say; she made the little finger-flick from her mouth. *I*, she signed. Then, frowning with thought, obviously not a practiced sign talker, she hesitated before making the sign *work*, then, *baby*. And with a shy smile, she looked down and touched her belly.

So she was in the work of making a baby. Her husband stood there beaming. He made the sign, *Question*. Then, *Medicine*. Then he pointed to himself and finally to Drouillard. And he laughed.

Drouillard nodded, then stooped and picked up his bedroll. He looked at their handsome faces. They were smiling at him with that same sweetness, but tears were standing in their eyes. He turned away, so as not to have to see those expressions anymore, and went down to the canoe, thinking, I don't know either, Brother. But whether it's yours or mine it seems to make you happy!

He slapped his neck. First mosquito of the season. Oh damn.

He watched the men carrying bundle after bundle of Mandan corn down to the boats, and saw the Mandan people going around trying to express themselves to the soldiers, and he wished the captains had tried somehow to thank these people for keeping their men alive and in good spirits through the cruelest of winters. And he hoped that somewhere in their long writings they had told their President that.

Fort Mandan April 7th 1805
Having on this day at 4 P.M. completed every arrangement necessary for our departure, we dismissed the barge and crew with orders to return without loss of time to S. Louis, We gave Richard Warfington, a discharged Corpl., the charge of the

Barge and crew, and confided to his care likewise our dispatches to the government, letters to our private friends, and a number of articles to the President of the United States . . .

At the same moment that the Barge departed from Fort Mandan, we embarked with our party and proceeded up the river . . . Our party now consisted of the following Individuals, Sergts. John Ordway, Nathaniel Prior, & Patric Gass; Privates, William Bratton, John Colter, Reubin and Joseph Fields, John Shields, George Gibson, George Shannon, John Potts, John Collins, Joseph Whitehouse, Richard Windsor, Alexander Willard, Hugh Hall, Silas Goodrich, Robert Frazier, Peter Crouzatt, John Baptiest la Page, Francis Labiech, Hue McNeal, William Werner, Thomas P. Howard, Peter Wiser, and John B. Thompson. Interpreters, George Drewyer and Tauasant Charbono also a Black man by the name of York, servant to Capt. Clark, an Indian Woman wife to Charbono with a young child . . . Our vessels consisted of six small canoes, and two large perogues. This little fleet altho' not quite so rispectable as those of Columbus or Capt. Cook were still viewed by us with as much pleasure as those deservedly famed adventurers ever beheld theirs; these little vessells contained every article by which we were to expect to subsist or defend ourselves . . . entertaing as I do, the most confident hope of succeading in a voyage which had formed a darling project of mine for the last ten years, I could but esteem this moment of my departure as among the most happy of my life.

Meriwether Lewis, Journals

Chapter 13

Nineteen days above Fort Mandan the expedition reached the juncture of the Missouri and the Yellow Stone, an unexpected garden of beauty and plenty. Here lay rich bottomlands five miles wide between steep, pale rock bluffs, grown up in more timber than they had seen for months: cottonwood, ash, and elm. And on a vast second bottom a few feet above the floodplain grew a profusion of gooseberry, chokecherry, currant, and honeysuckle bushes, mixed with open glades. They saw a pea vine sort of plant already in full yellow blossom, and expanses of bright green new grass. Here at last was relief from the violent, cold winds that had slowed their progress and some days kept them from launching the boats at all, winds so full of dust and fine sand that everybody had eaten and breathed it for days on end, sand that scoured and gritted up their eyes, already tortured by the glare of afternoon sun on water. This was a paradise of refreshing greenery and moisture and shade and shelter. And of course the most plentiful life swarming in this paradise was the mosquito.

Drouillard had never known that so much game could be found in one place. Immense herds of elk, buffalo, and pronghorns were everywhere, the timber was full of deer, and lately a kind of cliff-dwelling ram had been seen nimbly skipping from crag to crag on the steep bluffs. Buffalo in the bottomlands were so unaccustomed to man that they were as tame as cattle. One curious calf had attached itself to Joe Field and followed him four miles, right into the camp. Grown elk and antelope would come close and follow the men to see what they were. Grouse, rabbits, and porcupines were numerous, and in the watercourses the beaver had created dense populations. The captains were excitedly evaluating this place as the site of a fur-trading post and fort.

Most of the hoofed animals were still too lean and poor from the hard winter to be good eating, but some buffalo cows provided good marrow bones, and a buffalo calf was like fine veal. Beaver tail also provided some fat the men craved after their exertions in cold wind and river spray. Captain Lewis's dog had chased a wild goat into the river, drowned it, and swum back to shore with it.

The day before, Captain Lewis, Sergeant Ordway, Joe Field, and Drouillard had walked ahead to explore the juncture of the two rivers, and today when Captain Clark arrived with the boats and canoes, a camp was set up on a wooded point just below the Yellow Stone's mouth. A delicious, fat supper was cooked, whiskey rations were issued, and greenwood was thrown on the fires to make enough smoke to drive off some of the mosquitoes. Then the musical instruments were unwrapped, and by dusk the fiddle was pacing the dancers around the fire.

Drouillard helped York and Bird Woman erect a tepee frame and pull its skin cover around it. While this was being done, Captain Clark held the baby's cradleboard and made faces and lip sounds to entertain the infant, whose name was Jean Baptiste Charbonneau. Bird Woman's husband cavorted around the fire with the soldiers, his yellow teeth bared in a grin that looked like a grimace through his black whiskers. He grew winded quickly, being twice the age of most of the men, but tried hard and cheerfully to compensate for the bad impression he had made on the captains a few weeks ago. He had threatened then to quit his interpreting job if he had to stand guard or serve in work details and had demanded the right to drop out of the voyage any time he might grow discontented with his treatment. So the captains had simply dismissed him, hoping he would come crawling back, and he had done so a few days later. The captains secretly had been very relieved to see him recant, because they knew they would need his wife to interpret with her Shoshone people in the mountains.

Drouillard himself was perhaps even more delighted than the captains that Charbonneau had repented and stayed on. Though it had at first seemed foolish to bring a woman and baby on such a grueling journey, Drouillard had been changing that opinion little by little. The presence of this little family was growing to be strangely comforting to him, for various reasons, some of which he hadn't thought out yet but simply felt in his heart. The presence of a woman and child made this seem less like an army, more like a tribe. The soldiers, while not inclined to care much for Indians, had some regard for the presence of a married woman, and if Bird Woman's presence had done nothing else, it had muted their farting contests. And the sight of this slight, dignified girl with a baby at her breast seemed sometimes to make them wistful. He had seen the soldiers watching her by firelight with something deeper in their eyes than they used to have. Perhaps, as they now were heading farther and farther from their homes, this little nursing mother made them think more of their own sisters and mothers thousands of miles behind. Or for some of them, surely, she was a reminder of recent tender pleasures they had enjoyed in their long winter among the Mandan girls and their families. The baby Jean Baptiste was also an object of their gentler curiosity; there was hardly a man, even the most cocky and swaggering, who had not at least once enjoyed the small triumph of teasing a coo and a smile out of the little half-breed.

Half-breed, Drouillard thought, watching Captain Clark hand the cradleboard to the Bird Woman. One like me. He remembered that, just like Charbonneau, his father had been a French-Canadian interpreter for English-speaking white soldiers, with a petite Indian wife and a half-breed baby. Maybe that was a part of what he felt. Maybe this was how his family had looked among soldiers thirty years ago, back at that distant place called Detroit. His mother a Shawnee girl, this one a Shoshone girl.

Shawnee. Shoshone. Shoshawnee. He played with the words and brushed mosquitoes away from his face.

There were direct and practical reasons for appreciating this Shoshone girl too. She was an excellent forager. Wandering the riverbanks with her baby on her back and a pointed digging stick in one hand, she would come back to camp with tubers, roots, and sprouts that eased the monotony of the meat and meal diet.

So he watched this little family in the firelight with a deep and thoughtful pleasure. He doubted that Charbonneau was as educated or intelligent as his father Pierre Drouillard had been. On the other hand, Charbonneau likely had never been and never would be the sot that Pierre Drouillard had become. Maybe not. Though he was certainly gay and glassy-eyed with the dram he'd had this evening.

Drouillard was seated on a crate that he had never seen opened, though he had seen it in the keelboat's cargo, and now it was dutifully loaded and unloaded as the pirogues and canoes made their way up the river. It looked like a gun crate, with rope handles, and having helped lift it a few times, he knew it was one of the heaviest parts of their cargo. It was said to be a set of connecting iron bars that could be assembled to make the frame for a cargo boat. Captain Lewis intended to have it assembled at some point along the way and covered with skins, if there should be someplace where boats were needed and no timber to make them, as perhaps on the rivers beyond the Shining Mountains. It was in any case a tremendous burden for the soldiers who had to bring everything along up these rivers. Like many of the things Captain Lewis had brought, it had intelligent planning behind it but seemed more trouble than it was worth. Likewise the immensely heavy gunpowder canisters. They were made of lead, with screw-in lids that were sealed with wax to make them waterproof. When emptied, the canisters could be cut apart and melted down to make bullets. Apparently these were inventions that Captain Lewis and President Jefferson had dreamed up during the long years they had spent planning this adventure.

Drouillard sat on the crate watching the dancing, and listened to the campfire conversations. Potts was lamenting that the voyageur Rivet had left the party for St. Louis because "I'm sure there's many an Indian ahead who's never seen a man dance up-side down."

"Well, then!" exclaimed John Colter. "When that time comes, I'll dance on my hands for 'em!"

"Hah!" cried Potts. "You can hardly dance on your feet, Colter, let alone your hands!" Drouillard couldn't see Potts from where he sat, but recognized his voice and Dutchy accent. He re-membered a night more than a year ago when, coming up from Tennessee, he had lain by the campfire talking with Potts about dreams. He had been with these whitemen so long that he could recognize their voices in the dark.

"So y' say!" Colter cried. "Watch me!" He leaped into the fire-light, bent down and put his palms on the ground, kicked his feet skyward, went on over and landed with a thump on his back with his feet in Sergeant Pryor's lap. "Well, I need a little practice."

Among the soldiers for some days there had been much speculation about the white bears, or grizzlies, about which the Indians had given such dire warnings. "The Hidatsas," Captain Clark said, "told me that they actually put on paint and go through the war prayers before they hunt these bear, just as if they were going to war against men."

Captain Lewis waved a hand as if to dismiss the whole notion. "With bow and arrow, and those worthless muskets the British sell 'em, it well might be a frightful scrap. But with these rifles, and American riflemen, why, this bear will prove to be just an-other animal. Let's ask our bear hunter. Drouillard, are you fearful of the white bear?"

Several people were looking and listening for his answer. He thought for a minute, and then, having had his dram of whiskey, he replied, "Well, Cap'n, I guess I'd greet a white bear the way I'd greet a white man: with good manners and some suspicion."

There were still a few men with energy left to sing after the dancers had dropped with fatigue. Hugh McNeal and Tom Howard, accompanied only by a tambourine, were singing, one bass and one falsetto, with many elisions and slurs:

"I married a wife,
 Oh then, oh then,
 I married a wi-ife, oh then,
 I married a wife, the plague of my life,
 Now I long to be single again!
 Again and again, and again and again,
   again, again and again,
 I married a wi-ife, the plague of my life,
 Now I long to be single again!"

As their song went on, interrupted by disputes over what came next, whether the wife took fever and died in the same stanza, or waited to die in the next stanza, whether the husband "laughed and he cried" or "laughed *till* he cried," Drouillard got up and slipped out of the firelight to make water. He noted with gratitude that he had no discomfort from it, apparently having avoided the cock pox that almost every other man had caught. He moved in the darkness down toward the Yellow Stone's bank and stood watching the sentry who was guarding the boats. From ten paces away he could smell the man's dense odor: woolen clothes bearing countless days' dried sweat, cock dribbles, and shirttail smirch, and his breath reeking of tobacco quid. The sentry now and then tried to hum the tune that came so haltingly from the glowing camp off through the cottonwoods, and Drouillard would hear him spit. The breeze was busy with other odors. He could smell the latrine close by; he could smell the putrescence of old carrion, here in this rich valley where elk and buffalo carcasses lay so abundant that the wolves and buzzards and ravens couldn't pick them all clean, and left them for the flies and beetles to finish; he could smell buffalo dung and deer scat, and the rank boundary piddlings of wolf urine; he could smell fishy river-muck and beaver gland, campfire smoke and tobacco smoke, and, when the breeze shifted, that sentry again. But what he was trying to pick out was bear.

He had detected what he thought was a slight whiff of bear earlier today, while coming down the Yellow Stone's bank.

"My wife took a fever, oh then, oh then,
My wife took a fever, oh then,
My wife took a fever, I hope it won't leave 'er,
For I long to be single again . . ."

He wondered again whether the so-called white bears, or yellow bears, could really be so different in spirit from the bears he knew back home.

These days the captains themselves were doing much of the hunting. They took turns walking on shore as the pirogues and canoes came along, and both were spoiling for a fight with the bears. So their invasion of bear country would be hostile from the beginning. The bears would spread the word ahead: whitemen are enemies, not brothers.

Or, he thought, maybe the bear will smell these soldiers coming and say, Those must be bad! He and the Bird Woman were the only two members of this party who bothered about bathing their bodies or rinsing their clothes every day. She went to the water first thing every morning if possible, as he did, no matter how cold the water was. Her husband Charbonneau, like several soldiers of the corps, could not swim and thus was afraid to wade in and bathe, but she kept herself and her baby clean.

"My wife she die-ied, oh then, oh then,
My wife she die-ied. Ooooooh, then,
My wife she died, and I laughed till I cried,
For I finally was single again!"

In his years as a trader, Charbonneau had probably spread the pox, or at least gonorrhea, in many a village, and Bird Woman likely had it from him. And as she had been traded among several Hidatsa captors before Charbonneau got her, she might have been sick with it even before Charbonneau bought her, and the other Shoshone girl, from the Hidatsas.

It was by no means a love story. Yet she seemed a dutiful wife to him, and they occupied their own little circle of existence, with their baby at its center.

McNeal and Howard argued a little in the distance, and soldiers laughed, and then the song went on:

> *"I went to her graveside, oh then, oh then,*
> *I went to her graveside, oh then,*
> *By her graveside, a fair maiden I spied,*
> *And I longed to be married again . . ."*

When Charbonneau and his wife first visited Fort Mandan last fall, some flinching, cringing manner about her had made Drouillard suspect that he was brutal to her, but he had seen no sign of it since. Her timidity might have lingered from her girlhood ordeal among her Hidatsa captors. It was not a love story, it was a slave story.

> *"So I married another, oh then, oh then.*
> *I married another, oh then,*
> *I married another, she was worse than the other!*
> *Now I long to be single again!*
> *Again and again, and again and again . . ."*

The music was different now that the voyageurs were gone. Drouillard had liked their music. Fortunately, Cruzatte was still along with his fiddle, and Labiche now and then sang in French.

It was strange to him, how he was about this body of people. He was still the hunter, the Indian, independent from them. But in their minds he had become theirs. He knew they took pride in his prowess. And the truth was that he found himself concerned about them all the time. Keeping them fed fresh meat was his job, and at first that had been all of his concern. Now he was bemused to find himself worried about anything that might happen to them, be it sickness, drowning, or stirring up bears.

He shook his head, silently laughed at himself, and went back toward the firelight.

May 14, 1805

Drouillard was at the tiller of the white pirogue with a good east wind from astern, steering close to the south bank with the sail shading him from the afternoon sun ahead.

The captains had deemed him a "natural sailor," as they put it, and so now he seemed to spend more time crewing the captains' boat with Cruzatte than hunting. This boat carried all the medicine, sky instruments, books, journals, notes, and specimens— everything used in their work for the President. It also carried the people who couldn't swim, since it was the most stable vessel.

As a rule, one captain or the other stayed with this boat, which led their little fleet, but neither was aboard now. Cruzatte and Labiche were forward near the mast, tending the braces of the square sail. Three soldiers loafed and gambled amidships, and Charbonneau and his family were nestled amidst the cargo nearly at Drouillard's feet. Bird Woman had the baby out of his cradleboard and was repacking it with clean filler, which she made by pounding the inner bark of cottonwood until it was fluffy.

He heard on the wind four gunshots almost at once, then another, some frantic yelling, then another shot and more yelling.

Indian attack or bear attack? He was sure it was another bear incident. Astern he saw the red pirogue with sail up coming along behind, but only four of the six canoes following. Then he saw that a little way back, the other two canoes were on the bank, no men in them. Above on the bluff a huge yellow bear was chasing soldiers all over the place. Six shots. All the men had emptied their rifles and now the bear was doubtless wounded and in a fury. There had been several bear sightings since the camp at the Yellow Stone last month, and as he had feared, in each case the men—including Captain Lewis—had attacked the bears instead of just observing them.

Neither captain was anywhere near this bear fight. Both had gone ashore on the north bank an hour ago to stalk a buffalo herd. Everybody on board the white pirogue was gazing back at the distant melee in helpless dismay. Two of the canoes were turning, going to help. Drouillard saw that it was too far for him to shoot.

"Pierre!" he shouted to Cruzatte. "Drop the sail!" Drouillard turned the tiller, swinging the pirogue about, and told the soldiers to man oars and row. He hoped to get close enough to help before the bear caught and mauled any soldiers. He saw that two soldiers had tumbled down the bluff and were trying to get into a canoe.

There were two more shots; someone had reloaded. Still the maddened bear was roaring. He saw it chasing a man who was sprinting toward the edge of the bluff. He saw the man drop his gun, run straight off the bluff and plunge twenty feet down into the river.

The bear didn't stop. It hurtled off the bluff after the man. He couldn't tell whether the bear landed on top of the man. Now all of the other vessels were turning back to help.

The man in the water surfaced a short distance ahead of the bear and swam toward the oncoming canoes as fast as he could thrash water, but the bear was closing on him.

It was still too far to shoot at a target as small as a bear's head. Drouillard saw a man with a rifle on the bluff kneel and take aim. It looked like Colter. The muzzle flashed, banged; a puff of smoke billowed on the wind.

The bear jerked and its head vanished underwater. Triumphant shouts came from the bluff and the canoes. The swimming soldier slowed and looked back, then trod water waiting for the canoes to reach him. The men in the canoes pulled him from the water.

By the time the pirogue reached them, they had a rope on the dead bear and had towed it to shore.

Drouillard went ashore to examine the beast, and told Cruzatte to take the pirogue on up. The captains, far ahead on the other shore, must have heard all this shooting. The fleet moved back out into the river, except the two canoes of the hunters who had first attacked the bear. Drouillard was irritated at all of them for going out of their way to attack it, but said nothing; they were all nearly out of their minds with relief and excitement. They had got *la gloire*, though it had nearly been costly.

With its yellow-brown, white-tipped fur soaked, its massive torso and powerful limbs were terribly evident. The soldiers were guessing its weight at half a ton, but of course it looked enormous to them. Drouillard estimated it at six or seven hundred pounds.

It was leaking blood from everywhere. It looked as if eight rifle balls had hit it before the shot in the head had killed it.

He looked at the disheveled, wild-eyed, jabbering soldiers, and then down at the bear, its head as broad as a man's chest, its huge teeth outlined with blood from its own bullet-riddled lungs, its long tongue drooping pink against the gray mud of the riverbank. He thought of the powerful spirit that had just passed out of this animal, and he thought that spirit might just now be hurrying ahead toward the west to warn all the other bears ahead that there could be no peace with these whitemen coming up the river. The soldiers were laying claim to claws and teeth to keep as souvenirs of their thrilling battle.

"Get him aboard," Drouillard said, "and we'll catch up. Cap'ns'll want to know what all this shooting was about."

He sat in the canoe with the carcass and took up a paddle.

"Weather coming," he said. The pewter-colored water of the broad river was getting choppy. The sails of the pirogues ahead were pale against a purple-gray line of squall clouds running ragged on the western sky.

Now he could see the two captains on the narrow bottomlands on the other side of the river, tiny at nearly a half-mile distance, trotting downstream, waving to signal the pirogues, their calls barely audible in the wind. Probably they were trying to warn the crews of the oncoming storm. The canoes now all veered toward shore to avoid the rising chop.

Then Drouillard noticed that Cruzatte was not at the tiller of the distant white boat; he was forward near the mast. Charbonneau was steering. Cruzatte must have given him the tiller so he could go forward and shorten sail for the coming blow. Not a wise choice: Charbonneau had almost capsized the pirogue by steering her broadside to a gust the last time he had the tiller. He could not swim and had no sense of wind or sail. His wife with their baby sat low among the bundles and instruments. Cruzatte and Labiche were just getting ready to take in sail when the wind struck the vessel on her fore quarter and turned her almost broadside.

Charbonneau, instead of putting the pirogue before the wind, threw the tiller the other way to head into it. With a whap audible halfway across the river, the square-sail brace was jerked from Labiche's hand. The pirogue heeled over, part of the sail shivering, part in the water, side-slipping downriver and foundering in bursts of spray. Through the rush of wind Drouillard heard Cruzatte bellowing at Charbonneau, and Charbonneau wailing to heaven in his terror. Two gunshots banged on the far shore, the captains apparently trying to get the crew's attention; they were yelling but the wind carried their voices away. Drouillard saw Captain Lewis drop his rifle, sling off his gun bag, and start to strip off his coat as if to swim out, but Clark restrained him.

At last the halyard was cut and the sail was being hauled in. Cruzatte had drawn his pistol and was aiming it at Charbonneau, screaming in French that he would shoot him if he didn't recover the tiller. Charbonneau did so at last and slowly the pirogue came into the wind and her mast rose almost vertical. She was swamped within an inch of the gunwales, with every white-capped wave spewing in more water.

The canoes were ashore now, the red pirogue heading for the captains under oars and shortened sail, and Drouillard watched the desperate struggle of the white pirogue out there on the water.

Cruzatte had put two men to rowing and two others to bailing, and the vessel crept toward shore. As it came he could see the disorder inside; Bird Woman sitting in the icy water up to her ribs, holding the shrieking baby up on her shoulder with one hand, with the other hand tending to instrument cases, sodden journals, books, papers, and medicine stores that were immersed and afloat all around her.

It was dusk by the time the pirogue was beached and emptied, the officers rejoined with their fleet, the bear carcass brought ashore, and all members gathered in a camp. Over one campfire the men drank a dram and celebrated their deliverance from everything that had nearly happened to them, and over another they rendered six gallons of bear oil. Captain Lewis kept reminding everybody that if the pirogue and its contents had been lost, the expedition would have been utterly ruined. The soldiers knew he was in a state, and listened to his harangues patiently, waiting for him to simmer down and leave them alone to tell each other their bear story with all its elaborations. Drouillard's attention was mostly on Charbonneau's family. Charbonneau kept getting up and stalking around, not looking anyone in the face. Bird Woman was making sure her baby was warm and calm.

All that had actually been lost overboard were two cooking vessels, some gunpowder, a book, and the Indian baby's cradleboard. Everything else would need to be spread on the ground to drain and dry.

It was agreed that Charbonneau would not be allowed to steer a boat again.

Thursday May 16th
the Indian woman to whom I ascribe equal fortitude and reso-
lution, with any Person aboard at the time of the accedent,
caught and preserved most of the light articles which were
washed overboard
 this morning a white bear toar Labuiche's coat which he
had left in the plains.—

William Clark, Journals

For several days they had been coming into an increasingly hilly country where pitch pine grew on the slopes, a welcome change after a thousand miles of treeless plains. A less welcome change grew underfoot: a spiny cactus plant, low to the ground, with stiff spines that stabbed through moccasin leather. Anyone walking had to learn a new way of seeing his path because of this "prickly pear," and also because warm weather was bringing out rattlesnakes.

As they moved into this new country, they found fewer of the undercut riverbanks that used to cave in suddenly, endangering the boats. Now the firm, dry banks allowed the soldiers to walk easily onshore and pull the loaded vessels up the shallow river by long tow ropes of braided elk skin. They walked and pulled and sang. In the evenings some of the men shot beaver in the water, and the black dog Seaman would leap into the water, swim out and bring them ashore, which delighted his master. But one evening the dog retrieved one that was only wounded. With its great chisel teeth it bit the dog's hind leg and he almost bled to death from a cut artery before Captain Lewis was finally able to stop the bleeding.

That same evening, Captain Clark came in from a long advance trek, with more cheerful news. Climbing the highest hill he could find, he had seen ahead the mouth of a major river flowing into the Missouri from the south, one the Hidatsas had told of, and it was where they had said it would be. Even more satisfying to the captain was that in the distance, perhaps fifty miles west, he had seen a high snowy mountain.

Captain Lewis leaned back with a sigh. "Not fair, Clark. You get to see mountains first." He reached down and fondled the ear of his unconscious dog. "I'm not sure old Seaman here is going to make it to see a mountain."

That night in the lodge, Captain Lewis wrote late by candle while Charbonneau's family slept. Captain Clark was making pencil notes. Drouillard was trying to sleep, but there was some troubling spirit inside the shelter. When he would open his eyes, he would see Lewis gazing into the shadows instead of writing, and his eye sockets were black as caves. Drouillard didn't think the plight of the wounded dog was all of it, though that might have brought it on. Finally, Captain Clark sighed and asked, "What is it?"

Lewis was silent for a long while. Then he said, "We almost lost everything. It can happen so sudden." He was still thinking of the near loss of the boat, apparently.

"But we didn't. Don't fret over it. We're getting on splendid.

We'll be in those mountains in days! And from there on it's all downhill to the sea."

"Clark, friend." Lewis sighed. "Sometimes, when you carry so much of my load, I . . . I just get so ashamed of the rank thing, it—"

"We weren't ever going to talk about that," Clark said in a whisper.

"The President should have done something!" Lewis's whisper almost rose to a whimper.

"Never mind. The men don't know, and I thankee for that. I'm perfectly happy and having the time of my life. You should be too, damn it. Get your chin out of your chest. This is no time to let your faith go limp."

"Well, then . . ." Lewis corked his inkwell.

"Lights out? Are you through writing?"

"Leave it on till I go piss," Lewis said, and went out.

Clark glanced around and started when he saw that Drouillard was awake. He looked embarrassed. "Hello, George."

"Hello? I've been here all the time, Cap'n."

"Well . . ."

"Sir, I would like to know what that 'rank thing' is about."

"Nothing important."

"It seems important to him. Cap'n, you said when I hired on that I'd be privy to anything affecting this voyage."

Clark sighed. "You also said you could keep confidence?"

"You've never seen otherwise."

"All right, then." Clark leaned close, listening for Lewis's return. "Secretary of War didn't give me the co-captaincy Lewis promised me. Politics. Favoritism. Some folks in the capital hold grudges against my brother. They can't forgive him for the way they've treated him, I reckon that was a part of it. So, anyhow, I'm just a lieutenant, not a captain. Lewis was mad, then said, 'The hell with it, as far's anyone's concerned, you're co-captain.' And he's stuck by that, God bless 'im. But it eats on him. Now, by God, this is between you and me and we never speak of it again, right? Because Lewis and I can serve better this way."

"I can see that. Nobody will hear of it from me." He added, "Cap'n."

Drouillard pretended to be asleep when Lewis came back in. "Looks like good weather tomorrow," Lewis said. "How's old Seaman?"

"Snoring away in dogland. How about you? Better?"

"I guess. A good, steaming pee by starlight's like a prayer, I suppose."

"Am I supposed to report to Jefferson that you pray?"

The candle went out with a puff of breath. "Not really. But all those stars! They make one's worries seem pretty small, eh? Good night, Cap'n."

"Sleep well, Cap'n."

Drouillard lay there thinking about the "rank thing." He thought of all the force that was in this Lewis, and he thought of the dark spirit and the doubt that sometimes rose up around him.

But the "rank thing." It was actually one of those matters in which deceit seemed better than the truth. The way Drouillard had been taught, one deceived only enemies. But this seemed a good thing. And when he thought of Captain Lewis saying, "The hell with it, you're co-captain," the man rose far up in his esteem, narrow and uppity though he sometimes was. Those jealous Sioux chiefs could have learned something from these two whitemen.

Monday May 20th 1805
The Muscle Shell river falls into the Missouri 2270 miles above it's mouth. the waters of this river is of a greenish yellow cast, much more transparent than the Missouri . . . about five miles above the mouth of shell river a handsome river of about fifty yards in width discharged itself into the shell river on the Stard. side: this stream we called Sah ca gah we a or bird woman's River after our interpreter the Snake woman.

Meriwether Lewis, Journals

A Fork in the Missouri
June 2, 1805

Drouillard halted in the brush, sniffing the air, and held up his hand to warn Charbonneau, who was panting along behind him.

Charbonneau had asked to come hunting today in the hope that it would be easier than the ordeal of pulling the boats and canoes up through the rocky, muddy straits of the Missouri's rapids. Hauling on tow ropes, on banks so mucky their moccasins were sucked off their feet, much of the time in fast, icy water as deep as their chests, through rapids that swamped the canoes and time and again nearly overset the pirogues, the men were nearly as crippled by the stony river bottom as they had been by the prickly pear thorns out on dry ground. Though these narrow bottomlands were glorious with flowering berry and currant bushes and delicate spring greenery, they were full of danger and misery: blowflies, mosquitoes, and rattlesnakes of springtime vying with rainstorms and snow squalls to torment them as they labored along. But Charbonneau was finding out that keeping up with Drouillard was not much easier. He stumbled to a halt behind him, wheezing and blowing. *"Qu'est-ce que c'est?"* he gasped.

"Shh!" Drouillard warned. *"L'ours!"* Bear. He had smelled its barnlike odor; now he could hear its throaty breath. It was that close ahead, just upwind. But he couldn't see it yet in the foliage. He pointed back down the trail, several quick jabs of his forefinger. Charbonneau, his face gone ash-gray, needed no encouragement to retreat. But instead of slipping quietly back, he turned and bolted, crashing through the shrubbery and kicking rocks as he went.

Drouillard cocked his rifle. The bear surely heard Charbonneau's panicky rout.

It did. Above a cluster of blooming wild rose not ten yards away, the bear's broad, pale brown face and shoulders rose into view, ears up, listening. Immediately it dropped out of sight with a coughing grunt, and the foliage shook as it came running.

Drouillard leaped to one side and scrambled a few feet out of the bear's path, then spun about, hoping for an instant's clear shot at him in the open.

It tore past him at a distance of ten feet, looking as big and fast as a galloping horse. It didn't see him, and was going down the trail after the sounds of Charbonneau's flight. It would catch the Frenchman in moments. Drouillard yelled to warn him that the bear was coming, then ran after it.

Emerging into more open ground, he saw Charbonneau pelting along in full flight, the bear gaining on him. Charbonneau looked over his shoulder, saw his pursuer, fired his rifle straight up in the air, wasting its precious and crucial load, and sprinted toward a clump of brush with a leaning cottonwood tree in it.

Drouillard, catching up as fast as he could run, saw Charbonneau vanish into the thicket. The bear was about to go in after him.

Drouillard yelled, the war trill of his warrior ancestors. It fully captured the bear's attention. The beast spun and stood up. It opened its great maw and roared its reply to his war cry.

This time there were no soldiers standing around with loaded rifles in reserve to riddle this bear from every direction. Charbonneau's gun was empty and he was probably too distraught to reload it. It had to be this one load in Drouillard's rifle, and the only shot likely to kill the bear was a perfect one in the head. He sighted on its red palate as it roared, and squeezed the trigger. Before the gunshot had echoed away down the valley and the powder smoke dispersed, he was already sprinting around to flank the bear, reloading as he ran. Then he stopped.

The grizzly had toppled and hit the ground. It moved no more.

It was ten minutes before Charbonneau, scratched all over the face by the brush, could stop shaking enough to get a load into his rifle. He kept praying in rapid French, the old familiar Black Robe prayers. Finally Drouillard interrupted and asked him why he had shot into the air.

"*Je—Je ne sais pas.* I—I thought the noise would scare him."

"Eh! Next time, *mon ami,* don't try to scare the bears, eh? They are already annoyed."

*   *   *

They found the boats that evening at a point opposite the mouth of a major river. The camp was in a pleasant, narrow bottomland covered with cottonwoods. The captains were perplexed. The Hidatsas had not mentioned any juncture of rivers here. The next landmark the Hidatsas had told them to expect was the great falling water of the Missouri, where they would have to get out of their boats and walk a half a day to get above the falls. But now here were these two rivers coming together, one coming from the west, turbid, the other from the south and seeming too clear to be the Missouri. The evening being cloudless, the captains set up instruments to read moon and stars, and determined to send canoe parties up both streams the next day to explore them and determine which was the Missouri.

Monday June 3rd 1805
. . . to mistake the stream at this period of the season, and to ascend to the rocky Mountain before we could inform ourselves whether it did approach the Columbia or not, and then be obliged to return and take the other stream would not only loose us the whole of this season but would Probably so dishearten the Party that it might defeat the expedition altogether.

                                                    Meriwether Lewis, Journals

The soldiers were grateful for this day of indecision. Their feet were so bruised and mangled they could hardly bear to stand up, let alone labor on over more rough ground. Here they could sit and limp around, dressing hides to make clothes to replace the tattered remnants of their cloth uniforms, and make moccasins with double soles to deflect the prickly pear spines. They could eat to nourish their strained, exhausted muscles and get the ice-water ache out of their bones and joints.

And they could speculate and bet on the choice of rivers. They smoked and talked with Pierre Cruzatte, the expert riverman. He thought the right-hand river was the Missouri, because it looked like the same muddy water they had been on for more than a year, and the men were tending to side with him.

Drouillard, being much in the presence of the captains, found them leaning in favor of the south fork. "This is clear water," Lewis argued. "This is water right down out of the mountains. And we're almost in those mountains. And the Hidatsas said we'd make a heading southwest to reach the waterfalls."

Captain Clark nodded, agreeing with those inferences, but kept wondering how the Hidatsas, as well as they knew this country, could have failed to mention a major river coming in on the starboard. "Every other landmark they told of has proven true," he said. "I guess we won't, can't, be sure until we find the falls. I am almost sure they're up this left-hand stream. And no more than seventy miles, at most."

Drouillard sat fleshing the bear hide he had gotten yesterday, and cleaning the bear claws which would someday make a necklace, and as he worked he remembered his uncle Pierre Lorimier and how that man loved wagering. Lorimier had often said that one reason he loved the Shawnees was that they would bet on anything. After thinking on these things awhile, he scooted over to sit beside Charbonneau, who was just now cleaning the rifle he had fired into the air yesterday. Charbonneau beamed at his savior, and Bird Woman too looked up from the cradleboard she was making and smiled at him, quickly and shyly.

"Monsieur," Drouillard began, speaking low in French, "you could do me a small favor."

"Quelque chose!" he replied. Anything!

"Will you ask your wife if she remembers whether she came from that way," he pointed up the right-hand river, "or *that* way?" He could have asked her himself in sign, but did not want to be seen talking about this by those like Cruzatte and Lepage and Private Gibson, who could read a bit of signing.

"Mais oui, mon cher." Charbonneau spoke to her in Hidatsa. She raised her head, as if sniffing the air. She looked at each river, then squinted at the sun, which was just beginning to fade behind clouds. Then she looked down the Missouri in the direction from which they had come. Then she said something to her

husband, and pointed with her chin toward the south. Charbonneau said, "She was but a child then, but she feels her people were from that way, not the other."

"*Merci. Et vous, m'sieu.* When you were interpreting for Capitaine Clark at the fort, about rivers and falls and mountains . . . do you remember much of that?"

Charbonneau tilted his head and shrugged, his yellowed teeth bared in an embarrassed grin. "*Très peu.* It needed all my attention just to understand and change tongues. They spoke of so many rivers. I don't remember. But," he added, raising a finger, "those warriors come on horse, not boat. May be they miss some rivers? Eh?"

"*Peut-etre. Merci, mon vieux.*"

"*Pas de quoi, mon cher ami!* Heh heh!"

Drouillard worked on his bear skin and thought of all that for a while. He thought of the hunting camps and war-party camps he had seen all along the way, some fresh, some old, all abandoned. They had seen not one Indian party since their encampments on the Yellow Stone River. Most of the traces along the north bank had been Assiniboine, those called Stone Eaters because they cooked by dropping heated stones in the cooking water. Lepage had remarked that the Hidatsa usually traveled south of the river to avoid such people as those, and the Blackfeet. These last few days the boats had traveled between steep stone riverbanks and white cliffs as vertical as walls and towers, but the river had turned from west to northwest, then abruptly southwest again. It made sense that warriors or hunters on horseback would continue straight west toward their destination in the mountains, and thus might never have seen this fork. That might explain why they had not told Captain Clark about it.

He got up and wandered through the camp to find Cruzatte, and knelt by him. "Pierre, old *camarade*! It is said you believe *that* is our river."

"Oooh, *mais oui.* Everyone thinks so, except the *capitaines.*"

"We will soon know, after a little exploration. But while there is still doubt—"

"There is no doubt, *ami.*"

"Then, while it is still undecided—would you care to wager on it?"

"Wager what?"

He shrugged. "Our evening whiskey ration for a month, perhaps?"

Cruzatte leaned back, peering at Drouillard through his merry eye. "Oh, *non*. Even though I am right, surely, I would not risk losing *that*. Perhaps, instead, ah, wages?" He rubbed his palms.

That was what Drouillard had hoped he would say. "Wages?"

"*Oui*. When they pay us, back in St. Louis. Next year, *Dieu voulant*."

Drouillard cocked his head and pretended that he had not thought of such a thing. It was true that he had not had much thought of money lately, but if on his return he might gain even more than just his wages . . . "Perhaps. Tell me more."

Cruzatte laughed. "Ah, friend! You're too much with the officers. You believe what they say. But if you believe in that, you will bet on it, eh? Well, how much? Let us consider. . . ."

Since all the men believed with Cruzatte, Drouillard was able to go around and make small bets with half of them.

If he and the captains were right, he would have twice as much money as he had expected on his return. If the captains were wrong, he would have half as much.

He felt confident that he would be richer, and with all the others, he awaited the return of the scouting canoes with enhanced eagerness.

Five days later, after inconclusive reports from the two canoe parties, followed by scouting parties far up both branches, there was still no proof of which was the Missouri. Captain Clark had taken five men nearly sixty miles southwestward along the left branch and back in two days without finding the falls, while Captain Lewis with six, including Drouillard and Cruzatte, had made a strenuous four-day trek more than seventy-five miles up the other. These sorties were made in raw, rainy weather which turned the earth into a mud as slick as bear grease. Captain Lewis and Private Windsor one day had slipped and nearly fallen

to their deaths off a river cliff. During this trek the expert riverman Cruzatte convinced everyone—even Drouillard—that this
river was still the Missouri. But he did not convince Captain
Lewis.

They slogged on and on, sometimes in muddy water chest
deep. Drouillard was now afraid that he had lost half his fortune by putting too much faith in these damned stubborn white
captains.

But of course he could not rescind his bet on the other river,
even though he had lost his faith in it.

Sunday June 9th 1805
*. . . the party of all whom except Capt. C. still being firm in the
beleif that the N. Fork was the Missouri and that which we
ought to take; they said very cheerfully that they were ready to
follow us any wher we thought proper to direct but that they
still thought that the other was the river . . .*

*We determined to deposite at this place the large red per-
ogue all the heavy baggage which we could possibly do
without &c with a view to lighten our vessels and at the same
time to strengthen their crews by means of the seven hands
who have been employd in navigating the red perogue: ac-
cordingly we set some hands to diging a cellar or cache for
our stores*

Meriwether Lewis, Journals

Chapter 14

Great Falls of the Missouri
June 13, 1805

A hard wind from the southwest was beating and whiffing around his ears. Yet there was another sound, something deeper under the wind, like far off thunder. But the vast plain was shimmering under midday sun; there was not a sign of a storm in any direction. The sky was unbroken, vast blue, with flights of vultures wheeling over the plains, and white-headed eagles whistling and swooping above, sometimes dropping out of sight as if into the earth. Drouillard could not see the river course, but knew it was off to the south of him, where the eagles dropped out of sight. The treeless plain stretched away fifty or sixty miles in every direction, the western and southern horizons edged with dazzling white mountaintops, and a few bold hills beyond the river in the southeast. Massed on the green, wind-whipped plain were dark herds of buffalo, countless hundreds or thousands of them, some tramping up clouds of gray dust that billowed downwind from them. For, despite the pale grass that looked so verdant at a distance, the ground was dry, harsh and scrabbly underfoot, yellow with the flowers of the ground-hugging prickly pear, now so thick that even with double-soled moccasins and a watchful step, sore, pierced feet were a part of every day's discomforts along what Private Gibson had begun calling the "Misery River."

If it even *was* the Missouri River now!

Drouillard, Captain Lewis, Joe Field, Gibson, and Goodrich

251

had hoisted knapsacks two days ago and set out afoot up this branch that no one but the captains believed was the correct course. Before leaving the forks, they had tied the red pirogue upside down among trees on an island and hidden it under brush. On high ground, they had cached and buried extra lead, powder, tools, clothes, furs, kegs of pork and salt, flour and meal, which they intended to retrieve on their return next year. In the midst of all that preparation, Charbonneau's wife suddenly doubled over in pain and became sick and weak. The last sight Drouillard remembered that night was of Captain Clark kneeling beside her in the lodge, cutting her arm to let blood, which had seemed a thing of the poorest judgment, in his opinion. That, and their insistence on coming up this river despite Cruzatte's advice, had shaken his whole faith in them still again.

Drouillard was stalking a small herd of buffalo that he had seen wandering down into a draw, upwind from him. He intended to select a fat young cow or a calf to kill, and the only way to approach these herds without being seen on this treeless land was to use the gulches and draws. Far down to his left he saw Gibson trying to get within rifle range of another herd. Gibson, one of the tough young hunters Captain Clark had recruited in Kentucky, looked not much bigger than a mite in this immense landscape. Somewhere out of sight in the other direction, Silas Goodrich was hunting. The three had been told to get the best cuts of their kills and catch up with Captain Lewis at the river at midday. He was scouting the terrain ahead.

As Drouillard crested the bank of the gulch, he again heard that low thundering sound under the wind, coming with the wind, and, squinting against stinging sand and dust, he shaded his eyes and scanned the southwest, expecting perhaps to see thunderclouds rising over the mountains.

Instead he saw what appeared to be a cloud on the ground—a small, shimmering white cloud, not two or three miles away, it seemed, though not knowing what it was, he could hardly judge the distance. It seemed to shift shape and then dissolved from his sight. A little later it drifted up again, wavered and vanished.

He blinked and shook his head, and the wraith was gone. If

this had been early morning, he might have taken it for a patch of fog, but now the sun was high and the wind strong.

Below in the gully he heard the scuff of buffalo hooves and the snuffling of their snouts. A whiff of their dung and wool came up to him, and he knew they were very close. Slipping along behind a clump of sage, he looked down into the herd, about twenty, immediately picked out a plump young cow, prayed to the Keeper of the Game, and fired a ball into her heart. She dropped on her forelegs, then rolled on her side as the rest of the herd fled thundering away up the other side of the gully in a haze of dust. Turning his back to the wind, Drouillard reloaded, waved to the distant Gibson, then went down in the gully to skin the cow and cut out her hump and tongue. When he came back up, he found that the wind had died a bit and he could hear that low, drumming sound better. And there again was that wraith of mist. He realized then what it was.

It had to be the roar and spray of the falls of the Missouri. Those damned stubborn captains had been right after all. Their left branch *was* the Missouri.

"Ehhhh-*ya!*" he cried in the vast space, and turned to wave Gibson up. Gibson was one of the soldiers he had wagered, and he could hardly wait for him to come up so he could tell him that the captains had been right, and he would collect after all.

The three hunters descended into such an uproar of falling water that they could hardly hear each other speak, and found Captain Lewis sitting on a ridge of rocks gazing up into a shining turmoil of spilling, churning, spraying, thundering white water, foam, and spume. It filled the wide river canyon from cliff to cliff, a glistening torrent spilling straight down from a height that looked like a hundred feet into a swirling pool on the far side, but most of it dropped over great shelves of projecting rock which pulverized the falling river into a milk-white froth. The mist rose skyward, cool on sunbaked skin, and in the pale blue-green foam in the chute below, Drouillard saw the shadows of himself and the other three men with a rainbow around them. The very rock they stood on seemed to tremble. This was a spirit place. He could not breathe deeply enough. When the captain looked up from the notebook in his lap to notice his hunters' arrival, Drouillard saw something he had never seen before in the face of this stolid man: tears trickling from his shining eyes. Drouillard quickly looked away, far down the rapids below, and saw in the narrow, lush bottomland a grove of small cottonwoods, the bank littered with bleached driftwood and buffalo bones, and a small, abandoned Indian camp of stick lodges. He tried to imagine the people who came here. It would be terrifying to live down there.

But surely when a man was there, the spirits would sing to him.

Thursday June 13th 1805
I wished for the pencil of Salvator Rosa or the pen of Thompson, that I might be enabled to give to the enlightened world some Just idea of this truly magnificent and sublimely grand object, which has from the commencement of time been concealed from the view of civilized man; but this was fruitless and vain . . . at 4 OClock P.M. I walked down the river about three miles to discover if possible some place to which the canoes might be drawn on shore in order to be taken by land above the falls, but the river was one continued sene of rappids and cascades which I readily Perceived could not be encountered with our canoes, and the Clifts were from 150 to 200 feet high . . .

Meriwether Lewis, Journals

Sacagawea, the Bird Woman, was barely alive when Captain Clark arrived below the rapids with the white pirogue and the canoes. She had almost no pulse; her fingers and forearms were twitching, and she was seldom conscious to nurse the baby boy. Both captains were in a state of alarm over her, not just for herself and the prospect of having an unweaned motherless child on their hands, but because she would soon be needed as interpreter with her Shoshone people, who should be found somewhere above the falls, and whose help and horses would be needed to cross the mountains to the Columbia watershed. Without at least two dozen horses to carry supplies and Indian gifts over, there would be little point in trying to go on. Her condition was probably their most crucial concern at this point. Drouillard watched them hover over her with their hands on her brow and their thumbs on her wrist and throat, or with their fingertips probing her pelvis, and he looked at her trembling eyelids and graying face, and wondered if any whitemen anywhere had ever been this concerned with the health and life of an Indian.

Captain Clark had bled her several times in the last few days and had been making poultices for her husband to apply to her pubic and lower abdominal region, where the pain seemed to be centered. Captain Lewis believed the poultices should be continued, but was afraid she had been bled too much. Captain Clark had discovered a sulfurous spring in a hillside below the rapids, and some water from it was brought up for her to drink. Her husband was left to the task of dosing her while the captains attended to their other new problem.

In scouting upriver from the waterfall, Captain Lewis had found that the rapids and cascades continued for another six or seven miles up, including four other spectacular and precipitous falls. The whole distance was about twelve miles. The Hidatsas had said a half-day carry would get them past the falls—which would be true for men walking with their belongings on their backs. But for a troop of men with six fully loaded canoes and a large rowboat full of gear to transport over that much rough prairie ground, it would be a matter of days, not hours—if it were physically possible to accomplish at all. Moreover, the portage would have to veer far from the canyon to bypass several long gullies.

After several days, Captain Clark and five men had staked out, on the south bank, the shortest possible route of reasonably level ground. It terminated at a group of islands around a river bend and several miles upstream from the upper waterfall, and was eighteen miles long. Before this, the men had never had to haul the vessels over more than a few yards of ground.

And this was torturous ground. Wet prairie clay had been

trampled by thousands of buffalo hooves and dried to a rough, pitted, moccasin-tearing, ankle-twisting stucco, whose primary surviving vegetation was the dreaded prickly pear.

They can't do it, Drouillard thought. Even to please their Great Father Jefferson, they can't make these men carry all these tons of boats and belongings over such distance. If an Indian chief tried to make his people do such a cruel and crazy thing, they would get themselves a new chief, one who had some sense!

But these were whitemen. Drouillard was sitting with them in camp at the lower end of the rapids when Clark said, "Wheels! With wheels we can make the canoes into wagons."

So they sent out six men to find the right kind of wood to make four sets of wooden wheels, and the tongues, couplings, and axles to assemble truck wagons.

And as usual, the poor soldiers would be the oxen to pull the loads.

Drouillard remembered a saying whitemen used, that God looks after fools. There seemed to be only one tree large enough in the whole canyon to make wheels of, and it grew just below the portage camp. The trunk was perfectly round and two feet in diameter. Sergeant Gass sawed off sections six inches thick and made axle holes in the center of each. The mast of the white pirogue was cut in lengths to make axle trees, and the ends drilled to put in axle pins, then lubricated with bear grease. The white pirogue was too big to be portaged, so it was emptied and hidden near the camp just as the red one had been at the forks. Captain Lewis's iron-frame boat would be assembled at the end of the portage route to replace the pirogue as main cargo boat. He said it would carry four tons of baggage. He wanted elk hide to cover the hull. Several had been saved for that purpose, but not enough, so he sent Drouillard upriver to hunt elk, hoping there would be some in this vicinity. No one had seen any, or any trace.

Before Drouillard set out from the camp, he had the pleasure of seeing Bird Woman conscious, propped up, her baby suckling. It appeared that she was recovering after drinking the stinking water. She had eaten buffalo soup and meat, and was no longer twitching or grimacing with pain. As he hiked up the river, he was thankful for her recovery. The world felt right again. The Master of Life was allowing the little Shoshone mother to live and care for her child. The soldiers were busy preparing for the portage and were cheerful and dutiful. Drouillard was rejoicing in the sights of this powerful place where the Creator's work was so evident: the shining, wild waterfalls roaring and echoing within the cliff-bound river course, one above the other; the eagles, diving down to fish in the swift water; the countless thousands of buffalo feeding everywhere; the wildflowers and berry bushes blooming, blowing in the wind, life taking root in every rock crack. The magnitude of the Creator's work was heartening; surely not even the coming-through of whitemen could alter the Creator's mighty works here. It was true that whitemen had killed all the woods buffalo back in his homeland, but how could they ever diminish such numbers as these? He stood on the bluff with the churning white water far down below and watched a herd making its way down a gully to the river's edge to drink above the falls on the other side, half a mile away, one of the few places where they could even get to the river because of the towering cliffs. The buffalo in the front of the herd, wading down and drinking in the shallows, were crowded forward into deeper water by those still coming down, until they floated off their footing and were caught in the current. In the few minutes he stood there he saw a half dozen helplessly swept over the falls, crushed and torn apart on the rocks. Bears, buzzards, and wolves grew fat on the broken carcasses at river's edge below, leaving the countless bones and skulls that littered the narrow bottoms. Drouillard felt the Great Circle of Being, always turning, life giving to death, death giving to life. The more lives, the more deaths; this was the wheel the Master of Life had put in motion on this land, in the Beginning Times, and kept rolling—ages before the whitemen came, so proud of their rolling wheels that merely carried loads from place to place. Here was one of the Creator's places where the Great Circle could be plainly seen, with limitless power and infinite life. He was sure that even whitemen could not kill all these buffalo, stop these falling waters.

The Hidatsas had told the captains that at the top of the falls a black eagle lived in a nest in the top of one great tree standing on an island.

Drouillard saw the lone tree and the eagle's shaggy nest far up in it as he approached the waterfall. This waterfall thundered over a precipice, falling about twenty-five feet, and the island was just below it, faintly visible in the mist, but the treetop rose high out of the mist. He remembered this. He had dreamed of it!

He looked around the sky. In many places he saw buzzards circling, drifting against the cloudy sky. Higher up he saw two white-headed eagles in different quadrants of the sky.

On the hills and plains were countless buffalo, herded by the wolves who were always with them. He saw no sign of elk yet. Far up the river, where it began to bend to the south, he saw a yellow bear.

Above this waterfall the river was almost up to the level of the plains, the banks very low. The river canyon was deeper below every waterfall. From here he could see downriver to another bend, and beyond it there drifted the spray from the next waterfall, about two miles below.

Water thundered, wind blew, and now over it he heard the descending whistle of an eagle, close by. Looking up, he saw an all-black eagle swoop overhead and settle on the edge of the high nest in the cottonwood. It raised its great wings once, twice, slowly, then folded them down like a man closing his coat.

On the hoof-trampled ground he saw a long, black feather, the pointer-feather from an eagle's wing. He knelt and picked it up, twirled it between finger and thumb, thinking. He had no right to keep it. He put it where he had found it. He and the eagle regarded each other for a while over the distance, and he remembered the day when he had watched an eagle rise through the clouds above Fort Massac and dreamed of seeing over all its horizons. Then he turned to walk on up the riverbank, hunting for elk, thinking of the Hidatsa people, six hundred miles back down this river, who knew this wide land so well they could tell you where a bird would be and it would be there: the very one you had seen in your dream.

The portage unfolded as a labor of many days. It was all done with the captains' characteristic processes of planning, measuring, and organizing. George Drouillard again thanked the Creator that he was just the hunter, not a soldier laboring in the midst of their scheme. His responsibility was demanding enough, but as usual he had freedom to do it his way, at a distance. He would kill enough game to feed everybody, preserve the flesh, and prepare the hides for use as moccasins, clothing, and a cover for the iron-frame boat. He must especially try to get elk, if any were about, because Captain Lewis thought elk hide would be more waterproof and durable on the boat than buffalo.

The soldiers' ordeal as draft animals began every morning at the Portage Creek Camp below the lowest waterfall. From there they carried loads up a steep draw to the high plain and stowed them in the canoes-on-wheels. Then, six or seven to a canoe, they would put their shoulders into loop-harnesses, made of rope or hide, lean forward and strain until the clumsy wooden wheels began to turn. They would keep straining until all that tonnage was at Captain Lewis's Upper Portage Camp eighteen miles to the southwest, above all the falls and rapids. If weather or broken-down wagons didn't delay them too much, they might get there before dark. They would eat and fall into deep sleep, and the next morning pull the empty canoes back. Now and then favorable winds allowed them to raise sails on the wheeled canoes. The wind power made the pulling much easier.

That was how it was done on the good days. On bad days, when rain and hail turned the plains to slick, wheel-clogging mud, it was much more difficult. Bad days were frequent.

June 23rd Sunday 1805
the men mended their mockersons with double soles to Save their feet from the Prickley Pear and the hard ground which in maney Places So uneaven as to hurt the feet verry much.

added to those obstructions, the men has to haul with all their Strength wate & art. maney times every man all catching the grass & knobes & Stones with their hands to give them more force in drawing on the Canoes & Loads, and notwith-standing the Coolness of the air in high presperation and every halt are asleep in a moment. maney limping Some be-come faint for a fiew moments, but no man Complains all go Chearfully on—to State the fatigues of this Party would take up more of the journal than other notes which I find Scercely time to Set down.

William Clark, Journals

Drouillard's hunting camp was on the bank of a tributary river that flowed in from the west, four miles below Captain Lewis's camp, about halfway to the black eagle's nest. The Hidatsas had called this pretty little river the Medicine, because a magic drum sound often came down its valley from the mountains. His camp was basically a slaughterhouse. To it every day he carried the buffalo, deer, and elk meat and hides he harvested in the sur-rounding plains and bottomlands, and there, sometimes with the aid of another hunter and butcher, he cut the flesh into strips to dry on stick racks high in the sun, or over fires of driftwood and dried buffalo dung, and he flensed hides while the meat cured. Because of all the meat, bears were always around.

Eighteen miles below, downstream beyond the five great wa-terfalls, lay the lower portage camp under the charge of Sergeant Ordway, to which the exhausted soldiers returned after pulling their emptied wagons back to be reloaded. At that lower camp the cook was Charbonneau, who stayed there with the Bird Woman and their baby. Captain Clark and York were at that camp when they were not trekking back and forth with the wagons. From that camp every day came the welcome news that the young mother was regaining her health and strength.

Drouillard, though he had spent much of his hunting life alone, was surprised to find himself thinking and worrying about all these people spread out miles through this powerful place with all its winds, waters, and angry bears.

There were many bears. And they did seem angry. They kept making it plain that these whitemen were not welcome.

Tuesday, June 25th 1805
This morning I dispatched Frazier down for Drewyer and the meat he had collected, and Joseph Fields up the Missouri to hunt Elk. about noon Fields returned and informed me that he had seen two white bear near the river a few miles above and in attempting to get a shoot had stumbled uppon a third which immediately made at him being only a few steps distant; that in runing in order to escape he had leaped down a steep bank of the river on a stony bar where he fell cut his hand bruised his knees and bent his gun. fortunately for him the bank hid him from the bear when he fell and by that means he had escaped. this man has been truly unfortunate with these bear, this is the second time that he has narrowly escaped from them . . .

    in the evening Drewyer and Frazier arrivd with about 800 lbs. of excellent dried meat and about 100 lbs of tallow
                         Meriwether Lewis, Journals

After Drouillard and Frazier unloaded the meat from their canoe, Captain Lewis proudly took them over to show off the progress on his iron boat. The captain had named his boat-building camp White Bear Island, because those animals were always prowling around it. The vessel was being built on a scaffold so the crew could work under it and turn it over when they needed to.

"Thirty-six feet long, four and a half wide, and she'll carry four tons of cargo," Lewis exclaimed, "but light enough that eight men can carry her. Did you ever see such a clever vessel?"

Drouillard paid it the solicited compliment, although he found it much less ingenious and beautiful than an Indian bark canoe. Its basic frame was two hundred pounds of strap iron assembled with screws. Interwoven with the iron were flat-shaved slats of willow and box elder and strips of bark, which made the boat look like a big, long basket with pointed ends. Over it the workers were fitting a covering of elk hides, the hair singed or shaved off, sewn together to be form-fitting.

"I'm worried about sealing the seams," Captain Lewis said. "There's no pine around here for pitch. I'm experimenting. Tallow mixed with pounded charcoal might seal well enough. Drouillard, you— Oop! There it is again. I swear it sounds just like a cannon!"

It was the drumbeat sound from the mountains that the Hidatsas had spoken of. Drouillard had heard it several times a day in his hunting camp.

Lewis said: "Cap'n Clark and I have been speculating on what it is. Air pressure changing maybe. There has to be a rational explanation."

Of course, Drouillard thought.

"Do the bear bother you as much down in your camp as they do us?" the captain asked. "They prowl here so much that Seaman barks all night. We're too busy to deal with them the way I'd like to. When the time comes, I'd like to get enough troops to make war on 'em and drive them out of here."

Drouillard kept himself from saying something that he knew would be meaningless to the captain. He replied simply, "The meat draws 'em. I have to hang it high between trees at night."

"I won't let a man go alone anywhere in the bush, always in pairs. It bothers me that you're alone down there so much."

"I appreciate your concern, Cap'n, but I'm all right."

He spent that night, a night thick with droning mosquitoes, at Captain Lewis's camp. The next morning the captain woke him early for breakfast. Lewis was serving as the camp cook so his men could keep working every waking hour on the iron boat and the portage. He was making a great quantity of suet dumplings as a treat for the wagon crews when they should come up. The captain was in high spirits. "Fine meat you brought, George. We'll feed those hardworking fellows well. Ha ha! What do you think, a captain serving as cook for his men?"

"Guess they should feel real honored," he replied, telling the captain what he apparently hoped to hear.

"I want you and Joe Field to take that canoe upriver today and see if you can get more elk. I sent him up yesterday and a bear almost got him. Shields has fixed his gun, and he's ready for bear again."

"But what you really want is elk, sir. Not bear, eh?"

Lewis laughed. "Correct. Elk." He rubbed his hands and looked at his cookfire. "Another day or two they can bring up the rear camp. Be good to get Charbonneau up here. That fellow can cook! Captain Clark says the squaw's about well enough to make the walk."

"Good." She had been very much in his prayers,

The captain sighed and clenched his jaw, looking toward the mountains. "We've been here far too long. Near two weeks where I expected we'd be one day. I really want us out of this place."

Drouillard thought: The bears would be glad to know that.

June 26th Wednesday 1805
Some rain last night this morning verry Cloudy the party Set out this morning verry early with their loads to the Canoe . . .
I assort our articles for to be left at this place buried Kegs of Pork, ½ a Keg of flour, 2 blunderbuts, Caterrages a few Small lumbersom articles Capt Lewiss Desk and Some books & Small articles in it
in the evening the wind Shifted round to the East & blew hard, which is a fair wind for the two Canoes to Sail on the Plains across the portage . . .

William Clark, Journals

June 27, 1805

"Chief, I swear t' God they's a bear a-stalkin' to bushwhack us," Joe Field said in a low and tight voice from the stern of their canoe. They had started back down the Missouri to Captain Lewis's camp. Ominous dark weather was gathering in the southwest.

Drouillard knew. He had been seeing glimpses of a pale bear slipping through dense willow brush on the near riverbank, staying a good way ahead, and it looked as big as a buffalo.

The little narrow dugout was so loaded with elk meat and hides that it had scarcely three inches of gunwale above water. Their hunt for elk had been very rewarding: nine of them. Also the fat and hides of two small bears. Drouillard nodded toward shore. "Put over close." He wanted a look at the tracks. He didn't really want another bear just now. With weather rising and the canoe so burdened, they could be swamped easily, especially if they took on another bearskin. But he was interested in this bear's intentions.

From a few feet offshore he could see that the prints of the grizzly's hind feet in the mud were the biggest yet—about a foot long, not counting the talons. Joe Field said, "That big sneaky son of a bitch! I hate them bullyin' bastards!"

No wonder, Drouillard thought, Joe Field had reason to feel they were picking on him personally. What was beginning to worry Drouillard was that if this big warrior bear kept stalking ahead like this, he would head right into Captain Lewis's camp. And this one appeared to be more bear than the one last month that had needed eight bullets to die.

He thought of trying to get ahead of the bear to warn the camp. But probably this bear wouldn't allow anyone to pass him, not until he'd had his chance to ambush them on shore.

So it seemed there was nothing to do but go ashore. "Joe, put us in above that big leaning tree. And keep quiet." Field was probably good and scared now, but he was brave and he had a true bear grudge, and without a word he steered to the bank. The dugout was too heavy-laden to pull onshore, so Drouillard stepped off the bow and tied it to a willow clump, meanwhile looking, listening and smelling for the big bear. Wouldn't he like to come back and tear into this load of elk, he thought. But I think he'd want to tear us up first, and then maybe eat some elk. And then maybe go down and tear up the camp. Drouillard had a strong notion that this was a chief bear.

He motioned for Field to follow him into the brush, and led him to the base of the leaning cottonwood. Then he signaled for him to go up. They slung their rifles on their backs and started up. The thick, slanting trunk was easy to climb. Field rested in a fork twenty feet up. Drouillard straddled a limb below him, slipped out of his rifle sling and said, "Now call him."

"Eh? What? Me?"

"Let him hear your voice. You're the one they hate."

Field looked down at him oddly, but then hooted, "Hey, goddam bear!" They waited. Field whooped again. Drouillard felt a blast of cold air, smelled rain in the distance. Leaves turned underside up in the wind and the surface of the river darkened with shivering ripples. Their tree began to sway. A brilliant scribble and flash of lightning hit the trees nearby, followed instantly by a deafening thunderclap. "Jesus almighty! I want out of this tree!" Field gasped.

But Drouillard answered: "No, you don't. Look down there."

The pale bear had just burst out of the brush and was under their tree, where he heard their voices or caught their scent, and paused, swinging his enormous wedge-shaped head from side to side.

N'nochtu makwa, Pehthon aha 'y keeteh, Drouillard prayed. Chief war bear, I salute you to heaven. Just as it looked up and saw him with its intelligent eyes, he fired a ball between them. Another lightning bolt and thunderclap shook them, and hailstones now were tearing down through the foliage, shredding leaves. Drouillard bent over his rifle to reload it, hearing Field swear away in awe and amazement just above him. Then he slid down the tree trunk to inspect the dead bear. Field dropped to the ground beside him. Drouillard, hunched up against the hail that was beating his back, looked at Field and said, "Satisfied now?"

He was fleshing hides that evening at the White Bear Camp, and Joe Field kept telling all the soldiers about how Drouillard had killed the biggest of all bears while perched in a swaying tree in a lightning storm. Some of the soldiers had been terrorized by the storm and even blown down by the wind. Finally all that talk made Drouillard remember an old Shawnee story, and he started telling it as he scraped the hides.

"My people don't fear storms," he said. "We know they won't ever hurt us. Because of a promise from Wind Spirit." They looked at him strangely; it wasn't like him to just start telling about something without being asked a question. And they had never heard him discuss anything about spirits.

"Long time ago this was. Wind Spirit likes to blow things down, throw sand in your eyes, you know. Long time ago when he was young, he was even worse about that, like a bad boy. Blew people down and laughed about it. He blew houses down and laughed. So all the old Shawnee women held a council, said it was time Wind Spirit grew up. They would teach him manners. So here's what they did:

"Next time they saw Wind Spirit coming with a storm, they all lined up, all those old women, facing him. He came on, laughing. So they all grabbed the fronts of their dresses and pulled them up. When he saw that sight, all those old women fronts, he begged for mercy. They threatened him that if he ever bothered Shawnee people, they'd show him that again. So he promised he never would. And he never has again. That's why my people aren't afraid of storms."

The soldiers sat looking at him. It wasn't till they saw him slyly smiling that they all burst out laughing.

Two days later another violent hailstorm shrieked and pounded over the prairie. It was bad at the White Bear Camp, where it seemed every tree would come crashing down. That night the canoe wagons didn't come up from the lower camp, and Lewis grew tense with anxiety. By midnight not even a messenger had come up, and worry kept everyone from sleeping well.

The next day they learned that the hailstorm had punished the wagon-haulers brutally, and had come within a hair's breadth of wiping out the lives of Captain Clark, Charbonneau, Bird Woman and her baby, and York.

Caught in the open on the portage trail without even hats or shirts, the men had been beaten to the ground by a deluge of hailstones the size of apples. Many were bloodied, some knocked unconscious, others so badly bruised they could hardly walk or use their arms. After the storm they had left the wagons on the trail and staggered back to the lower camp.

At that same time, Captain Clark, York, and Charbonneau's family were hiking up by way of the riverbank. Clark had needed to rewrite some earlier waterfall measurements that were blown away in the wind. He'd taken Charbonneau's family with him because they had not been out of the lower camp yet to see the spectacle of the waterfalls. York veered off toward a small buffalo herd in hopes of shooting a calf for a meal along the trek. They viewed the grand waterfall and then proceeded a quarter of a mile above it when the black storm cloud suddenly mounted the sky, the wind howling up with such force that it threatened to blow them all off the cliff into the river. They had taken shelter under overhanging rocks in a dry ravine just ahead of a deluge of rain and hail that looked and sounded as powerful as the grand waterfall itself.

In moments a flash flood of muddy water came roaring down the ravine, and would have swept them into the river above the grand waterfall had the captain not seen it coming; by the time he had pushed Charbonneau and Sacagawea, with her baby in her arms, up the muddy bank and out of the ravine, the torrent was fifteen feet deep and he was half submerged, pulling himself up to the lip of the ravine by his fingertips. He saved his rifle but lost his compass. Charbonneau lost his gun, shot pouch, and tomahawk. Sacagawea saved her baby, but for the second time the child's cradleboard had been swept away by water, and his clothes went with it.

When everybody was finally reunited at the upper camp, Drouillard had the strange, sweet feeling in his breast that he was in a family household again. Here were the brown faces of the quiet and self-contained Bird Woman and her cheerful baby Jean Baptiste, whose eyes were both coal-black and star-bright. And here too was the only other one who was not a whiteman, the brawny slave, York, in whose black face a hundred unspoken emotions were always passing in succession. Now York sat with his arms embracing his knees, telling his own view of the hailstorm on the plain:

"Broth' Droor, I thought I losted ev'body! They was on 'at clift 'bove them horrenjus waterfall one minute. Then come a wind 'at blown me down, and when I got up and look for 'em, they was gone! When I see 'em come up out o' that ravine, I got on my knees an' pray thanks to the Lord! Yeah, got prickly pear in my knees, but I di'n mind. Heh heh!" He was chuckling now, looking at his master and the Charbonneau family, but tears ran down his cheeks.

The whole island was a thicket of willow, a vertical maze so dense a man could hardly see thirty feet ahead, the worst kind of place to hunt bears. But both captains believed that this island was where all the bears came from to bother their camp, and so here they were with half their soldiery thrashing through the thickets to kill or drive them out for good. Every man was at great risk, not just from bears that might charge through the bush at short range, but from the other soldiers' bullets, which would be flying in every direction the moment anyone saw or thought he saw a bear. Captain Lewis was seething with frustration over the details that delayed the completion of his dream boat, and was taking it out on the only other annoyance he couldn't control: the bears. York and Captain Clark were somewhere on Drouillard's right, and Captain Lewis far off to his left, but he got only glimpses of them now and then: York's sun-faded red headkerchief, sun-glint on a gun lock beyond twigs and green leaves. He could hear them breathing and their feet crackling in old twigs on the ground. He could smell the men—indeed could recognize almost everyone by odor—and there was some faint bear scent on the island. He saw strands of their fur on twigs here and there, and footprints from before the rain. But Lewis's hope of finding an army of bears here to engage in battle seemed in vain.

They had pushed through almost all the way across the island when Drouillard heard a grunt and a rumbling growl just ahead, saw willow slips shaking and swishing, then saw the broad brown snarling face crashing toward him. Straight for him, not for anyone to his left or right. He heard warnings and questions shouted nearby as he cocked the flintlock and aimed just below the chin. The grizzly was two loping strides from him when his ball hit it in the heart.

The bear was knocked down by the shock, crashing to the ground almost at his feet, but it was up instantly with a roar. Without an instant to reload, Drouillard sprinted away to the left, crashing through the willows as fast as he could flee, with the roaring, gurgling animal at his heels and men's alarmed voices shouting from every direction. In a few seconds the pursuit was over. He heard the animal fall silent behind him. He was reloading his rifle when the captains, following the trail of noise and blood, emerged through the willows and looked down on its carcass.

It was a young male of about four hundred pounds, and after another hour of beating the bush it was evident that this had been the only bear on the island.

Bird Woman and her little son were nearby that evening as Drouillard flensed the bear hide. She looked as if she wanted to say something about it—perhaps to offer to help with a task that was considered woman's work. He kept working. He was thinking some curious thoughts about this bear, or rather, feeling something. Finally he leaned back and, with greasy hands, signed to her: *You question?*

She nodded and with a sweeping hand indicated everything outside the camp. Then she signed: *Question all bears war against men who wear hats?* That meant whitemen. She had noticed, then, that it had been this way since the first conflicts near the Yellow Stone. She had noticed the many bears around this camp last night.

He signed: *War yes.* Then he signed: *I killed chief bear five days before. This bear come to kill me back.*

She nodded. She had no difficulty believing it. Probably she was the only person in all this party who would believe such a revenge story. But with all the soldiers hunting bears on that island, the one bear on the island had sought him out and tried to kill him.

And yesterday while out hunting, Joe Field had another of his narrow escapes, chased into the river by a bear that went straight for him. It was Joe who had been in the tree with Drouillard when he killed the chief bear. Joe had been lamenting that he was having more than his share of bear troubles; maybe he would come to understand why.

It was getting too personal, this bear war, and Drouillard wasn't sure he was on the right side.

> *July 4th Thursday 1805*
> *a beautiful clear pleasant waarm mornng . . . we finished putting the Iron boat together and turned hir on one side to dry. it being the 4th of Independence we drank the last of our ardent Spirits except a little reserved for Sickness. the fiddle put in order and the party amused themselves dancing all the evening untill about 10 oClock in a Sivel & jovil manner.*
> *Sergeant John Ordway,* Journals

July 9, 1805

The day dawned fair. Then a dark cloud settled over the island, but it was not a storm cloud. Drouillard felt a chill, hearing a strange fluttering and squawking din. Glancing up, he saw the sky over the camp full of wheeling blackbirds, some landing in brush and trees, some staying aloft. This seemed a bad sign. He glanced at Sacagawea, herself called the Bird Woman, to see her reaction, and he could see in her face too that this was bad. Whatever it meant, he would have to pray and be watchful.

Captain Lewis had finally finished assembly of his hide-covered iron boat, with a coating of charcoal, tallow, and beeswax over the entire hull to seal and waterproof it. It had been a maddening and anxious time, and the task had kept them here a week since the completion of the portage. Now the boat had been launched, and it floated like a swan, waiting to be loaded. Captain Lewis kept pacing on the shore, slapping the back of one hand into the palm of the other, looking at his creation from every angle, grinning and chuckling with his bottom lip between his teeth. The six dugout canoes had already been caulked and loaded, ready to proceed at last on up the Missouri to the snow-topped mountains. The load for the iron boat sat on shore.

Just then the blackbirds all flew away to the east, and a violent windstorm swept in after them. The Missouri was whipped up into high, whitecapped waves which sprayed over the canoes, wetting their baggage before it could all be unloaded. Another delay.

The wind continued until evening. Captain Lewis had stayed hunkered down in the spray-drenched camp, keeping an eye on his precious boat, and by the time the wind slacked, he was slumping, grim-faced.

The hull of his iron boat was delaminating. The caulking compound was slipping off the elk skin, leaving the seams exposed, and through each one of the thousands of needle holes where the skins had been sewn together, river water was leaking. Even without any load in, she was sinking. Captain Lewis looked so gray and defeated, no one knew what to say to him.

Maybe this was what the blackbirds had foretold.

Eventually Captain Clark said, "I've had the hunters looking out for timber good enough for making dugout canoes. There's some really big cottonwoods a few miles upriver. I'll take a crew of our best axmen up in the morning, and a hunter, and we'll have two or three dugouts made by the time you get up there. Two should carry what that basket-boat o' yours was supposed to."

It was plain that Clark had not had much faith in the iron boat. Captain Lewis glared into the fire, cracking the knuckles of one small, thick hand and then the other. Finally he muttered, "If I'd only *singed* the elk hair instead of shaving it, the composition might have stuck on. At least till we got to some pitch pine country. But there's no time to experiment anymore. I've piddled away a week, on top of what that portage cost us." He shook his head slowly. "I don't know whether this place is enchanted, or cursed, or both. Seems like we've been here for years, not weeks."

He sighed mightily, then went on: "Well, my friend, all right. I'll take apart this favorite boat o'mine and bury her tomorrow, and say adieu. We've got to get up to the end of this damned Missouri River and find Shoshone horses if we're to cross the mountains before winter. God knows, our biggest portage is still probably ahead of us!" They all sat looking at him, thinking about what he had just said. They had barely survived this one. After a while he said, "Notice how quiet the bears are? Lord, I hope I never have to meet another one!

"But, my God!" Lewis looked as if he would cry. "Hasn't it been worth it all, just to see these waterfalls?" There was a desperation in his eyes that Drouillard could hardly bear to see. Then he saw something gather and straighten up inside Lewis, who laughed and exclaimed, "Damn, what a time to run out of whiskey!"

Monday July 15th 1805
We arrose verry early this morning, assigned the canoes their loads and had it put on board. We now found our vessels eight in number all heavily laden, notwithstanding our several deposits . . . we find it extreemly difficult to keep the bagage of many of our men within reasonable bounds: they will be adding bulky articles of but little use or value to them. At 10 A.M. we once more saw ourselves fairly under way much to my Joy and I believe that of every individual who compose the party.

Meriwether Lewis, Journals

Chapter 15

The Three Forks of the Missouri
July 27, 1805

Drouillard raised his head to sniff and listen, because there was something important about this place that he felt he was supposed to know.

He thought that it was one of the most beautiful places he had ever seen, a long, wide, fertile basin with snow-topped mountains on every horizon, berries and currants growing thick, extensive stands of timber, and considerable game. It appeared to be the best beaver country he had seen yet.

It was a coming-together place of rivers; here, within a short walk, three rivers came together, cold, clear waters, to become the Missouri. The captains had seen a high, level limestone plateau which they with their military eyes thought of as a naturally fortified place for a fort and trading post. So it was in many ways one of those proper places where his uncle had said a man should establish himself early. Drouillard could see that.

Charbonneau's wife, the Bird Woman, said she remembered it as the valley where the Hidatsas had killed her relatives and captured her. This was hunting country of her Shoshone people. That news excited the captains, who urgently wanted to find the Shoshones and acquire horses that could carry their tons of goods over the Shining Mountains to the westward-flowing rivers. Captain Clark had scouted far ahead up the western fork with Frazier, the Field brothers, and Charbonneau, looking for Shoshones. They had found horse tracks and burned prairie but no sight of a living Indian. Clark had finally returned this afternoon sick from heat exhaustion and fatigue, feet bleeding and infected from prickly pears. In the course of his scouting he had saved Charbonneau from drowning in a swift stream, had climbed high hills to view the basin and river courses, and killed two grizzly bears who were unfortunate enough to cross his path.

The rest of the soldiers were in no better shape; they had been poling and dragging the eight dugout canoes up through swift, cold, rocky-bottom shallows and riffles, and were almost too weak to move. The two hundred miles since the Great Falls had exhausted them almost as much as the portage itself. There had been no evening whiskey to alleviate their miseries since the Fourth of July. The season was deep into summer, the days scorching even at this altitude, and the whole height of the Shining Mountains lay before them yet to be crossed before fall snows would close the passes, those passes they hadn't even found yet.

Those were the anxieties of the captains, and Drouillard felt their tension. Captain Lewis was ready to take a sortie up the west fork, which he called the Jefferson River, and not stop until he found Indians who would sell him horses and show him the way through the mountains. Drouillard knew he would be one of those going on such a sortie. This was one of those times when Lewis was desperate. But Drouillard also felt something apart from this journey of the whitemen, something about himself and the voices of the ancestors, the faint voices that sang in the wind from high places. As he gazed around and smelled the air now, he thought he could hear those voices.

They sang not just about what had happened here before, or was happening here now, but about something farther ahead around the circle of time.

August 12, 1805
The Continental Divide

Up and up the long, scruffy slope they trudged, keeping an eye on the Indian path, through prickly pear, short dry sedge, thistles and dusty sage, looking ever ahead for the ridge where this treeless slope eventually would have to culminate. Drouillard walked before and to the right of Captain Lewis, Shields left of the captain a few yards, and McNeal following, each carrying a knapsack and blanket roll and a rifle. They scanned the slope in every direction for a sight of the Indian horseman they had seen yesterday, who had waited curiously and nervously as the captain came within a hundred yards of him, signaling to him with trinkets, waving a blanket in the parley sign, and calling out to him over and over a Shoshone word that was supposed to mean "I am a whiteman." In other words, not your enemy.

But that wary Indian suddenly had wheeled his elegant horse, leaped a creek and vanished among the willow brush.

Later they found the hoofprints of several horses, and places where Indians had been digging roots, but no people. The captain was in a nasty state of anxiety, desperately wanting to make contact with any Indian, but afraid that any Indian who saw them would run to warn the rest and they would disappear.

They were deep in Shoshone country. For two weeks Bird Woman had pointed out places she remembered, and in those two weeks the captains had taken turns scouting far ahead of the slow-moving canoes, searching desperately for the elusive Shoshone. Unfortunately, the Shoshone were an extremely wary people. They had no guns, but their enemies did.

They were excellent horsemen with fine herds, who in late summer made furtive forays eastward onto the plains to hunt buffalo with their bows and arrows, but most of the year lived on the scarce game of these mountains, eating roots and fish, and trying to avoid raiding parties from the tribes who knew whitemen and had gotten guns from them. Bird Woman's husband had told the captains, "She say, anyone they see they fear to be an enemy." And her tribe of the Shoshones had never seen whitemen. When she was a girl, they had only heard of them, of those far to the south, where, in the old days, horses had come from. That, the captains presumed, would mean the Spaniards.

So it was no wonder these people were so hard to find. They lived in a vast, high country and did not want to be found. Even the hunters' guns, which were needed to feed the expedition, might be frightening these Shoshones farther and farther into hiding.

But they had to be found, and befriended, and persuaded to sell at least two dozen horses. If not, the expedition could never go across the mountains.

Captain Lewis was grim in his desperation. He had blamed his men for scaring off the man on horseback. He had angrily sworn that he would find the Shoshones if he had to hike these mountains for a month. After that, of course, it would be too late because of the seasons. But he had laughed today, once:

Coming up a narrow, grassy stream bed on this endless slope, Private McNeal had stood with one foot on either side of the clear trickling rill, fumbled with his breeches, and yelled: "Thank God! I've lived to bestride the end of the goddamn endless Misery River! And now I'm going to take a piss 'at goes plumb to the Gulf of Mexico!"

Drouillard gave him a hard look and said: "Among my people, it's the women who straddle to piss."

Captain Lewis laughed out loud, but then scowled at McNeal. "Stop that. Our people are downstream." Shamed, McNeal quit.

A little farther up they found the source of that stream to be a clear, ice-cold spring emerging from the earth. Here Captain Lewis had drunk and sat to rest, and he said, with a long, long look in his eyes, gazing back down the long slope, "I've done it! Drunk from the very fountainhead of the greatest river of this continent. Boys, we've come three thousand miles up this Missouri. Now, let's cross over this ridge and get us a drink from the fountainhead of the Columbia."

And so now here they were, trudging up onto the ridge that separated the east-flowing from the west-flowing waters. The Shoshone trail led over a pass; the ridge rose higher both north and south. If the Shoshones had a village, it must be over on the west side of the divide. That way went their path. And from this ridge it was supposed to be all downhill to the Pacific Ocean in the west. They climbed toward the ridge. In his mind's eye Drouillard anticipated a long, easy slope down the other way, with wide rivers for boats. These captains had been right so many times, he was ready to see what they expected to see.

What they did see when they crested the rise, into a howling updraft, left them speechless.

The western slope fell away steeper than the one they had just climbed, and was the same sere, brown, treeless kind of ground.

But as far as they could see to the west, rose range after range of immense, craggy, snowcapped mountains, some shining in sunlight, some somber and almost black in the shadows of drifting clouds.

For a year he had heard the captains speak of the western mountains as if they were a single range, to be easily crossed by going up one side and down the other. But here lay before them an endless maze of obstacles. Any one of those peaks was higher and steeper than anything they had yet climbed. And there were scores of them ahead.

This was the most beautiful and magnificent sight Drouillard had ever beheld, greater even than his eagle dreams.

It was not good. The captain now must speak of turning back.

But when Lewis at last spoke, he said, "Let's head on. We *really do* have to find some horses."

Drouillard took the women to be a grandmother, a mother, and a daughter. They were digging and talking, and had gathering baskets and root-digging sticks of the kind Bird Woman used.

They would flee like the pronghorn if they saw the whitemen at a distance, so Drouillard led the soldiers close in the defilade of a long ravine.

When the three saw the soldiers rise a few yards away, they looked like startled rabbits, but only the young woman ran, leaving her basket and stick. The old woman and the young girl stood stunned. Captain Lewis laid his gun on the ground and turned up his sleeve to show his white skin, saying "Tab-ba-bone! Tab-ba-bone," trying to tell them he was a whiteman. Drouillard raised his right-hand palm forward, with the forefinger and middle finger pointing up, believing that "friend," would be more reassuring than something as alien as "whiteman." As the soldiers approached, the woman and girl sat on the ground with their heads down, apparently awaiting inevitable death or capture.

Captain Lewis took their hands, opened them, and put in gifts: awls and small pewter looking glasses. When they looked up, confused and still wary, the captain smiled at them and said, "Drouillard, tell this old one to call the woman back. Don't want her to go and alarm the people to run off! We've got some in hand at last!"

Drouillard knelt before her and signed, *Call woman back. Friends.* He could see the young woman lurking in the distance, almost out of sight, still as a deer. The old woman's eyes were red-rimmed, deep in wrinkled sockets, and suspicious. He signed again, adding, *Bring good.* She looked intently in his eyes, and he saw trust take hold. She was small and scrawny, but when she turned and called, her voice was strong as a bugle.

Slowly, the distant woman emerged into view and came back, looking as if she would dart off at any minute. Drouillard smelled horse and had the feeling that someone else was out there watching, but could see no one.

When she came up, Captain Lewis made soothing noises, and with his thumb he dipped into a little packet of vermilion powder and put red marks on their cheeks that meant Peace. The women and girl had been trembling, but now they were surreptitiously admiring the little gifts in their hands and talking rapidly and softly to each other. In their voices was the lilt of relief and deliverance. McNeal and Shields were already making admiring eyes at the young woman, and she was aware of them and not displeased. Though the soldiers must have seemed very strange to someone who had never seen bearded faces, they might have appeared splendid. They were tall and lean, with sun-bleached whiskers, sun-browned faces, and bold blue eyes.

"Tell them we wish to go to their camp and meet their chiefs and warriors," the captain said.

Soon, then, the three women were leading them down alongside a small, clear river on the worn footpath. Captain Lewis kept up cheerful banter with his men in hopes that his tone of voice would reassure the women. Drouillard knew that Lewis must be as nervous as the women. Captain Clark and all the men, canoes, and gear were on the other side of the continental divide, anywhere from fifty to a hundred miles back, utterly out of communication for nearly four days, except for a note Lewis had left on a willow pole two days earlier at a fork in the stream, telling Clark to halt the boats there and wait for further word. As narrow and shallow as the streams had become, the boats might not even have reached that note yet. It might not even be there anymore; a similar message pole several days ago had been cut down by a beaver, causing the scouts and the main party to diverge at a lower fork and lose each other for a day. There was getting to be too much chance and remoteness as this desperate search for the Shoshones continued. The western mountains were daunting; time was running out.

And geese were already flying south.

"It'll be up to you, Drouillard," Lewis said as they hiked along with the cheerful but nervous women. "I expected we'd have Charbonneau's wife to translate when we found 'em. But she's clear over on the Missouri watershed, and God knows when we'll get her here. I sure hope they use the same gesture talk on this side of—"

"We find out now," Drouillard said. "Here they come."

Drouillard had been noticing that the women were becoming more animated, and then he heard hoofbeats. Now he pointed ahead. Dust was drifting above a rise, then a great body of horsemen came into view over the crest: more and more, bristling with long lances and painted shields. By now the riders had seen the soldiers and whipped up their horses, coming at full gallop; there seemed to be sixty or seventy of them.

"Ooooh, my God," Shields groaned.

"Been nice knowin' ye, gents," McNeal murmured, starting to raise his rifle even though the odds were hopeless.

Lewis said: "Drouillard, send the old woman to inform 'em we're peaceable. Don't let the young ones go; they're hostage if we need 'em. McNeal, get the flag out of your pack and give it to me. Quick! Look, they're reining in!"

The horsemen had stopped a hundred yards distant. When they saw the old woman coming, three riders separated out and came forward at a trot. Lewis said, "Ease down your guns. Don't even look hostile!" He slid the ramrod out of his rifle, shrugged his knapsack off onto the ground, and laid his rifle on top of it. Quickly he tied the little flag on the ramrod and said, "Stay back. I'm going up there. If anything happens to me, try to get back to Cap'n Clark. You've got range on their weapons and you've got their females; you might make it. Here I go." He paced out with the little flag high over one shoulder and the other hand held up in the peace gesture. He was five paces forward when the young woman and the girl, not being restrained, suddenly ran past him toward the warriors. He muttered "Damn you!" but continued forward. The three women were talking excitedly to the horsemen and showing them their gifts.

The three riders dismounted. With immense relief, Drouillard watched the Indian leader put his left arm over Captain Lewis's right shoulder and press his cheek against the captain's, saying, *"A hi ee! A hi ee,"* an utterance he had heard often enough from Bird Woman to know it meant "Thank you," or "I am pleased." Then the other two embraced Lewis, making the same sounds, and soon all the other riders had come up and dismounted to get in on the hugging. The captain called his men forward to join in. Drouillard thought he would burst with gratitude and kindly feelings as all these beautifully decorated warriors, smelling of grease, wood smoke, and horse sweat, milled about, greeting these strangers with such open delight. This was good, this was how people could be when they were not afraid of others. This was a greeting of joy that made him remember the Missouria youth named Hospitality, a year ago. The three women were happy with all this; they stood flexing their knees and patting their palms.

"Drouillard," said Lewis, whose cheeks and shoulders were by now thoroughly smeared with grease and face paint, "I'm anxious to talk with these people about us and what we need."

So Drouillard slipped off his knapsack and got out the pipe. Soon all the Shoshone warriors, except a few boys left tending the horses, were seated in a circle, with the captain and his men in the center. The Indians had taken off their moccasins. Drouillard explained: "It means they will go barefoot if they don't keep their word, whatever we say here."

"Oohoo! Pretty serious pledge, considering the prickly pear!" McNeal exclaimed.

It was hot in the afternoon sun on this scrabbly slope, and the passing of the pipe took a long time. Drouillard had to remind the captain not to let his impatience show. "The pipe's not just a preliminary, sir. It's the main thing. The rest's just details."

"All right. Thankee. Now I take it the long-face with short hair's their chief?"

Drouillard began signing, and watching the replies. Fortunately, their signs varied little from the plains peoples', and the understanding would not be difficult.

The chief gave his name as Cameahwait, meaning He Does Not Walk. He said his men had come out so aggressively because they expected enemies; lately they had been raided by enemies with guns and had lost some horses and lodges, and that the men with hair cut short were in mourning for lost relatives.

"I'm going to give them some beads and vermilion," Captain Lewis said. "Then tell them we want to go to their camp because we have much to explain and to ask them. That a council should be held nearer to water than this, because it will take a long while."

Drouillard told them all that with signs, and it seemed to go well enough with them. They accepted the token gifts very gracefully, got up and put on their moccasins. "Now I'll give this Cameahwait our flag," Lewis said. "Tell him it is an emblem of peace, and bonds us to him in a union, sort of like taking off your moccasins."

These Shoshone were rich in horses and hospitality but poor in almost everything else. The destructive raid of the Atsinas had left the band with only one skin tepee lodge. All their family shelters and their council house were cleverly made but crude tepees and huts of willow brush. There seemed to be only three firearms in the whole band, cheap smoothbores of the sort the English traders sold to the Missouri tribes.

The Shoshone camp was in a fertile, level bottom on the east bank of a clear, wide, shallow river, quick-flowing north over many-colored round stones and gravel. It was a beautiful place in the shadow of the mountain range. Captain Lewis seemed gaunt and exhausted but his eyes glowed when he looked out and saw the horse herds.

Cameahwait had prepared seats for the whitemen, green boughs covered with antelope skins, in the brush council house. The chief and his people were excited and fascinated. They had never seen whitemen, and these had suddenly appeared in their land like spirits. The chief told Drouillard by hand language that the people wondered if they were children of the Great Spirit. Everybody had crowded around the council lodge to look at them. Drouillard understood that he was himself an object of curiosity, a real person traveling with these pale ones and speaking for them, but Cameahwait was too civilized to ask him a personal question about that. Instead he asked Drouillard to request that the pale men now be barefoot so that their sincerity could be assured. After that was done, the Shoshones could scarcely keep their eyes off the visitors' bare feet, which were even whiter than their sun-weathered faces and hands, and showed much sign of abuse: bloody punctures from the prickly pears, bruises, and red-rimmed toenails.

A strange thing about this camp-village was that there was no smell of cooking, usually the most pervasive and compelling stimulus in any Indian town. Drouillard was particularly aware of that absence because he and the soldiers had eaten nothing since the previous evening. Feeding guests was usually the first act of hospitality. He could tell by the gaunt look of all these people that the reason they offered no food was that they had none. This was a bleak and terrible realization, and his urge as a hunter was to borrow horses from these people, go out in the remaining daylight and get meat for everybody. No one was supposed to go hungry when George Drouillard was present.

But the pressing matter for Captain Lewis was not eating

but talking, and Drouillard was the only one who could make that happen. Therefore the chief began a long and meticulous pipe ceremony which would enable everyone to speak well and truthfully.

To the sound of burbling and groaning stomachs, Drouillard put his talking hands to work, to explain that whole complex story of the Great White Father Jefferson and what he wanted, and the part these Shoshones of the western slope would be expected to perform in it. He passed on the usual promises, about the guns and goods the Shoshones might expect to get if they were good and true and helpful.

But he did not translate the threats, the threats about how they would be left out of the prosperity and how they would be punished by countless soldiers if they didn't cooperate. The captain spoke to them in his usual veiled and diplomatic way, but Drouillard didn't translate this because he knew the captain had taken off his moccasins and smoked the pipe, and thus must not lie. But Lewis could not tell these people of the western slope that the White Father in the East was their new father whom they must obey, because he knew that Jefferson had purchased the country only as far as the dividing ridge, and these people were beyond that. Any help they chose to give they could give of their own free will, in response to promises.

They did not *have* to do anything, which was the way it always should be, and Drouillard felt good about it. His people, the Shawnees back on the far side of the continent, had expended their lives for generations in refusing to obey orders the whitemen had had no right to give them.

It was dusk by the time Captain Lewis got around to explaining what help he needed immediately from the Shoshones. He had Drouillard describe the main party coming up the other side with canoes full of goods, with the other soldier chief in charge. He told of their need for Shoshone horses and for people to help them bring all the goods across the ridge. All this was fairly easy to tell. Although most of these mountain people had seldom seen canoes or boats, they knew about them and understood what Drouillard was saying.

He was an excellent sign talker in the same way he was an excellent hunter: he could see and sense more than just the apparent. Now he was seeing and sensing that some of the Shoshones were growing fearful and suspicious. He saw little side glances and squints in the eyes of even the agreeable Cameahwait. He saw warriors on the outer circle of the council stiffening, leaning to whisper to each other, and he saw fear replacing curiosity in the faces of the women and children who were crowding the periphery of the lodge to watch the whitemen. Cameahwait changed the subject to say that his people had just been getting ready to cross the divide and descend into the plains to hunt buffalo, and that they needed to do this soon or they would starve here in the mountains when winter came. They had to rendezvous with their friends the Flatheads very soon to go down in strength for the buffalo hunt.

All this carrying for the whitemen, the chief suggested, might delay their crucial hunt too long. The winter was hard in these mountains. There were pronghorns and a few deer here now, but they were so swift that even hunters on good horses could not catch them except by surrounding them and running them to exhaustion. And with cold weather, the hoofed ones would be going away, down to the good grazing. Drouillard saw that this was a genuine concern of the chief, but he sensed there was more to it.

He translated those statements to Lewis and saw the captain beginning to puff himself up for a demanding argument, so he added: "Cap'n, the real trouble is, they don't trust us. Asking them to follow us out of their haven here has got some of 'em nervous. If I were these people, I'd be wondering who we've got coming up the other side: enemies waiting there for you and me to trick 'em out? Hidatsas? Blackfeet? They've already been hurt by the Atsinas. Don't get mad, Cap'n, but I think we're worrying 'em and I think that's why."

Lewis clenched his jaw and thought. He said, "Tell them that if they help us, the United States will bring them trade and good guns so they won't even have to hide here from their enemies. That they could go out and live where the buffalo are. And while they're thinking that over, tell them that we haven't eaten for more than twenty-four hours."

"I'll tell them that, sir. From the looks of 'em, they might reply that they haven't eaten for a week. I think we'd do ourselves and them the most good by killing them some meat tomorrow."

Lewis nodded. "That would be good. And impress on them what American rifles can do, while you're at it."

This was the most exciting but least effective hunting he had ever done.

He rode at a headlong gallop through the short vegetation of the valley, a Shoshone horseman far off to his right and several to his left, chasing a small herd of pronghorn that the horses could not possibly overtake. White rumps, reddish backs, bounding and flashing ahead, the antelopes diminished rapidly in the distance. It was like chasing birds.

Far down the valley, two miles beyond the fleeing herd, a line of Shoshones on fresh horses would gallop out and turn the herd of pronghorns in another direction, toward another waiting line of horsemen on rested mounts. Drouillard and his fellow hunters now veered off toward a knoll where boys were awaiting them with fresh horses. This was the third horse Drouillard had ridden to exhaustion so far. Almost all the riders who had come out to meet them yesterday were here on the plain surrounding the fleeing antelope, chasing them five miles one way, then six another, in hopes of eventually wearing them down enough to be able to ride within bow shot. Thus far he could see no hope even of getting within long rifle shot of one. Private Shields was with another group of Shoshone riders elsewhere in the valley. The chase had been in progress for more than two hours, usually in sight of the Shoshone town, but not one antelope had succumbed yet. This morning Captain Lewis had requested horses to allow his best hunters to go hunting. But the Shoshones, reluctant to let them ride out of sight, had joined them, and, seeing this herd, had drawn them into this thrilling but futile pursuit, which seemed more like a racing sport than a way to feed the hungry people. The white visitors, and the whole band of Shoshones as well, had gone to bed last night with nothing more to eat than cakes of dried berries and a bite or two of leathery dried salmon. The Shoshones had honored their visitors with a dance until late. The captain had declined, saying he was too tired to do anything but write a few notes by firelight and then go to sleep in his mosquito net. The soldiers, professing to be too hungry to sleep, had stayed up watching the Shoshones do their circle dances and showing them some of their own high steps—as well as they could without benefit of fiddle music.

Now the pronghorns found a gap between two racing groups of Shoshone hunters and sped up a draw to freedom. The fifty riders returned to camp on their lathered horses, hungrier than ever. Drouillard wanted to go out and hunt his own way, but by now Captain Lewis had spent the morning unable to ask Cameahwait anything or tell him anything, and was prowling with impatience for his interpreter. McNeal had made a sort of pudding with flour, water, and berries, which was at least edible and assuaged the hunger pangs a little. "Now," Lewis told Drouillard, "I want to talk to this Never Walks chief about geography. About the way through those mountains, and some navigable way to the Columbia. We should allow another day for Clark to get the boats up to that fork, so we should use the day well. Now, Cap'n Clark did well talking maps out of the Hidatsas last winter. Think you and I might do as well here?"

Drouillard said, "If Never Walks has ever walked out that way, and if he can draw lines in the sand, I guess so." He sighed. Map talk was a most tedious kind of interpreting. Where he really wanted to be was out in this valley along the streams, finding game to ease the hunger of these people. Too much hunger makes people small in spirit. These Shoshones were becoming dull and fearful.

If whitemen were this hungry, they would be eating their horses, he thought.

It was going to take much cajolery, many promises, to persuade these furtive people to postpone their buffalo hunt and cross the divide, risking exposure to enemies, just to help these mysterious people with their strange request. But Cameahwait had promised to help.

Drouillard saw the deer jerk its head up. It had seen one of the Shoshone horsemen and was about to flee, so he would have to shoot it now at this long range instead of stalking closer to it. He made his prayer to the Keeper of the Game and the deer itself and aimed high to compensate for the distance.

It was the second day out of the Shoshone camp, and now that they were back on the east side of the divide, the Shoshones were as fearful as they had been before their chief shamed them into coming. When he and Shields had ridden out this morning to hunt, the Indians insisted on sending riders along to keep an eye on them. Captain Lewis had argued to the chief that the presence of such scouts could scare off any game, but the Indians were afraid that if the two hunters got out of their sight, they might go down and call in the dreaded imaginary enemies. The more Lewis protested the escort, the more suspicious the Shoshones became, and so now Drouillard and Shields were hunting with the handicap of highly visible horsemen off on their flanks. These people were nearly starved, having eaten absolutely nothing for days, but apparently they feared their enemies worse than they feared hunger. They had wanted to turn back last night, but Lewis told them that one of their own long-lost relatives was with the white men in the boats, a young woman captured by the Hidatsas five years ago. They remembered that raid and nodded.

And Drouillard had told of a black-skinned man with hair like a buffalo's poll. It was as if they had to stay, to see such a thing.

He had dismounted a few minutes ago and left the horse tied to a willow in order to stalk this close to the deer, which was not close enough to suit him, because if he missed, this gunshot would scare any game even farther down, and it was scarce enough already.

He squeezed the trigger; the rifle cracked and bucked, and the deer sprang forward three times, then fell. Up on the slope one of

the Shoshone horsemen whooped. Drouillard watched him lash
his horse and ride full tilt back along the draw to tell his people
of meat. Drouillard reloaded, ran back to get his horse, rode up
and gutted the deer. He waved to Shields, whom he could see
half a mile away on the other side of the valley, pointed down at
the carcass, then mounted and headed on down the valley to hunt
for more. He knew this one would not last long when the captain
and the hungry Indians arrived, and also that one deer would
scarcely begin to feed seventy starving people.

Within an hour he had killed a second deer, hung it by a
stream and gone on down looking for another. Before mid-
morning he had got a third, and he butchered it and slung it behind the saddle to take back to the Shoshones. Three deer would
at least take the edge off their hunger, and he looked forward to
cooking and eating a solid breakfast with these poor people.

He had taken a bite out of each deer's heart—spiritual food,
not enough to ease his own ravenous hunger. Remembering this
country, he guessed it would take until late afternoon to get
down to the creek fork where Lewis had left the note for Clark.
No doubt the Shoshones were getting more and more nervous as
they came down. He knew some of the women were certain they
were being led into a trap. If Captain Clark wasn't at the forks
with the boats, the Shoshones' suspicions would seem confirmed, and they probably would just turn and retreat back over
the divide. Lewis had him explain, as well as he could, about the
note he left on a stick for the other white chief. It had been very
difficult to explain what a note was; Drouillard had to first explain such a mysterious thing as writing.

When he got back to Lewis and the Shoshones, he expected to
see them cooking the other two deer, but there was nothing left
of them but bones and hides. Lewis exclaimed with a grimace
that when he gave them the major portions of the two animals,
they had devoured them raw, down to the guts and even the soft
parts of the hooves.

"You're their savior, Drouillard. Now let's cook this one
proper for a good breakfast, all of us, if they can be patient

enough. I'll be able to eat if I don't let myself remember these wretches chewing raw guts. Eugh!"

Later Shields killed a pronghorn. The Shoshones rewarded Lewis and his hunters with fur capes. Lewis gave the chief his cocked hat. Now, to any lurking enemy, they all looked indistinguishable.

"Damn, look at 'em," Lewis muttered. "Now they fully doubt us again! Where's Clark?"

The Shoshones did look as if they were ready to turn and hightail back up the valley to their hideaway on the other side of the divide. Above the fork where Lewis had promised them the other whiteman chief with the boats would be waiting, there was not a sign of Clark's party. Some of the most dubious warriors were crowding around Cameahwait and it was all too obvious they were telling him they were being tricked, that they should go no farther.

"I've got to restore their faith," Lewis said, "or we'll never see them again and we're out of luck for horses ever. Listen . . . I'm going to give Never Walks my rifle . . . tell him that if I've tricked him and there's any enemy in the brush down there, by God, he can shoot them or he can shoot me, that I'm not afraid to die. Got to challenge their courage again . . . We'll all give 'em our rifles."

The soldiers looked stunned. Shields protested: "S'pose there really *are* Blackfeets or somethin' around? What if Cap'n Clark run into some? Maybe that's why he ain't here!"

"I think they're just slow coming. Tell them, Drouillard."

So Drouillard told them, and the men handed their weapons up to the horsemen. The Indians fondled and examined the fine weapons, and it was obvious that they would love to keep them forever—especially now that they knew from how far away they could kill deer. Drouillard had no illusions about men and weapons, and he knew that Lewis in his desperation had just enabled the Shoshones to kill the four members of the expedition, who had come in and troubled their lives and delayed their buffalo hunt, with their very own weapons.

But it seemed to be working. This gesture, and his hand-sign explanation of it, now had the chief and his warriors nodding and talking rapidly among themselves, and the looks in their faces were changing. Faith in Cameahwait's integrity was well-placed.

Now the captain said, "Here's something else we can do. You remember the note I left for Cap'n Clark to wait here for us? Drouillard, I want you to tell them again about that note and then take one of their scouts down there with you and get it. I want him to see you pick it up. Then bring it back to me."

So he told them about the note. They nodded and waited, still fondling the rifles.

Then, with one of their scouts to keep an eye on him, Drouillard rode down to the point in the forks and took the paper off the stick, brought it back to Lewis and handed it to him. Lewis untied it and seemed to be reading it with growing delight.

What's he doing? Drouillard thought. He already knows what it says—he wrote it himself!

Lewis waved the paper in front of Cameahwait, smiling broadly. "Now, George, tell them that this is a note from our other captain. That he comes so slow that he sent a messenger here today with this note, and took away my note. That this one asks us to wait here for him with the Indians. And that if the Indians don't believe it, one of their braves should ride down with you to meet Clark and tell him we're waiting. Got all that?"

Drouillard, incredulous, said, "But that's the same note you left there. I recognize—"

"They don't know that. Tell them what I said."

"But that isn't true, it's lying."

Lewis narrowed his eyes. "It isn't really a lie. It's a stratagem. You've got to tell them that or we lose them, and probably our guns and our lives too. This is no damned time for niceties, and I'm ordering you to tell them what I said!" He kept his voice low and pleasant but there was ice in his eyes.

Drouillard turned slowly to the Indians, cupped his hand behind his ear and pointed to them, meaning, *Listen.* And for a moment he wasn't sure what he was going to tell them. He did not ever want to lie to Indians for whitemen, especially friendly Indians who were sure they were risking their lives to help them. But to undermine the captain's "stratagem" would destroy their trust, probably with fatal consequences for these soldiers and himself, and cause a failure of the whole mission. Would that be better than a small, inventive deceit?

He sighed. There was a way to say it. He began signing:

My chief wants me to tell you this story about the message on the white leaf. That it came from our other chief. He wants me to say it was put here just today . . .

This was going to be an uneasy night.

Saturday August 17th 1805
This morning I arrose very early and dispatched Drewyer and an Indian down the river. I made McNeal cook the remainder of our meat which afforded a slight breakfast for ourselves and the Chief . . .

Meriwether Lewis, Journals

It was cold and Drouillard was glad when the sun rose over the eastern mountains, ever so slightly warming the right side of his face. The Shoshone warrior who had agreed to accompany him down was glancing about warily, but now and then he took out and examined the shiny steel knife Captain Lewis had given him for this service. Drouillard's rifle had been returned to him for protection on the way down, and the young warrior was watching him as carefully as he watched the countryside for enemies. This was one who had seen Drouillard shoot the first deer at such great distance yesterday, and it must have required considerable courage for the warrior to come with him. But Captain Lewis, Shields, and McNeal in effect were hostages until this warrior returned safely, and perhaps he took some courage from that.

The sun was just starting to melt the frost when Drouillard saw cawing ravens fly up from the willows downstream, and at the same time he heard a man's voice, faint and distant, but sounding like Charbonneau's. The warrior had heard it too, and reined back. Drouillard smiled, pointed down and signed, *Come. Friends.* He put his heels in the horse's flanks and they trotted down, the unshod horses' hooves thudding softly. He heard another voice now, and it was a woman's. He felt laughter bubbling up in his bosom. Sacagawea. The ravens had said, Bird Woman comes.

They came walking up the shore, Charbonneau and his wife with their baby on her back, and they stopped suddenly, seeing him and the other rider. He raised a hand in greeting.

And then the Bird Woman gave a squealing whoop. She put two fingers in her mouth, her sign of kinship, meaning, *We eat together,* and began dancing in a small circle where she stood. At that moment a big man came running into view from behind them, carrying a rifle and clad in deerskin and a wolf-skin cap and virtually skidded to a stop beside them, his ruddy face open with astonishment. Drouillard leaned back in his saddle, laughed aloud and yelled:

"Cap'n Clark! It's me, Drouillard! Come on up! We got Shoshones with four hundred fine horses!"

It was like a fair, a festival, here at the fork of the narrow stream: people milling and staring, Indian men and women, whitemen in ragged and fringed deer hide, wet to the waist from pulling the canoes up the shallows and over riffles; saddled horses being led about; groups of Indians gawking at a huge black man and a huge black dog and at countless bundles of material riches being unloaded from the beached canoes and opened and spread on the grass to dry in the sunlight; women gasping and prattling about beads and colorful cloth garments with gold ribbons and buttons; Indian men hugging brawny, rawboned whitemen with face hair that hung to their collarbones. Cameahwait was tying pearly shells into locks of Captain Clark's coppery red hair, which was in itself an object of the crowd's fascinated attention, and Lewis was demonstrating his dog's obedience.

John Colter grinned at Drouillard's Shoshone trappings and exclaimed, "Hey, old friend! Y'look like a real Indian now!"

"Haha! That's the thing, eh, to look like one?"

Women gathered around Bird Woman to eye her Hidatsa dress and ornaments and to make a fuss over her baby. Drouillard wandered here and there, greeting soldiers, his heart feeling big as the world, stopping occasionally to do hand-signing for soldiers and Shoshones who had statements or questions for each other. He was hearing all the happy babble in his ears, but in his spirit he was hearing a song, a song that some of the Shoshones had sung as they came along the riverbank watching the boats come up, a happy but bittersweet greeting song with throat trills that made him long for his boyhood days in the Shawnee town at Lorimier's.

He was looking at Bird Woman, who was speaking in her own tongue with the curious women, when she abruptly went speechless. Her eyes grew big and she clapped her hand over her mouth. He heard a girl's voice exclaiming behind him and turned to see a pretty Shoshone approaching Bird Woman with her hands reaching. They embraced, almost collapsing on each other with laughter and tears. Drouillard grabbed Charbonneau by the sleeve and asked him what this was about. The Frenchman queried his sobbing wife in the Hidatsa tongue, then raised his eyebrows, nodding.

"This two were caught together by t'Hidatsa, same day, but t'at one got away and run back to her people! They see each other now! Five years! Ha haaa!" Charbonneau clapped his big, dirty hands together and shook his head sharply from side to side, yellow teeth grinning through his black beard, tears in his eyes. Drouillard had learned just today that Captain Clark reprimanded Charbonneau severely just days ago for striking his wife, yet the man seemed genuinely joyous over her reunion.

The Shoshones had erected a circular arbor of tall young willows, and the soldiers had put up a sail as a shade awning. Captain Clark called for Drouillard and Labiche and the Charbonneaus, waving them toward the awning. The captains and Cameahwait and some subchiefs were gathering there. Apparently they were getting ready to parley a little and wanted the interpreters. When Drouillard slipped into the shade, stopping to shake hands with Labiche, the captains had already seated themselves and the Shoshone headmen on the deerskins he had so recently obtained. A pipe lighting ember was being made up by Sergeant Ordway, using his burning glass just outside the bower with a tin pan to hold the tinder. The Charbonneaus came in out of the sunlight and were directed to seat themselves near the center, where they could translate, and the young woman glanced at Cameahwait. She gasped, and again made that motion of clapping her hand over her mouth. She stepped in front of the chief and dropped to her knees, face crumpling with either anguish or joy, eyes gleaming with tears. The chief's bony face at first showed just surprise. Then recognition. They uttered soft cries to each other and she embraced him, wrapping the edge of her blanket around him, now in full, unrestrained sobbing while he held her shoulder in a tight grip and tried in vain to keep a chiefly composure, his own face streaming with tears. Shoshones nearby were murmuring to each other in wonder. *"Qu'est-ce qui passe?"* Drouillard asked Charbonneau, who was watching with mouth ajar.

"Il me semble qu'il est son frère, croyé mort!"

The captains too were looking around for an explanation, and when Clark's eyes met his, Drouillard said, "Never Walks is her brother! She thought he was dead!"

"Good God almighty! Lewis, did you hear that? Good God almighty!"

Sunday August 18th 1805
began the operation of forming the packages in proper Parsels for the purpose of transporting them on horseback. Drewyer Killed one deer this evening. This day I completed my thirty first year, and conceived that I now had existed about half the period which I am to remain in this sublunary world. I reflected that I had as yet done but little, to further the happiness of the human race, or to advance the information of the succeeding generation. I viewed with regret the many hours I have spent in indolence . . . but since they are past and cannot be recalled, I dash from me the gloomy thought and re-

solved in future, to redouble my exertions, and to live for
mankind, as I have hitherto lived for myself.—

Meriwether Lewis, Journals

August 22, 1805

Drouillard gutted the fawn he had just shot, tied it behind the crude Indian saddle, and mounted to ride on down the fork, toward the camp where Captain Lewis was transferring everything from the canoes to packsaddles so the Shoshone horses could carry them west over the ridge to the town. The canoes would be sunk in a pond, weighted down with rocks, to keep them from drying out and splitting or being burned in prairie fires before the troop's return next year—in the event they did come back this way. Some extraneous items were being stored in another secret cache, hidden from the eyes of the Shoshones.

On the other side of the divide, Captain Clark was exploring the watershed for a navigable stream that would lead to the Columbia River, beyond the maze of the Shining Mountains. Here, between the two soldier parties, Drouillard hunted day by day for meat to feed both soldiers and Shoshones.

At midday he smelled smoke, saw it drifting over a rise, and rode toward it.

It was a family group of Shoshone foragers. They were eating a meal and were startled to see him ride in, but he quickly informed them by sign that he was a friend, dismounted and visited with them long enough to explain the presence and purposes of the whitemen. There were three women, a boy, an old man, and a very nervous warrior with the longest nose and narrowest face Drouillard could remember ever seeing. The warrior had no gun and could hardly keep his eyes off Drouillard's rifle; probably he was so nervous because this stranger was so much better armed than he. Drouillard was impressed by the quantity of food these people had found in this steep, stark land. In hand-woven bags they had about two bushels of dried service berries and chokecherry cakes, and another bushel of dried roots. They also had several prepared hides of buffalo, rolled to carry their belongings. They were friendly but watchful, and had the boy stay near their horses as if to protect them. Seeing that he was making them nervous, and needing to get on with the hunt, Drouillard gave them parting signs and walked off to get his horse, which was grazing away from the camp. It kept moving away and he finally caught it about fifty paces away from the fire. He heard hoofbeats then, turned, and was astonished to see the whole family mounted on their horses and galloping away, leaving their fire burning and all their belongings on the ground. He had had no idea they were that scared of him, and regretted it. He led his horse back toward the fire to get his rifle, which he had left where he was sitting.

With a chill and a flush of shame he saw that it was gone. He looked after the fleeing Indians and saw that the warrior was carrying it in one hand and desperately quirting his horse with the other.

Cursing himself for his carelessness, for turning his back on his most critical possession, he swung into the saddle and lashed the horse into an all-out run in pursuit.

He knew this was not a wise thing to be doing. His only weapon was his sheath knife, and the man he was chasing had his long rifle, loaded, and a bow and a quiver of arrows. But by damn, he thought, no man was going to steal George Drouillard's rifle and vanish without fighting for it!

Drouillard's pistols were in his gear with Lewis's party miles below. If this Shoshone thief decided to turn and fight, he had all the advantage.

As he chased them up the pass, Drouillard reflected that the Shoshone was a stranger to the gun, had only the one load that was in it, and hadn't gotten the shot and powder horn.

But the Shoshone had arrows.

There was plenty of time to weigh these things, because the chase was over open ground, and his horse was no better than theirs, if as good. He wasn't gaining. Now and then the distant warrior turned and brandished the rifle, but didn't shoot.

The race went on and on. The lean, spare Shoshone horses had

admirable endurance. Drouillard thought of throwing off the
dead fawn to lighten the load, but was too intent on staying up to
fumble with knots.

The pursuit had gone perhaps eight or nine miles when he saw
that the family's horses were not keeping up with the warrior's.
He was overtaking them. The women were crying out in fright.

Now Drouillard could see a chance.

He caught up with the family and rode in the midst of their
flagging horses. He grabbed reins and pulled them to a halt, in a
flurry of dust and confusion. He convinced them by sign that he
was not going to hurt them. They sat on their heaving mounts
looking ashamed.

Their plight had caused their warrior to circle back. Drouillard imagined he was torn between coming back to protect them
and getting away. He did what Drouillard expected of a warrior.
He kept riding nearer, pointing the rifle and crying *"Pahkee!"*
which was their word for enemies, and his face was full of torment and doubt. He couldn't shoot at Drouillard in the midst of
his family, and he looked frustrated enough to cry.

Then, in a moment when the warrior was occupying himself
with the unfamiliar workings of the flintlock, Drouillard lashed
his horse into a charge straight at him, and with every bit of his
angry strength and quickness grabbed the rifle barrel with such
force that the gun gouged and wrenched the warrior's trigger
hand, likely breaking a finger. All the warrior could do before he
relinquished the rifle to Drouillard's superior strength was flip
up the frizzen and spill out the priming powder—very quick
thinking.

The thief whipped his horse and fled, leaving the others to
fend for themselves.

Drouillard in an instant reprimed the gun and was about to
shoot the fleeing man from his saddle when he thought of the
consequences of shooting a Shoshone in Shoshone country
while the captains were crucially reliant on their cooperation.

So he left them and rode back. On the way to Lewis's camp, he
picked up the food baskets and hides they had abandoned and

loaded them on the tired horse. He was pretty sure the warrior and his family would never show up to claim them.

Despite many opportunities to steal the goods of the soldiers, the Shoshones had never taken one item. In their society, it seemed, it was not done. That one warrior apparently had just been overcome with desire for the best weapon he had ever seen, and it likely would be a long time before he would show his face among his people.

That evening, Captain Lewis had a feast prepared for the Shoshones. He had corn and beans boiled, and dried squash from the Mandans, and hundreds of fresh trout the soldiers caught by making a dragnet of brush. Part of the feast was the fawn and the roots and berries Drouillard had brought in. The always hungry Shoshones were delighted.

Chapter 16

Bitterroot Mountains
September 1805

Drouillard was too disgusted with Captain Lewis to look at him, and so was glad to be riding out ahead as hunter.

The poor and kindly Shoshones had finally fulfilled their promises to the whitemen, then with relief had hurried their migration toward their buffalo hunting grounds.

The demands of the whitemen had delayed their hunt for two weeks and had eventually tried the Shoshones' patience to the limits. After they had helped the soldiers carry all their tons of goods westward over the divide, and helped them plan a route through the western mountains, even providing an old man to guide them to the Nez Perce country, Captain Lewis had found occasion to scold Cameahwait and make him apologize for putting his own people's hunger before Lewis's desires. And then the Shoshones had been forced to wait still longer while the whitemen haggled over the prices of twenty-nine horses. What a self-important ass Lewis could be!

The soldiers now led those horses, and one mule, along rocky riverbanks into a jagged maze of mountains steeper and higher than they had ever imagined, mountains already capped with snow and sometimes shrouded in purple clouds that would leave more snow. Drouillard was aware that his days of easy hunting were over. Here there were no buffalo. Elk were seldom seen, and the few deer were hard to track on the stony mountainsides, quick to vanish in the pines. It was no wonder the Shoshones were so lean and hungry, and so impatient to go to the plains for buffalo.

Drouillard was riding a buckskin-colored gelding among tumbled, mottled boulders and gnarled driftwood alongside a rapid, rocky-bottomed stream that ran almost straight north—back north, after coming so far southwest from the falls. Long way around, it seemed.

The smells of this valley were clean, crisp: pine, crystal water, moss, cedar, berry bushes—but the only animal smell most of the time was that of his own horse. Beaver now and then. He remembered the stench of plenty at the Great Falls: the countless dead buffalo rotting at the river's edge, whiffs of animal dung on every breeze, the acrid urine of wolf boundaries, the last putrid odor of elk carrion declining to the worms and beetles after the bears and buzzards and wolves were through—where there was much to eat there was much to smell. This cleanness, to a hunter, was the scent of hunger. The only life prolific in this mountain valley was insect life: mosquitoes and biting flies, clouds of them, annoying him and his horse to twitchy distraction, swarming at eyes and mouth, whining in the ears.

Behind came the grating hooves and the snorting horses and the voices of the troop. These were not very good horses. The Shoshones had had hundreds of excellent horses, but the captains had not been willing to pay enough, and had come away with these. At first the Shoshones had been so bedazzled by the whitemen's novelties that they would give a decent horse for a cheap knife, a used cloth shirt, a few metal trinkets. But they had learned quickly about value. Theirs were the only horses to be had, and they could hold out for the true worth of their animals; good battle axes, considerable quantities of ribbon and beads, awls and mirrors. In the end, Captain Clark had yielded up a pistol and a musket and some ammunition for a final pair of horses, despite their policy of not trading away any firearms.

From the indifferent quality and condition of the packhorses, and the scarce sign of game, Drouillard could predict that the soldiers would taste horse meat before they were through these mountains—if they ever got through.

As he rode, his mind kept going back to those wild, spare Shoshone people. He had felt everything with them in two weeks: affection, anger, exasperation, joy. Every one of that people was free to do or not do according to conscience or judgment. The chief could not order, only persuade or inspire, which of course the two army officers had found maddening, even contemptible. Children were not punished, for fear it would break their spirit. And yet the Shoshone were cheerful, tough, generous; they kept their promises, and, in Drouillard's judgment, had more elegant manners than Lewis: When the chief, driven by his people's desperate hunger, had begged to hurry on to the buffalo hunt, it was Lewis who reminded him of the deer Drouillard had shot to feed his hungry Indians. He clenched his jaw when he thought of that. To remind someone of a kindness you've given him was boorish. Had Cameahwait reminded Lewis of the berries and fish his people had fed the hungry whitemen when they first arrived?

When the canoes were unloaded and all the treasures spread out to dry, no Shoshone had stolen a single object. All had asked permission even to examine things.

As for the warrior who had picked up his rifle and fled with it, that had been more of a *coup* than a theft. Warriors were admired for taking things from their enemies, and maybe the warrior had believed Drouillard was a *pahkee*, as he had called him.

Besides, Drouillard reflected, he had deserved that *coup* for leaving his rifle where someone could grab it. In getting it back, he just did a better *coup*. How he had hated telling Lewis of that incident! If he had been a soldier, he probably would have been tried and whipped. And of course there were other reasons besides censure not to leave your gun unwatched. He and that warrior had taught each other good lessons that day.

They were going back north because Captain Clark had found the west-flowing river too violent and its banks too steep and rocky. Cameahwait and the old guide had said the only safe way to go beyond the mountains was by the trails and passes the Nez Perce people traveled to hunt buffalo in the plains. That route, the old man said, was about nine sleeps north; there they must turn west and climb over the pass.

Among the voices from the column behind, Drouillard could hear, faintly now and then, the Bird Woman's. She spoke in her tongue to the old guide. He was wiry, brown and wrinkled as jerky. The captains had given him the nickname Toby, because it sounded something like the first part of his unpronounceable Shoshone name.

To Drouillard it was strange that the Bird Woman was still with the expedition. Seeing her reunion with her relatives, he had thought she would never leave them again. In the first few days she seemed to have felt that way too. She had spent as much time as possible with the few people she remembered, especially with her brother the chief, and had begged sugar and other little gifts from the captains to give them. Drouillard had presumed that Charbonneau would go on with the expedition, according to his contract, and perhaps on the way back reunite with his wife and son among her people. She seemed to love her blood people more than she loved her husband. And he, though he had some pride in his little son, demonstrated no deep attachment to Bird Woman. She could have stayed with her people and been rid of Charbonneau, who was three times her age. And smelled bad too.

But in the period of crossing the divide and trading for horses, something had changed. Drouillard had noticed it; some of the women had cooled toward Bird Woman. Maybe her far-ranging adventures had made her something beyond a Shoshone. Perhaps she, full of those adventures and enjoying prestige among these powerful white strangers, had lorded it over these poor mountain women whose lives had been lived on a smaller scale.

There was also among the Shoshone men one to whom she as a child had been promised in marriage by her now-deceased parents. That man now had two wives and had long presumed her dead. While asserting that he had a right to her, he told the captains that he didn't want her anyway because she had borne Charbonneau a child. Perhaps some of the men and women in the tribe had assumed some of his disdain.

Any or all of those considerations might have made her feel she no longer belonged among her tribe. But probably the strongest reason she was still coming along was that the captains still needed her for a while.

Only she could talk fluently with old Toby, the one man who knew, or claimed he knew, the way through the terrible maze of these mountains.

September 2nd Monday 1805
a Cloudy Mornin, raind Some last night . . . without a roade preceded on thro' thickets in which we were obliged to Cut a road, over rockey hill Sides where our horses were in pitial danger of Slipping to Ther certain distruction & up & Down Steep hills, where Several horses fell, Some turned over, and others Sliped down Steep hill Sides, one horse Crippeled & 2 gave out. with the greatest difficuelty risque &c. we made five miles & Encamped in a Small Stoney bottom.

William Clark, Journals

September 4, 1805

He held his little mirror and tweezered out his chin hairs. Sergeant Pryor, whose face was all blond whiskers from the cheekbones down, said, "Drouillard, you'll wish you left every hair on your face when it gets winter, which ain't that far off, feels like."

Whitehouse, nearby, said, "Him care 'bout cold? Him 'at takes a bath every morning even if he has to break ice? Damn fool Indian!"

Drouillard motioned toward Whitehouse with the mirror. "I can smell you coming a long way. Game have a better nose than mine. You like meat, so be glad your hunter rinses off."

Whitehouse laughed. "I *am* glad. I'm glad that's you in ice water of a morning, not me."

Snow was ankle deep on the ground. The soldiers had been

without tents for weeks, as the canvas had rotted and been shredded by the winds on the plains. They slept crowded together under the ragged remains of boat sails and old tarpaulins and skins. The officers and their retinue stayed well sheltered in Charbonneau's tepee, rigged with any available support. The surveying and navigating instruments, whose cases and boxes had become battered, were additionally wrapped in the skins of wolves killed along the way. The captains now shared Clark's small desk, Lewis's having been cached back by the Great Falls. Yesterday, rain had turned to sleet, and several more horses were hurt, slipping and falling down mountainsides. In one of those accidents their last thermometer was broken. The hunting had been so poor that supper consisted of nine grouse stewed with corn, a mere taste compared with the amount of meat these men were used to consuming. Drouillard had seen bighorn sheep, but too high and far to be shot or retrieved.

Private Frazier, who had been keeping a journal and making map sketches, complained about how much time and effort could have been saved if they had simply come straight over this way from the falls, instead of so far south and now back north. When Lewis got wind of it, he reminded everybody that the President's orders were that the Missouri was to be explored and mapped to its head. It had also been necessary to get Shoshone horses, which could only have occurred where it did. That closed that discussion.

Still, the soldiers needed something to grumble about, so they began lamenting that so much of the tobacco had been left in the caches to lighten the loads. Almost all the men were addicted to smoking or chewing it, and the supply dwindled fast. The prospect of being without tobacco as well as liquor was dreadful. Drouillard had been showing them several plants the Indians used to stretch their tobacco into kinnikinnick, such as red willow bark, sage, and wood punk. "You'll be used to kinnikinnick by the time you run clear out of tobacco," he said, "and hardly miss tobacco at all." His solution didn't interest them much; they *needed* to complain. Fortunately, as always, they had miseries aplenty. This morning the men moved about aching and shivering, hugging themselves, their breath clouding, and as usual making the crazy-head sign when they saw Drouillard go down to the edge of the fast water, naked, and wade in. It was so cold he could not breathe, only gasp, and many minutes in this water would have made his bones ache for the rest of the day, so he didn't stay in long.

Whitehouse shivered and shook his head. "I got bone-chill enough when I was pullin' those damn canoes. S'cuse me, Drouillard, I just cain't bear to watch y' do that!"

"I'll bring you a deer for supper," Drouillard gasped. "You'll be glad your hunter doesn't smell like you!"

Two years ago Whitehouse would have torn into him as a cheeky redskin for talking that way to a whiteman. Things sure had changed since then. Nowadays they didn't even brawl among themselves, or call York a nigger. Out here in the wilderness they were getting almost civilized.

> *September 4th Wednesday 1805*
> *a verry cold morning every thing wet and frosed, I went in*
> *front, & Saw Several of the Argalia or Ibex . . . our hunter*
> *killed a Deer which we made use of . . . I was the first white*
> *man who ever wer on the waters of this river.*
>
> *William Clark,* Journals

Drouillard found fresh hoofprints and moccasin tracks. One man had stood here in the snow, dismounted, watched from a thicket, then left, recently. Drouillard checked his flintlock and rode forward, sniffing and scanning. A raven was gurgling and croaking not far ahead. Near it, he thought he saw something of a buckskin color retreating through the bush. When he got to that spot, there were the fresh prints again, the scent of horse still in the air.

Someone was spying on their approach and withdrawing as they came. When the captains caught up, he told them. They concluded that any Indians in this vicinity probably were Flatheads—the tribe the Shoshones were planning to meet down at the three forks for their fall buffalo hunt.

Now the valley broadened to open their view on sloping ground with copses of evergreens, like a wide bowl ringed by snowy mountains, easier travel for the limping horses and foot-sore soldiers. As they rode along the bold stream, Lewis proposed naming it Clark's River, since he had been the first to come upon it. Old Toby and Bird Woman were chatting cheerfully as the guide walked alongside the packhorse she was riding. She rode balanced atop the packsaddle, wrapped in a blanket that sheltered also the cradleboard on her back. Her baby, seven months old now, seldom cried. He slept, or rode with calm, dark-eyed curiosity through magnificent landscapes. When released from the confining cradleboard, he was always eager to kick up his fat legs and wave and reach, coo and laugh, and was most lively when he heard any kind of music, the singing of men or the squeak of the fiddle. Captain Clark had nicknamed him Pomp the Dancing Boy.

Drouillard now saw several sets of hoofprints in the snow and soft ground, so he quickened his pace and went out ahead, swinging eastward away from the river toward pine timber, to have some cover as he studied the valley ahead.

He smelled wood smoke.

He rode among the pines and passed through, and when he came through to the other side, saw smoke hazing the dark pines of the distance, then the source of the smoke: tepee lodges, about thirty of them, beside the river and in the path of the oncoming soldiers. People were milling about on the near side of the camp, mostly men with lances and shields, some mounted, others holding horses by their bridles. Whoever had been watching the soldiers come had alerted the community, but for some reason the warriors had not ridden out yet.

So Drouillard rode his horse out of the pines straight down toward the camp with his hand up and two fingers together in the Friend or Brother sign. This would be better than running back to tell the captains, he thought; doing that, he would look like a war scout going to give a warning. As he came out from the pines, he saw their horse herd on a grassy bottom beyond the camp, and there were hundreds.

Just then someone saw him coming and yelled, and four mounted men broke from the crowd and rode toward him at a trot.

They were dressed in beautifully tanned skins and robes, and their horses were superior. All the men wore their hair neatly plaited, with the braids wrapped in otter skins and hanging forward on both shoulders. They were gaunt like the hungry Shoshones, but did not seem timid or suspicious. The gray-haired rider in front returned Drouillard's peace sign.

They talked by hands without dismounting. The old one said he was glad the strange men were coming in peace. He had been watching them come and had seen a man among them with his face blackened, as for war. But he had seen that they had a woman with them, unlike a war party. The old man was Three Eagles, a chief. He called his people Ootlashoots; some tribes called them Flatheads. Drouillard told him that the people behind him were whitemen who were going to see the ocean, that they sought friendship with all peoples, and had recently been with the Shoshones. He said they would want to camp here because of the lateness of the day, and smoke and talk. That they gave gifts to express their desire for friendship.

When the soldiers came down, a crowd rushed out to meet them. Many put robes over the whitemen's shoulders; it was presumed they must be cold, because they were so pale.

Thursday 5th Sept. 1805
a clear cool morning. the Standing water froze . . . the Indian
dogs are so ravinous that they eat Several pair of the mens
Moccasons . . . these natives have the Stranges language of
any we have yet Seen. they appear to us as though they had an
Impedement in their speech or brogue on their tongue. we
think perhaps that they are the welch Indians. &C. they are
the likelyest and honestest we have seen and are verry
friendly to us. they Swaped to us Some of their good horses
and took our worn out horses and appeared to wish to help us
as much as lay in their power.

Sergeant John Ordway, Journals

Neither Bird Woman nor Toby spoke the gurgling, throaty language of these people, and it appeared that Drouillard might have to sign-talk everything. But living among these people was a bright Shoshone boy who was fluent in both tongues. He translated the Flatheads' words into Shoshone; Bird Woman translated Shoshone into Hidatsa; Charbonneau translated Hidatsa into French, which Labiche translated into English for the captains. That process was reversed as the captains explained their mission and trade prospects, offered gifts and medals, and swapped for more and better horses. It gave Drouillard time to go and hunt, as the Indians had nothing but dried berries and roots to share with their guests. He brought in a deer toward evening, which was stewed and gave at least a taste of meat to many hungry people, Indian and white. By then the captains had obtained three colts for emergency eating, and enough good horses to bring the number of pack animals to forty—enough to carry all the packsaddles, with a few relief horses, and to allow four hunters to go out mounted all the time.

Neither group could linger. The tribe was running late for its buffalo-hunting rendezvous with the Shoshones. The whitemen needed to get through the mountains westward before too much snow fell. Some of the Flatheads said the trek across the mountains could be made in five sleeps.

Chapter 17

The Nez Perce Trail
September 1805

Five days travel had become ten, and there was still no sign of an end to the mountains. They had gone four days northward just to reach a creek that came down from the pass they were seeking, then two days up that creek on a brutally rough climbing trail often blocked by fallen trees, camping at night on slopes so steep there was no level place to lie down, and barely enough grass to keep the horses going. They had seen stone circles and charred wood from old Indian camps, which Toby said were former Nez Perce camps, evidence that they were now on that tribe's trail over the mountains. Near the crest of the pass was a plume of steam, rising from a spring whose water was so hot it was painful to hold a finger in it a second. Several paths led to this spring, and a rock dam had been built below to form a bathing pool. A few miles farther up they had crested the divide to stand in the wind and look at an endless array of towering, snow-topped peaks thickly clothed with evergreen timber on their slopes. The next day Toby had taken a wrong turn and led them down to a clear, shallow creek rushing over round, many-colored cobbles and boulders, where the discovery of fishing weirs showed him that he had chosen a fish-camp trail instead of the correct route.

In that steep-sided valley amidst gloomy forests of pine, spruce, and fir, wet and chilled by rain and hail, with no fresh meat, losing faith in their guide, they had killed and butchered a colt for meat to supplement the "portable soup" of bouillon powder, carried from the East in tin boxes and more than two years old. They named a branch creek near that wretched camp Colt Killed Creek, then set out the next morning to climb several miles up a steep, rocky, deadwood-strewn switchback trail to regain the Indian road at the ridge, a climb that took all day and ruined two of the packhorses, which had to be abandoned. Other horses had tumbled unhurt down the mountainside, one such accident smashing Captain Clark's portable desk. On regaining the snow-covered trail atop the mountain that night, they found no water, and had to melt snow for boiling the last of the colt meat.

The next morning they all awakened nearly chilled to death and found themselves covered with snow that had fallen before daybreak. Drouillard had watched with pity as the soldiers, who had no socks, wrapped their benumbed feet in rags and pulled their frozen moccasins on over them. There was no game to be found on this snowy mountain, and the Indian path had become so filled in with snow that sometimes it could be discerned only by finding trees that had been worn and rubbed by the Indians' packsaddles in past migrations.

By the middle of the month they were on steep mountainsides whose thick pine forests were so laden with snow that the passing pack train was constantly covered with wet snow that cascaded from the branches upon them. The air was frigid, their clothes and thin moccasins soaked, and the fear of slipping down steep slopes kept them so tense that they were doubly fatigued at every day's end. Then there was no level place to sleep. Visibility was poor, either because it snowed or because the mountaintops they traveled were in the clouds. More horses fell and were injured. On several days, the departure from camp had been delayed because of strayed packhorses. It seemed to Drouillard that he spent almost as much time hunting for horses as for game.

By September 18 the third and last colt had been devoured. Game was so scarce that the hunters had not fired their rifles for days. The reconstituted soup gave no strength; the men were gaunt, losing flesh visibly, plagued with dysentery and skin eruptions, and were finally becoming drained of spirit. Provisions had been depleted to a few more canisters of the soup, a very little bear oil, and about twenty pounds of tallow candles. Some of the men were already gnawing their candles, which, though tasteless, helped their craving for fat to stoke their ever-chilled bodies. Drouillard, though more accustomed to cold and fasting than the others, found his hands going so shaky he wondered whether he could hit an animal if he ever saw one to shoot. Some of the soldiers, remembering the old guide's mistake on the divide, feared that he had gotten them permanently lost. But Toby confidently asserted that they were still on the Nez Perce trail and would soon be descending into a rich lowland where everyone could eat well.

18th Septr. 1805
I deturmined to take a party of the hunters and proceed on in advance to Some leavel Country where there was game kill Some meat & Send it back &c. a fair morning cold at 20 miles I beheld a wide and extencive vallie in a West & SW Direction at a great distance. Drewyer shot at a Deer we did not get it, made 32 miles and Encamped on a bold running Creek which I call Hungery Creek as at that place we had nothing to eate.
                                    William Clark, Journals

They awoke before daybreak famished and shaky. Reubin Field and John Shields blinked dumbly around in the firelight, all their hunter keenness gone. Their eyes were so hollowed and dark the men looked like skulls with whiskers. As morning dusk lightened the snowy copse, they looked around in vain for even a grouse to shoot. There was nothing.

The seven men mounted at daylight and clambered back up the rocky banks of Hungery Creek to regain the high trail. After about six miles without a sight of game, they entered a long glade full of snow. Drouillard rode shivering, yearning for the lowland plain they had seen yesterday from a mountaintop, afraid it might have been just a vision. Captain Lewis and the main party by now might have reached the height of that mountain from which the plains were visible. Drouillard imagined old Toby pointing down at it and smiling in the face of his doubters, proving that an Indian can be right. He hoped they had seen it by now; if not, their hope might be dead.

To his left, motion: snow cascading off the branches of a pine. Then in all that white snow and dark evergreen he saw a tiny spot of reddish-brown, like an animal's hair. With cold-numbed fingers he readied his rifle and focused on the place. The animal must have brushed the tree and shaken loose the snow. He veered toward it, rounding a thicket, and saw it: a gaunt horse in shaggy winter coat, pawing snow, seeking grass, unaware of his presence. But then his own mount saw it and whickered. The wild one, a stray perhaps, raised its head and pricked up its ears, and came wading through deep snow to investigate. Drouillard heard Reubin say, "Horse meat, Cap'n!"

"Shoot it, then," Clark said.

The horse heard the voices and shied. Drouillard and Reubin fired at the same instant. With a grunting sound the horse fell kicking in the snow, and went still.

The horse meat was lean but not poor. The anticipation of meat was almost unbearable. While Collins and Colter were butchering the horse, Drouillard rode out in one direction, Shields and Field in others, hunting for other horses or any game. Captain Clark was hoping that with this horse meat and a fair quantity of anything else, his hunters could turn back toward the main party and feed them today.

But there was not even a track of anything else, so Clark decided to hang the major portion of the horse carcass up out of the reach of wolves, where the main party would find it by the trail, and keep hunting down toward the plain. As the meat was broiled and served around, Drouillard saw some of the men shut their eyes and move their lips. Praying, in this expedition, was an individual matter. Lewis, like his president, didn't believe in a god who listened or intervened, so he neither encouraged nor discouraged prayer. Clark seemed to believe, but the captains never disputed over it. Lewis claimed that man's reason was sufficient to guide him. Lewis sometimes talked to Clark about what seemed to be a sort of brotherhood or clan of principled men everywhere in the world who were called "Masons." Lewis was extremely proud to be one of them and told Clark that he should become one when he returned to civilization. Those in that brotherhood, he said, always knew what was right, so Drouillard figured that would be just the thing for Captain Lewis.

Drouillard, in the manner of his people after a long hunger, put his first morsel of meat into the fire as thanks to the protecting spirit. He was salivating like a wolf as he put the meat in his mouth, and as he chewed he kept thanking the horse for its body and the protecting spirit for guiding the horse to this place.

Friday September 20th 1805
we were detained this morning untill ten oclock to collect our horses. we had proceeded about 2 miles when we found the greater part of a horse which Capt Clark had met with and killed for us. he informed me by note that he should proceed as fast as possible to the leavel country to the S.W. of us, which we discovered from the hights of the mountains on the 19th there he intended to hunt untill our arrival. at one oclock we halted and made a hearty meal on our horse beef much to the comfort of our hungry stomachs . . .

Meriwether Lewis, Journals

They went from dank cold to dry heat, from mottled boulders and gray cliffs to level prairies of short grass and open pine glades, all in a few hours of descending from that last terrible mountain. They had made it at last through the inhospitable maze of the Rocky, or Shining, Mountains. Drouillard looked back at the rocky ridge they had descended, seeing how a river came around each side of the mountain to join here in the gentle lowland. He had ranged in prairies and wooded hills and along creeks and rivers all his adult life as a hunter, seldom confused by stream courses or the lie of the land, but in those mountains he had been disoriented as never before. He had memorized as well as he could every knob and cliff and chasm, with as much detailed concentration as Captain Clark used in his measurements and maps. Always, if Drouillard had come by a way, he could go back by it. But there was something that had shaken him in those mountains. Rivers and roaring creeks zigzagged through the cold canyons with no apparent regard for the Creator's rules of water flow. In that precipitous maze he had sometimes had to steady himself to keep from believing that a rapid rushing downhill had reversed its flow while his back was turned and started running uphill. Water rushed everywhere at the feet of those mountains, and it was hard to tell whether you were crossing five different streams in a day or the same one five times.

While he was looking back at that wall of mountains, he heard Reubin Field say, "Lookee, Cap'n! Young'uns!"

Three Indian boys had just seen them, turned, scattered, and hid in the grass. Captain Clark said, "Don't want them to alarm their people. Reubin, take my gun." The captain turned and fumbled into his saddlebag. He brought out short pieces of bright ribbon. Dismounting, he walked out into the grass, holding up the ribbons with one hand, making the Friend sign with the other. He came upon two of the cowering boys and urged them to stand up. Smiling, he gave them the pretty ribbons. Then he signed to them, *Go. Say friend men come.* The boys, eight years old perhaps, looked at the ribbons, looked at the big, red-haired, blue-eyed creature before them, their expressions a mixture of fear and fascination, and ran. Clark mounted and they followed the boys at a walk. Beyond the pines they saw a camp, twenty or thirty tepee lodges of various sizes, covered not with hide but with rush or reed mats, situated in a pleasant bottomland, mostly overgrown with the slender leaves of a plant that looked like wild onion. As they rode toward the camp they saw trampled areas and large piles of bulbous roots.

"Wonder if those are good," Collins said. "I'm pretty damn hungry."

"Here comes a man out," the captain said. "I reckon we're about to meet the Nez Perce at last."

"Hope we don't scare him away," Colter said. "We look like the league o' death."

It was true. Scrawny, sunken-eyed, hair and beards in filthy disarray, skin and ragged clothing smudged from resin-pine campfires, they looked like skeletons raked out of a pyre.

"Now, Drouillard," Clark said, "tell him about us."

Drouillard bent nearly double with the pain in his gut. But he straightened up quickly because the gassy swelling of his stomach squeezed his lungs and he could scarcely breathe. The bulbs harvested by these people were delicious and plentiful, and the natives had been generous with them. Captain Clark and his hunters, ravenous after their descent from the mountains, had stuffed themselves. They had eaten the roots steamed, and eaten them dried. They had eaten a delicious sweet bread whose main ingredient was a flour made from the dried roots. And the Nez Perce women had also served them dried berries and dried salmon.

Then the hunters went out for meat to send back to Lewis in the mountains, but found no game. So Clark scraped together all the goods and trinkets he had in his saddlebags and pockets, and traded them for a packhorse load of dried roots and salmon.

With a young Nez Perce as a guide, Reubin Field was sent back up the mountain trail to meet the others with the load of food.

After that had been sent, the recent meal began to take effect. The men swelled up and belched. Then they began farting like buglers, but in the middle of their noisome serenade they suddenly were spewing and scouring. They flinched with cramps and stabbing pains.

Drouillard hurried down to the stream to purge and clean himself in the way his mother had taught him, inside and out. He stripped, rinsed his filthy clothing, and scrubbed his body with sand. Then he went upstream a few yards, spread his clothes in the sun, ignoring the scores of curious women and children, went into the water and drank from his cupped hands. He drank until he could drink no more. Then he stooped and gagged himself until he had emptied his stomach, drank his fill again and expelled it again. Then once more. The water was cold and he was trembling and wretched, and would have been embarrassed by all the public attention had he let himself care about it. But he knew it was more important to purge himself, because he could not afford to be sick. He thought there was something going on among these people, and he would have to be well and alert. He stood naked in the sun sluicing water off his body and limbs with the edges of his hands, noticing that he had never been this spare; every vein, cord, and sinew of his arms and legs was as visible as if he had been flayed. He would need to eat to restore his strength, but could not eat, as he and the others just had, too much at once. They had been eating nothing but meat for months, and then had nearly starved, then eaten a great amount of something too different. That had made the gassy swelling, he thought. But the rest, the spewing and scouring: when he had eaten the salmon, his nose had warned him it might be too old. Sometimes one had to eat meat that was not fresh; he was used to that. But this had been fish, old dried fish, and had he not been so famished, he would not have eaten it.

Captain Clark was now visiting with one of the headmen, and was so swollen and sick he could hardly breathe, but was pretending to be well. Clark needed to purge himself the Indian way. So did the rest of the hunters. They were all so sick they could hardly walk or ride. They were helpless. They needed to be well, because something might happen.

The Nez Perce, who called themselves Ni Mi Pu, or True People, were generous, and seemed to be fascinated by the whitemen and eager to help them. They said they had heard of whitemen, by word from the tribes far down the Columbia who had met whitemen on big trading boats. But these were the first they'd seen. The Indians hung around and watched the whitemen, but Drouillard smelled nervous fear on them. It was something down deep that was troubling them. Not witchcraft; it was not anything like that. It was more like the fear of not knowing what to do. One minute a crowd would be following the red-haired captain along, joyously admiring him. Then something would make them draw back, even run away.

For one thing, their chief, Broken Arm, was not here. He was away raiding enemies far in the southwest. Few men of warrior age were here, just boys and older men, and many women who had come to harvest the great quantities of roots. Sometimes when Drouillard would look up and around from his hand-signing with the old men, he would see men looking at the captain darkly.

The one person among these Nez Perce who had seen white-men, and in fact had known them well, was a respected elder woman, Watkuweis. When she was young she had been captured by enemies in the north and treated badly. Then she had come into the care of whitemen traders in Canada who had treated her well. Drouillard had watched her during the talks. She looked favorably on the captain but was nervous. She stayed nearby while Clark talked with a sturdy and friendly old chief whose name was Twisted Hair. Clark had learned to talk fairly well with his hands, but he was usually so busy thinking of his own next signals that he missed things. So Drouillard stayed with him most of the time to help.

Twisted Hair said the Nez Perce were expecting whitemen to come, and were not surprised when they came down off the mountains. They'd had foreknowledge of it. Captain Clark presumed they were claiming some kind of a vision. "Indians often pretend that they knew something was going to happen," Captain Clark told his men.

Oh yes, Drouillard thought, superstitious savages.

Sunday September 22nd 1805
we met Reubin Field one of oure hunters, whom Capt. Clark had dispatched to meet us with some dryed fish and roots that he had procured from a band of Indians. I was happy to find a sufficiency to satisfy compleatly all our appetites. the plea-sure I now felt in having tryumphed over the rocky Mountains and decending once more to a level and fertile country can be more readily conceived than expressed, nor was the flattering

prospect of the final success of the expedition less pleasing. on our approach to the village most of the women fled to the neighboring woods on horseback with their children, a circumstance I did not expect as Capt. Clark had previously been with them and informed them of our pacific intentions towards them.

Meriwether Lewis, Journals

Clark took Drouillard's advice and puked himself empty. It relieved him, but he was still wincing from sharp belly pains. And the sudden change to hot weather was wearing him down.

The captain rode downriver, scouting for good trees for making dugouts, and discovered thick, straight cedars that looked very suitable. Chief Twisted Hair helped him draw a map of the river courses to the great seaward river, told him how many sleeps it would take to get from one place to another, and told him of a great waterfall on the big river. The chief told him that uncountable numbers of Indians of many tribes lived along the rivers below, most of them fishers and traders, and that those people far down the river knew the whitemen of the big boats. Drouillard signed between the captain and the chief, and his respect for both kept growing. It looked as if Captain Clark would have everything arranged by the time Lewis descended from the mountains with the rest of the soldiers.

Even though most of the warrior-age men were gone, the remaining men had keen eyes for rifles. Drouillard saw them always looking at the rifles so intently that he did not dare set his aside unless he handed it into the care of the captain or one of the hunters. The chief several times complained that enemy tribes in the north had been getting more and more guns from the traders, and it was becoming ever more dangerous for the Nez Perce to go over the mountains for buffalo hunting.

These Nez Perce were a friendly, good-looking people who dressed in beautifully made skin clothing, decorated themselves with blue beads and brass and copper jewelry, and owned many good horses. They were not a desperately poor, furtive people like the Shoshones. But his intuition told Drouillard it was good that the chief and warriors were away. Old men and boys might not dare overpower whitemen to get their rifles, even a few sick whitemen. But a handful of warriors might not be able to resist the opportunity. Drouillard had faith in the hospitality and honor of the tribes, as they had proven those things. But he was becoming aware of something he had not expected to find so far west in advance of whitemen: guns were affecting the lives of all the Indians. It was a hard reality. No one wanted to be the people without guns.

The men of the expedition, now stumbling and plodding into the Nez Perce camp, were filthy, scruffy, and dull-eyed. The mountains had humbled them. Their ashen faces—what little could be seen through their whiskers—were greasy, smudged, scabby, peeling, broken out in eruptions. Their eyes were swollen and mattering from snowglare, and their noses looked like organ meat. It was no wonder the Nez Perce women fled from them with their children.

Captain Lewis's bow-legged walk was exaggerated by pain. The fur hat pulled hard down on his head pushed his prominent ears out even farther, and his intense eyes, blazing from his sooty face, looked crazy. He was desperately gut-sick.

Cruzatte's one eye was swollen nearly shut. Lepage and Labiche looked like trolls. The big men looked small and old: Pryor, Gass, Ordway, Shannon, Willard, Potts, Whitehouse, Frazier. Charbonneau, much older than anyone else, was still on his feet. Atop the packsaddle of the skinny, limping horse he led, Bird Woman sat swaying, the baby still in its cradleboard on her back, and she smiled when she saw Clark and Drouillard. The only visible change in her was that her face was bonier. Somehow she had come through with a clean face, her hair still shiny and well-combed, and had kept the baby nourished—he was still chubby-faced and seemed in no distress. And somehow she had never fallen off the horse, nor had the horse carrying her ever fallen down a mountain. York came limping along, the last of his portliness totally wasted off. He hardly looked any blacker than the rest of them now, and he grinned and waved when he saw his master.

"Hello, York," Clark said. "Missed you, old pickaninny. I had to do for myself."

Sick though he was, Captain Lewis felt he had to drag out flags and medals and assemble whatever chiefs were on hand and give his Jefferson talk. This was obviously a major tribe along the narrow trail to the western sea. And even though they lived far beyond the limits of the great land purchase, they and their fine horse herds could be important in the future when American commerce started crossing the mountains. So, looking as if he might die any minute, Lewis pressed on through the whole council until he got these subchiefs to say what he expected to hear.

By the next day, almost all of the men were too sick to mount horses and had to be helped up. Captain Lewis was sicker than anybody, and could hardly bear the short rides between Nez Perce camps. The soldiers were so gassy and full of pain that many of them had to stop and lie down by the path from time to time. They were so miserable, in fact, that they hardly paid any attention to the many comely women and girls who followed along on foot and horseback, marveling at them. The women were in the midst of their harvest of the roots, which they called quamash. Bird Woman was familiar with the food, which was *pasheco* in her language, but she had never seen it grow in such profusion as it did in these bottoms. She was awed.

At Twisted Hair's camp, the old woman Watkuweis at once fixed on the young mother as someone needing her care and protection. She recruited women from her band to help the Bird Woman with the baby and to mend and clean for her. Watkuweis and the Bird Woman did not understand each other's language, but both were capable at handsigning. When each learned that the other had been carried off in raids by enemy tribes, and thus drifted into the company of whitemen, their hand signs began to flutter like butterflies. Even from the other end of Twisted Hair's brush lodge, where Drouillard was translating for the captains, he could follow their conversation. The old woman was asking if

Bird Woman too had been treated well by whites. It was obvious that both had been.

The captains were making arrangements to leave their weary horses here with the Nez Perce to recover. They would be marked by a burning brand with Captain Lewis's name. If the whitemen met ships at the ocean and didn't return this way, the Nez Perce could keep the horses. If the expedition found no ships and had to come back, they would renew friendship and take the horses back over the mountains. In either event, cooperation by the Nez Perce would assure them of future friendship with the whitemen's great council far in the east, and the whitemen to come in the future would have wonderful goods for the Nez Perce, including guns of such good quality and dependability that their enemies would never be able to dominate them again.

Twisted Hair grew more intensely interested after the talk about getting guns. Drouillard saw some shrewdness working behind that pleasant old face. After a while the old man began talking about the many tribes living down these rivers toward the west. He spoke of their association with his own people, and smiled thoughtfully, then suggested that if he went down the rivers with the whitemen's canoes, he might be able to help them pass among those peoples in a friendly way.

Many of these Indians had sore, mattering eyes, and Captain Clark began treating them with eyewash from the medicine chest. Soon he was also treating bad backs and opening abcesses. Before long he was serving hours a day as physician, for his own men and the tribe alike.

The hunters were scouring the country far and wide, but found barely enough deer to supplement the root and salmon diet. By the time Captain Clark had set up a boat-building camp at the river fork below the Nez Perce towns, Captain Lewis was so sick in the bowels that he did not even bother to write. He spent most of his time reclining and gasping, nearly a total invalid. Some of the men were sick all of the time, and all were sick some of the time. Captain Clark, wheezing, farting like a horse, selected four magnificent, straight trees to be felled and hewn for long canoes, assigned the able-bodied men to ax teams, and doled out Thunderbolt pills, jalap, tartar emetic, and salts to keep the men purging. When he was not doctoring or supervising, squatting at the latrine or treating his Nez Perce patients, he was making terse entries in his journal and notes. He was pasty-faced or flushed, always with a sheen of sweat, but never idle. The heat in the valley remained oppressive day after day, and even men who started the day well enough to work were often sick by midday. The axes were small camping axes, made for chopping and splitting, not for hewing, so the old native technique of burning out and chopping was adopted. The constant dense smoke made the heat seem worse, but it did help keep away mosquitoes and biting flies, and this wood burned with a pleasant, tangy aroma that Drouillard loved to smell when he rode in from hunting in the uplands. One day he killed two deer and Colter killed one, but most days there were just no deer to be found. This was a heavily populated country and had long been hunted.

Of the whole party, only Bird Woman did not get sick. Roots and fish had been much of her diet in childhood. Toby the guide was well too, and spent his days patiently sitting in the shade with flint rocks and a deer antler tip, chipping and flaking arrow points. He seemed to be a ghost from the ancient times, with no interest in guns. Drouillard wondered why the captains didn't pay him for his services and let him go home.

Because the dugout logs were so large and so much wood had to be removed, the burning, chopping, and scraping went on for ten days. As the month of October came on, cooler winds blew through the camp, and a look back at the mountains showed the snow to be heavier and farther down the slopes with each new day, a reminder of how narrowly they had avoided being trapped and lost up there, where they surely would have died.

While most of the men were improving a little in health, Captain Lewis lay still in pain and misery, sometimes hardly able to draw breath. Captain Clark had bad days and terrible days, but kept going. He had map notes to revise, doctoring to do, and a designer's attention to the shaping of the dugout hulls. He had watched Indians navigate their dugouts past this place and had noted the degree of rake they had carved under the bows and sterns of their vessels for stability and maneuverability in these rapid waters. And he was still making arrangements about the keep of the expedition's thirty-six horses. Two brothers and a son of the chief would take responsibility for the branded horses, in return for knives, two muskets, and other articles.

Drouillard fared better on the Nez Perce diet than most of the men because he ate only as much as he had to, just a bit at a time, and would eat no salmon unless it was fresh. Even then, one day he came down too sick to go hunting, and had to purify himself with water again. He declined the pills and the salts. The next day he was well enough to hunt, and got two deer. When there was venison, the men got a bit better, but most days they had to keep trading beads and cloth to the Indian women for the quamash roots that made them so gassy. Whitehouse had a new song:

> *Quamash roots, quamash roots!*
> *The more I eats, the more I poots!*
> *The more I poot, the better I sound,*
> *So dig me quamash from the ground!*

In the evenings at the canoe camp, Cruzatte would get his fiddle out, pray thanks that it had not been smashed when it tumbled a hundred yards down a cliff on Private Frazier's horse, tune it up approximately, and try to rouse the spirits of these weary, skinny, gut-scoured soldiers. His prayer of thanks, though Catholic and in French, was clearly prayer, and always brought solemn nods of affirmation from the soldiers. They seemed to feel that whatever grace had brought the Frenchman's fiddle through the mountains intact had done the same for them. And in tribute to it, they would get up and dance. Now and then Cruzatte would announce, "I now shall play you an air!" And, raising a leg and grimacing, he would emit a note, pick it up on the strings, and be off on a merry improvised tune.

*   *   *

The canoes were nearly finished. The forelocks of the expedition horses had been cut short and they had been marked with Lewis's brand:

Cruzatte played by the fire, and the men who could dance were dancing. Drouillard sat near Bird Woman. The baby was dancing in her lap, waving his arms as if to the music, making an expression that looked like a toothless grin. Bird Woman looked thoughtfully at Drouillard, then turned and spoke to her husband, who sat on a crate behind her. Charbonneau translated from Hidatsa into his laborious French:

"La vieille femme s' dit, les Nez Perce déjà connus que les anglais . . . ou, les hommes blancs . . . viennent. Depuis longtemps."

Drouillard said, *"Oui.* They knew from a vision that white people would come from the east. I heard of that."

Charbonneau talked to his wife, and she shook her head and said more.

"Yes, that vision. But also, some Nez Perce went there this spring, to Hidatsa towns near your winter fort. They went to buy guns from the English traders. They learned of these captains coming this way. So they were not surprised. Only a little afraid. They knew your captains come with many guns."

Drouillard thought on that, smiling. A foreknowing, by dream or vision. Then learning that it will be so. Then it is so. It was a thing that often happened, that way. Whitemen called it superstition.

It also seemed to mean that some Nez Perce already had guns, new guns. Perhaps that was why the chief called Broken Arm had gone to the southwest to war on the Paiutes. Drouillard said: "What else did the old woman tell her, of such interest?"

They talked, and then Charbonneau turned to him, eyes bugging wide. "Some Nez Perce considered that they should kill us, that the whitemen are a bad thing coming. That we were so weak they could kill us and take the good guns. But that old woman told them no, whitemen are kind, they treated me well, do not harm them. And so, they chose to be friends. The old woman told my wife, fear not, they have promised me. *Eh, mon Dieu!*" Charbonneau pursed his lips and slapped his cheeks with both hands. "I am having almost too much excitement! Wheeu!"

Only now that it was time to leave these Chopunnish Nez Perce towns and head downstream did the soldiers start feeling well enough to be intrigued and stirred by the young women, who were uncommonly lovely.

These women were friendly and generous, but seemed to have no desire for connection with the whitemen, for either social or spiritual reasons. Perhaps the wretched soldiers coming down out of the mountains had been too pitiful and filthy to seem attractive at all. Only Clark, with his beacon of red hair and his solidity, dignity, and healing hands, had a strong female following. But he was too busy running the whole show to have time for dalliance.

Chapter 18

On the Kooskooskee River
October 1805

They had labored for almost two years to get to the top of the continent, always thinking how easy it would be to coast down the western side to the ocean. But the troubles started at once, and there was an omen that put a darkness upon Drouillard's spirit. It was an omen tied to remembered dreams.

Both captains were still sick, but Clark was functioning. A fifth canoe was made, a small pilot vessel. These rivers were clear and swift. Twisted Hair and another chief named Teto-hoskee had agreed to ride down in the canoes and help the whitemen make friendships with other tribes. But the two chiefs did not arrive when it was time to shove the canoes off. And some Nez Perce, among those gathered around for the excitement of the departure, stole some tomahawks. One had been Sergeant Floyd's, and another was an elegant pipe-tomahawk Clark considered his good luck piece. Drouillard hand-talked, saying it was a spirit thing of the captain. Soon it reappeared, with no one having to take blame. Then the little hewn-log fleet set out.

There were tricks to be learned about going downstream in fast water. The expedition was in the third of many rocky rapids under a cloudy sky when the little pilot canoe, with Captain Clark riding in it, struck a rock just hard enough to make a long crack along the grain, and water began leaking in. That was patched with tin and pitch at the evening camp.

The river twisted fast down through rocky, piney lands. The next day, the canoes raced through a dozen stretches of roaring rapids, passing islands occupied by salmon fishing camps. Thus the banks were often crowded with Indian spectators as the education of the fast-water boatmen continued. At one of the camps they were greeted by the smiling Twisted Hair and Tetohoskee, and after a smoking ceremony the chiefs were taken aboard. At another camp the officers bought some fresh salmon and roots. Captain Lewis was not fully recovered and thought red meat would help him, but because there was no time for hunting, he took the notion that dog meat might serve, and two dogs were purchased and killed.

It was Sergeant Gass, steering a long canoe that carried most of the nonswimmers, who had the first of many wrecks. His vessel struck a rock in the middle of the rapid, swung around and hit another. Strain cracked the hull and water poured in. The men hung on, with cold water roaring over and around them until they were rescued by the crew of another canoe, with the help of two Indian fishermen in a small dugout. A tomahawk and several light articles were swept away and lost.

Sergeant Gass personally took the responsibility for repairing the vessel he had wrecked, and no one else could have done it as well. He found a few pieces of driftwood and shaved them down to make knee-braces that spanned the cracks, set them in place with handmade wooden pins, and then caulked the repair with pine resin, and the vessel was stronger than ever.

The excitement of the whitewater was lifting the spirits of most of the soldiers, while terrifying a few. In camp that evening it was finally noticed that Toby the Shoshone guide was gone. Someone who had been collecting resin remembered having seen him running back up the riverbank with his bow and quiver and blanket roll, right after the boat wreck. Apparently this was all a little too thrilling for him. The captains asked Twisted Hair if he might send someone to bring Toby back so that he could be paid the goods he had been promised for his guide services. But the old chief advised against it. He said that a little old Shoshone man passing through many camps with valuables would have nothing left anyway.

Drouillard hung back from the campfires, a cold anger eating in him as he stared at Captain Lewis. The captain was up and about now, still weak, ravenously chewing roasted dog meat and exclaiming how good it was. Even better than a coyote they had killed and eaten the last day in the mountains. There were many Indians around the camp, watching the soldiers with great curiosity, and sentinels had been placed around the wet baggage to ensure that Indians took nothing. Captain Clark was shaking his head, telling Lewis that he still couldn't bring himself to eat a dog. Pierre Cruzatte had left the fireside to fetch his fiddle.

As he brought it back in its battered, scuffed carrying case, he paused and said to Drouillard: *"Pourquoi la colère, ami?"*

Cruzatte had Indian blood, and Drouillard wondered if he felt this anger. He tilted his head toward Lewis. "Him."

"Le capitaine? What?"

"If he gave the least damn for an Indian, he'd have got on his knees and kissed Toby's hand as soon as the old man had brought him through the mountains. You know why Toby came down this river, farther and farther every day from his home? Probably because he was waiting for the captain to remember to pay him what he promised."

"Peut-être." Cruzatte nodded. "He should have asked."

"Eh, so? He should have to remind a man he saved his life? All these lives? The whole Jefferson mission? All you hear from the cap'n is how *he* triumphed over those mountains!"

"Hm. Mmm." Cruzatte nodded, thinking. *"Eh bien.* Maybe some music from my wondrous feedle will brighten your spirit, eh, *mon sauvage?"*

"Heh! Never mind my spirit. I'm just a damned Indian. Play for the captain. His stomach hurts."

Surely there had never been a sound anything like this fiddle here in this rough valley where the mountain waters rushed headlong toward the western sea. It squeaked and squawked and groaned and whined, faster and faster. At first the Indian fishermen and their women and children winced and put their hands

over their ears. The fiddler himself must have looked like some
sort of one-eyed demon, hopping, stamping one foot, his tongue
lolling out of one corner of his mouth then the other, concen-
trating on the clublike thing he held tucked under his chin and
the whiplike thing in his right hand with which he tortured it,
making it scream and whine.

And the noisemaking demon seemed to be casting a spell on
all these other Hairy-Faces; they stamped and whirled, grabbed
each other's hands and arms as if fighting, and swung each other
around. And among them was another demon, huge and black, .
leaping and stomping and wriggling in some kind of ecstatic
spell, while everyone whooped and clapped hands. It was not
long before some of the Indian men and women began whooping and trilling in the margins of the firelight, and then one, and
two and three, hopped in among the hairy-faced dancers and
began twirling and hopping with them.

Drouillard was used to this, and was usually glad to hear the
whitemen's laughter. But tonight he was affected in a different
way. He was angry and was troubled deep inside, felt himself
pulling away from these men. This music and dancing, which he
usually knew as just a frolic to reward the soldier-slaves for their
courage and labor, now looked to him like a manic ceremony;
men were laughing while a merciless force thrust through the
delicate balance of the Sacred Circle. He was not of those men
now; they seemed strangers. He was one with the fishermen who
had been here taking salmon from the pure water for generations; he was one with the root-diggers and the buffalo-chasers,
and he was also one with man's brother the bear, and with the
ground-snuffling buffalo, and with the eagle in the treetop, and
with the eagle's eye at the edge of a cloud looking down on a vast
circle of horizon. It was at this moment that a woman began
singing, and came out from the shadows into the center of the
firelight.

She was a striking, square-jawed woman with intense eyes
and long, loose-flowing gray hair, an erect, spare, but broad-
shouldered figure. He had seen her come into the camp before
sunset with a fisherman who was probably her husband. She had

come carrying a large basket of quamash roots, while he brought dried salmon. She wore an ankle-length dress of fringed elk hide, almost white in color, ornamented with dangles of brass and some pearly kind of shell. The dress had long sleeves, open under the arms so the arms could be bared by slipping them out of the sleeves, which were then thrown back to hang behind the shoulders. Now this woman came out with arms bared, revealing many brass bracelets.

This woman emerged into the firelight, her eyelids quivering and blinking, eyes rolled far up as if looking into her own skull. Her mouth drooped open, emitting a tremulous Indian song of terrible poignancy, beginning high in her nose and descending to a low, bass groan, then suddenly starting again at the top and descending again. She carried her big basket of roots before her. Suddenly the whole camp was aware of her.

Her song was so powerful and heart-wrenching that it made Cruzatte come out of his fiddling trance and lift the bow off the strings to look at her. The dancers stopped, to stand gaping.

Her song seemed to be coming not from her throat but up through her from the ground. Drouillard felt the hair prickle on the back of his neck. On the far side of the fire Bird Woman and her baby were motionless, staring at the singing woman. This was the oldest of all songs.

The singing woman began offering the quamash roots to everyone around the fire, the standing dancers and the sitting spectators. No one reached into the basket; they drew back instead of reaching, as if afraid of her. She held the basket against her belly with her left hand and held handfuls of roots out to them with her right. A few men gingerly held out their hands and took them. When others drew back, she just tossed the handfuls at them, still singing. Her face was glistening with tears, her eyes still rolled up, yet she seemed to see. When her basket was empty she dropped it on the ground and began shaking the bracelets on her forearms; they clinked and rattled. She kept moving around the circle with a shuffling step like a dance, slipping the bracelets off over her hands and offering them. Her song was not of words, but Drouillard thought that she was asking them all to take everything she owned, pleading with the whitemen to take the gifts and go away.

Captain Lewis was watching her intently.

Some of the soldiers reached and accepted the bracelets she was offering, but some hung back as if afraid to take them. She tossed them into their laps. Then she came to Captain Lewis. He crossed his arms over his chest and shook his head. His refusal caused her song to become more shrill, a sound of agony and fury, and suddenly with a shriek she spun and threw the rest of the bracelets into the fire. She darted to her husband and said something to him, and he put something into her hand. On the far side of the fire Chief Twisted Hair was trying to say something in sign talk to the captains. The woman moved back into the firelight.

Soon she was standing in front of Captain Lewis. Her song changed; it was still that achingly plaintive fall of notes, but with a sob at each note of descent. Her teeth were fiercely bared. With a flint in her right hand she began hacking at her left arm, then at the right with the left, and a murmur of shock went up around the crowd as blood began streaming down both arms. Drouillard had seen this in dreams. The woman stopped singing. She ran her right hand up her left arm, scooping blood into her palm, and then she drank and licked the blood from her palm. She did the same with her left hand; her mouth and chin were red with blood. The amount pouring from her wounds was astounding. It gushed from the cuts faster than she could scoop and drink it, and her dress was soon spattered and smeared with it like a butcher's apron. Though her eyes looked inward, her power pressed on Lewis.

Everyone seemed immobilized. The captains were frozen in place. Lewis was flinching and seemed to be bracing himself. Meanwhile, the Nez Perce chiefs were just looking on with resigned, saddened faces, as was the woman's husband, as was Bird Woman. Only the captain's dog moved; he whimpered suddenly, leaped up and slunk away into the darkness with his tail between his legs.

The woman stood like a fountain of blood in the center of the camp for a long time, or it seemed a long time, singing her song again, which suddenly ended with a groaning whimper as she pitched forward on the bloodsoaked ground. All the whitemen were still too spellbound to move, but women emerged from the shadows and hovered around her. They cleaned her wounds and face with cold water from a pot, and when she came out of her trance, they helped her stand and escorted her away. The only sounds were the rushing of water over rock and the whiffling and cracking of the fire burning in the wind. Then men began talking, in querulous, hesitant voices. Cruzatte put his fiddle away. The captains tried to talk to Twisted Hair and Tetohoskee by sign, but they seemed not to understand, so Drouillard decided this was a good time to vanish.

As he edged away, Sergeant Ordway put a hand on his sleeve and asked: "She had a fit, eh?"

He put the sergeant's hand off. He was not going to say anything about the Ancient Ones coming, or about the omen directed at Lewis. He said, "Looked like a fit, didn't it?" and vanished before Ordway could ask why she hadn't bled to death.

October 9th 1805
a woman faind madness &c. &c. Singular acts of this woman in giveing in Small potions all She had & if they were not received She would Scarrify her Self in a horid manner &c. Capt Lewis recovring fast.

William Clark, Journals

Captain Lewis was getting over the digestive problems that had nearly killed him, but there was a darkness growing in his spirit, or so it seemed to Drouillard, who was now watching for it.

Lewis's forward force, always intense but methodical, now was heedless, like a boulder rolling down a hill. He was impatient to get to the coast and he seemed to aim straight down the rivers instead of studying everything along the way as he always had before.

Lewis remarked from time to time that dog meat had cured his bowels and that it was the most nourishing and strengthening flesh he had ever consumed. So now in their rush down the rivers toward the Columbia, whenever he stopped to barter for food from the Indians, he tried to buy dogs.

Captain Clark would eat the salmon and roots they bought, but not dog. He would snap his fingers and call, "Here, Seaman! I'll protect you. I see how he's lookin' at you and licking his lips!"

Drouillard noticed that Lewis's pet had been growing more detached from his master since that evening when the dog had slunk away from the woman's spirit power, and he did seem to stay closer to Captain Clark now. Clark was the only person who didn't eat dog. The rest of the soldiers, hungry for the flesh of Four-Leggeds, had gotten used to dog and welcomed it as a relief from fish and roots. Drouillard himself found it acceptable.

The river called Kooskooskie had run into the one called Snake. The chiefs said this one would flow into the great river itself, soon. That would be the long-sought Columbia. Captain Clark elected to rename the Snake, calling it Lewis's River. And one day, passing a fast, clear river that poured in from the north bank, the captains decided to name it after Drouillard, in honor of his many services. Captain Clark wrote on his map: *Drewyer's R.*

There was almost no game along this densely populated route. And wood for fires was as scarce as the game. No wood grew on the hills and plateaus near the river, only on lightly timbered hills seen at great distances from the rivers. It was as if the corps were floating down into a desert. The only wood anywhere was driftwood from the rivers, and the Indians apparently scoured the riverbanks for it, making lodges and fish-drying racks out of straight pieces, stacking the rest up on scaffolds to dry for fuel. It became necessary to barter or beg for wood as well as food, which worsened Lewis's state of mind because it diminished his store of trinkets and trade goods faster than he had planned. Sometimes the riverside Indians helped the soldiers at boat wrecks, and if the captains didn't offer to pay them, they would help themselves to whatever lay unguarded. Lewis's mood was as grim as the craggy dark basaltic cliffs of the canyon: Indians were supposed to be obedient children. And gullible too, Drouillard thought.

He wondered if Lewis's dark anxiety was part of what the woman with bloody arms had been warning about.

There were many rapids where good sense would have called for unloading the cargoes and carrying them around, letting the lightened canoes skim the swift water to pass through. But Captain Lewis was desperate about the lateness of the season and did not want to be delayed. On the cold morning of October 14 the vessels approached a long rapid that the Nez Perce chiefs had warned was bad, but Captain Lewis went into it in the little scouting canoe, with Cruzatte in the bow as his pilot. Then one of the four long, heavily laden vessels dipped into the head of the rapid and safely headed into the chute, but the last three boats ground to a halt, lodged on rock, and had to be worked off at great risk in the roaring current. Drouillard was steering the last one, and got it free only by leaping out, standing on the rocky bottom and lifting the stern, then flinging himself back aboard the moment the vessel was free. Then for three miles he steered with all his strength and skill as the heavy, cumbersome vessel slid, plunged, and bucked through three miles of roaring sluiceway. The subchief Tetohoskee rode in the bow, waving left or right as signals for him to steer by. Tetohoskee was added weight in the bow. That worried Drouillard. Often he heard the hull grate and bump rocks, the men whooping in alarm each time, flailing ineffectually with their paddles or fending the canoe off rocks with their hands. At last all the canoes were safe below that long watery gauntlet, and the party put ashore shaky and giddy for rest and food. Tetohoskee decided he would stay with Drouillard's canoe.

Two miles farther down an island split the river into two short but roaring chutes. One by one the vessels slid past the island. Drouillard, praying that the chief's extra weight in the bow would not make the canoe run too deep, followed into the chute. At once the laden bow scooted onto a flat rock just under the surface and the stern was swung out across the current. In an instant it was broadside, tilting. Tetohoskee leaped into the water and swam, and the soldiers abandoned ship and jumped onto the rock, leaving Drouillard in the stern with no ability to steer. The soldiers grabbed the bow and held on. The stern rode up on another rock and the canoe listed into the current, quickly filled and sank in the chute, with Drouillard scrambling forward trying to grab the most valuable items before they floated away. He grabbed a few shot pouches and two rifles and threw them to the men on the rock, who were shin-deep on the slippery rock in the fast water. Some of the soldiers' bedrolls, some hides being saved to make clothing, and two tomahawks went overboard before he could reach them. All the quamash roots recently bought for food went floating over the side. The men were yelling at the top of their lungs, and the canoe that had gone through just ahead turned toward shore, where its crew started heaving bundles onto the bank so they could try to come back up and rescue the men from the rock. Drouillard was too busy even to curse. Probably the most important thing in the vessel was gunpowder, in powder horns and in one of the lead canisters whose waterproof seal had already been broken. There were two unopened canisters in the bilge, but they had been tied down and were safe. But a great deal of gunpowder was already wet. The canoe paddles were floating down the river, and the crews of the boats below would probably pick them up.

When there was nothing left light enough to save, Drouillard at last clambered out over the bow onto the rock and helped the men hold the canoe steady so she wouldn't roll over underwater and lose even more. He was fully soaked and chilled, and ashamed and furious with Captain Lewis for his reckless haste, which had caused this.

"Hey, skipper!" Private Shannon yelled in his ear over the rush of the water, "Why'd ye go an' hit that rock?" The young man was grinning.

"Cap'n's orders!" he yelled back.

And in the midst of the watery uproar, Shannon laughed.

*   *   *

Here was the smell of plenty again: decaying flesh. Now it was not buffalo carcasses rotting, but dead fish, dead fish in prodigal quantities in the water and along the banks. And even though Drouillard was by now thoroughly used to the smell of salmon in the fishing camps, where the Indians split them and hung them to dry in the arid breeze from the west, uncountable tons of fish drying, this fish-rot was overpowering.

Here was abundance greater than all the buffalo and antelope and elk of the plains, yet it was all in a desert. And it supported bigger populations than he had ever imagined. Even in the great gathering place of rivers on the Mississippi, near St. Louis and Cahokia and Kaskaskia and St. Genevieve and Cape Girardeau, where he had spent his youth, there were not populations to compare with these in their mat-covered shacks along the lower stretches of Lewis's River. At every rapid there were scores of spectators lining the shores to watch the bearded strangers crash on the rocks, to help rescue them and pick up any unwatched item as their due toll. They were not afraid of the whitemen; Twisted Hair and Tetohoskee usually went ahead to explain who was coming, and any lingering apprehension was dispelled when Bird Woman and her baby came into view.

These fish people were different from the game-and-fish Nez Perce people. Their language was similar; the two chiefs could still speak with them without resorting to much signage, but they seemed to have little use for horses. Their lives were all about fish and they traveled by canoe. They made rock weirs at the rapids to narrow the channels, and with fish traps and gigging spears they simply scooped and snagged their food out of the water from morning to night. They didn't have to go hunting. Their food came to them. And they said that was the way it always had been, from the beginning of the world.

And so, Drouillard thought, they probably believe that it will always be so. Why should they fear a few whitemen? How could a few hairy-faced people in five canoes change something that had been unchanged since the beginning of the world?

Once long ago on the east coast, when the Shawnee ancestors had seen a few whitemen coming in ships, they had thought that same way, and had welcomed them, as these people were welcoming these whitemen from the east. How were they to know?

October 16, 1805

In the afternoon the canoes were unloaded above a violent raceway of water and everything was carried almost a mile down below the rapids; the canoes were eased down through on elkskin ropes and reloaded in the calm water. They then shot through four smaller rapids and passed three bare islands. Indians on horseback were watching them from the south bank. Stopping at another rapid, the party was joined by five horsemen. Drouillard talked sign with them and they smoked with the captains. Their dress and language were similar to the Nez Perce. Their horses were excellent, stout, with speckled coloration. The captains gave these horsemen some tobacco to take home and smoke with their people, and they rode off at full gallop, until they were out of sight.

One more hour in the canoes brought them around a bend and into a wide expanse of water and low, sloping desert land.

"Eeeaay-*hah*!" came Captain Clark's mighty voice from ahead. "Columbia!" And a loud cheer rose up from all the crews. Drouillard knew this was one of those landmarks, like the divide, that the captains had fixed in their minds. Now when the afternoon sun peeked through windblown clouds of rose and lilac, its glare sparkled on the expanse of swift water. The stench of dead fish blew even stronger into their faces. Another shout was relayed back: "Put ashore starb'd, on the point! There's our Indians!"

Twisted Hair and Tetohoskee had roused up a huge welcoming party of several hundred people from several villages around the confluence of rivers. A few miles above the mouth of the Snake, or Lewis's, River, another flowed into the Columbia from the west, called the Yakima. The people had not seen whitemen before, but knew of them from tribes farther down the Columbia, and in fact wore brass trade ornaments and a few woolen blankets. They milled about, gawking at these strange men with their guns and bundles and strange devices, awed by the big black man York. Their dogs were similarly awed by the big black dog Seaman, whose intrusive cold nose made many of them go sidewinding away with their tails between their legs and fearful snarls on their lips.

The soldiers were that curious about the posteriors of some of the women in the crowd. Unlike the Nez Perce women, whose long, fringed dresses concealed their bodies to the ankles, some of these women wore no skirts at all. They had waist-length jackets, but were bare the rest of the way down, except for a leather thong tied around their hips and passed between their legs. Some of the soldiers couldn't keep their eyes off the bare buttocks and the barely concealed crotches.

Not one tree was visible in any direction, but soldiers were sent along the riverbank and managed to gather enough driftwood for small fires. Then, as the camp took shape in the evening, a murmur of voices and a rhythmic drumming caught their attention.

Into the camp came a parade of two hundred men, beating on small drums with sticks and singing a wailing song, another of those songs in which Drouillard heard the sounds of the ancient ages, like those he had heard atop the mound by the faraway Mississippi, at that other gathering of rivers. He watched their chief, a tall, sturdy, stately man, lead them in a half circle between the soldier camp and the riverbank; there they halted and faced the campfire and continued to sing.

Later the chief, Cutssanem, and his subchiefs were given medals, handkerchiefs, and elegant shirts. A pipe was passed, and with Drouillard's hand signs and the help of the Nez Perce chiefs, Cutssanem was given the usual Jefferson message. He gave no sign of being much impressed, perhaps because Twisted Hair and Tetohoskee themselves had such vague conceptions of the ideas they were trying to convey to him. But he let it be known that he was happy to meet these whitemen and that some of his people wanted to present them with a little firewood and a large basket of good dried horse meat. Then Cutssanem took his men back up to their own camp, a short distance above, and the tired soldier camp settled down.

"B' damn, these ones close down early, don't they?" Cruzatte mused. He hadn't even had an opportunity to show off his fiddling to these fishing people.

Drouillard glanced down at the dwindling campfire, which was made of driftwood sticks, weed-stalks, and any other combustible woody material anyone had been able to scrape up, which was very little. He said, "When the lights go out, it's time for bed. I'd guess they're used to it."

Colter scooted in by the fire. Reubin and Joe Field appeared out of the darkness and sat looking at the last little flames. Fortunately, it was not cold. The captains' lodge stood a little way up the bank, its skin covering aglow with candlelight from within, where they were writing. Colter said: "Did y' ever see the likes of those women? Hams! Hams! Man, I miss ham and bacon!" The soldiers laughed.

"Hams, was it?" said Reubin. "Smelt more like fish t'me, when them ladies was squattin' 'round here."

"Still does," Drouillard said.

"Yeah, but I mean to say you know what I mean to say."

Joe Field looked upriver into the darkness. Stars were brilliant and the great river rushed by. "Tell ye," he said, "I don't know whether I'm glad them ladies went home or wish they'd stayed. Y' have to admit, they ain't very perty. It was all I could do to git up a cockstand. But it's like John said, when y' ain't had ham for so long . . . Those other women, up the river, was a lot better looking, but I was too sick to give 'em a passing hard-on."

"Passin', yeah. Passin' gas," Reubin said.

"But now these," Joe went on. "Frankly, they're ugly. They smile and it's just gums. But when they just willingly show you a half-acre o' hams . . ."

"You al'ays liked fat women, Joe," Reubin said with a snort.

Drouillard raised his nose to the wind. He was sorting out odors. And he was remembering some things he thought these people had said in sign. He said, "I've been wondering how they could eat all the fish they take out o' this river. I even saw 'em scoopin' up the dead ones. Tell you something I just figured out. I think they eat some, trade some, and the dead ones I bet they just dry them and burn them for fuel, since there's no wood anywhere."

This had drawn the men's thoughts away from those other yearnings. "Burn?" Reubin said.

Drouillard was remembering all the uses the plains Indians made of their buffalo. He remembered the grassy, smoky smell of dried buffalo dung burning on a campfire. "Think of all the oil in a salmon. Look." He produced a small slab of the dried fish from his shoulder bag, tore a strip off the edge and leaned forward to touch it to the flames. It caught and burned like a candlewick.

It was the same odor as on the night breeze over the river.

Gifts from the Creator, he thought.

October 18th 1805
The Great Chief Cuts Sah nim gave me a Sketch of the rivers & Tribes above on the great river & its waters on which he put great numbers of villages of his nation & friends—The fish which was offerd to us we had every reason to believe was taken up on the Shore dead, we thought proper not to purchase any, we purchased forty dogs for which we gave articles of little value, Such as beeds, bell, & thimbles, of which they appeared verry fond, at 4 O'Clock we Set out down the Great Columbia accompand by our two old Chiefs.
                                              William Clark, Journals

Drouillard listened to Captain Lewis venting his indignation about the bad fish "those wretches" had tried to sell, and smiled and shook his head. He was pretty certain they had meant to sell it as fuel, not food. But Lewis seemed to enjoy being contemptuous of Indians and scornful of their ways, whether he understood them or not. Whiteman has to look down his nose at somebody, Drouillard reminded himself. So he said nothing about it, and steered down the curving course of the great river toward the sea.

Chapter 19

On the Columbia River
October 19, 1805

Drouillard at day's first light took off his clothes and waded into the cold river, taking the clothes with him. It was the only way to keep from being overwhelmed by the fleas. The soldiers didn't bathe or rinse their clothes in the mornings, so they had more and more fleas every day, and complained, and scratched, and slept poorly.

He went down into the clear water over his head and scrubbed at his scalp with his fingernails and then around his genitals and under his arms. Then he stood in the shallows and scrubbed at the seams of his deer-hide shirt and leggings, and worked his loincloth back and forth over a rock, rinsed it again and wrung it out. He got on shore to wring out the rest of his clothes, which he would have to wear damp and clammy until they dried from the exertions of the day and the desert air. He saw that Indians from the fishing villages were already gathering along the riverbank in the early light to go and watch the soldier camp. Some of them were watching him.

Standing naked in the cold air, he braided his hair into a queue at the back, then signaled to the Indians, *Day sunrise good,* a morning greeting. Some answered with hand signs, others with cheerful voices. His greeting would be about all the cheer they would get. The captains and soldiers were grouchy because of the fleas, which they blamed on the Indians, and because the

341

Indians were always around watching the camp and picking up untended articles.

Drouillard put on his wet clothes and climbed the riverbank. He watched the sky fill with pale light above the stark, craggy canyon walls. Looking downstream he saw, ghostly in this early light, one of the faraway, snow-topped mountains that could be seen before them sometimes even from the canoes, depending on the course of the Columbia between its cliffs. The captains called one of the mountains Mount St. Helens and another Mount Hood, names given them by a ship captain who had seen them years ago. The Columbia River, they said, was named after an American ship that had charted its mouth thirteen years ago. The mountains had been named by an English captain who had sailed a distance up the river from the Pacific later the same year. This meant, as Lewis liked to say, they were at last reentering the known world. Even before they left the Mississippi, they knew they would eventually see these mountains, and now they saw them.

The captains were impatient. Everyone was sick of salmon and more salmon, and some were even getting tired of dog meat. The fishing places all along this river were piled with unbelievable quantities of dried salmon, in stacks, in baskets, buried in lined pits. The ground at those places was littered with fish skins. The riverbanks were strewn with dead fish, which drew countless pelicans and ravens. At the rapids, salmon jumped out of the water to get above, sometimes almost leaping into the canoes. In deep water, the river was so clear that salmon could be seen swimming twenty feet below the canoes.

The salmon were an encouragement to the captains. They felt that if salmon could come up from the ocean, the waterfalls must be only a few feet high, nothing like those on the Missouri that had required weeks of portage.

As Drouillard went up the riverbank toward the camp, he was greeted with toothless smiles by some of the Indians. He had hardly ever known a toothless Indian of any age, but by middle age many of these salmon-eaters were. Clark guessed their teeth were worn down to the gums by grit from stones with which they pounded their dried fish and roots, and also perhaps by the considerable amount of fish scale they took in with their salmon. That seemed likely. Drouillard had ground his own teeth on plenty of grit and scale lately.

He had also known very few fat Indians; Big White the Mandan chief had been one. But many of these river Indians were thick in girth, with chubby faces and thick legs, and jowls that quaked when they walked. They were a slow-moving people; only youngsters were quick. Some of the women had so much fat on their lower bodies that their little crotch thongs were invisible within the folds of flesh. He wondered if they were fat because there was so much food all the time and they scarcely had to exert themselves to obtain it.

These unattractive characteristics only increased the disdain the captains felt for them, much of which was due to their "thieving" tendencies and their intrusiveness about the camp. Drouillard sometimes seethed when Captain Lewis complained about their intrusiveness, he who had come uninvited into their country. All the soldiers, irritated by fleas and flies, vented their wrath in ferocious language about the "filthy Indians." Drouillard had observed that the Indians bathed more and stank less than the soldiers. But their living environs were so permeated with fish and fish waste that the people must be helpless against the fleas and flies. It seemed as if fleas lived even in the ground and in the poles and mats of the lodge-houses. He knew that merely by sleeping on the ground in this land, he got fleas. The only way these people could get rid of fleas would be by moving away. And they couldn't do that. They were salmon people and always had been here. How could they even imagine life without fleas? And their ancestors were here, buried on islands in family or community graves surrounded by picket fences and covered by wooden houses and elaborately carved canoes. The captains had stopped and examined many such burial places, poking about, making notes for Jefferson. Drouillard stayed back, as he had last year at the hill of the little devils. There were countless skulls, and signs of even older burials. These people must have been here since the Beginning Times; thus they had become the way they were. It mattered little, Drouillard thought, if these whitemen coming through found them disagreeable.

> *October 21st 1805*
> *a verry cold morning we Could not Cook brakfast before we embarked as usial for the want of wood or Something to burn.—one of our Party J. Collins presented us with Some verry good beer made of the quar-mash bread, the remains of what was laid in . . . at the head of the Kosskoske river which by being frequently wet molded & Sowered &c. we made 33 miles to day.*
>
> *William Clark, Journals*

By the next day they were out of the desert. Mountains and cliffs rose high on either side of the river, and high up there were trees. Moisture and the scents of greenery were on the cool breeze, vaguely detectable even through the pervasive smell of fish. The gorge of the Columbia was deep. It appeared to have bored its way through a mountain range; in some places it was half blocked by huge boulders as if whole cliffs had fallen in. They ran through fast, roaring channels, skillfully avoiding boulders as big as houses. The long canoes were clumsy to steer, but they had become skillful, confident that if they had a foot of water under the hull and two feet of paddling space on either side, they could go anywhere. They swept by Indians fishing on flimsy pole scaffolds and in graceful, wide-bottomed canoes. They swept by the mouths of spectacular little rivers that fell into the Columbia on the south side through steep canyons. They passed big fishing towns that appeared to be permanent, not seasonal, nestled on picturesque rock ledges. They saw smoke drifting over the villages and sniffed the welcome odor of real wood smoke, tangy and piney.

Now Twisted Hair and Tetohoskee were tense and alert, and suddenly the old chief signaled toward the right bank, almost frantically.

And up the high-walled gorge rolled a sound deeper than the familiar rush of river and rapid: that familiar roar of a waterfall.

Ahead a mile or so the broad river appeared to end at a wall of rock, and from beyond it rose a mist. Near the head of a rock ledge the five canoes were brought to shore on a rocky beach, above which a large village perched on a high, straight ledge. Behind that ledge rose high hills that dwarfed the town, echoing and magnifying the booming roar of the falling water.

This was the great waterfall the Nez Perce had been telling of for days, at the village of the Eneeshur nation. Here they would have to get out and carry everything.

They walked out, exploring a huge island of rock cut through by several narrow channels of racing water. Toward the other bank lay another rock island of about a quarter mile in length. A cascade of five steps thundered between the two islands, falling perhaps forty feet in a beaten, greenish-white froth. Drouillard felt the water force through the solid rock beneath his moccasins and inhaled deeply of the fresh wet air, his face up into the re-freshing mist. His spirits were higher than they had been for days. What a place this was to see: cliffs, mossy rock, pure water churning, mist full of sunlight, eagles, pelicans, cormorants against a blue sky straight overhead, dizzying to watch. And by facing a particular way he could see no whitemen.

The carry path was a little more than half a mile, along the north bank, down to a little cove around the bend, and the Eneeshurs had a few horses for hire to carry the bundles of goods. There the bundles were set under guard and the corps camped. The next day Clark took the canoes upriver a way and then brought them down and landed on a rock bank just above the sheer pitch of the falls on the south side of the river. Most of the men were needed to carry the water-soaked vessels down a dry channel about a third of a mile to emerge below the main pitch of the falls. Unfortunately, that portage channel was a sun-warmed trough of silt and fish skins and rotting vegetation, pu-trid and infested with so many fleas that the men were covered instantly. Below this portage remained a fall of eight feet, down which the canoes had to be lowered by ropes. All the men took off their clothes and did this work in the water to wash off the fleas. The natives gathered on high banks and ledges on both sides to amuse themselves with the sight of the naked, white-skinned men shouting and easing their long log canoes down through white water. An elk-skin rope broke when one of the canoes was being let down, the men shouted and the vessel bobbed and floated loose below, but some Eneeshur fishermen in their canoes rounded it up, and it cost the captains a bit of merchandise for their trouble.

That evening Captain Lewis traded for one of the finely crafted native vessels, giving the little pilot canoe, a hatchet, and some trinkets for it. Eight dogs were purchased for food. The men rinsed as many fleas out of their clothes as they could, and settled down for a tired camp with real wood to burn and the thunder of the vanquished falls behind them.

The next morning, the Nez Perce chiefs wanted to leave and go home. They explained in sign language that the people below the falls—the Chinooks—had a different kind of language and were not friendly to the Nez Perce. They expected that they would be killed if they went on down.

But Captain Lewis was not through with them yet. The next falls, near below, they had said were very dangerous, and he wanted their help in approaching them.

And the captain had not forgotten his peacemaking mission. If the people below were hostile, that should be changed.

No, they said. They wanted the goods that had been promised them for their services to this place, and they wanted to go home.

The only control Captain Lewis had over their choice was by withholding their reward. Frightened and sullen, they got into the canoes and prepared for the worst.

October 24th Thursday 1805
At 9 o'Clock A.M. I Set out. at 2⅕ miles the river widened into a large bason to the Stard Side on which there is five Lodges of Indians. here a tremendious black rock high and Steep appearing to choke up the river . . . the Current was drawn with great velocity to the Lard Side of this rock at which place I heard a great roreing. the natives went with me to the top . . . I could see the difficuelties we had to Pass . . . The whole of this

*great river must pass thro' this narrow channel of 45 yards
wide as the portage of our canoes over this high rock would be
impossible . . . I thought (as also our principal waterman
Peter Crusat) by good Stearing we could pass down safe . . .
notwithstanding the horrid appearance of this agitated gut
Swelling, boiling & whorling in every direction*

William Clark, Journals

Charbonneau with his family, and all the men who could not
swim, were assigned to carry the papers, instruments, ammunition, and guns overland to a likely campsite on calm water below
the roaring narrows. When the natives of the vicinity got word
that these strange visitors were going to get in their canoes and
go through that churning chute on purpose, they hurried to
gather on the heights. Drouillard looked around at the two dozen
designated paddlers who were nervously securing everything in
their five vessels. He went over to York, who would be in the elegant Chinook canoe with Captain Clark and his paddlers, and
shook hands with him. Then he pointed at the spectators. "Ready
to watch us perish, I reckon." York swallowed and nodded.
Drouillard motioned with his chin toward numbers of Indian
men and women who were hurrying down the riverbank.
"Those, I bet, are going down to the eddy where they reckon our
pieces and remains'll wash up. This could be a profitable day for
them, eh?"

" 'F you tryin' t' scare me," York said, "it's too late. I already am."

Drouillard feigned surprise. "Eh? I'd never've known it!
You're the only one of us not gone pale!"

York managed to laugh. Then he licked his lips and looked all
around, put out his hand again and said, "Mist' Droor, I been
please t' know ye."

"Likewise. You and your boss man both." He glanced over at
Captain Clark, who was talking to the men, inaudible against the
roar of the water, but making gestures that apparently had to do
with steering. Drouillard watched the rugged, cheerful, red-
haired captain and remembered all the bragging York had done
about him, and considered that just about every day in nearly

two years since, that man had proven that York wasn't so much bragging as understating. Clark had basically been running everything, and doing most of the writing as well, since the descent from the mountains. Lewis was physically recovered now but had been in a surly, melancholy state for a long time, occasionally rousing himself to study some novel plant or halfheartedly do his Jefferson ceremony in the fishing villages.

Now, Clark whooped and waved to summon York. Drouillard took a deep breath and went to his canoe, which would be the last through.

In single file, well-spaced, the canoes were paddled upstream and then curved around to aim straight down the chute. Captain Clark's canoe, Cruzatte steering, headed down, all paddles flashing. Cruzatte had taught everyone that a canoe can be handled better in fast water if it is going a little faster than the water, instead of just being carried along with current pushing the stern. That Indian-made canoe might be the only one to make it through, Drouillard thought, if any did. It was wide, lightweight, tapered and high at both bow and stern. He watched it enter the chasm, skimming like a leaf, speeding up, then receding from sight like a toboggan going down a hill. Whooping voices were lost in the roar of water. Then the second canoe went, then the third, then the fourth, and now his own canoe was in the fast current, entering the high rock funnel, stern tending to drift to the right until he reminded his paddlers with a rude shout to dig in. Then the chasm walls were blurring by on both sides and they were racing downhill on a dimpled sheen of water, the crew howling with exhilaration. Drouillard could see the other canoes ahead, all paddles rising and dipping furiously, every canoe going arrow-straight, none sideways. His heart rose up and he couldn't contain his voice: it trilled out of his throat like the old war cry of his people.

They were all giddy and wishing they could have that much fun again when Captain Clark walked up from scouting below and said there was another chute much like it two miles below, but a longer funnel and not quite so narrow. Once again the nonswimmers set off overland with the valuables, and the canoes sped through another roaring, dark chasm, with vertical cliffs high on either side. By the end of this day they all felt they were ready to take on any kind of rapid that God saw fit to put in their way. Or at least they were saying they felt that way; there were a few who waded into the shallows below and pretended they were washing fleas out of their breeches. Potts, who had been a paddler in Drouillard's canoe, was forthright about what his breeches were full of, saying, "Hell, I was just fine, till ye give out that 'ere heathen war cry, damn ye!"

Clark had walked down to a Chinook village, where he met its principal chief and invited him to come up to the canoe camp, where the crews had unloaded the canoes to dry their cargoes.

When the Chinook headman came up with a few of his men, the initial wariness between them and the two Nez Perce chiefs was soon dispelled, and all the Indians gave the captains their pledge to be peaceable toward each other. The Chinook leader was given a medal and other gifts, which he accepted with pleasure, and then Cruzatte played on the fiddle and the men danced for the visitors. The captains smoked with the Chinooks until late at night, and did what they could to begin recording a Chinook vocabulary for the President.

While the corps paused here to mend canoes and dry cargoes, there was time for Drouillard to take some hunters up out of the river gorge and onto a mountain to hunt, up into the pines and oaks. It was a joy to hunt again. They came back with four deer, the first venison in weeks. The men drooled while it was roasting. The captains had learned from the Chinooks that more dangerous falls and rapids lay yet between there and the sea they were seeking. That below these mountains lay tree-covered mountains inhabited by deer and elk, and other animals good to eat. That more salmon were in the rivers than one could count, and more swimming birds, and swimming animals with beautiful fur. The captains presumed those would be seals or sea otters.

They learned that they would find another range of mountains below these, mountains full of fog and ferns, where streams of water fell from cliffs and rain fell from the sky most days, where the trees were so thick and tall and dark on the mountainsides, they looked black—trees so big and straight that perfect, wide planks could be split from them.

They learned that they would meet Indian nations down there who knew the white men who came from the sea in huge boats with wings. Those Indians spoke the Chinook tongue but knew also how to talk trade with the whitemen, and had obtained many metal things from the whitemen who came every year in their big boats. The captains learned that there was a good bay in the mouth of this river where the whitemen's boats came in, for protection from the sea storms and to trade with those Indians down there.

These Chinooks knew all about what lay below, because those people from the ocean came up here to sell whiteman things and seashells and waterproof baskets and mats they made, and a kind of cloth they made of cedar bark, and a kind of root they harvested in great quantity, called *wapato*, not the same as the quamash roots the Nez Perce brought down from the mountains to trade, but just as good. These Indians here knew the tribes from up the river very well too, because here where the upper river and the lower river were separated by the falling waters was the center of the trade, and these people who lived here controlled the trade; all had to pass through them. This was a statement of their own importance. These chiefs had skins from the mountain animals and furs from the water animals below, and they had brass buttons and ornaments and bells, and metal knives and awls, and woolen blankets, even a few muskets and swords. These people took fingers instead of scalps from dead enemies. The chief had fourteen.

Drouillard and the Nez Perce chiefs translated all this. Some things for which they knew no hand signs could just be pointed to in the Chinook houses—such as the wide planks and the *wapato* roots and the seashells. The language of these Chinooks was spoken with tongue-clicks and throat-clucks. Most of the women here were short and obese, with the worn-down teeth. Their foreheads were broad and sloped sharply back from the brow to culminate in an almost pointed crown of the skull. They achieved that shape by compressing their babies' skulls with an angled board attached to the cradleboard. Thus the profile of a Chinook woman at her most beautiful was a slope from the crown of the head to the end of the nose or even the upper lip, as if to imitate the shape of the head of the fish that dominated their lives.

Old Twisted Hair and Tetohoskee had served their promised role in the voyage down the Columbia. They had been fine friends and helpful comrades throughout this strenuous downstream journey of some four hundred miles. Back at their home in the mountains they still had the responsibility of keeping the whitemen's horses for them until next year. They would all meet again and renew their great friendship then, if the soldiers returned east by the way they had come.

As the captains readied their canoes to go on down, they paid the two chiefs in goods. It was an emotional parting. The chiefs could not hide their affection or their sadness no matter how hard they clenched their jaws. They promised that their people would always be the whitemen's friends and would always watch for them to come into sight, whether up the rivers or down the mountains.

"Tell them," Captain Clark told Drouillard, "that we deem them the finest Indians we have met, all across this whole land. And tell them those are words from my heart."

It was time to get in the canoes and go on. Depending on the course of the river, it could be between a hundred and two hundred miles yet to the Pacific. It would soon be winter, and as they had learned, even downstream was not easy.

Chapter 20

The Columbia Estuary

November 7th Thursday 1805
Great Joy in camp we are in View of the Ocian, this great Pacific Octean which we been So long anxious to See. and the roreing or noise made by the waves brakeing on the rockey Shores (as I Suppose) may be heard disticly

William Clark, Journals

Joy, disappointment, and misery. What the captains had thought was the seacoast was only a rocky point jutting into the wide mouth of the Columbia, a mouth so wide and fog-shrouded that they could not see across it, and so beaten by swells and rollers that the canoes could neither proceed to the coast nor retreat to calmer waters.

And there was no level ground on which to make camp. They could not camp on beaches at the foot of the cliffs because the waves roared in and swept over them, and the tides came in and inundated them. Huge driftwood logs, five and six feet thick and two hundred feet long, washed in and piled up, rubbing and groaning against the cliffs, threatening to smash the canoes. The soldiers found niches and crevices in the face of the cliff and hung on, cold, soaked with rain and spray. There was nothing to eat but the rancid pulp of dried, pounded salmon they had bought from natives.

The hunters couldn't go up and hunt, because the cliffs were too steep to climb, and thick with undergrowth and fallen deadwood. To lie down, the soldiers had to spread their mats on jumbles of stones. Their weatherworn deerskin clothes were rotting on their bodies. Rain poured down day and night, loosening stones on the cliffs, which came clattering and bouncing down among the hunkering men. The winds were gales much of the time, sending tremendous waves bursting against the rocks.

When they tried to board the canoes to find better campsites, they were nearly swamped by the surging, gray seas, and forced to take shelter in other alcoves as bad as the previous one, or worse, and by then they were seasick. Bird Woman was among those with the most violent seasickness. And several of the men had got nausea and diarrhea by drinking the brackish river water instead of collecting rain.

Their tenacious and miserable foothold was further complicated by something new to them: tides. They would make a camp on a beach or ledge, secure the canoes among the gigantic drift logs, rigging shelters there, only to have the tide rise and set them afloat, grinding and thumping with crushing force. It was an unending battle to keep the canoes from being destroyed. All the soldiers had been wet for so long that their skin was wrinkled and fish-belly white.

Even in these circumstances, the whitemen wrote. Clark looked up from his notebook one day and said, "November eleventh, Drouillard. Two years since the day we met you, at Massac fort."

Drouillard remembered the eagle leading him. "Let's celebrate," he said, rain dripping from the end of his nose.

It had been raining and blowing for eleven days, varied only on one day by thunder, lightning, and hail. When the seas diminished a little, three men set out in the Indian-made canoe to scout for a cove or beach ahead, but were turned back by the force of the seas. They tried again the next day. On November 14, Colter swept around the point in the canoe with the welcome news that they had found a beach with a good canoe harbor not far around the point, and two Indian camps. He had left Willard and Shannon at the beach to hunt and explore the river farther down, and to look for ships in a bay.

Captain Lewis decided to grab the opportunity to take a small party around the point while it was feasible. He selected Drouillard, the Field brothers, and Private Frazier, took a canoe with a crew of paddlers, and launched into the bashing waves. By the time they had struggled around the sheltering point, the canoe was half full of water and the men were soaked by spray. But they did get around and were landed on a sandy beach in the rain, and at a timely moment: Willard and Shannon ran to meet them with the news that the young Chinooks in the camp had deftly stolen both their rifles. The arrival of many soldiers so alarmed the Indians that they meekly delivered up the guns and submitted to a scolding and severe threats delivered by Drouillard in sign language. The canoe was sent back with word for Captain Clark to bring the rest around to this habitable place as soon as the seas permitted. They made a comfortable, though flea-infested, camp in one of the many abandoned Indian houses. There, Captain Lewis showed them a map and laid out his purpose.

The map was a copy of one made in 1792 by a British captain, named Vancouver. It showed where an anchorage was supposed to lie in the river's mouth on this northern bank. If there were any ships in the vicinity, they would likely be there. And just over the outer arm of that bay lay the ocean itself, that ocean so close yet so maddeningly unreachable. "Are you ready to see the ocean?" Lewis asked. They were indeed. "We'll set out on foot in the morning," he said.

The bay had not a sign of a ship in it, and Indians they met said there had been no ships for a long time. The rain stopped and started as they marched with squishing steps through the marshy ground on the bay's north side. They swam across the mouth of a small river, floating their rifles and knapsacks on a raft of bundled driftwood, climbed a long, rocky eminence on the west side of the bay, and headed south toward the point. Captain Lewis said this place was called Cape Disappointment, because a British sea captain in 1788 had wrongly concluded that no major river met the ocean here. The captain laughed as he told that story; he hated the English and enjoyed telling of their mistakes and failures.

The sky was clearing. From over the ridge came a deep, regular sound, like the breathing of a giant. A shadow passed over the scrubby ground before them and they looked up to see a huge, buzzardlike bird soaring on the wind, its wings appearing to be ten feet from tip to tip. "Let's go over," the captain shouted in the wind. They climbed a rocky hill, which was almost bald except for long grass blowing, and came over the crest. The deep, rolling sound now burst upon their ears unmuffled, a hissing boom, a long roar, then another hissing boom, and they looked down over the seaward side to illimitable graygreen water. The horizons were lost in spume and mist, but beams of sunshine illuminated vast areas to the southwest. Below the cape the high waves came marching shoreward, curling, white-topped, to burst against the rocks below, sending towers of white water straight up to dissipate in the onshore wind and fall seething away, followed momentarily by the burst of the next wave.

There was nothing to say. They had all seen immense wonders beyond imagination in these two years, and should have been immune to amazement by now. For the first time the other side of the Columbia's mouth could be seen, faintly, perhaps five miles to the south, all wooded lowlands and dun-colored expanses of sand. Eastward across the bay the Columbia was full of such a maze of islands and points that the river course was hard to distinguish. A sea captain easily might have presumed it was just an inlet, not a river.

George Drouillard stood in the wind and the noise watching the light play over the endless water. This was the last edge of the land known as Turtle Island by his own people. Once, the Shawnees had lived on the eastern coast, the Atlantic, but they had been pushed away from there a hundred years ago. Drouillard had never seen an ocean until now. Probably no other

Shawnee had ever seen this one, and it was unlikely that any ever would, unless somehow they got on ships.

He thought far back. Two years ago it was that he had met the captains and they asked him to come with them to this ocean, and he had almost said no. Then he had heard the songs of the Ancient Ones and decided to come. Now he was here where they had promised they would come to; he had often had good reason to doubt that they would get here, but here they were. He looked at Lewis, that strange, hard, troubled man. The captain was standing silent looking out, and Drouillard had a notion that he was thinking as much about Jefferson as about his own feelings.

Drouillard reached into his pouch and got sacred tobacco. He crumbled some between his thumb and fingers and turned in a circle, kneeling in each of the four directions to sprinkle some on the ground. This was a time to pray, and so he prayed with the wind beating against him and the ocean booming in his head. He stood with the whitemen behind him so he couldn't see them and imagined himself an Indian alone.

> *Ocian 4142 Miles from the Mouth of Missouri R.*
> *William Clark,* Journals

November 24, 1805

The sun was actually shining. For the first time in weeks here was a chance to break out the instruments and make observations at this culmination point of their journey. The men in the meantime spread the wet cargoes and bedding out to dry.

Drouillard took five hunters and set out into the rough hills, but found virtually no sign of deer or elk. They shot one goose, a brant, and that was all they brought in after a full day's hunt.

He reported to the captains that the party would starve if they tried to spend the winter here. "Not even nibblings," he said. "There hasn't been any game here for a long time."

During the day some Chinooks had come from their villages to the north with a sea otter skin and a little food to trade, and that had been a disheartening experience. These Indians had been dealing with ship merchants for several years and had learned the art of overpricing. They had seen all kind of white-men's goods, and were not impressed by the dwindling store of tarnished, moldy, water-damaged goods the corps could produce. The only thing they seemed to want badly was blue beads, not red ones or white ones but blue ones, and there were precious few of those left. Bird Woman a few days earlier had given up her most cherished possession, a belt of blue beads from her waist, so the captains could trade it for an otter-skin robe.

The captains and the men soon built up a seething dislike for these Chinooks, not just for their avarice in trade but also because of their thievery. In every one of their few encounters with them so far, they had caught them stealing or trying to steal something or other, and Captain Lewis had put the word out that the next Chinook who tried to steal a rifle would be shot instantly. That condition was declared to every Chinook who came to visit.

So there was no game here on the north bank of the Columbia, no evident place for winter shelter, and surely no chance of being able to afford food bought from the Chinooks at their prices. And yet the captains wanted to stay close by the mouth of the Columbia, in hopes that ships would come.

The soldiers, after their initial satisfaction in having reached the Pacific Ocean, were sick of this place. Here they had suffered three weeks of incessant rains and gales, seasickness, a short-ration diet of rancid, moldy fish-pulp, infestations of fleas, sodden clothes and bedding, and the proximity of the most disagreeable Indians they had seen since the Sioux. To order them to stay in these circumstances through a whole winter against their will, just in the wan hope of seeing a ship, might well undermine their morale and even lead to mutiny. Drouillard had a quiet discussion with the captains. He and his hunters recommended a return up to the falls, where they had seen signs of more varied game, where a man could wear dry clothes, and where the Indians had inexhaustible stores of good fish and would sell it cheap.

"No," Captain Lewis argued. "There will be ships. I have the President's letter of credit. It will buy us provisions, or enough goods to trade for food even with these greedy Indians. And a ship could take word back to the States that we're alive and well. And all our reports to Mr. Jefferson. I want him to know that I've done what he sent me to do! If we don't get back, no one will ever know we got here! Do you think anybody back there imagines we're still alive?"

Captain Clark was in agreement about staying near the coast in expectation of meeting a ship, but he believed that living near the sea was not healthful. He was in favor of exploring the other shore of the Columbia. Some of the Indians had said elk lived in the woods over there. "If there are elk there, we can live there. If there are elk, we can make clothes and moccasins. In those woods we can build shelter from this damned sea wind but still be near if ships come."

"Unless it gets colder than this, Cap'n, meat won't keep," Drouillard said. "We'll need a smokehouse. If we jerk elk meat, we'll have to do it over fire. Nothing will dry here."

"Salt," Captain Lewis said. "We'll boil down seawater for salt. We're out of it. Elk's awful without salt. And if we can make enough salt, that'll help us preserve meat. Salt meat and jerky. Drouillard, if there's any elk over there, you and your hunters can keep us fed."

"*If* there is elk. If there is plenty of elk. I need to see that country," he said. "And even then, my hunters and I would rather be at the falls. Better country."

"Understood," Clark said. Then he turned to Lewis and said, "We need to let our boys have a say in this. Like when nobody believed which fork was the Missouri. Once they had their say, they were happy to go along with our judgment. If we stay here without letting them have their say, they're like to mutiny on us before winter's over."

So they called a council that evening.

As Drouillard said, most of his hunters wanted to return to the mountains near the falls. Ten other men wanted to go to Sandy

River, back up the Columbia about a hundred miles—a wide, lush, wooded bottomland they had passed on the way down, a place teeming with game birds, far above this dismal coastal weather and within view of the beautiful cone-shaped mountain called Mount Hood.

The other twelve men were agreeable to scouting the south side of the Columbia for game and a protected site for a winter bivouac.

And as Captain Clark had predicted, once every man had had his say, they were ready to do what the captains wanted: look for a place on the other side of the river. Only John Shields objected to the other shore; he still wanted them to go to the Sandy River, which had looked like a paradise to him.

Even York was allowed his say. In the past two years he had proven himself anybody's equal and was liked by everyone; in the isolated little society of this corps, he was temporarily more than just a Negro and a slave.

And then Charbonneau startled everyone by standing up and pointing to his wife and saying, *"Elle veut voter aussi."*

Drouillard hid his smile with a hand. This was a delightful surprise.

"What's this?" Captain Lewis said.

Drouillard said, "His wife wishes to vote."

Captain Lewis frowned. "Nonsense. She's just an Indian!"

"I'm an Indian too, Cap'n," Drouillard reminded him.

Lewis hissed, "Women don't vote. Let's get on—"

"Pardon, Cap'n. Indian women do vote."

Charbonneau spoke again in French.

"Sir, he says if she doesn't vote, he doesn't," Drouillard said.

"Well, then, strike his damned vote. Of all the damned cheek!"

Captain Clark interrupted. "What might her vote be, Mr. Drouillard?"

He and Bird Woman talked with hands. "She says she would like us to go live where there are plenty of *wapato* roots."

Clark smiled at Drouillard and scribbled with his pencil. "Sounds reasonable to me," he said.

"Assieds-toi, m'sieu," Drouillard said to Charbonneau. *"C'est accompli. Merci."*

Charbonneau told her, and she gave one firm nod and drew the edge of her blanket closer about the baby's face.

Drouillard thought he understood what had caused that protest: both Sacagawea and her husband were still angry about her blue bead belt being traded away. It had been her only valuable possession.

The Chinooks and Clatsops, with their wide, high-prowed canoes, came and went in the estuary in any weather. They were incomparable boatmen. The low, narrow dugouts of the corps were just not suitable for such high seas. The soldiers had to paddle miles up the Columbia and cross the wide river in the lee of islands because of the high waves that raced up the channel from the sea.

Elk were seen at places on the south shore, but it was impossible to shoot any because of the downpours. Most of Lewis's hunters gave up and returned to his party because the woods were so thick they couldn't make their way through them. Drouillard stayed out, slithering like a snake through the woods, ferns, briars, alder, salmonberry, and skunk cabbage, finding and memorizing animal trails, getting the lie of the land, eating squirrels when he could find them, salmon pulp from his pouch when there was nothing else. It was good to be alone for a while, away from all those miserable soldiers with their fleas and diarrhea and swellings and scabs. Captain Lewis and his men were somewhere below. Clark and the rest were somewhere above. And he was by himself, as he had been so seldom in these last two years, as he used to be almost all the time before. Although he was soaked to the skin, and the tall trees above him waved and groaned as if they would topple on him, he was in his old, lone predator state now, learning where everything lived, learning where the prey went, and when. If those thirty men were going to depend upon him for food all winter in this strange, dark, wet, evergreen place, he had a whole new territory to learn.

Netul River
December 13, 1805

There was barely enough light left to aim at the elk, but Drouillard sent his prayer message to it just as it turned to see him, and he fired. He heard it thrash in the foliage as the gunshot echoed, and then he couldn't see the animal. But it was soon still among the ferns and the evergreens and he knew it was dead. He made a picture in his mind of the place where it was standing when he shot it. He reloaded. He turned back down to the edge of the river and slipped through the foliage, down to the fork where he had left Shannon butchering. It was raining softly and the woods were wet and dripping. It was always raining here. The expedition had reached the mouth of the Columbia more than a month ago, and in all that time the rain had not stopped for more than an hour or two.

He edged through the underbrush and stepped into the grass at the river fork so suddenly and silently that Shannon was startled. Shannon said, "I heard you shoot twice. I s'pose that means you got two more?"

"That's right. Too dark to find them tonight. Better head home before it gets too dark. And bring canoes up tomorrow for them. I hope they've got that smokehouse built. Nothing keeps long in this weather. Ready?"

"Lead on."

They each shouldered an elk hide with about thirty-five pounds of the best cuts in it and set out through the dusk. Shannon had all he could do to keep up with Drouillard's walking pace, which was like anyone else's fast trot.

It was dark by the time they reached the partially finished huts. They smelled smoke and saw the ruddy glow of campfires and heard voices. Shannon was still coming along, but he was wheezing like a winded horse when they came into the firelight. The soldiers' garments were so tattered and rotten from rain and wear that they were half naked. Fortunately, there seemed not to be any truly bitter cold in this region, just a constant dank chill.

They desperately needed elk hides to make new winter clothes for everybody. Several men at a time were sick with colds.

"Hey, boys! Here come Drouillard and Shannon!"

"Thought y' was lost, boys!" They had been out four days.

Captain Clark came out from under an awning attached to a log wall and said, "Sure glad to see you two! Had us worried." As Drouillard swung his meat bundle off his shoulder and eased it to the ground, Clark looked at it wistfully and said, "That all?"

"All we could carry. We'll need canoes tomorrow to go up for the rest."

Friday 13th December 1805
Drewyer & Shannon returned from hunting, haveing killed 18 Elk & left them boochered in the woods near the right fork of the river about 6 miles above this place all except 2 which they Could not get as night provented ther finding them . . .
                                        William Clark, Journals

Sergeant Gass liked to say, "This whole goddamn fort was built in weather that would've been a carpenter's days off."

It stood in a clearing dotted with the stumps of the tall, straight fir trees that had become its walls. The wood split so neatly that a nearly perfect plank could be made without a ripsaw. By Christmas Eve the men had finished their huts and moved in out of the rain and hail that had fallen every day of the construction. All their fleas moved in with them.

Stocky men and women of the Clatsop tribe had been coming to the site of the fort during its construction, bringing roots and berries, baskets and mats, and the skins of panthers and sea otters, but were such tight bargainers that the soldiers bought very little, and the Indians usually left disgruntled. They were a mild-mannered people with pleasant faces, some of the women and girls very pretty, saucy and bawdy. They covered their heads and upper bodies with cone-shaped hats and mantles so tightly woven that they shed rain, but went basically naked from the waist down. Captain Lewis remarked that he could do a venereal diagnosis of a whole party just by glancing around, and they all seemed to be infected. Soon the soldiers' venereal symptoms were back, and the calomel came back out of the medicine chest. These coastal Indians apparently had been ravaged by diseases off the trading ships; they told of being a very numerous nation within the lifetime of their fathers and mothers, but they were just a few hundred now. The captains were little inclined to be bothered by Indian visitors now, but had to maintain friendly relations for practical reasons, and were obliged to learn what the President would want to know of them. Captain Lewis was counting on Indians to bring news of any ship that might come too, so he had to feign more cordiality than he felt.

The dampness and the warmth made the preservation of meat very difficult. Even with a smokehouse constantly tended, much of the meat spoiled. A great deal more was ruined before it even got to the smokehouse, because terrain and weather combined to make its transportation slow and difficult. Wherever Drouillard and his hunters slew elk, some circumstance made it difficult to bring in. If it was near the Columbia, the violent waters often made it impossible to fetch the meat in canoes. If it was up in the hills to the south, dense undergrowth was the problem. And if it was in the quaking bogs down toward the coast, men carrying any load of meat would sink so far they couldn't wade to solid ground. This terrain, and the inability to see the sun, bewildered almost everybody, and hunting parties frequently got lost and spent long nights squatting in total darkness, soaked to the skin, unable to build fires. And so, much of the meat that Drouillard and his hunters tracked, chased, killed, and butchered was wasted, or had to be eaten in degrees of spoilage.

A few days ago Captain Clark had taken Drouillard and several soldiers about fifteen miles down through the mountains and out to a windy, sandy beach piled with driftwood, a perfect place for a saltmaking camp. They had blazed a trail between that place and the fort to keep the men from getting lost between the two places. It was a beautiful but forbidding coast, a sight Drouillard knew he would never forget. There, the dark gray ocean thundered and sprayed against gigantic dark pinnacles and towers of rock that stood separated from the grim, high cliffs above the beach, cliffs jutting miles and miles southward, each point of rock and headland and mountain fainter than the one before it, dimmed by fog and spume, until the farthest vanished in mist. A party of salt-boilers had already been picked to go down with kettles after Christmas and start making salt: Bratton, Gibson, Willard, and Weiser, with Joe Field as their overseer and hunter. The captains wanted salt badly, and the men craved it.

They were out of salt. Out of liquor. Out of meal and flour. Almost out of tobacco. And they were four or five thousand miles from their homes and families, and most of them had been sick or pained in one way or another for so long that they couldn't remember real comfort.

> *Wednesday 25th Decr. 1805*
> *rainy & wet. disagreeable weather. we all moved in to our new Fort, which our officers name Fort Clotsop after the name of the Clotsop nation of Indians who live nearest to us, the party Saluted our officers by each man firing a gun at day break. they divided out the last of their tobacco among the men that used and the rest they gave each a Silk hankerchief, as a Christmas gift, to keep us in remembrence of it as we have no ardent Spirits . . . we have nothing to eat but poore Elk meat and no Salt to Season that with but Still keep in good Spirits as we expect this to be the last winter that we will have to pass in this way.*
>
> *Sergeant John Ordway,* Journals

The soldiers and captains gave what poor gifts they had. The most surprising exchange was from Sacagawea to Captain Clark, a beautiful shoulder mantle made of two dozen weasel tails. Her brother, Cameahwait, had put it on her shoulders last summer as she set out westward from their homeland with these soldiers. Apparently she harbored a true but unexpressed affection or admiration for Clark. No one had thought of giving her anything.

No one had given Drouillard anything either. Apparently, their Christmas was just for Christians, not Indians. So his gift to himself was the completion of a necklace of grizzly bear claws he had been drilling and stringing in his spare time. He had no warrior feather, but he had earned bear claws.

Two wide, split boards had been planed smooth to make writing surfaces for the captains, and they went into heavy use. Any time Drouillard entered their smoky room for anything, he found them bent over their writing boards, hats and boots on against the dankness, scratching away with pencils and quills. The daily life in the fort was so monotonous—sending out hunting parties, receiving Indian visitors, treating the colds, influenza, venereal complaints, and the sprains and strains of the soldiers—that the journal entries were cursory. The captains' tireless writings on everything else were information on the three local tribes and their headmen, names of some ship captains the Indians traded with and when they might be expected to come, information and measurements of plants and animals, descriptions of geography, weather, and edibles, the dress and handicrafts of the local Indians—it was as if Captain Lewis had nothing on his mind but Thomas Jefferson's curiosity, and killing time until they could leave this wet, moldy place and start home in the spring. Writing killed time better than anything. And, in the event that some American ship might show up in the Columbia, as much information as possible would be ready to send home.

At his table, Captain Clark concentrated on assembling his hundreds of sketches, compass headings, distances, and map scribblings taken from Indian interviews, and connecting them to make a vast map of everything from Fort Mandan to the Pacific. The concentration in their dim little room was so strong one could almost feel the pressure of it. And all the time, rain roared or pattered on the roof of riven wood shakes.

Drouillard stayed out as much as possible with his hunters, ranging farther and farther with every passing week to find the diminishing elk. Being out away from the fort, he could avoid the torments of the fleas and the gloomy complaints of the bored troops. They lived for their smoking and chewing tobacco, and for those days when they got some of the bawdy Indian girls into their quarters. The wife of one of the chiefs seemed to be a sort of madam who escorted groups of saucy, bare-bottomed girls to the fort so often that she was a special object of Captain Lewis's disdain. Much of Lewis's discontent he took out on the Indians: harping on the eternal threat of treachery and thievery, making rules about when they could and could not be in the fort, and what offenses should justify their ejection. A strict regimen of guard duty was scheduled, and a roofed booth to keep a sentry out of the rain was built on the picket wall of the fort.

Drouillard's relentless search for game had turned up some good beaver habitat, so he started taking traps out with him. The pelts he brought in were in excellent condition, and now and then he got an otter, whose fur the captains especially coveted. And whenever he caught a beaver, there was of course a tasty, fat variation to the monotonous diet of lean, half-spoiled elk.

When the first quarts of white sea salt were brought into the fort from the coastal brine works, it helped make the elk diet a little more palatable. But in this dank climate, the men craved fat even more than salt, and it happened that the soldiers who brought the salt also brought a little whale blubber. A few miles below the salt works, a whale had beached and died, and the Clatsop villagers nearby were cutting and rendering its meat and fat. The captains at once determined to take a large party down and get some before it was gone. One of the selected men being Charbonneau, his wife suddenly stood up with fire in her eyes and stated in swift, strong sign language that she wanted to go too. She declared that she had traveled a long, hard way with these soldiers to see the great waters, and had not yet been permitted to see the ocean. And now there was a great fish such as she would never have another chance to see, and she knew no reason why she should not get to go. She stood with her chin up and eyes glittering and waited for an answer.

Drouillard translated every part of her demand with pleasure, inspired, seeing the quiet little Indian woman assert herself again. Clark gazed at her. Then he nodded. "Drouillard, tell her she can go with us if she's sure she can keep up, carryin' that baby and all. Going to be a long trek."

They returned four days later with three hundred pounds of blubber and a few quarts of whale oil. It had been a grueling trip through creeks and marshes, on stony seashore, and an exhausting climb up the steep side of a mountain well over a thousand feet high. Bird Woman with her baby on her back had kept up without any complaint. All that was left of the whale was bones by the time they got there, and Captain Clark had bargained hard to get the Indians to sell any blubber or oil at all. But the soldiers were delighted to have both fat and salt for their diet, and the trek was considered to have been worth all its effort. Bird Woman was content. She had seen the bones of a fish that was forty paces long, and wherever she might live hereafter, she would be able to tell of it to people, and see their disbelief. And she told Drouillard that no one would believe the size of the ocean she had seen either.

It seemed that the sight of the ocean had fulfilled any desires or expectations she had nurtured on this long and grueling journey. The whitemen, of course, had never even considered whether she had any desires or expectations. Now some of them were beginning to see her in that new light—Captain Clark, in particular. Drouillard saw the officer studying her by firelight now and then, as if considering what her world within might be.

No ships yet. No word of ships. The officers worked week after week on their writing and planning. They were killing time. They had until May to get back up the Columbia and the Snake and the Kooskooskee to the Nez Perce country where Twisted Hair was keeping their horses, the horses they would need to recross the mountains to the Missouri. Because of snow in the mountains, they could not expect to cross them before May. They estimated that if they left here in late March or early April, they would have time to ascend to the mountains by then. Here they had their fort for shelter until spring, and could subsist without expending the remains of their trade goods too soon on the way up. They didn't like it here; it was like being in a flea-infested jail of their own making. But they would live here, and make all their preparations for the journey home to the United States.

Sunday the 12th January 1806
This morning Sent out Drewyer and one man to hunt, they re-
turned in the evening Drewyer having killed 7 Elk; I scercely
know how we Should Subsist, if it was not for the exertions of
this excellent hunter; maney others also exert themselves, but
not being acquainted with the best method of finding and
killing the elk, and no other wild animals is to be found in the
quarter, they are unsucksessfull in their exertions.

William Clark, Journals

Chapter 21

Drouillard steered the canoe to the bank of the Netul where the corps kept its little fleet of canoes on shore, and the other canoe followed. It was deep dusk. It had taken hours to bring the canoes along the Columbia shore from the Kathlamet town because of the rough water, then up the Netul to the fort. He had a severe pain in his left side and was glad the trip was over. It was raining and blowing as usual. The soldiers with him climbed out of the vessels and pulled them onto the shore. With them were two Kathlamet headmen wearing cone-shaped hats and capes woven so tightly of cedar and bear grass that they shed rain perfectly. The canoes were leaking through cracks, and the rain and bashing waves had poured even more water in them. Constant travel in canoes half full of water apparently was the reason these river peoples wore nothing below the waist and went barefoot.

Drouillard and his party had been trying to buy a few canoes from the Clatsop and Kathlamet villages so they would have enough for the return trip up the Columbia, and it had been a frustrating effort. Canoes were among these tribes' most useful and valued possessions, and they would not sell them cheaply. The Clatsops had kept their price for one out of reach. Drouillard finally had obtained one from the Kathlamets, paying in tobacco and Captain Lewis's fanciest army coat. The corps was almost out of trade goods, and even the soldiers had given most

369

of their valuables away to the local girls who came selling carnal pleasures.

Drouillard, with the soldiers and the two Kathlamets, went up the muddy path to the fort, smelling chimney smoke, latrines, and rotten elk meat. He clenched his teeth against the pain in his side. He hadn't figured out what it was, but did not want the captains to see that he was sick, because they would probably want to bleed him or fill him with four or five kinds of their evil little pills.

Unfortunately, Lewis saw him wince at a stab of pain, and in no time he was lying on a bunk with blood dripping from a slit arm vein into a bowl. It made him think of the woman far up the river who had slashed her arms. Lewis was saying, "Too many sick. This is no time for it, just when we're trying to get ready to leave this place."

"Well, mine's not cock pox, Cap'n. Whatever this is, I didn't bring it on myself."

"I'll say that for you," Lewis said, then looked at him thoughtfully. Drouillard was just very careful. He was one of the few men who had visited and socialized in the Clatsop towns, and not for romance. He often stopped to visit with such chiefs as Coboway and Warhalot and Shanoma while ranging in their vicinity, and smoked and ate and hand-talked with them, trying to soothe their ruffled feelings, to make them feel that their new white neighbors weren't really hostile and arrogant, as they seemed, but just whitemen soldiers, unlike the traders, who were the only other whitemen these people knew. He tried to tell them that these whitemen lived by codes they had learned on the far side of the land and that they didn't understand Clatsop ways any better than Clatsops could understand theirs. When Drouillard was in their towns he made it clear that he himself was an Indian from a tribe a year's travel eastward, and being an Indian he did not have goods to trade for women's favors. A few times, out of plain Clatsop hospitality, he had been offered bed companions. A couple of times he had accepted, but only after discreetly determining that there was no risk of disease. In those households he was always cheerfully welcomed. And he already was legend among the tribesmen as a hunter. Back in January some Clatsops had seen him shoot several elk at a distance they could scarcely believe even when they witnessed it with their own eyes. The captains had been very pleased with that incident; they thought that just in case the Clatsops had ever considered attacking the soldiers, their opinion of American marksmanship and superior rifles likely would discourage them. Drouillard doubted that the Indians had ever considered it. They were a happy, congenial people who were competitive only in trade. Their greatest joy seemed to be in getting a real bargain.

Lewis stopped the bleeding with pressure and told Drouillard to lie quiet and hold a cloth over the slit. He said, "We still need another canoe. The Clatsops won't give one up at a price we can afford. I hate to do it, but I guess we'll just have to take one. I'll send a party out tomorrow to get one."

"Wouldn't do that, Cap'n. These people don't care a lot for us, but one thing they can't say is that we steal."

"They steal from us. I think that elk meat they took from your cache last month, that's justification enough."

"That's been smoothed over. Coboway apologized and gave us three dogs, remember?"

"Hardly compensation for six elk," Lewis retorted. "You said so yourself."

"Cap'n, I took it too personal at the time. I'm on good terms with him now." He didn't mention that he had counted the Clatsop girls as personal compensation.

"It's not that I want to do this," Lewis said. "But we have to have another canoe. They'll never know. They'll think it drifted, like that one of ours."

Drouillard sighed in anger and annoyance. Lewis would do what he wanted to. It would be easy. The tribes didn't guard their canoes because they all had a code against stealing each other's vessels. It was just the opposite of the horse-stealing games of the plains tribes. Here the honor was in *not* stealing each other's essential transportation. It took weeks to make a canoe, whereas horses reproduced themselves and the tribes had hundreds of them. Drouillard admired the respectful understandings these coastal tribes had among themselves, by which they kept peace.

It seemed strange to him that the captains had no such admiration. For all their talk about peace among the tribes, they seemed to have nothing but disdain and suspicion for these peaceful peoples. They hardly ever let Indians stay after dark in the fort, even if they had come too far to travel home. At Fort Mandan they had let more warlike chiefs stay overnight and had afforded them attention and hospitality. All winter Drouillard had tried to imagine why they so disliked these coastal peoples, beyond their appearance.

Sometimes it seemed to Drouillard that the real reason these whitemen scorned the natives here was because these people were not particularly impressed by the whitemen. The officers had been accustomed to being a novelty and the center of attention and awe across much of the continent, with their white skins and their instruments and manufactured goods, with their great black man, with their amazing message from their new Great Father. Here, none of that amounted to much. These coastal people had traded for at least ten years with whitemen on big ships, ships carrying more and better goods than these whitemen had. They had seen plenty of black men on the ships. They apparently had heard fiddles and horns and Jew's harps before, and Cruzatte was so little in demand that he had all but stopped playing. He excused himself by saying the rain and dampness would ruin the instrument and the strings had no tone in this humidity.

And perhaps even more to the heart of the matter, here the captains could not proclaim power over the country. This was beyond the land Jefferson had bought from France. Coming down the Columbia, the officers had quit demanding allegiance or trying to win the natives with promises of alliance. The whitemen just weren't very important to these people.

The captains had chosen to build their winter quarters in a place they hated, among people they scorned, so they would be nearby if a ship came into the bay. But then they had built in a place from which they couldn't see the bay, and had been barely civil to the Clatsops and Chinooks who might bring them word i a ship did come. That was one of the reasons why Drouillard had tried to remain friendly with the Clatsops near the mouth of the Columbia. If a ship did come while the corps was here, he wanted them to let the captains know it.

They needed another canoe because they had acquired so many Indian-made treasures to take back to Jefferson, and preserved plant and animal specimens. Even though they had traded away most of the goods they struggled so hard to bring west, they had traded them for bulkier things: otter and ermine skins, fur capes, fine basketry, weapons, robes.

Drouillard suggested they lighten their load by leaving things with the Clatsops, with instructions to Chief Coboway to turn them over to the first American ship that came. But Lewis didn't trust the Indians. He thought they would keep it all themselves. All he might agree to entrust to Coboway would be a letter or report that could go back to the United States by ship. And then there were the paper things, including the first map of all the rivers and mountains and Indian lands ever made between the Mandans and the coastal mountains, all of which had been blank in previous maps of the continent. Of course, Lewis would not entrust this to a slant-headed, bare-bottomed Indian chief to give to a ship captain, if one came. Therefore a canoe was needed to take it all back up the Columbia.

So Drouillard sighed and agreed. He wouldn't steal the canoe himself. But if one was taken and Coboway found out about it, Drouillard would say it was because of the meat stolen from his cache. Lewis needed to steal a canoe, but needed an excuse so he wouldn't think of himself as a thief. Now Drouillard just wished the captain would go away and let him lie here and rest.

It was good, being a man who could always be relied upon, but sometimes he wished he didn't have to be a part of everything.

He winced with a new stab of pain in his side, held the compress on his cut arm and tried to go to sleep. He remembered how hard it had been coming down the rivers from the mountains, and wondered if it would even be possible to go back up.

The captains had been working on a plan to split the corps in the mountains, with Lewis taking the Nez Perce shortcut to the

Great Falls and then going up to see how far north Maria's River originated, and thus perhaps claiming more land for the United States, and Clark going back down to the Shoshone land and crossing over to explore the upper Yellowstone, then the two groups rejoining at the mouth of the Yellowstone for the rest of the way down the Missouri. Leave it to them to find a way to make a hard task harder, Drouillard thought. He might have enjoyed going with Clark to see some new lands, in company with York and Bird Woman and her baby; they had come to feel like his family. But Lewis had already named him as his own hunter and scout for that northern exploration.

If indeed they even made it up to the mountains.

PART THREE
March, 1806–September, 1806

we determined allways to be on our guard as much as the nature of our situation will permit us, and never place our selves at the mercy of any savages. we well know that the treachery of the aborigenes of America and the too great confidence of our countrymen in their Sincerity and friendship has caused the distruction of many hundreds of us ... the well known treachery of the natives by no means entitle them to such confidence ... our preservation depends on never loosing sight of this trait in their character. and being always prepared to meet it in whatever shape it may present itself.

—Meriwether Lewis

Chapter 22

Columbia River
March 24, 1806

A bad and embarrassing start home: rain, wind, ebb tide, and the fleet of canoes wandered into the wrong shallow channel among islands. An Indian man in a small canoe came to guide them. He was very tense as he guided them through, then finally worked up the courage to tell them that he recognized one of the canoes. It was his.

There followed a long silence. Captain Lewis did not admit that his men had stolen the canoe, but offered the Indian an elk skin in exchange. Being in the midst of a party of well-armed soldiers, he had no choice. After the fleet was through the maze, the Indian vanished in the blowing rain. Lewis was glum and silent for a long time after that.

The fort had been abandoned to the custody of the nearest chief, Coboway of the Clatsop tribe, in the expectation that his people would likely make use of it anyway. It was a gesture the captains hoped would incline him to speak well of them after their departure. They also had given to him and other neighboring Indians a written roster of the members of the corps, inscribed:

The object of this list is, that through the medium of some civilized person who may see the same, it may be made known to the informed world, that the party consisting of the persons whose names are hereunto annexed, and who were sent out by

*the government of the U'States in May 1804 to explore the
interior of the Continent of North America, did penetrate
the same by way of the Missouri and Columbia Rivers, to the
discharge of the latter into the Pacific Ocean, where they
arrived on the 14th November 1805, and from which they departed . . . March 1806 on their return to the United States by
the same rout they had come out.—*

All the men on the list were yearning eastward, sick of the
constant rain, wind, dankness, boredom, weary of the unvaried
diet of scrawny elk and root mush and rancid fish. To them the
fort had been a gloomy, moldy, flea-infested prison. They knew
they had a continent to recross and it would be hard and haz-
ardous and they might not make it—but they were going home-
ward, and that was their inspiration now. Men were talking of
their families; Captain Clark had mentioned his betrothed, Miss
Hancock. Lewis had been overheard wondering whether his
mother was still alive, or President Jefferson. He had half a continent to deliver to Jefferson, in the form of maps and sketches
and hundreds of thousands of words, and in specimens of plant
life and Indian clothing and handiwork, all in canoes full of wa-
tertight skin bundles. But ahead lay roaring rivers, snowy mountains, Indians, grizzly bears. Beyond that a big question: the rest
of their lives, if God granted them any more.

The Columbia Narrows
April 21, 1806

Drouillard wasn't sure they would get out of this mess alive. The
demon was in Lewis, the worst he had ever seen it.

When they had sped down these roaring water chutes between
the high cliffs last fall, Drouillard had wondered how they could
ever get canoes back up, either through or around.

And there had not been so many Indians along the river then
compared to the thousands who were now waiting for the spring
salmon run to start up. Worse, they were all kinds of Chinooks

whom Lewis had come to hate and scorn. Still worse, they were being themselves and Lewis was being himself. They were pushy and insolent and thieving. He was angry and impatient. There had been threats.

The river was in spring flood, faster and higher than it had been then. The captains needed to get up to the Nez Perce by May so they could cross the mountains. They had expected to feed the corps by purchasing dried fish from the tribes along the Columbia, but then rumors came down that the Indians were in famine upriver. So Drouillard and his hunters had scoured the Cascade country to kill and dry meat, slowing progress. At the portage, doubly hard and dangerous because the river was high, Indians crowded around, picking up anything the moment it was unguarded. Three men had even run off with Lewis's dog one evening, and Seaman had to be retrieved at gunpoint. Private Shields bought a dog to eat, and had to pull his knife to scare off some young braves who tried to take the dog carcass from him. During the strenuous portage along a steep, slick path, a few Indians entertained themselves by throwing stones down on the soldiers. Tomahawks and other items were stolen; Indians were grabbed and searched. A small gang of swaggering youths jumped John Colter and tried to get his tomahawk away from him; they all ended scattered and bruised in the dirt. At every town, Lewis came to the point of telling the natives they would be shot if they touched another thing, that he would burn their towns.

Now these narrows. There was no way to take the canoes up the roaring chutes, and the big ones couldn't be portaged. The natives were swarming and belligerent. The captains had decided to obtain enough horses to carry the cargoes overland to the Nez Perce country. Captain Clark had gone above the falls on the north side of the river and set up a trading station to bargain for horses with the few trade goods that remained. He wasn't doing very well. After two days of being tantalized and toyed with by Indians who knew it was a seller's market, Clark had three poor horses for which he had traded his best blanket, his sword, and his military coat, and now he was almost as ill-disposed toward the natives as Lewis.

Lewis, meanwhile, had gone into the darkest and meanest frame of mind. When the horses carried the goods to the upper end of the portage, instead of trading the abandoned canoes or giving them to the Indians as a parting gesture of conciliation, Lewis ordered them chopped up, piled with oars and poles, and set ablaze with the Indians watching. He looked like a malevolent whiteman devil standing there in the heat and smoke. And when one Indian boy tried to salvage an iron pole socket from the edge of the pyre, Lewis gave him a severe beating, every blow a relief and a venting of the captain's fury, and had the soldiers kick him out of camp. That was when Drouillard resigned himself to the possibility of ending his days here in a windswept, fishy-smelling desert with a river roaring through it. There was nothing, it seemed, to keep these hundreds of people from rushing and annihilating the thirty whitemen, either now or in their camp at night.

But the captains staged an impressive display of rifle target practice with a large Indian audience. Soon thereafter, the people left.

Drouillard himself had been annoyed and embarrassed by the behavior of these wretched representatives of the race; he felt that somehow their tribal discipline and decorum had failed, that the elders perhaps had lost their influence.

But irritated as he was with them, he still saw the spiteful burning of the canoes through their eyes. He knew that if he were an Indian living here, and witnessed that mean and wasteful act done by strangers coming through, he would never want to see any more men like them in his country again. Lying that night in a cold, nervously guarded soldier camp, nipped by fleas, without even any campfire fuel because Lewis had burned the canoe wood in a venomous fit, Drouillard went to sleep and dreamed again of the woman staring at Lewis and cutting her arms with flint.

In a changing part of the dream, flint blades were cutting flesh and the woman was staring straight at him. Drouillard woke up with a racing heart, and where in his dream he had started to feel flint edges cutting his groin, fleas were biting him. They kept him from going back to sleep for a long time.

Nez Perce Country
May 5, 1806

One of Tetohoskee's cheerful young warriors was apparently amused that soldiers liked to eat dog meat. It was good to be among friendly Indians again. The Walulas at the great bend of the Columbia had held a dance and feast for the soldiers and had helped them obtain about twenty good horses, and now a few days later the corps was climbing up into the country of the amiable and handsome Nez Perce. Tetohoskee, one of the Nez Perce chieftains who had traveled by canoe with them down the Columbia last fall, had joined them as they came back up, and it was good to see the old friend again.

They had also had the good fortune to encounter a Nez Perce elder whose lame knee Captain Clark had treated last fall with liniment and hocus-pocus. The old fellow was perfectly well now, and Clark's reputation as a great healer had spread. This enabled him to trade doctoring for food—mostly roots and dogs, as the salmon run had not reached these streams yet. The corps had come out of the desert and sage country into a land of grazing grasses and some pine woods. The weather was cold, windy and rainy, sometimes with hail, and the paths were slick and dangerous, but contact with the Nez Perce had lifted the spirits of the troops. It had also lifted the spirits of many ailing Nez Perce people with eye problems and other health troubles, who had heard that the red-haired healer was back. They kept coming in, and left Clark with little time for other duties.

One ailing man Clark had not been able to help was one of his own soldiers. Private Bratton's back had first crippled him while he was working at the salt camp on the coast. It had improved little since last winter, and last month he aggravated it during the portage at the cascades. Since then he had been unable even to

walk, becoming just another load for the packhorses. Bratton's
agony and despair were pathetic to watch. He was lying under a
hide shelter nearby as the young Nez Perce laughed about the
dog-eating whitemen.

A puppy wandered in, sniffing at the roasting dog meat. A
youth scooped it up with one hand and tossed it toward Lewis's
plate, which was on his lap, as if to say, "Pups are more tender
than dogs."

Lewis snatched up the squirming pup as if it were a rock and
hurled it with all his strength at the young man's face.

With a yip of pain it fell thrashing to the ground, and Lewis
leaped to his feet with his tomahawk cocked to strike. "Damn
you! One more impertinence from you and I'll split your head!"

The young man turned and left without looking back, while
Drouillard stood looking in astonishment at Lewis. He had
hoped that getting away from the Chinooks and being among the
friendly Nez Perce would settle Lewis down, but apparently it
had not.

May 10, 1806
The Clearwater River

Drouillard examined the deer decoy and learned how it was
used, and realized how hard hunting was for these Nez Perce
who still used bow and arrow. The decoy was the skin from the
head and neck of a deer. It would be put over a frame of sticks to
look natural, then a concealed hunter would move it in the motions of a deer feeding, until live deer would see it and graze
within bowshot. This was how they hunted deer in the wooded
and rocky country when they couldn't chase them down on
horseback.

Drouillard saw other signs of how bad the hunger could be in
the mountains in winter. He found pine trees cut down and
peeled for their edible inner bark, their cones twisted open for
the seeds inside, and learned that a kind of hanging lichen was
also gathered off the pine limbs and boiled for food. It was n

wonder these people had such a yearning to obtain guns for easier hunting. But even more, they wanted guns because their enemies in the north and northeast had been obtaining guns from the English traders in Canada. Drouillard had no illusions that the Nez Perce liked the Americans. It was obvious they hoped this cooperation would help them obtain more and better guns than their enemies had.

Relieved as the captains were to have found the Nez Perce, some troubling matters had come to light. They were now close enough to the mountains to see them heavily clothed in the snows that had almost fatally entrapped the expedition last fall. Even here in the foothills they were riding through seven and eight inches of snow.

Another trouble was that Twisted Hair, whom they had been so anxious to see, was cold and nervous, and evasive about their horses, which he had agreed to take care of over the winter. The branded horses were not all there at his village, a situation that seemed to have something to do with other chiefs.

As Drouillard had feared, the situation required that he be put right in the middle of the quarrel, as only he could use and read hand-sign well enough to understand and interpret it. He spent several days going from one chief's camp to another, getting them to come individually, then together, to hash it out before the captains. There was a Shoshone boy, a captive, among the Nez Perce, who understood Nez Perce and could have translated to Bird Woman, but the youth had enough sense to refuse to interpret a dispute between chiefs.

The other chiefs were Broken Arm and Cutnose, who had been absent last fall, away raiding Paiutes, when the expedition came through. Cutnose was a not very impressive man whose most memorable feature was the result of getting a lance up his nostril during a long ago fight against the Shoshones. Broken Arm was formidable of physique, and proud.

Old Twisted Hair said that when those two had returned from their raids, they accused him of taking too much importance upon himself in agreeing to care for the whitemen's horses. Probably they were jealous of the two muskets and ammunition he had been promised in payment. He said the two chiefs had so troubled him that he had neglected the horses and let them stray.

The version of the story told by Cutnose was that Twisted Hair had not been taking good care of the soldiers' horses, that he had let his young man use them so hard that some had been hurt. He said Twisted Hair was a two-faced, bad old man.

The deep snow on the Bitterroot Mountains made it obvious that the expedition would be here longer than expected—perhaps as much as a month—and so this sore spot among the chiefs would have to be doctored as tenderly as the abcesses and sore eyes of Captain Clark's patients, who kept coming in from the hills, several a day. The troops would need Nez Perce cooperation with food, horses, and camp resources, and, when the snow eventually melted in the mountain passes, Nez Perce guides to lead them back through the maze by which old Toby had brought them last fall. Even to Drouillard, who had done his best to remember it, the route was broken and baffling. He recalled how streams had seemed to turn around and run uphill.

So the captains decided to stick by their old agreement with Twisted Hair, if his young men could indeed round up the horses and bring them in, and then council with the other chiefs to elevate their sense of importance to the level where they would no longer resent the old man. As long as the expedition was stuck here, it should do as much Jefferson diplomacy as possible, and build an alliance with these strong and likely people. That would, of course, mean promising they would be rewarded with goods and guns—someday.

When two more of the leading Nez Perce headmen came, Bloody Chief and Five Big Hearts, it was deemed a proper time for a major council with the Nez Perce nation. Captain Lewis gathered his wits and braced himself for his biggest presentation in a year. It was done with a pipe ceremony, the presentation of medals, the demonstration of magnets, compasses, mirrors, telescopes, and the air gun. The Shoshone captive participated by translating Nez Perce to Shoshone, which Bird Woman then passed to Charbonneau in Hidatsa, and his French then was translated to English by Drouillard and Labiche. Thus the talk took most of the day. In the meantime, Captain Clark in a nearby lodge of Broken Arm's town dispensed eyewash, liniments, pills, and laudanum, and performed minor surgery, back rubs, and adjustments with his capable and powerful hands. While Lewis was giving the council difficult new political and commercial concepts to mull over—trading posts, peace missions, arms sales, and delegates to the Great Father in the East—four men carried an especially important and difficult patient to Clark: a big, fleshy chief, beloved by his people for his wisdom, in apparent robust health with good pulse, appetite, and digestion, but paralyzed from the neck down for the last three years. This appeared to be a case that might at last put limits on the captain's burgeoning fame as a medicine man. Clark told the Indians that he doubted he could help the man but would soon begin trying.

The second day of the council was the time for the Nez Perce to answer Captain Lewis's proposals. Another forty or fifty patients had showed up for Clark, most needing eyewash. The Indians held a morning council in which all the Americans' proposals were discussed. Then Broken Arm mixed some root flour in water and distributed it to every man in the council. He told them that if they agreed to follow the advice of the whitemen, they should eat the mush; anyone opposed should not. Drouillard watched carefully from the edge of the council. Some women outside the circle began wailing and pulling their hair, as if afraid of such an alliance, but it appeared to Drouillard that every man tipped his bowl and swallowed the contents.

The chiefs went to where the captains and their interpreters sat waiting. Drouillard told them of the method and outcome of the vote. Then commenced an outpouring of good cheer and generosity such as he had seldom seen. The captains were approached by two young Nez Perce men, who presented each with a fine horse. Then Cutnose came forth and gave Drouillard an excellent gray gelding. Clark grinned at him and said, "By God! Reckon they think you're an officer, George!" Drouillard was so moved he could only look at Cutnose and nod and smile, swallowing hard.

The captains gave each chief a flag, a pound of powder, and fifty musket balls, and also gave powder and shot to the two young men who had presented them with the horses. Broken Arm said the council's answer would now be presented by their best orator, the father of Bloody Chief. But first, he said, there were more people in pain waiting to see the red-haired medicine man. And so Dr. Clark returned to his waiting room while Lewis remained to hear the Nez Perce's declarations of agreement.

When Clark returned in mid-afternoon, he brought a vial of white vitriol and sugar of lead to Broken Arm, and had the interpreters tell him how to dilute it to make eyewash for his people after the whitemen were gone. The war chief washed his own eyes out with sudden uncontrollable tears. "Cap'n," Drouillard told him, "if you don't mind me saying it, you'd make a good Indian."

Lewis closed the business by giving Twisted Hair a musket, a hundred balls, and two pounds of gunpowder for taking care of the horses, and promised to give him another gun and a like amount of ammunition when the last nine horses were delivered. Then, as if to make as good an impression on these people as Clark had, he held a shooting match with the Indians, hitting a small mark twice at 220 yards.

Ah-huh, Drouillard thought. Yes. They'll do whatever you want to get guns like that. But if they ever get any American guns, they won't be good rifles like that. They'll be cheap muskets. My Shawnee people can tell you about whiteman promises.

By early June the snow in the mountains still showed no signs of melting, and Lewis was getting frantic. It was three thousand miles to St. Louis from here, and at this rate it would be late summer before they even reached the Missouri River. The possibility of being somewhere on the Great Plains when the Missouri froze next fall or winter was almost too dreadful to contemplate. The men wanted to go.

Drouillard, aside from that worry, felt that if one could not go anywhere, this was the best place one could be. It was not just the high, beautiful country, the smell of evergreens and moss and the music of fast water, or the challenge of hunting the scarce deer, mule deer, and bears; it was these people.

For all their hard life, they were kind and generous, high-spirited, brave and playful, and their joy on receiving anything was beautiful. They reminded him of his own Shawnee people as he remembered them from childhood. The troop had found a campsite with good graze and water, and the round pit of an old winter lodge in which to store the goods. They had asked Twisted Hair and his followers to camp nearby, and he had taken that as a great honor. These Nez Perce sang a friendship song when they approached the camp. When they found a stray horse or anything else lost by the soldiers, they brought it to camp. Even Captain Lewis was hard put to criticize these Indians. After a visit from Bloody Chief, who wore the scalps and fingers of his enemies on his breast yoke, Lewis was very thoughtful and subdued.

Tuesday May 27th 1806
The chief told us that most of the horses we saw runing at large in this neighbourhood belonged to himself and his people, and whenever we were in want of meat he requested that we would kill any of them we wished; this is a peice of lib-erallity which would do honour to such as bost of civilization: indeed I doubt whether there are not a great number of our countrymen who would see us fast many days before their compassion would excite them to a similar act of liberallity.
Meriwether Lewis, Journals

The captains noted that these people were uncommonly kind and attentive to their old people, and treated their women with more respect than did the plains tribes.

For many days the family of the paralyzed chief kept re-turning to Captain Clark, expressing faith that he could heal him, even though no medicines had worked. Private Shields had suggested a sweat pit treatment for Bratton, and in a few days it had cured him fully after his weeks of immobility. Clark considered that a similar treatment might work on the helpless Indian, but he was too large for Bratton's sweat pit, so his companions enlarged the pit. Then he could not sit up on the wooden seat. So his father, a very old man, got in with him and held him in the sitting position, and sprinkled water on the superheated earth in the hole, which was covered with blankets. Everyone expected the old man to die, but when the ordeal was over he stood and helped them lift his son out. The next morning the chief was able to move his hands and arms and sat up much of the day, declaring that he had not felt so good in a year and would recover. Clark himself looked as if he would drop to his knees any minute and yield up prayers of thanks for the miracle. Other things added to the joy in camp that day. The Bird Woman's child, who had been severely sick with fever and a terribly swollen neck, was beginning to respond to the captain's medicines. And a long spell of futile hunting seemed to be broken when Drouillard, Cruzatte, and Labiche brought in five deer.

It was days like those that made Drouillard not altogether unhappy with the delay enforced by those snowy mountains.

It was not surprising that the gratitude of these people to Captain Clark took many forms. Soon he began disappearing into the village on those occasions when he had leisure from his doctoring, mapmaking, and journal writing. One day he made a journal note that, while the Nez Perce men plucked all the hair from their faces, only the women kept the hair plucked from a lower part.

"How do you know that?" Lewis asked.

Clark turned almost as red as his hair. "Uh—Uh, well, you—you know that I give a great number of rubdowns and massages as their, um, medicine man."

Bird Woman had been in a state of quiet distress during the weeks of her little boy's fever, but nevertheless remained useful, gathering roots and greens. Although she kept apart from the main society of Nez Perce women, she did have a friend and confidante in old Watkuweis, the woman who had first spoken in favor of the whitemen when they came through on their way west. Watkuweis, it was suspected, was a link in the chain of communication that had started the run on Captain Clark's services.

Clark did not have any illusions about his doctoring skills. He relied heavily on information and guidance from Lewis, who knew more about cures and simples. But Lewis recognized the great value of Clark's popular reputation, and they both vowed to prescribe nothing harmful, and hoped their luck would hold out.

His medical services had become the main currency for obtaining food from the Nez Perce. Almost everything that could be traded was gone. These people were not much interested in beads and ribbons and trinkets. They preferred useful items like awls and knives and other small tools. When a damaged length of surveyor chain came up for discard, the soldiers crafted moccasin awls from its links and traded those. One ornamental item became popular with the women, perhaps more as souvenir than decoration: brass uniform buttons. In a few days what was left of uniforms were bereft of all metal buttons, and the men were making buttons of antler for their own use.

With the Nez Perce warriors, Drouillard for the first time in his adult life felt that he was among peers, if not brothers. He relished their pride and their cheerful disregard of discomfort or injury. They admired him as a hunter and marksman. He and his team of hunters shared game with the tribe as much as they could. And he was the one they could talk to best in hand sign. Though Captain Clark and Private Gibson had learned some, and Charbonneau, Labiche, and Cruzatte were adequate, Drouillard seemed to be the Talking Chief of the soldiers, and important talks simply were not attempted unless he was present.

While the captains waited and waited for the mountain snows to melt, they worried that the soldiers—except Drouillard's hunters—were growing slothful and getting out of condition. And so they encouraged athletic competitions with whatever bands of Nez Perce hunters and warriors visited. Drouillard and

Reubin Field had over the last two years edged out Colter as champion sprint-runners in the corps, but there was one rangy brave of Bloody Chief's band who always finished right beside them. As for distance, no one had a chance against Drouillard. When he went into his running trance, all the soldiers eventually staggered out in his wake. The Nez Perce relied on their horses for distance travel, and that kind of running was beyond their experience. So Drouillard became also the Running Chief.

The Indian men best loved games that were easy to bet on, like races, archery, and shooting arrows or throwing lances at rolling hoops. But the Americans drew them into team games, like tag and prison base, all dust, sweat, and hilarity, with occasional bruisings. Sometimes Drouillard would ride in from the hunt and at half a mile distance would know what was going on at the camp and village; he would hear the shouts of the soldiers, the whooping of the Indians, and the women's incessant pounding of roots, which Lewis said reminded him of a nail factory.

Another year here, he thought sometimes, and these soldiers might just forget about wanting to go back to that wretched and complicated tangle of trouble they called civilization.

The corps now had more than sixty horses, most in good condition—enough for each man to have a riding mount and a packhorse on the trek over the mountains. A corral had been built near the camp. When the young stallions became troublesome, it was Drouillard's duty to geld them, because no one else in the party admitted to having any experience with that odious process.

One of the stallions was the horse Lewis had ridden west across the mountains last fall, a very special horse to him, and Drouillard suggested to Captain Clark: "Maybe you should do him. You're the doctor."

Clark laughed. "Sorry. I've got to go give a lady a liniment rub."

"I could do that for you, while you do this."

"Go cut."

Two Nez Perce men were hanging around the corral. They

watched as Drouillard and three soldiers roped the stallion's legs, threw it on its side, sat on it and drew up the rope rig that pulled its hind legs up tight and forward. Drouillard told one man to blindfold the stallion, then leaned over its quivering haunch, cut the scrotum, pulled, cut again, tied a ligature, all in swift motions while the horse surged and screamed. It was a hot day but he was sweating more from concentration than from heat or effort. When he jumped up and told the men to release the leg ties, he saw the two Indians shaking their heads and making signs at him.

He went to see what they wanted, holding the bloody testicles in his hand while the soldiers led the whinnying new gelding away, leaving the blindfold on because a horse that can't see moves cautiously. He thought the warriors might be asking for the testicles; some people thought them a delicacy. But they were telling him not to do something. They were saying, *Do not tie off.* They were saying, *Let bleed is good.*

Tying off was how it had always been done around Lorimier's. The horse would be in pain a few days and have swelling, with a little chance of getting infection. But these two men said they would show whitemen how to do it so the horse didn't hurt so long and wouldn't get sick.

He knew this tribe gelded most stallions young and let only the best ones breed; that was why their horses were so good. He sent a soldier to ask Lewis if the Nez Perce could do a couple of stallions their way, and Lewis came out to watch.

They did it with a flint knife, without tying off, and although these two horses bled freely as they were taken away, they settled down quicker, and seemed to forget about it even while Lewis's horse was still in distress.

Two weeks later Captain Lewis's horse was still in agony and had fallen off in flesh and spirit so badly that Lewis ordered him shot. The other two were nearly recovered.

There was much to be learned about horses and riding from these people. The soldiers had thought they were good in the saddle, but these riders put them to shame. They could shoot arrows quickly and accurately at a rolling hoop while controlling a horse at full gallop with their knees. At a full run they could hang off the horse's side and snatch an object off the ground, or throw a slipknot loop over a free horse's neck and capture it. The soldiers watched bug-eyed as the Indian riders went headlong down slopes almost too steep for a man to stand on. They rode with a rein-rope trailing twelve or fifteen feet on the ground so that if they fell they could grab it and keep the horse from running off. Horses were the main wealth of these people. A man might have a personal herd of fifty. Horses were interwoven with many aspects of their spiritual life. Not long ago, it was learned, Cutnose's wife had died; he and her relatives had sacrificed twenty-eight horses at her rock-pile grave, a testimonial of their great love and esteem for the woman.

Cutnose seemed to believe that Drouillard was as important a chief as the captains, because he was the whitemen's Talking Chief, and nothing could be more important than a Talking Chief. He taught Drouillard that Coyote had created all people, giving them his own weaknesses and faults and cunning. That he had made them from chunks of meat of a monster he had slain. But the Ni Mi Pu, the True People known as Nez Perce, had grown from drops of monster blood that Coyote had washed from his hands. "Ah-huh!" Drouillard exclaimed, remembering his mother's old stories: his people had become Shawnees when their ancestor hero killed the Horned Serpent that was terrorizing all the creatures. He was beginning to feel as if Cutnose and all his people were his own relatives.

Monday June 2nd 1806
McNeal and York were Sent on a tradeing voyage over the river this morning in order to prepare in the most ample manner in our power to meet that wretched portion of our journy, the Rocky Mountains, where hungar and Cold in their most regorous form assail the waried traveller; not any of us have yet forgotten those mountains in September last. I think it probable we never Shall.

William Clark, Journals

A week later the formerly paralyzed chief was standing on his own legs. The troops were in fit condition from their athletic contests and excited to move eastward to their families; they danced to the fiddle after dark. But the mountains were still covered with snow.

June 21, 1806

Chief Cutnose and Drouillard smoked in the chief's lodge and talked of many things, and for a while they sat together and admired the young pair of nestling eagles that perched, tied by their legs, on a rack made from a branched sapling. Cutnose had gone down the river a few days ago to capture them from their nest. He would raise them here in captivity, and when they molted, he would have their feathers to award to his warriors when they earned them. He said it might seem sad that eagles should spend their lives in captivity, but that it was their honor to decorate brave men, and they understood it. Despite the disfiguring scar, Cutnose was a man whom Drouillard was always delighted to see. This man had given him the best horse he had ever owned. And recently he had gone with Drouillard to the lodge of a Nez Perce man who had stolen a tomahawk from Captain Clark, to help him get it back. It was a tomahawk that had belonged to Clark's relative, Sergeant Floyd, the soldier who had died two years ago on the Missouri, and the captain cherished it because he had meant to take it back to the United States and present it to Floyd's relatives. Cutnose and Bloody Chief helped Drouillard persuade the thief's family to return the tomahawk. It was just one more of the many kindnesses that made Drouillard's affection for this man so strong that he had told him his private joke name, Followed by Buzzards. Cutnose loved to call him that.

Cutnose took Drouillard's bear-claw necklace as proof of his courage, and admired him for it. Now and then Cutnose asked Drouillard about his tribe, and gave him the rare opportunity to talk about the Shawnees, about their long wars against the whitemen far back in the East, about their role as traders and peacemakers and warriors, about their ancestors who had been the builders of temple mounds and burial mounds as big as hills. Cutnose was uplifted by those stories, even though they were told slowly and painstakingly in hand language. The hand-signing was a practical, day-to-day language, by which it was hard to convey such ideas as honor and spirit-life.

Cutnose signed that Drouillard's people must have been a fine people, like the Nez Perce. Then he said they must have worn many eagle feathers. Then he said, *You wear none. Question: You have not been in war?*

Drouillard had to admit that he had not, because his people had been defeated when he was still a boy. He didn't tell him that his real Shawnee name was Without Eagle Feathers. It would be hard to put that in sign, and he didn't like to talk about it.

What he had to talk about now was difficult and essential. The captains and their soldiers had started over the mountains; they couldn't wait any longer, or they would not get back to their country this year. But the snow was still so deep in the mountains that the trail could not be seen. They needed guides, and they had sent him and Shannon back to try to enlist some.

Cutnose thought for a while, lighting a pipe and sharing it with Drouillard. Eventually he said, *Our people have been afraid you would ask this. We knew you would. Any Nez Perce who go east over the mountains might be killed by the Atsinas and the Blackfeet. Therefore we go over all together in strength, only in fall to hunt the buffalo.* Then he told Drouillard something he did not know: the Atsinas lately had killed many of the Ootlashoots and the Shoshones, the people of the Bird Woman. Cameahwait's people. Cutnose didn't know whether Cameah-wait had been killed.

Again they smoked for a while in a sad silence. Outside was the steady pounding noise of women making flour of roots. And in the air was the smell of salmon being smoked. The salmon finally had arrived in these rivers, late, alleviating the food short-age the Nez Perce and the soldiers had endured for so many weeks. Shannon was out there in the village, probably saying his last goodbyes to a girl. Shannon was a beautiful young soldier and had a sweetheart in every village. It was another of those things that would make it hard to leave the Nez Perce.

Finally Cutnose said, *I have a brother who knows that trail well, snow time or summer. He might go with you. What will your officers pay? Will they pay guns?*

Drouillard signed, *They have two guns they can pay. They hope for two or three guides.*

Cutnose smoked and looked at the eagles. Then he said, *Remember two men, last moon, each gave one of your captains a horse at the council. The day I gave you the gray.*

I remember those men. One was Twisted Hair's son. The other was Bloody Chief's son.

Yes, Cutnose said. *They are brave men. They have much respect. They know the trail over the mountains. If I asked their fathers, they might ask those two young men. I would ask them, if it would please my friend Followed by Buzzards.*

It would please me, Drouillard said. *It would make my heart like sunrise.*

He thought, *Megweshe, Weshemoneto.* Thank you, Creator.

June 25, 1806

The Indian guides, with great cheerfulness, took pine torches from the campfire and ran out into the darkness. They had said they were going to do something that would make good weather for the trip over the mountains.

Suddenly, a column of fire shot up through the darkness with a rush and crackle, then a fireball separated from it and exploded in the air a hundred feet above the ground with a deep boom. Then another column of fire, another fireball, a little off the left, then another to the right. The soldiers whooped and whistled in amazement.

"Like fireworks, b'God!"

"Independence Day early!"

"Yee-ha!"

Another half-dozen blazes shot up and roared, and the

meadow was bathed in light. Then the Indians came back into the camp laughing. Out in the field, nine fir trees glowed for a while and sparks rose and swirled and drifted. The Indians had ignited the dead branches that covered the lower trunks of the tall trees. Now, they said, it would not snow in the mountains while they were passing over. The captains were delighted to have guides, and they were particularly pleased to see whom Drouillard had brought to lead them.

June 27, 1806

Indeed it did not snow anymore. But there was still deep snow on the mountains. It averaged seven feet deep along the ridges and slopes of the trail. Fortunately, the spring sun had been shining on it and it was crusted and packed deep enough to support the horses and riders and their loads. They rode carefully and nervously over this slippery crust. A hoof usually would sink two to four inches in, giving some purchase, but there were slips and falls. This was the reason why the Nez Perce had kept telling the captains not to leave yet. On the fifteenth they had first tried to start over—without guides, because the Indians had said it was impossible to go yet—and ran into soft drifts fifteen feet deep. They had had to turn back and camp in the quamash prairie for a week, thwarted and impatient, until Drouillard came with the guides.

In one way, this ordeal of riding on crusted snow was better than no snow: the awful tangles of brush and fallen trees that had been such obstacles last fall were now buried several feet below. But also buried far below were the rubbed and blazed traces of the Nez Perce road.

On a high mountain, the guides pointed to a stripped pine pole sticking up from a rock pile. They asked to stop at this route marker to smoke a spirit pipe. This appeared to be the very peak of their Road to the Buffalo, as they called it. In every direction lay more stupendous, snow-covered mountains to the limits of vision, and here Drouillard heard the captains admit to each